along, Bosch's internal monologue about legendary Dodgers broadcaster Vin Scully and his phrase, 'The deuces are wild,' and how it relates to the case are examples of how Connelly elevates the genre. In the closing pages, the author offers a taste of a possible love interest, something that longtime readers can look forward to in the next book."

—Colleen Kelly, *Minneapolis Star Tribune*

"Bosch's masterly examination of the murder books— as he digs out a whisper of a contradiction here, a fact that needs fleshing out there—is a pleasure to watch…Connelly has created a subtle gem. Among the always-inventive drama and fireworks of the investigation, he gives us a more mature Bosch, one who is dealing with radical upheavals in his world, though not necessarily changes for the worse. The brooding and gloom have lessened…The newness in his life may have him blinking at the brightness, but by the end he has found a way to stand tall once again."

—Barry Lancet, *New York Journal of Books*

"[A]n unusually cerebral case…a classic whodunit…an extra treat for the reader is being able to follow the case from the dual perspectives of the prosecution and the defense…Bosch is well versed in the professional tactics of a police investigation…Haller's vocational talents, being on the shady side, are more like the sleight-of-hand tricks of a con man…Brothers they may be, but at times they seem a lot like an ego and its id."

—Marilyn Stasio, *New York Times Book Review*

"Masterly…Indeed, the notion of crossing resonates on different levels—the intersection of predator and prey, cops gone rogue, and for Bosch, the transition from one part of his life into something exciting and new."

—*Publishers Weekly* (starred review)

"One of the pleasures of a Connelly novel is how he delves into the minutiae of a police procedural, making the most mundane aspects of an investigation exciting. In this case, Harry uses his decades of investigative skills—and instinct—to follow the trail of an expensive watch...Readers may be taken aback a bit to find this iconic character without a badge, but Connelly proves he still has much to uncover about Harry. Harry's lifelong "mission" of police work never wavers, even without his detective shield. Mickey may see evidence as a way to help his client, but for Harry, evidence will always be 'a bridge to the truth.' Watching Harry reinvent himself—as so many new retirees have had to do—brings even more energy to this series that never lags. *The Crossing* again proves Connelly as a master of the genre."   —Oline H. Cogdill, *Sun-Sentinel*

"Thrilling...Harry is back in his groove...As always Connelly makes expert use of the city as a setting, from the glitzy offices of a Beverly Hills plastic surgeon to the lonesome alley behind an auto repair shop where a prostitute's body is found. Finding the connections between the parts of the case—the crossings of the title, the places where apparently unconnected people encounter one another—gives readers Harry at his best. We get the bonus of seeing Mickey take that case to court for one of his bravura performances."

—Colette Bancroft, *Tampa Bay Times*

"Compelling...loaded with extremely clever sleuthing by Bosch, with a trail that brings him under fire from the cops, in more sense than one. All of this is rendered in confident Connelly prose that glues the reader to the page."   —Jack Batten, *Toronto Star*

"Tense and effective."
                          —Tom Nolan, *Wall Street Journal*

"Bosch's investigations take him all over his beloved L.A. and beyond, from swank watering holes to hot sheet motel rooms. All the while, Bosch himself is being tracked by killers and dogged by obscenity-laced phone calls from irate former Los Angeles police colleagues who've learned of his defection to the enemy country of criminal defense. As always with a Bosch novel, the delight is in these 'inside police' details...What Bosch does discover in *The Crossing* is a vile conspiracy and a new vocation as an independent investigator that should keep him busy—and Connelly fans happy—for years to come."
                          —Maureen Corrigan, *Washington Post*

"We get a twofer in Michael Connelly's latest sordid tale of murder among the Los Angeles freeways...Bosch still drinks too much and he still can't handle a relationship with a good woman without messing it up. But he's dogged, and Connelly does this stuff so well...It's a great read, and sees Connelly on top of his game."
                          —Nick Martin, *Winnepeg Free Press*

THE CROSSING

BOOKS BY MICHAEL CONNELLY

THE HARRY BOSCH NOVELS

The Black Echo
The Black Ice
The Concrete Blonde
The Last Coyote
Trunk Music
Angels Flight
A Darkness More than Night
City of Bones
Lost Light
The Narrows
The Closers
Echo Park
The Overlook
Nine Dragons
The Drop
The Black Box
The Burning Room
The Crossing
The Wrong Side of Goodbye

THE LINCOLN LAWYER NOVELS

The Lincoln Lawyer
The Brass Verdict
The Reversal
The Fifth Witness
The Gods of Guilt

OTHER NOVELS

The Poet • *Blood Work* • *Void Moon*
Chasing the Dime • *The Scarecrow*

NONFICTION

Crime Beat

E-BOOKS

Suicide Run • *Angle of Investigation*
Mulholland Drive • *The Safe Man*

THE
CROSSING

A NOVEL

MICHAEL
CONNELLY

VISION

New York Boston

Copyright © 2015 by Hieronymus, Inc.
Preview of *The Wrong Side of Goodbye* copyright © 2016 by Hieronymus, Inc.

Cover design by M80 Design LLC / Wes Youssi. Cover photos: holbox / Shutterstock (skyline); Viore; Sima / Shutterstock (man)
Cover copyright © 2016 by Hachette Book Group, Inc.

Vision
Hachette Book Group
1290 Avenue of the Americas, New York, NY 10104
grandcentralpublishing.com
twitter.com/grandcentralpub

Originally published in hardcover by Hachette Book Group
First oversize mass market edition: October 2016, December 2016

Vision is an imprint of Grand Central Publishing, Inc.
The Vision name and logo are trademarks of Hachette Book Group, Inc.

The publisher is not responsible for websites (or their content) that are not owned by the publisher.

The Hachette Speakers Bureau provides a wide range of authors for speaking events. To find out more, go to www.hachettespeakersbureau.com or call (866) 376-6591.

ISBN: 978-1-5387-2750-8

Printed in the United States of America

OPM

10 9 8 7 6 5 4 3 2 1

In memory of Simon Christenson

THE CROSSING

APRIL FOOLS' DAY

Ellis and Long were four car lengths behind the motorcycle on Ventura Boulevard. They were eastbound, coming up to the big curve where the road would turn south and head down through the pass into Hollywood.

Ellis was behind the wheel, where he preferred to be, even though he was the senior partner and could dictate to Long who drove and who rode shotgun. Long was looking down at the screen on his phone, staring at the video feed, watching over what they called their investments.

The car felt good. It felt strong. There was little play in the wheel. Ellis felt solidly in control. He saw an opening in the right lane and pushed his foot down. The car jumped forward.

Long looked up.

"What are you doing?"

"Getting rid of a problem."

"What?"

"Before it's a problem."

He had caught up and was now riding next to the motorcycle. He glanced over and saw the rider's black boots and the orange flames painted on the gas tank. The flames matched the color of the Camaro.

He pulled a few feet ahead and as the road curved

right he allowed the car to drift into the left lane, following the laws of centrifugal force.

He heard the rider yell. He kicked at the side of the car and then gunned it to try to move ahead. That was his mistake. He should have braked and bailed but he tried to gun his way out of it. Ellis was ready for the move and pinned the accelerator. The Camaro surged into the left lane, completing the cutoff.

Ellis heard brakes squeal and a long sustained blast of a car horn as the motorcycle went into the oncoming traffic lanes. Then he heard the high-pitched scraping of steel and the inevitable impact of metal against metal.

Ellis smiled and kept going.

1

It was a Friday morning and the smart people had already taken off for the weekend. This made traffic into downtown a breeze and Harry Bosch got to the courthouse early. Rather than wait for Mickey Haller on the front steps, where they had agreed to meet, he decided to look for his lawyer inside the monolithic structure that covered half a block of space nineteen floors into the air. But the search for Haller would not be as difficult as the size of the building suggested. After clearing the lobby metal detector—a new experience for him—Bosch took an elevator up to fifteen and started checking courtrooms and using the stairs to work his way down. Most of the courtrooms assigned to criminal cases were on floors nine through fifteen. Bosch knew this because of the time he'd spent in those courtrooms over the last thirty years.

He found Haller in Department 120 on the thirteenth floor. Court was in session but there was no jury. Haller had told Bosch he had a motion hearing that would finish by their lunchtime appointment. Harry slipped onto a bench in the back of the public gallery and watched as Haller questioned a uniformed Los Angeles police officer on the witness stand. Bosch had missed the preliminaries but not the meat of Haller's examination of the officer.

"Officer Sanchez, what I would like you to do now is go through the steps that led to your arresting Mr. Hennegan on December eleventh of last year," Haller said. "Why don't we start with what your assignment was that day."

Sanchez took a moment to compose an answer to what seemed to be a routine question. Bosch noticed that he had three hash marks on his sleeve, one for every five years with the department. Fifteen years was a lot of experience and that told Bosch that Sanchez would be very wary of Haller as well as skilled at giving answers more helpful to the prosecution than the defense.

"My partner and I were on routine patrol in Seventy-seventh Street Division," Sanchez said. "We happened to be traveling westbound on Florence Avenue at the time of this incident."

"And Mr. Hennegan was also traveling on Florence Avenue?"

"Yes, that's correct."

"Which direction was he going?"

"He was also going west. His car was directly in front of us."

"Okay, and then what happened?"

"We came to a red light at Normandie and Mr. Hennegan came to a stop and then we stopped behind him. Mr. Hennegan engaged his right turn signal and then turned right to go northbound on Normandie."

"Did he commit a traffic code infraction by turning right when the light was red?"

"No, he did not. He came to a complete stop and then made the turn when it was clear."

Haller nodded and checked something off on a legal pad. He was sitting next to his client, who was in county blues—a sure sign that this was a felony case. Bosch guessed it was a drug case and that Haller was trying to suppress whatever was found in his client's car by claiming it was a bad stop.

Haller was questioning the witness from his seat at the defense table. Without a jury, the judge was not requiring the formality of standing when addressing a witness.

"You made the turn as well, following Mr. Hennegan's car, correct?" he asked.

"That is correct," Sanchez said.

"At what point did you decide to conduct a traffic stop on Mr. Hennegan's vehicle?"

"It was right away. We lit him up and he pulled over."

"Then what happened?"

"The minute he stopped the car, the passenger door opened and the passenger bolted."

"He ran?"

"Yes, sir."

"Where did he go?"

"There is a shopping plaza there with an alley behind it. He went into the alley in an easterly direction."

"Did either you or your partner give chase?"

"No, sir, it would be against policy and dangerous to separate. My partner got on the radio and requested backup and an airship. He broadcast a description of the man who ran."

"An airship?"

"A police helicopter."

"Got it. What did you do, Officer Sanchez, while your partner was on the radio?"

"I exited the patrol car and moved to the driver's side of the vehicle and told the driver to put his hands out the window, where I could see them."

"Did you draw your weapon?"

"Yes, I did."

"Then what happened?"

"I ordered the driver—Mr. Hennegan—to step out of the vehicle and lie down on the ground. He complied and then I handcuffed him."

"Did you tell him why he was under arrest?"

"At that time he was not under arrest."

"He was handcuffed facedown on the street but you are saying he was not under arrest?"

"We didn't know what we had and my concern was for the safety of myself and my partner. We'd had a passenger bolt from the car, so we were suspicious about what was going on here."

"So the man bolting from the car was what set all of this in motion."

"Yes, sir."

Haller flipped some pages on his yellow pad to look at notes and then checked something on the screen of his laptop, which was open on the defense table. His client had his head tilted down, and from behind, it looked as though he might be asleep.

The judge, who had been slumped so low in his seat that Bosch had only been able to see the top of his gray head, cleared his throat and leaned forward, revealing himself to the courtroom. The placard at the front of the bench identified him as the Honorable Steve Yerrid. Bosch didn't recognize him or his name, which didn't mean a whole lot, since the building housed more than fifty courtrooms and judges.

"Nothing further, Mr. Haller?" he asked.

"I'm sorry, Your Honor," Haller said. "Just checking some notes."

"Let's keep this moving."

"Yes, Your Honor."

Haller apparently found what he was looking for and was ready to proceed.

"How long did you leave Mr. Hennegan handcuffed on the street, Officer Sanchez?"

"I checked the car and once I was sure there was no one else in it, I went back to Mr. Hennegan, patted him down to check for weapons, then helped him up and placed him in the backseat of the cruiser for his own safety and ours."

"Why was his safety in question?"

"Like I said, we didn't know what we had here. One guy runs, the other guy is acting nervous. It was best to secure the individual while we determined what was going on."

"When did you first notice that Mr. Hennegan was acting nervous, as you say?"

"Right away. When I told him to put his hands out the window."

"You were pointing a gun at him when you gave that order, weren't you?"

"Yes."

"Okay, so you have Hennegan in the backseat of your car. Did you ask him if you could search his car?"

"I did and he said no."

"So what did you do after he said no?"

"I went on the radio and called for a dope dog to come to the scene."

"And what does a dope dog do?"

"It is trained to alert if it smells drugs."

"Okay, so how long did that take, to get the dog out to Florence and Normandie?"

"About an hour. It had to come from the academy, where they had a training demonstration."

"So for an hour my client was locked in the back of your car while you waited."

"That is correct."

"For your safety and his."

"Correct."

"How many times did you go back to your car, open the door, and ask him again if you could search his car?"

"Two or three times."

"And what was his response?"

"He kept saying no."

"Did you or other police officers ever find the passenger who ran from the car?"

"Not as far as I know. But the whole thing was turned over to the South Bureau Narcotics Unit after that day."

"So when this dog finally arrived, what happened?"

"The K-9 officer walked him around the subject's vehicle and the dog alerted at the trunk."

"What was the dog's name?"

"I think it was Cosmo."

"What kind of vehicle had Mr. Hennegan been driving?"

"It was an old Toyota Camry."

"And so Cosmo told you there were drugs in the trunk."

"Yes, sir."

"So you opened the trunk."

"We cited the dog's alert as probable cause to search the trunk."

"Did you find drugs, Officer Sanchez?"

"We found a bag of what appeared to be crystal meth and a bag of money."

"How much crystal meth?"

"Two point four pounds, it turned out to be."

"And how much money?"

"Eighty-six thousand dollars."

"Cash?"

"All cash."

"You then arrested Mr. Hennegan for possession with intent to sell, correct?"

"Yes, that was when we arrested him, read him his rights, and took him to South Bureau for booking."

Haller nodded. And was looking at his notepad again. Bosch knew he had to have something else. It came out when the judge prompted him once again to proceed.

"Officer, let's go back to the stop. You testified earlier that Mr. Hennegan turned right on a red light after coming to a complete stop and waiting for the moment that it was clear and safe for him to make that turn. Do I have that right?"

"Yes, correct."

"And that was correct under the law, yes?"

"Yes."

"So if he did everything right, why did you light him up and force him to pull over?"

Sanchez made a quick glance toward the prosecutor, who sat at the table opposite Haller. He had so far said nothing but Bosch had watched him taking notes during the police officer's testimony.

The glance told Bosch that this was where Haller had found the weakness of the case.

"Your Honor, can you ask the witness to answer the question and not look at the prosecutor for the answer?" Haller prompted.

Judge Yerrid leaned forward again and told Sanchez to answer. Sanchez asked for a repeat of the question and Haller complied.

"It was Christmastime," Sanchez said. "We always give out turkey tickets at that time of year and I was pulling them over to give them turkey tickets."

"Turkey tickets?" Haller asked. "What is a turkey ticket?"

2

Bosch was enjoying the Lincoln Lawyer show. Haller had expertly put all the details of the arrest on the record, had circled back to the Achilles heel of the case, and was about to exploit it big time. Bosch now thought he knew why the prosecutor had been silent throughout the procedure. There was nothing he could do about the facts of the case. It was going to come down to how he argued them to the judge later.

"What are turkey tickets, Officer Sanchez?" Haller asked again.

"Well, there is a chain of markets in South L.A. called Little John's and every year around Thanksgiving and Christmas they give us these gift certificates for turkeys. And we give them out to people."

"You mean like a gift?" Haller asked.

"Yes, a gift," Sanchez said.

"How do you choose who gets these turkey tickets?"

"We look for good deeds, people doing what they are supposed to be doing."

"You mean drivers obeying the traffic laws?"

"That's right."

"So in this case you pulled over Mr. Hennegan because he did the right thing on that turn at the red light?"

"Yes."

"In other words, you stopped Mr. Hennegan for not breaking the law, correct?"

Sanchez looked at the prosecutor again, hoping for some help. None came and he struggled through an answer.

"We did not know he was breaking the law until his partner bolted and we found the drugs and money."

Even Bosch saw it as a pathetic stance. But Haller wasn't letting it go by.

"Officer Sanchez," he said, "I ask you very specifically, at the moment you put your car's lights on and sounded the siren in order to pull Mr. Hennegan over, Mr. Hennegan had done nothing you saw to be wrong, nothing illegal. Is that correct?"

Sanchez mumbled his answer.

"Correct."

"Please say your answer clearly for the record," Haller said.

"Correct," Sanchez said in a loud, annoyed tone.

"I have no further questions, Your Honor."

The judge asked the prosecutor, whom he called Mr. Wright, if he wanted to cross-examine the witness, and Wright elected to pass. The facts were the facts and nothing he could ask could change them. The judge dismissed Officer Sanchez and addressed the lawyers.

"This is your motion, Mr. Haller," he said. "Are you ready for arguments?"

A brief dispute followed as Haller said he was ready to proceed with oral arguments and Wright suggested that written arguments be submitted instead. Judge Yerrid threw it Haller's way and said he wanted to hear oral arguments and then decide if written arguments were necessary.

Haller stood and moved to the lectern between the prosecution and defense tables.

"I'll be brief, Your Honor, as I think the facts of the case are pretty clear. By any measure of those facts, not only is the probable cause to make this traffic stop insufficient, it simply doesn't even exist. Mr. Hennegan was obeying all traffic laws and not acting suspiciously in any way when Officer Sanchez and his partner put on their lights and siren and forced him to pull to the side of the road."

Haller had carried a legal tome with him to the lectern. He now looked down at a highlighted section of text and continued.

"Your Honor, the Fourth Amendment requires that a search and seizure be pursuant to a warrant supported by probable cause. However, there are exceptions to the warrant requirement under *Terry,* one of which is that a vehicle may be stopped when there is probable cause to believe that an infraction has been committed or there is reasonable suspicion to believe that the occupants of the vehicle are engaged in a crime. In this instance we have none of the requirements for a *Terry* stop. The Fourth Amendment places strict limitations on the state in its exercise of power and authority. Handing out turkey tickets is not a valid exercise of constitutional authority. Mr. Hennegan committed no traffic offense and by the arresting officer's own admission was driving in a perfectly legal and correct way when he was forced to pull over. It does not matter what was found to be in the trunk of his car later. The government trampled on his right to be protected from unlawful search and seizure."

Haller paused, perhaps attempting to gauge if he needed to say more.

"Additionally," he finally said, "the one hour Mr. Hennegan spent locked in the back of Officer Sanchez's patrol car constituted an arrest without warrant or probable cause, again a violation of his protections against unlawful search and seizure. Fruit of the poisonous tree, Your Honor. It was a bad stop. Everything that came out of it was therefore tainted. Thank you."

Haller walked back to his chair and sat down. His client gave no indication that he had listened and understood the argument.

"Mr. Wright?" the judge said.

The prosecutor stood and reluctantly approached the lectern. Bosch had no law degree but he did have a solid working knowledge of the law. It was clear to him that the case against Hennegan was in trouble.

"Your Honor," Wright began. "Every day of the week police officers have what we call citizen encounters, some of which lead to arrest. As the Supreme Court says in *Terry,* 'Not all personal intercourse between police officers and citizens involves seizure of persons.' This was a citizen encounter — the intention of which was to reward good behavior. What turned this in a new direction and provided the probable cause for the actions of the officers was the passenger fleeing the defendant's vehicle. That was the game changer."

Wright checked the notes on the yellow pad he had brought with him to the lectern. He found the string and continued.

"The defendant is a drug dealer. The good intentions of these officers should not preclude this case's going forward. The court has wide discretion in this area and Officer Sanchez and his partner should not be penalized for carrying out their duty to the fullest."

Wright sat down. Bosch knew his argument had been tantamount to throwing himself on the mercy of the court. Haller stood up to respond.

"Your Honor, if I could make one point. Mr. Wright

is Mr. Wrong here. He quoted from *Terry* but left out that when an officer, by means of physical force or show of authority, restrains a citizen, then a seizure has occurred. He seems to have a slide rule with which he likes to move the point of seizure vis-à-vis probable cause. He says there was no seizure until the passenger jumped from Mr. Hennegan's car and probable cause arose. But that logic does not work, Your Honor. Through the siren and lights on his car, Officer Sanchez forced Mr. Hennegan's car to the side of the road. And for an arrest of any kind to transpire, there had to be probable cause for that stop. Citizens are free to travel and move about unimpeded in this country. Forcing a citizen to stop and chat is a seizure and a violation of the right to be left alone to lawful pursuits. The bottom line is, a turkey ticket is not probable cause. It is this case that is the turkey, Your Honor. Thank you."

Proud of his last turn of phrase, Haller returned to his seat. Wright did not get back up to throw out the last word. His argument, what there was of it, had been submitted.

Judge Yerrid leaned forward once again and cleared his voice right into the bench's microphone, creating a loud blast in the courtroom. Hennegan sat bolt upright, revealing that he had in fact been sleeping through the hearing that might decide his freedom.

"Excuse me," Yerrid said after the ringing sound receded. "Having heard the testimony and the arguments, the court grants the motion to suppress. The evidence found in the trunk of—"

"Your Honor!" Wright shouted as he jumped up from his seat. "Clarification."

He held his hands out wide as if he were surprised by a ruling he certainly had to have known was coming.

"Your Honor, the state has no case without the evidence from the trunk of that vehicle. You are saying the drugs and the money are tossed?"

"That's exactly what I am saying, Mr. Wright. There was no probable cause to make the stop. As Mr. Haller stated, fruit of the poisonous tree."

Wright now pointed directly at Hennegan.

"Your Honor, the man is a drug dealer. He is part of the plague on our city and society. You are putting him back out on—"

"Mr. Wright!" the judge barked into his microphone. "Do not blame the court for the failings of your case."

"The state will be filing a notice of appeal within twenty-four hours."

"It is the state's right to do so. I will be most interested in seeing if you can make the Fourth Amendment disappear."

Wright dropped his chin to his chest. Haller took the moment to stand and pour salt on the prosecutor's wounds.

"Your Honor, I would like to make a motion to dismiss the charges against my client. There is no longer any evidence in support of the filing."

Yerrid nodded. He knew this was coming. He decided to grant Wright a small dose of mercy.

"I am going to take that under advisement, Mr. Haller, and see if the state actually does file an appeal. Anything else from counsel?"

"No, Your Honor," Wright said.

"Yes, Your Honor," Haller said. "My client is currently incarcerated in lieu of half a million dollars' bail. I ask that he be released on recognizance pending appeal or dismissal."

"The state objects," Wright said. "This man's partner ran. There is no indication Hennegan won't do the same. As I said, we will be appealing this ruling and returning to prosecute the case."

"So you say," the judge said. "I am going to take consideration of bail under advisement as well. Let's see what the state does after considering the case further. Mr. Haller, you can always request a rehearing on your motions if the District Attorney's Office moves too slowly."

Yerrid was telling Wright not to sit on this or he would take action.

"Now if there is nothing else, we're adjourned here," the judge said.

Yerrid paused a moment to see if there was anything else from the lawyers, then stood up and left the bench. He disappeared through the door behind the clerk's desk.

Bosch watched Haller clap Hennegan on the shoulder and lean down to explain to his client the great victory he had just won. Bosch knew the rulings didn't mean that Hennegan would immediately waltz out of the courtroom or the county jail. Not even close. Now the dealing would begin. The case was no doubt a wounded duck that couldn't fly. But as long as Hennegan was being held in jail, the prosecutor still had some leverage in negotiating an end to the case. Wright could offer a lesser offense in exchange for a guilty plea. Hennegan would end up looking at months instead of years and the D.A. would still get a conviction.

Bosch knew that was how it worked. The law could bend. If there were lawyers involved, then there was always a deal to be made. The judge knew this, too. He had been faced with an untenable situation. Everyone in the courtroom knew that Hennegan was a drug dealer. But the arrest was bad and therefore the evidence tainted. By keeping Hennegan in county lockup he was allowing a resolution to be worked out that might prevent a drug dealer from walking away. Wright quickly packed his briefcase and turned to leave. As he headed toward the gate, he glanced at Haller and said he would be in touch.

Haller nodded back, and that was when he noticed Bosch for the first time. He quickly finished conferring with his client as the courtroom deputy came over to take Hennegan back to lockup.

Soon afterward, Haller came through the gate to where Bosch sat waiting.

"How much of that did you catch?" he asked.

"Enough," Bosch said. "I heard 'Mr. Wright is Mr. Wrong.'"

Haller's smile went wide.

"I've been waiting years to get that guy on a case and be able to say that."

"I guess I should say congratulations."

Haller nodded.

"Tell you the truth, that doesn't happen too often. I can probably count on my two hands how many times I've prevailed on a motion to suppress."

"You tell your client that?"

"Somehow the subtleties of the law are lost on him. He just wants to know when he's getting out."

3

They ate at Traxx in Union Station. It was a nice place that was courthouse close and favored at lunchtime by judges and lawyers. The waitress knew Haller and she didn't bother giving him a menu. He simply ordered the usual. Bosch took a quick look and ordered a hamburger and French fries, which seemed to disappoint Haller.

On the walk over they had talked about family matters. Bosch and Haller were half brothers and had daughters the same age. In fact, the girls were planning to room together in September at Chapman University down in Orange County. Both had applied to the school without knowing the other's intention until they celebrated their acceptance letters on the same day on Facebook. From there their plan to be roommates quickly formed. The fathers were happy about this because they knew they would be able to pool their efforts to monitor the girls' well-being and adjustment to college life.

Now as they sat at the table with a window that looked out on the train station's cavernous waiting room, it was time to get down to business. Bosch was expecting an update on the case Haller was handling for him. The previous year Bosch had been suspended from the LAPD on a trumped-up beef when he had picked the lock on a captain's office door so he could look at old police records connected to a murder investigation he was actively working. It was a Sunday and Bosch didn't want to have to wait for the captain to come in the next day. The infraction was minor but could have been the first step in the firing process.

More important, to Bosch it was a suspension without pay that also halted payments to his Deferred Retirement Option Plan. That meant he had no salary and no access to his DROP funds while he fought the suspension and took it to a Board of Rights—a process that would take a minimum of six months, pushing him past his retirement date anyway. With no money coming in to cover living expenses and college around the corner for his daughter, Bosch retired so he could access his retirement and DROP funds. He then hired Haller to file a lawsuit against the city, charging that the police department had engaged in unlawful tactics to force him into pulling the pin.

Because Haller had requested a meeting in person, Bosch expected that the news would not be good. Previously Haller had given him updates on the case by phone. Bosch knew something was up.

He decided to put off discussing his case by going back to the hearing that had just ended.

"So I guess you're pretty proud of yourself, getting that drug dealer off," he said.

"You know as well as I do that he's not going anywhere," Haller responded. "The judge had no choice. Now the D.A. will deal it down and my guy will still do some time."

Bosch nodded.

"But the cash in the trunk," he said. "I bet that goes back to him. What's your piece on that? If you don't mind my asking."

"Fifty K, plus I get the car," Haller said. "He won't need it in jail. I got a guy handles that stuff. A liquidator. I'll get another couple grand out of the car."

"Not bad."

"Not bad if I can get it. Need to pay the bills. Hennegan hired me because he knew my name from a bus bench right there at Florence and Normandie. He saw it from the backseat of the cruiser they put him in and he memorized the phone number. I've got sixty of those benches around town and that costs money. Gotta keep gas in the tank, Harry."

Bosch had insisted on paying Haller for his work on the lawsuit, but it wasn't anything as stratospheric as the potential Hennegan payday. Haller had even been able to keep costs down on the lawsuit by having an associate handle most of the non-courtroom work. He called it his law enforcement discount.

"Speaking of cash, you see how much Chapman is going to cost us?" Haller asked.

Bosch nodded.

"It's steep," he said. "I made less than that the first ten years I was a cop. But Maddie's got a couple scholarships. How'd Hayley do on those?"

"She did all right. It certainly helps."

Bosch nodded and it seemed as though they had covered everything but the thing the meeting was about.

"So, I guess you can give me the bad news now," he said. "Before the food gets here."

"What bad news?" Haller asked.

"I don't know. But this is the first time you called me in for an update on things. I figure it's not looking good."

Haller shook his head.

"Oh, I'm not going to even talk about the LAPD thing. That case is chugging along and we still have them in the corner. I wanted to talk about something else. I want to hire you, Harry."

"Hire me. What do you mean?"

"You know I have the Lexi Parks case, right? I'm defending Da'Quan Foster?"

Bosch was thrown by the unexpected turn in the conversation.

"Uh, yeah, you've got Foster. What's it have to do—"

"Well, Harry, I've got the trial coming up in six weeks and I don't have jack shit for a defense. He didn't do it, man, and he is in the process of being totally fucked by our wonderful legal system. He's going to go down for her murder if I don't do something. I want to hire you to work it for me."

Haller leaned across the table with urgency. Bosch involuntarily leaned back from him. He still felt as though he were the only guy in the restaurant who didn't know what was going on. Since his retirement he had pretty much dropped out of having day-to-day knowledge of things going on in the city. The names Lexi Parks and Da'Quan Foster were on the periphery of his awareness. He knew it was a case and he knew it was big. But for the past six months he had tried to stay away from newspaper stories and TV reports that might remind him of the mission he had carried for nearly thirty years—catching killers. He had gone so far as to start a long-planned-but-never-realized restoration project on an old Harley-Davidson motorcycle that had been gathering dust and rust in his carport shed for almost twenty years.

"But you've already got an investigator," he said. "That big guy with the big arms. The biker."

"Yeah, Cisco, except Cisco's on the DL and he's not up to handling a case like this," Haller said. "I catch a murder case maybe once every other year. I only took this one because Foster's a longtime client. I need you on this, Harry."

"The disabled list? What happened to him?"

Haller shook his head like he was in pain.

"The guy rides a Harley out there every day, lane-splitting whenever he wants, wearing one of those novelty helmets that is total bullshit when it comes to protecting your neck. I told him it was only a matter of time. I asked him for dibs on his liver. There is a reason they call them *donor*cycles. And it doesn't matter how good a rider you are, it's always the other guy."

"So what happened?"

"He was cruising down Ventura one night a while back and some yahoo comes up, cuts him off, and pushes him into head-on traffic. He dodges one car and then has to lay the bike down—it's an old one, no front brakes—and he skids through an entire intersection on his hip. Luckily he was wearing leathers, so the road rash wasn't too hideous, but he fucked up his ACL. He's down for the count right now and they're talking about a total knee replacement. But it doesn't matter. My point is, Cisco's a great defense investigator and he already took a swing at this. What I need is an experienced homicide detective. Harry, I'm not going to be able to live with it if my guy goes down for this. Innocent clients leave scars, if you know what I mean."

Bosch stared at him blankly for a long moment.

"I've already got a project," he finally said.

"What do you mean, a case?" Haller asked.

"No, a motorcycle. A restoration."

"Ah, Jesus, you too?"

"It's a nineteen-fifty Harley like the one Lee Marvin rode in *The Wild One*. I inherited it from a guy I knew in the service way back. Twenty years ago he wrote it into his will that I get the bike and then he jumped off a cliff up in Oregon. I've had the bike in storage since I got it."

Haller waved a hand dismissively.

"So it's waited all that time. It can wait longer. I'm talking about an innocent man and I don't know what I can do. I'm desperate. Nobody's listening and—"

"It'll undo everything."

"What?"

"I work a case for you—not just you, any defense lawyer—and it'll undo everything I did with the badge."

Haller looked incredulous.

"Come on. It's a case. It's not—"

"Everything. You know what they call a guy who switches sides in homicide? They call him a Jane Fonda, as in hanging with the North Vietnamese. You get it? It's crossing to the dark side."

Haller looked off through the window into the waiting room. It was crowded with people coming down from the Metrolink tracks on the roof.

Before Haller said anything the waiter brought their food. He stared across the table at Bosch the whole time the woman was placing the plates down and refilling their glasses with iced tea. When she was gone, Bosch spoke first.

"Look, it's nothing personal—if I did it for anybody, it would probably be you."

It was true. They were the sons of a fabled L.A. defense attorney but had grown up miles and generations apart. They had only come to know each other in recent years. Despite the fact that Haller was across the aisle from Bosch, so to speak, Harry liked and respected him.

"I'm sorry, man," he continued. "That's how it is. It's not like I haven't thought about this. But there's a line I can't bring myself to cross. And you're not the first one to ask."

Haller nodded.

"I get that. But what I am offering is something different. I got this guy I'm convinced was somehow set up for murder and there's DNA I can't shake and he's going to go down for it unless I get someone like you to help me—"

"Come on, Haller, don't embarrass yourself. Every defense lawyer in every courthouse says the same thing every day of the week. Every client is innocent. Every client is getting railroaded, set up. I heard it for thirty years, every time I sat in a courtroom. But you know what? I don't have a second thought about anybody I ever put in the penitentiary. And at some point or other every one of them said they didn't do it."

Haller didn't respond and Bosch took the time to take his first bite of food. It was good but the conversation had soured his appetite. Haller started moving his salad around with his fork but he didn't eat anything.

"Look, all I'm saying is look at the case, see for yourself. Go talk to him and you'll be convinced."

"I'm not going to talk to anybody."

Bosch wiped his mouth with his napkin and put it down on the table next to his plate.

"You want to talk about something else here, Mick? Or should I just take this to go?"

Haller didn't respond. He looked down at his own uneaten food. Bosch could see the fear in his eyes. Fear of failure, fear of having to live with something bad.

Haller put his fork down.

"I'll make a deal with you," he said. "You work the case and if you find evidence against my guy, you take it to the D.A. Anything you find, no matter how it cuts, we share with the D.A. Wide-open discovery—

anything that doesn't fall directly under attorney-client privilege."

"Yeah, what will your client say about that?"

"He'll sign off on it because he's innocent."

"Right."

"Look, just think about it. Then let me know."

Bosch pushed his plate away. He'd taken only one bite but lunch was over. He started wiping his hands on the cloth napkin.

"I don't have to think about it," he said. "And I can let you know right now. I can't help you."

Bosch stood up and dropped the napkin on his food. He reached into his pocket, peeled off enough cash to pay for both sides of the check, and put the money down under the saltshaker. All this time Haller just stared out into the waiting room.

"That's it," Bosch said. "I'm going to go."

4

Bosch successfully put off thinking about Haller's offer for most of the weekend. On Saturday he and his daughter drove down to Orange County so she could visit her future school and get a feel for the surrounding town. They ate a late lunch at a restaurant on the edge of campus that served everything on waffles and later took in an Angels game in nearby Anaheim.

He reserved Sunday for working on his motorcycle restoration. The task he had waiting for him would be one of the most vital parts of the project. In the morning he dismantled the Harley's carburetor, cleaned all the parts, and laid them out on a spread of old newspapers on the dining room table to dry. He had previously bought a rebuild kit at Glendale Harley and had all new gaskets and O-rings for the job. The Clymer rebuild manual warned that if he mis-seated a gasket, left the pilot jet dirty, or mishandled any of a dozen things during the reassembly, then the whole restoration would be for naught.

After lunch on the back deck, he returned to the table, jazz on the stereo and Phillips head screwdriver in hand. He carefully studied the pages in the Clymer manual one more time before starting the assembly by reversing the steps he had followed while taking the carburetor apart. The John Handy Quintet was on the stereo and the song was "Naima," Handy's 1967 ode to John Coltrane. Bosch thought it was up there with the best live saxophone performances ever captured.

With Bosch following the manual step-by-step, the carburetor quickly began to take shape. When he reached for the pilot jet, he noticed that it had been lying on top of a newspaper photo of the state's former governor, cigar clenched in his teeth, a broad smile on his face as he threw his arm around another man, whom Bosch identified as a former state assemblyman from East L.A.

Bosch realized that the edition of the *Times* that he had spread out was an old one that he had wanted to keep. It had contained a classic report on politics. A few years earlier, in his last hours in office, the governor had used his authority under executive clemency to reduce the sentence of a man convicted in the killing of another. He happened to be the son of his pal the assemblyman. The son had been involved with others in a fight and fatal stabbing, had made a deal with prosecutors and pleaded guilty, but then was unhappy when the judge handed him a sentence of fifteen to thirty years in state prison. On his way out the door at the end of his term of office, the governor knocked it down to seven years.

If the governor thought nobody would notice his last official act in office, then he was wrong. The shit hit the fan with charges of cronyism, favoritism, politics of the worst kind. The *Times* cranked up an extensive two-part report on the whole sordid chapter. It sickened Bosch to read it but not so that he recycled the paper. He kept it to read again and again to be reminded of the politics of the justice system. Before running for office the governor had been a movie star specializing in playing larger-than-life heroes—men willing to sacrifice everything to do the right thing. He was now back in Hollywood, trying to be a movie star once again. But Bosch was resolved that he would never watch another one of his films—even on free TV.

Thoughts of injustice prompted by the newspaper article made Bosch wander from the carburetor project. He got up from the table and wiped his hands on the shop cloth he kept with his tools. He then threw it down, remembering that he used to spread murder books out on this table, not motorcycle parts. He opened the sliding glass door in the living room and walked out onto the deck to look at the city. His house was cantilevered on the west side of the Cahuenga Pass, offering him a view across the 101 freeway to Hollywood Heights and Universal City.

The 101 freeway was choked with traffic moving both ways through the pass. Even on a Sunday afternoon. Since his retirement Bosch had reveled in not being a part of it anymore. The traffic, the workday, the tension, and the responsibility of it all.

But he also thought of it as a false sense of revelry. He knew that, no matter how stressful it was being down there in that slow-moving river of steel and light, he belonged there. That in some way he was needed down there.

Mickey Haller had appealed to him at Friday's lunch on the grounds that his client was an innocent man. That of course would have to be proved. But Haller had missed the other half of that equation. If his client was truly innocent, then there was a killer out there whom no one was even looking for. A killer devious enough to set up an innocent man. Despite his protestations at the restaurant, that fact bothered Bosch and was not far from his thoughts throughout the whole weekend. It was something he had trouble leaving alone.

He took his phone out of his pocket and hit a number on the favorites list. The call was answered after five rings by the urgent voice of Virginia Skinner.

"Harry, I'm on deadline, what is it?"

"It's Sunday night, what are you—"

"I got called in."

"What's going on?"

"Sandy Milton was involved in a hit-and-run last night in the Woodland Hills."

Milton was a conservative city councilman. Skinner was a politics reporter for the *Times*. Bosch understood why she'd be called in on a Sunday. But what he didn't understand is why she had not called him to tell him, maybe pick his brain about who she should call in the LAPD to try to get details. It underlined for him what had been going on in their relationship for the past month or so. Or rather not going on.

"I have to go, Harry."

"Right. Sorry. I'll call you after."

"No, I'll call you."

"Okay. Are we still having dinner tonight?"

"Yes, fine, but I need to go."

She disconnected. Bosch went back inside the house to grab a beer out of the refrigerator and to check its stores. He determined that he had nothing he could tempt Virginia with to come up the mountain. Besides, Bosch's daughter would be coming home from her Police Explorer's shift at about eight and it could get awkward with Virginia in the house. She and Maddie were still in the early stages of getting to know each other's boundaries.

Bosch decided that when Skinner called back, he would offer to meet her somewhere for dinner downtown.

He had just opened a bottle and switched the CD to

a Ron Carter import recorded at the Blue Note Tokyo when his phone buzzed.

"Hey, that was fast."

"I just turned in the story. It's just a sidebar on the political implications for Milton. Richie Bed-wetter will call me in ten or fifteen minutes to go over the edit. Is that enough time to talk?"

Richie Bed-wetter was her editor, Richard Ledbetter. She called him that because he was inexperienced and young—more than twenty years her junior—but insisted on trying to tell her how to handle her beat and write her stories and a once-a-week column on local politics, which he wanted to call a blog. Things would be coming to a head between them soon, and Bosch was worried that Virginia was the vulnerable one, since her experience translated into a higher paycheck and therefore a more appealing target to management.

"Where do you want to go? Somewhere downtown?"

"Or near your place. Your call. But not Indian."

"Of course, no Indian. Let me think on it and I'll have a plan when you're close. Call me before you reach Echo Park. In case."

"Okay. But listen, can you do me a favor and pull up some stories on a case?"

"What case?"

"There's a guy that got arrested for murder. LAPD case, I think. His name is Da'Quan Foster. I want to see—"

"Yeah, Da'Quan Foster. The guy who killed Lexi Parks."

"Right."

"Harry, that's a big case."

"How big?"

"You don't need me to pull stories. Just go on the paper's website and punch in her name. There are a lot of stories about her because of who she was and because he didn't get arrested until like a month after it happened. And it's not an LAPD case. It's Sheriff's. Happened in West Hollywood. Look, I gotta go. Just got the signal from Richie."

"Okay, I'll—"

She was gone. Bosch put the phone in his pocket and went back to the dining room table. Holding the corners of the newspaper, he pulled the carburetor project to the side. He then took his laptop down off a shelf and turned it on. While he waited for it to boot, he looked at the carburetor sitting on the newspaper. He realized he had been wrong to think that restoring the old motorcycle could take the place of anything.

On the stereo Ron Carter was accompanied by two guitars and playing a Milt Jackson song called "Bags' Groove." It got Bosch thinking about his own groove and what he was missing.

When the computer was ready he pulled up the *Times* website and searched the name Lexi Parks. There were 333 stories in which Lexi Parks was mentioned, going back six years, long before her murder. Bosch narrowed it to the current year and found twenty-six stories listed by date and headline. The first was dated February 10, 2015: *Well-Liked WeHo Asst. Manager Found Murdered in Bed.*

Bosch scanned the entries until he came to a headline dated March 19, 2015: *Gang "Shot Caller" Arrested in Parks Murder.*

Bosch went back and clicked on the first story, figuring he could at least read the initial story on the murder and the first on the arrest before heading to his car for the drive downtown.

The initial report on the murder of Lexi Parks was

more about the victim than the crime because the Sheriff's Department was revealing few details about the actual murder. In fact, all the details contained in the report could be summarized in one sentence: Parks had been beaten to death in her bed and was found by her husband when he returned home from working the midnight shift as a Sheriff's deputy in Malibu.

Bosch cursed out loud when he read the part about the victim's husband being a deputy. That would make Bosch's possible involvement in the case for the defense an even greater offense to those in law enforcement. Haller had conveniently left that detail out when he urged Bosch to look into the case.

Still, he continued to read, and learned that Lexi Parks was one of four assistant city managers for West Hollywood. Among her responsibilities were the departments of Public Safety, Consumer Protection, and Media Relations. It was her position as the chief spokesperson for the city and the front-line media interface that accounted for the "well-liked" description in the headline. She was thirty-eight years old at the time of her death and had worked for the city for twelve years, starting as a code inspector and rising steadily through promotions.

Parks had met her husband, Deputy Vincent Harrick, while both were on the job. West Hollywood contracted with the Sheriff's Department to provide law enforcement services and Harrick was assigned to the station on San Vicente Boulevard. Once Parks and Harrick got engaged, Harrick asked for a transfer out of the West Hollywood station to avoid the appearance of conflict of interest with both of them working for the city. He worked at first in the south county out of the Lynwood station and then transferred out to Malibu.

Bosch decided to read the next story in the digital

queue in hopes of getting more detail about the case. The headline promised he would: *Investigators: Lexi Parks Murder a Sex Crime*. The story, published one day after the first, reported that Sheriff's homicide investigators were looking at the murder as a home invasion in which Parks was attacked in her bed as she slept, sexually assaulted, and then brutally beaten with a blunt object. The story did not say what the object was or whether it was recovered. It made no mention of any evidence that had been collected at the scene. After these scant few details of the investigation were revealed, the story transitioned into a report on the reaction to the crime among those who knew Parks and her husband, as well as the horror the crime had invoked in the community. It was reported that Vincent Harrick had taken a leave of absence to deal with the grief arising from his wife's murder.

After reading the second story, Bosch looked back at the list of stories and scanned the headlines. The next dozen or so didn't sound promising. The case remained in the news on a daily and then weekly basis but the headlines carried a lot of negatives. *No Suspects in Parks Murder, Investigators Drawing Blanks on Parks, WeHo Offers 100K Reward in Parks Case*. Bosch knew that going out with a reward was in effect announcing that you had nothing and were grasping at straws.

And then they got lucky. The fifteenth story in the queue, published thirty-eight days after the murder, announced the arrest of forty-one-year-old Da'Quan Foster for the murder of Lexi Parks. Bosch opened the story and learned that the connection to Foster seemingly came out of the blue, a match made on DNA evidence collected at the scene of the crime. Foster was arrested with the help of a team of LAPD officers at the Leimert Park artists' studio where he had just finished teaching a painting class as part of an after-school program for children.

That last piece of information gave Bosch pause. It didn't fit with his idea of what a gang shot caller was all about. He wondered if Foster was booking community-service hours as part of a criminal sentence. He kept reading. The story said that DNA collected at the Parks crime scene had been entered into the state's data bank and was matched to a sample taken from Foster following his arrest in 2004 on suspicion of rape. No charge was ever filed against him in that case but his DNA remained on file in the state Department of Justice data bank.

Bosch wanted to read more of the stories in the coverage but was running out of time if he wanted to meet Virginia Skinner. He saw one headline that came a few days after Foster's arrest: *Parks Suspect Had Turned Life Around.* He opened the story and quickly scanned it. It was a community-generated story that held that Da'Quan Foster was a reformed Rollin' 40s Crips member who had straightened his life out and was giving back to his community. He was a self-taught painter who had work hanging in a Washington, DC, museum. He ran a studio on Degnan Boulevard where he offered after-school and weekend programs for area children. He was married and had two young children of his own. To balance the story, the *Times* reported that he had a criminal record that included several drug arrests in the '90s and a four-year stint in prison. But he paroled out in 2001 and other than his arrest on the rape case, for which no charge was ever filed, he had not run afoul of the law in more than a decade.

The story included statements from many locals who expressed either disbelief at the charges or outright suspicion that Foster had somehow been set up. No one quoted in the article believed he had killed Lexi Parks or been anywhere near West Hollywood on the night in question.

From what he had read, it was unclear to Bosch whether Foster even knew the victim in the case or why he had targeted her.

Harry closed the laptop. He would read all of the stories later, but he didn't want to leave Virginia Skinner waiting for him—wherever it was she would choose to meet. They needed to talk. The relationship had been strained as of late, largely because she was busy with her work and Bosch had not been busy with anything other than restoring a motorcycle that was as old as he was.

He got up from the table and went back to his bedroom to put on a fresh shirt and nicer shoes. Ten minutes later he was driving down the hill to the freeway. Once he joined the steel river and cleared the pass he pulled out his phone and hooked up the earpiece so he'd be legal. When he carried a badge, he used to not care about such minor things, but now he dutifully buckled his seat belt and put in his earpiece. He could be ticketed for talking on a cell while driving.

From the background sound, he guessed he had caught Haller in the backseat of the Lincoln. They were both on the road, going somewhere.

"I've got questions about Foster," Bosch said.

"Shoot," Haller said.

"What was the DNA—blood, saliva, semen?"

"Semen. A deposit on the victim."

"*On* or in?"

"Both. In the vagina. On the skin, upper thigh on the right. Some on the sheets, too."

Bosch drove in silence for a few moments. The freeway was elevated as it cut through Hollywood. He was passing by the Capitol Records Building. It was built to look like a stack of records but that was a different time. Not many people listened to records anymore.

"What else?" Haller asked. "I'm glad you're thinking about the case."

"How long have you known this guy?" Bosch asked.

"Almost twenty years. He was my client. He was no angel but there was something gentle about him. He wasn't a killer. He was either too smart or too soft for that. Maybe both. Anyway, he turned things around and got out of the life. That's why I know."

"Know what?"

"That he didn't do this."

"I read some of the stories online. What about the rape arrest?"

"It was bullshit. I'll show you the file. They brought him and about twenty other guys in. Let him go in less than a day."

"Where are you in discovery? Did you get the murder book yet?"

"I got it. But if you are getting interested in this, I think you need to talk to my client. You read the book, and you're going to get the other side's case. You're not going to—"

"I don't care. It's all about the book. It begins and ends with the book. When can I get a copy?"

"I can get it put together by tomorrow."

"Good. Call me and I'll come get it."

"So then you're in?"

"Just call me when you have the book ready."

Bosch clicked off the call. He thought about the conversation and what he was feeling after reading the newspaper stories. He had made no commitment yet. He had crossed no line. But he couldn't deny that he was getting close to the line. He also could not deny the growing feeling that he was about to get back on the mission.

5

Bosch and Skinner met at the Factory Kitchen off Alameda. It was a trendy Italian place in the Arts District. It was her style and her choice. His suggestions had been shot down.

It was crowded and voices echoed and clattered off the old factory's brick walls. It was definitely the wrong kind of place to discuss the dissolution of a relationship but that was what they did.

Over a shared plate of tagliatelle with duck ragù, Skinner told Bosch that their time together as a couple was at an end. She was a reporter who had spent almost thirty years covering police and politics. She had a direct, sometimes abrupt, delivery when discussing any subject, including romance and the fulfillment of her needs. She told Bosch he had changed. He was too consumed by the loss of his career and finding his place as a man without a badge to keep the relationship on the front burner.

"I think I need to step away and let you work things out, Harry," she said.

Bosch nodded. He was not surprised by her pronouncement or the reasoning behind it. Somehow he knew that the relationship—not even a year old—could not go the distance. It had been born in the excitement and energy of a case he was working and a political scandal she was writing about. The nexus of the romance was those two things. When they were gone, they both had to wonder what they still had.

She reached over and touched his cheek in a wistful way.

"I'm only a few years behind you," she said. "It will happen to me."

"No, you'll be fine," Bosch said. "Your job is telling stories. Stories will always need to be told."

After dinner they hugged at the valet stand while waiting for their cars. They promised to stay in touch but they both knew that would not happen.

6

Bosch met Haller at 11 a.m. Monday in a downtown parking lot beneath the outstretched hands of Anthony Quinn painted on the side of a building on Third. Bosch pulled his old Cherokee up close to the rear passenger door of the Lincoln and the window came down. Because of a bad angle and the tinting on the Lincoln's windows Bosch could not see who was driving.

From the backseat Haller handed a thick, rubber-banded file out the window to him. Bosch had somehow thought it would be contained in a blue binder the way murder books were in the detective bureau. Seeing the file full of photocopies was a glaring reminder that what he was about to do wasn't remotely close to working a case for the police department. He was going far out on his own here.

"What will you do now?" Haller asked.

"What do you think?" Bosch replied. "I'll go off somewhere and read through all of this."

"I know that, but what are you looking for?"

"I'm looking for the things that are missing. Look, I don't want to get your hopes up. I read all the newspaper coverage this morning. I'm not seeing what you're seeing. The guy's a criminal. You know him because he's a criminal. So right now all I'm promising to do—

the one thing—is look through all of this and render an opinion. That's it."

Bosch held the unwieldy file up so Haller could see it again.

"If I don't find something missing or something that flares on my radar, then I'm giving it all back and that'll be it. *Comprende, hermano?*"

"*Comprende.* You know, it must be hard to be like that."

"Like what?"

"Not believing in rehabilitation and redemption, that people can change. With you it's 'once a con always a con.'"

Bosch ignored the accusation.

"So the *Times* says your client's got no alibi. What are you going to do about that?"

"He has an alibi. He was in his studio painting. We just can't prove it—yet. But we will. They say he's got no alibi but they've got no motive. He didn't know this woman, had never even seen her or been in that neighborhood, let alone her house. It's crazy to think he would do this. They tried to connect him somehow to the husband when he worked down in Lynwood— some kind of a gang revenge scheme, but it's not there. Da'Quan was a Crip and the husband worked Bloods. There is no motive because he didn't do it."

"They don't need motive. With a sex crime the sex is motive enough. What are you going to do about the DNA?"

"I'm going to challenge it."

"I'm not talking about O.J. bullshit. Is there evidence of mishandling of the sample or test failure?"

"Not yet."

"'Not yet'—what's that mean?"

"I petitioned the judge to allow for independent testing. The D.A. objected, saying there wasn't enough material recovered, but that was bullshit and the judge agreed. I have an independent lab analyzing now."

"When will you hear something?"

"The court fight took two months. I just got the material to them and am hoping to hear something any day. At least they're faster than the Sheriff's lab."

Bosch was unimpressed. He assumed the analysis would conclude what the Sheriff's analysis concluded—that the DNA belonged to Da'Quan Foster. The next step would be to go after the handlers of the evidence. It was the kind of tactic defense attorneys took all the time. If the evidence is against you, then taint the evidence any way you can.

"So aside from that, what's your theory?" he asked. "How'd your client's DNA end up in the victim?"

Haller shook his head.

"I don't think it was. Even if my lab says it's his DNA, I still won't believe he did it. He was set up."

Now Bosch shook his head.

"Jesus," he said. "You've been around the block more times than most of the lawyers I know. How can you think this?"

Haller looked at Bosch and held his eyes.

"Maybe because I have been around the block a few times," he said. "You been at it as long as me, you get to know who's lying to you. I got nothing else, Harry, but I have my gut and it tells me something's wrong here. There's a setup, there's a fix, there's something somewhere, and this guy didn't do this. Why don't you go talk to him and see what your gut tells you?"

"Not yet," Bosch said. "Let me read the book. I want to know everything there is to know about the investigation before I talk to him. If I talk to him."

Haller nodded and they parted ways, Bosch promising to keep in touch. Each man drove off to a different parking lot exit. While waiting for traffic on Third to open up for him, Bosch looked up at Anthony Quinn, his arms stretched out as if to show he had nothing.

"You and me both," Bosch said.

He pulled out on Third and then took a right on Broadway, driving through the civic center and into Chinatown. He found street parking and went into Chinese Friends for an early lunch. The place was empty. Carrying the file Haller had passed to him, Bosch took a table in the corner where his back would be to the wall and no one would be able to look over his shoulder at what he was reading. He didn't want anyone losing their appetite.

Bosch ordered without looking at the menu. He then took the rubber bands off the file and opened it on the table. For more than two decades he had put together discovery packages for attorneys defending the men and women he had arrested for murder. He knew every trick there was when it came to planting obfuscation and misdirection in a murder book. He could write a how-to manual on the art of turning the discovery process into a nightmare for a defense attorney. It had been his routine practice back in the day to redact words in reports without rhyme or reason, to intermittently remove the toner cartridge from the squad room photocopier so that pages and pages of the documents he was turning over were printed so lightly they were impossible or at least headache-inducing to read.

He now had to use all he knew in assessing this murder book. And experience dictated that his first job here was to put the book in the proper order. It was routine to shuffle the stacks of reports like a deck of cards, throw in a takeout menu or two, just to say *fuck you* to the defense attorney and his investigator. Each page turned over in discovery was stamped with a page number and date. This was done so that in court the attorneys from each side of the aisle could refer to the same page by a uniform number. So it didn't matter if Bosch reordered the pages. He could put his own system in place. All Haller would have to do is use the stamped page number if he wanted to refer to one of the documents in court.

There was not a lot of difference between the reports filed by Sheriff's investigators and the reports Bosch had authored for the LAPD. Some headings were different, a few report numbers as well. But Bosch easily had the book reshuffled and in correct order by the time his plate of thin-sliced pork chops arrived. He kept the stack of records front and center and the plate to the side so he could continue to work as he ate.

On top of the reordered stack was the Incident Report, which was always the first page of a murder book after the table of contents. But there was no table of contents—another *fuck you* from prosecution to defense—so the IR was on top. Bosch glanced at it but was not expecting to learn anything. It was all first-day information. If it wasn't wrong, then it was incomplete.

The pork chops were thin and crispy, piled on top of fried rice on his plate. Bosch was using his fingers to eat them like potato chips. He now wiped his hands on the paper napkin so he could turn the pages on the stack without soiling them. He quickly went through several ancillary and meaningless reports until he got to the Chronological Log. This was the murder bible, the heart of any homicide investigation. It would detail all the moves of the lead detectives on the case. It would be where case theory would emerge. It would be where Bosch would be convinced of Da'Quan Foster's guilt or find the same doubt that had crept into Mickey Haller's gut.

Most detective pairings had a division of labor that was worked out over several cases. Usually one member of the detective team was charged with keeping reports and the murder book intact and up to date. The Chronological Log was the exception. It was kept on computer as a digital file and routinely accessed by both detectives so each could enter his or her movements on a case. It was periodically printed out on three-hole paper and clipped into a binder, or in this case added to a defense discovery package. But the most active version was always a digital file and it was a living document, growing and changing all the time.

The printout of the chrono in the discovery file was 129 pages long and was authored by Sheriff's investigators Lazlo Cornell and Tara Schmidt. Though over the years Bosch had had many interactions with Sheriff's homicide investigators, he knew neither of them. This was a handicap because he had no measure of their skills or temperaments as he moved into their written work. He knew some of it would surface as he learned of their investigative moves and conclusions but Bosch still felt like he was behind the curve. He knew other investigators in the Sheriff's homicide bureau he could call to discuss the pair, but he didn't dare do that and possibly reveal that he was working against them. Word of Bosch's betrayal to the cause would spread rapidly and jump from the Sheriff's Department to the LAPD in hours if not minutes. Bosch didn't want that. Yet.

The first seventy-five pages of the chrono documented the moves of the investigation before the DNA connection was made to Da'Quan Foster. Bosch carefully read these pages anyway because they gave insight into the investigators' initial case theory as well as their thoroughness and determination. Lexi Parks's husband was fully investigated and cleared and the efforts were well documented in the chrono. Though he had an ironclad alibi—involved in the pursuit and arrest of a car thief—for the time of his wife's murder, the investigators were smart enough to know that he could have set the murder up to be carried out by others. Even though aspects of the murder—the sexual attack and brutality of the fatal beating—tended to point in another direction, the investigators were undaunted in their look at the husband. Bosch found a growing respect for Cornell and Schmidt as he read through these sequences in the chrono.

The early investigation also went in many other directions. The investigators interviewed a multitude of sex offenders living in the West Hollywood area, probed the victim's personal background for enemies, and looked through her job activities and history for people she may have angered or who could have held grudges.

All of these efforts hit dead ends. Once they had DNA from the killer, it was used to clear anyone who even remotely approached suspect status. The victim's personal background produced no deep conflicts, no spurned lovers, and no extramarital activity on her or her husband's part. As an assistant city manager her reach into the city's bureaucracy and politics was substantial, yet she carried the final say on few items of business and on none that were controversial.

A profile of the murderer drawn from the details of the crime scene was what eventually pointed the investigation away from the victim's personal and professional life. The profile, put together by the Sheriff's Department Behavioral Science Unit, concluded that the suspect was a psychopath who was filling a complex of psychological needs in the murder of Lexi Parks. *No kidding,* Bosch thought as he read the conclusion.

The profile stated that the killer was most likely a stranger to Parks and that she could have crossed his path anywhere recently or long ago. Because she was a public figure who appeared regularly on West Hollywood's public-access cable channel as well as at public events, the circle of possibilities was even greater. Her killer could have simply seen her on the news or at a televised city council meeting. The crossing could have happened anywhere.

The killing seemed to be both carefully planned and reckless in terms of the overkill in violence and the DNA evidence left behind. Other crime scene details that influenced the profile included the fact that the victim had not been tied up in any way—indicating the killer did not need bindings to overpower and control her. The victim was also found by her husband with a pillow over her face, hiding the intense damage of the fatal beating from view and possibly indicating remorse on the part of the killer.

Since her husband was a law enforcement officer, several security measures had been installed in the home, including an alarm system and multiple locks on all doors. The killer had gained entrance through the window of a home office, removing a screen and leaving it leaning against the back wall of the house, then jimmying the lock on the window. The victim apparently had not set the alarm system and her husband said that she rarely did so despite his often-repeated request that she set it when he was working at night and she was home alone.

All of this and other details added up to the profile of a suspect who was opportunistic and relentless as a predator. Parks had gone to the Pavilions supermarket on Santa Monica Boulevard on the evening of her murder. For several days the investigators scoured security video from the store and shopping plaza where it was located, tracking Parks's visit and hoping to find the point of intersection between victim and predator. But nothing came of it. In the store, Parks saw and acknowledged several acquaintances whom she knew socially or from her government work. But all of them were checked out and eventually cleared, either through voluntary DNA comparison or otherwise.

It all added up to spinning wheels, but they were wheels that needed to be spun. Bosch's review of the first eighty pages of the chrono left him with the belief that Lazlo Cornell and Tara Schmidt had conducted a very thorough investigation—one that he would be proud to have put his name on himself.

And all of it was for naught. That is, until the twenty-seventh day of the investigation when they received a letter from the California Department of Justice informing them that the DNA sample they had submitted to the state's CODIS database had been matched to a convicted offender named Da'Quan Foster.

Until that moment, neither Cornell nor Schmidt had ever heard of Da'Quan Foster in regard to Parks or any other case. But they started planning for when they would eventually meet him. He was placed under twenty-four-hour surveillance to see if he made any moves that could be useful in his prosecution or threatened to harm another woman. Meanwhile, he was backgrounded and the investigation proceeded under the tightest security so that no word would leak to the media or to the husband of the victim.

Eleven days after the DNA match came in from the

state, the two lead investigators entered the artist's studio where Foster was alone, having just finished teaching a small class of children about primary colors. Leimert Park was in the City of Los Angeles. The investigators were accompanied by two uniformed LAPD officers from the South Bureau Gang Unit. Cornell and Schmidt asked Foster if he would accompany them to the Homicide Unit, where they wanted to ask him questions.

Da'Quan Foster agreed.

Bosch looked up and realized he had worked through the lunch rush in the restaurant. His check was sitting on the edge of the table and he had not noticed it. Feeling sheepish about not turning the table over during lunch, he put thirty dollars down on the table for the ten-dollar check, then gathered the reports back together and headed out. He cursed his luck when he found a parking ticket under the Cherokee's windshield wiper. He had paid for two hours on the meter but had been in the restaurant for two and a half. He took the ticket from beneath the rubber blade and shoved it into his pocket. He never had to worry about parking tickets when he was driving a city car, when he carried a badge. It was another reminder of how his life had changed in the last six months. He used to feel like an outsider with an insider's job. From now on he would be a full-time outsider.

For some reason Bosch didn't want to go home to finish reading the chrono and the rest of the discovery reports. He felt as though reviewing the case at the dining room table where he had worked on so many cases as an LAPD homicide detective would be some kind of betrayal. He took Third Street out of downtown and out to West Hollywood. Before reading further into the chrono log, he wanted to drive by the house where Lexi Parks had been murdered. He thought it would be good to get out of the paper and to see some of the physical touchstones of the case.

The home was located on Orlando south of Melrose in a neighborhood of modest bungalows. Bosch pulled to the opposite curb and studied the house. It was almost entirely hidden by a tall privacy hedge with an arched entry cut through it. He could see the front door beyond the passage. There was a FOR SALE sign posted in front of the hedge. Bosch wondered how difficult it would be to sell a house where a brutal murder had recently occurred. He decided that living in the house where your wife had been the victim of that murder would be even more difficult.

His phone buzzed and he answered while still staring at the house.

"Bosch," he said.

"It's me," Haller said. "How's it going?"

"It's going."

"You still reading the discovery material?"

"About halfway through."

"And?"

"And nothing. I'm still reading."

"I just thought maybe you might have—"

"Look, don't push me on this, Mick. I'm doing what I have to do. If I want to take it further when I'm finished, I'll tell you. If I don't, I'll drop all of this stuff back with you."

"Okay, okay."

"Good. I'll catch you later."

Bosch disconnected. He continued to look at the house. He noticed that there was a BEWARE OF DOG sign posted in a planter beside the front door. He had not read anything in the discovery so far that mentioned

Parks and her husband having a dog. He drummed his fingers on the steering wheel as he thought about that. He felt strongly that if the couple owned a dog it would have been noted up front in the reports. House pets always leave trace evidence in a home. It was something that had to be accounted for in an investigation.

Bosch's conclusion was that there was no dog and that the sign was posted as a deterrent. The next best thing to having a dog was pretending you had a dog. The question was did the killer know there was no dog? And if so, how?

Finally, he drove away and went up Orlando to Santa Monica Boulevard. He turned east toward home but pulled over again when he spotted a Starbucks at Fairfax. This time he bought four hours of time on the meter and went in with the discovery file.

With a cup of steaming black coffee in hand, he settled into a chair in the corner with a small round table next to it. There was no room to open the file and spread the stack, so he just pulled out the chrono to continue reading where he had left off. Before doing so he took a pen out of his shirt pocket and wrote a quick note on the outside of the file folder.

DOG?

He needed to confirm his conclusion about the dog. Jotting the one-word question down was an almost involuntary response to what he had seen while sitting outside the murder house. But as soon as he wrote it, he realized that something as small as writing a single word on the file was a big step toward buying into the case. He had to ask himself the question. Did he miss the work so much that he could actually cross the aisle and work for an accused murderer? Because that was what it would be. Haller was the attorney of record but the client was sitting in a cell accused of raping a woman and beating her to death. If he accepted the job offer, Bosch would be working for him.

He felt the burn of humiliation on the back of his neck. He thought of all the guys before him who retired and the next thing you know they were working for defense lawyers or even the Public Defender's Office. He had dropped relationships with those guys as though they were criminals themselves. The moment he heard someone had crossed, Bosch considered him persona non grata.

And now…

He took a sip of scalding coffee and tried to put the discomfort aside. He then took up the investigation where he had left off.

After picking up Foster at his studio, the Sheriff's investigators drove him to the Lynwood station, where they borrowed a room in the detective bureau. The interview was short and its entire transcript was placed into the chronological record. Foster was asked only a few questions before realizing the depth of the trouble he was in and asking for Mickey Haller by name.

Cornell and Schmidt never told him that they had connected his DNA to a murder scene. They attempted to pad their case by flushing out an admission from Foster. But the effort failed. Cornell began the session by reading Foster his constitutional rights—always a quick way to put a willing interview subject on high alert.

Cornell: Okay, Mr. Foster, are you willing to talk to us a little bit, maybe answer some questions and clear up some details?

Foster: I guess so, but what's it about? What do you people think I did?

Cornell: Well, it's about Lexi Parks. You know her, right?

Foster: That name, it rings a bell for some reason but I don't know. Maybe I sold her a painting or she's one of the mothers of the kids I got come in the studio.

Cornell: No, sir, Lexi Parks didn't buy a painting. She is the woman up in West Hollywood. You remember you visited her at her house?

Foster: West Hollywood? No, I ain't been to West Hollywood.

Cornell: What about Vince Harrick, do you know him?

Foster: No, I don't know no Vince Harrick. Who's he?

Cornell: That's Lexi's husband. Deputy Harrick. Did you know him when he worked in this station?

Foster: What? I don't know him. I've never been here before you took me.

Schmidt: Can you tell us where you were the night of February eighth going into the morning of February ninth of this year? That was a Sunday night. Where were you that night, Mr. Foster?

Foster: How the fuck would I know? That's like two months ago. Tell you what, every night I'm either at home with my family, puttin' my boys to sleep, or at the studio, doin' my work. I stay over a lot at night to get things done. I'm not teachin' anybody anything and I get to work on my own stuff, you understand? I mean, like I got people who want my pictures and they'll pay. So I do the work. So you can take your pick between me bein' at home or me bein' at the studio because that's it. There's no other place. And I know my rights here and you people are up to no good on me. I think I want my lawyer now. I'm thinking I want Mickey Haller to represent me in this matter—whatever the fuck it is.

Cornell: Then let's get it on the record right here, Mr. Foster. Tell us why you chose Lexi Parks.

Foster: Chose her for what? I don't know her and I don't know what you're talking about.

Cornell: You killed her, didn't you? You beat her and you killed her and then you raped her.

Foster: You people are crazy. You're really fucking crazy. Get me my goddamned lawyer. Now.

Cornell: Yeah, you bet, asshole. One lawyer coming right up.

Schmidt: You sure you don't want to clear this up right here? Now's the time. You bring a lawyer into this and it goes out of our hands.

Foster: I want my motherfucking lawyer.

Schmidt: You got it. But he's not going to be able to explain how we found your DNA in Lexi Parks. Only you can—

Foster: DNA? What DNA? Lord, what is happening here? What is—I can't believe you motherfuckers. I ain't killed nobody. I want my lawyer and I'm not saying another word to you people.

Cornell: In that case, stand up, sir. You are under arrest for the murder of Lexi Parks.

End of Interview

Bosch read the entry twice and then made a note to remind Haller to get a video version of the interview. The interview room was most likely outfitted with a camera. If he stayed with the case, he would want to see Foster's body language and hear the tone of each voice. It would tell him more than the words on the printout. Still, knowing that, his take on the transcript of the brief interview was that Foster had not seen the questions about Lexi Parks coming. There appeared to be real surprise and then panic in his words. He knew that didn't really mean anything. Sex murders were usually the work of psychopaths and with that psychology was an innate ability to lie, to act, to feign surprise and horror when it was needed. Psychopaths were great liars.

Bosch noted one of the lines in the transcript. Cornell had accused Foster of beating and killing Lexi Parks and then raping her. Harry had not reviewed the autopsy yet but the question from Cornell was the first hint that the rape had occurred postmortem. If that was what the evidence revealed, then it rolled a whole new set of psychological factors into the case.

Bosch continued to read. The rest of the chrono outlined the efforts of Cornell and Schmidt to find a connection between Da'Quan Foster and Lexi Parks, either through her husband and his work, which would put the motivation in the arena of revenge, or through a random intersection of predator and prey, which would better fit the profile and type of assault. But neither effort was fruitful. As Foster said during his brief interview, he had never been to the Sheriff's Lynwood station, where Vincent Harrick had last worked five years ago. The investigators could find no evidence to the contrary and the reality was that there would be no logical reason for a Rollin' 40s Crip out of Leimert Park to be conducting gang business all the way east in Lynwood. That was Bloods territory and it didn't add up.

Cornell's focus was on the Lynwood/Harrick angle and backgrounding Foster, while Schmidt worked the sexual predator angle. Schmidt's task was the more difficult to investigate and prove because it relied upon the happenstance of Lexi Parks somehow, somewhere crossing the radar of a sexual sadist on the hunt. Bosch, like Cornell and Schmidt, had already read and seen enough to know the murder was not a crime of opportunity. There was more than enough evidence that the victim was stalked and the crime planned. The BEWARE OF DOG sign was the starting point of this supposition.

According to the discovery, there was no dog in the house, and the killer seemed to know it. That suggested that the house on Orlando had been cased. Other factors such as the alarm system not being engaged and the husband working a midnight shift also added to the theory.

Schmidt carefully documented the victim's activities in the six weeks prior to her death, trying to find the place where Foster and Parks crossed paths. She looked at hundreds of hours of video taken from cameras along Lexi's path but she never found Foster in one digital frame. Bosch knew that this was the juncture where cases could go wrong. They had a suspect in custody and a DNA match. Some would already call that a slam-dunk case. But the investigators were being thorough. They were looking for more and in doing so they were sliding into the tunnel. The tunnel was the place where vision narrows and the investigator sees only the bird in hand. Bosch had to wonder if Schmidt had been looking for any other faces on those videos besides Foster's.

Bosch made another note on the outside of the file, a reminder to tell Haller he should make a discovery request to be allowed access to all of the videos Schmidt had studied.

The chrono had an oblique reference to a witness interviewed by Cornell and identified only as AW— which Bosch recognized as shorthand for *alibi witness*. It was not uncommon to use coded abbreviations in reports to safeguard witnesses who were not officially given confidential informant status. Bosch also knew that AW could be a witness fortifying or knocking down a suspect's alibi. In this case the chrono said that Cornell met with the AW seven days after Foster's arrest and that the meeting lasted an hour.

Bosch skimmed through the remaining pages of the chrono and nothing else caught his eye. There were routine entries on preparations for the case to move toward trial. Cornell and Schmidt found nothing that directly tied Foster to the victim but they had his DNA, and apart from the O.J. Simpson case twenty years before, DNA was as good as it got when it came to closing out a case. Cornell, Schmidt, and the prosecutor assigned to the case were locked and loaded. They sailed through a four-hour preliminary hearing in April and were now ready for trial.

The prosecutor was a woman—always a good edge to have when it was a sex crime. Her name was Ellen Tasker and Bosch had worked with her on some big cases early in her career. She was good and lived up to her name when it came to making sure cases were ready for trial. She was a lifer in the D.A.'s Office, a prosecutor who kept her head below the level of office politics and just did her job. And she did it well. Bosch could not recall Tasker ever losing a case.

Before moving on, he called Haller.

"You said that your client had an alibi but you just couldn't prove it."

"That's right. He was in the studio painting. He did that a lot—worked all night. But he worked alone. How am I going to prove that?"

"Did he have a cell phone?"

"No, no cell so no pinging record. Just the landline in the studio. Why?"

"There is a reference in the Chronological Log to one of the detectives meeting with an alibi witness. You know anything about that?"

"No, and if they found somebody who supports DQ's alibi, they have to bring them forward."

"DQ?"

"Da'Quan. He signs his paintings DQ. By the way, you know that's how I'm getting paid, right? In paintings. I figure we get an acquittal and the value will go way up."

Bosch didn't care how Haller was getting paid.

"Listen to me. I'm not saying this witness supports his alibi. It's probably the opposite. It was referenced in the chrono and I just wanted to know if you were aware."

"No, I didn't see that."

"It was coded and brief—which makes me think it might be significant. I'll look through the witness reports and see if I can find anything."

"If you don't find it, then that's trouble for them. Violation of discovery."

"Whatever. I'll call you later."

Clicking off, Bosch realized he needed to be more guarded with Haller and not just throw things out to him that he might tee up and take into court, dragging Bosch along with him.

Bosch looked through the printouts until he found the stack of witness statements. He started paging through them, checking the summaries for who they were and what they said. The great majority were witnesses from the Lexi Parks side of the investigation: friends, co-workers, professional acquaintances who were interviewed as the investigation took shape. There were also statements from her husband and several Sheriff's deputies who knew Parks through him. The second half of the stack contained interviews from people who knew Da'Quan Foster. Many of these were LAPD officers who knew of him from his active gang days. There were also statements from former parole officers, neighbors, fellow shopkeepers, and the suspect's wife, Marta.

Bosch found what he was looking for on a twofer—
a report page that had statements from two witnesses
summarized on it. It was an old discovery trick. Turn
over reams of paper as a way of hiding the one thing
you don't want the defense attorney to notice. The prosecution had not violated the rules of discovery but had
made finding the important piece of information a needle in the haystack.

The top half of the witness report contained the
summary of an interview with a neighbor of Da'Quan
Foster's who said he did not see Foster's car parked in
front of his house on the night of the murder. It was
a relatively harmless comment because Foster was not
claiming that he was at home. He was claiming he spent
the night painting in his studio.

But just a line below the neighbor's statement was
the start of another statement from someone identified
only as M. White. This statement said M. White
stopped by Foster's studio on the night of the murder
to see Foster but the painter was not there. That was
all that was included in the report but it was enough
for Bosch to know that Cornell and Schmidt had found
someone who could counter Foster's claim that he had
spent the entire night in the studio painting.

The subterfuge employed by the detectives to hide
the identity and value of the witness known as M.
White didn't really bother Bosch. He assumed that "M.
White" was not the witness's name but rather his gen-
der and race. He knew all Haller would have to do is
file a motion citing insufficient discovery and the sheriffs would have to cough up the real identity. It was all
part of the game and he had pulled the haystack move
himself on occasion as a cop. What troubled him was
the fact that now there was an alibi issue added to the
DNA match that put Foster at the crime scene.

It was enough to make him want to drop the review of the case right there and then.

Harry thought about it for a little bit while he finished his coffee and gave his eyes a rest. He took off his reading glasses and looked out through the window at the busy intersection of Fairfax and Santa Monica. He knew he still had the autopsy and the crime scene photos to go through to complete his review of the murder file. He had saved the photos for last because they would be the most difficult to look at—and were not something he would risk doing in a public place like a coffee shop.

His eyes suddenly caught on a familiar face across the intersection. Mickey Haller smiling from the back of a bus moving south on Fairfax. The advertisement carried a slogan that made Bosch want to dump the whole file in the trash can.

**Reasonable Doubt for a Reasonable Fee.
Call the Lincoln Lawyer.**

Bosch got up from the table and went to the trash can. He dropped his empty cup in and headed out the door.

7

Entering his house, Bosch looked at the empty dining room table and was tempted to sit down and spread out the printouts and photos from the case. But he knew his daughter would be getting home at any time and he didn't want to risk her stumbling onto a bad scene. He went down the hallway to his bedroom, closed the door, and started spreading things out on his bed—right after he made it and smoothed the top covers.

What he spread out were the 8 x 10 color copies of the crime scene photos from Lexi Parks's house. These included several dozen of the victim's body as it had been found on her bed. They were shots taken from many angles and from many different distances ranging from full room shots to extreme close-ups of specific wounds and parts of the body.

There were also photos taken from many angles of all the other rooms in the house, and his plan was to look at them second.

The crime scene photos created a grisly tableau on the bed. The murder of Lexi Parks had been excessively violent and the harshness of it was not buffered by the one-step-removed process of viewing the scene through photos. There was a stark quality to the shots that Bosch was familiar with. Police photographers were not artists. Their job was to unflinchingly reveal all, and the photographer on the Parks case did just that.

Bosch had spread the photos out in a matrix of eight across and eight down and he stood at the end of the bed, taking in the overall murder mosaic. He then picked up individual photos one by one and studied them. He took a magnifying glass from a drawer in his dresser so that he could see some aspects of the photos even closer up.

It was difficult work. Bosch never got accustomed to viewing crime scenes. He had been to hundreds of them and seen the result of human inhumanity too many times to count. He always thought that if he got used to it, then he had lost something inside that was needed to do the job right. You had to have an emotional response. It was that response that lit the match that started the fire of relentlessness.

What lit the match this time was Lexi Parks's hands. She had obviously tried to fight her attacker. She had struggled and put her arms up to ward off the assault. But she was quickly overpowered by repeated blows to her face. Her hands fell back on the bed, palms up, almost as if she was raising them in surrender. It touched Bosch. It made him angry, made him want to find and hurt whoever had done this.

How could Haller defend the man who did this?

Harry went into the bathroom to fill a glass with water. He drank it while standing in the doorway and looking at the photos from the side. He worked to calm himself so that he could continue to professionally assess the photos and the crime scene.

He went back to the bed and studied the photos again and soon started drawing conclusions about the crime. He believed that the victim had been asleep in her bed. She was on the right side of a king, having left room for her husband on the left. It appeared to Bosch that the killer had surprised her in her sleep, straddling her and taking immediate control as she awoke. He probably put one hand over her mouth, maybe held a weapon with the other. She got her hands loose to fight and then he started striking her.

And he didn't stop. Long after her defenses were down and she was incapacitated, she was struck over and over again with a hard object. The face of the victim in the photos bore no resemblance to the face Bosch had seen accompanying the many newspaper stories generated by her murder. The face of the victim in the photos in fact bore no resemblance to any face at all. The nose was literally gone, interred in the pulp of blood and tissue that had been her face. Both eye sockets were crushed and misshapen, pieces of broken teeth and bone shone brightly in the blood. The eyes were half-lidded and the normal singular focus was broken. One stared forward, the other down and to the left.

Bosch sat down on a chair in the corner of the room and looked at the grid of photos from afar. The only thing worse would have been his being at the real scene, which would have added a multisensory dimension to his revulsion. No murder scene ever smelled pleasant. No matter how fresh, no matter how clean the environment.

His eyes kept going to the hands and he noticed from his new position a slight discoloration to the victim's skin on the left wrist. He got up to go back to the bed. The photo was a wide shot that displayed the entire body in situ. He bent over the photo with the magnifying glass and saw that the woman's wrist had slight tan lines left by a thick bracelet or, most likely, a watch.

Since he had seen nothing in the summaries or reports about the murder being possibly motivated by robbery, the missing watch was curious to Bosch. Had the victim been wearing it at the time of the attack? Had she taken it off to sleep? Had it fallen or been pulled off during her struggle to live? Had it been taken by her attacker as a souvenir?

Bosch studied the bed table next to the body. There was a bottle of water, a prescription bottle, and a paperback novel, but the watch wasn't there. He went back to the printouts and looked at the property report. Since the victim was murdered in her own home, the property report dealt primarily with items from the crime scene and the house that were specifically examined by the investigators or forensics team. There was nothing here about the watch. It had apparently not come off in the victim's struggle. It had not been noted as having been found in the bedding, on the floor, or anywhere else.

Bosch next flipped back into the Chronological Log to check if he had missed a mention of the watch in the early stages of the investigation—before there was a focus on Da'Quan Foster. He found nothing and wrote a note about the watch on the outside of the file below his other notations.

He collected all the photos of the body from the bed and put the stack to the side in case his daughter came home. He then moved to the second stack of photos, which were the shots taken of every room in the victim's house at the time of the on-site investigation. This was a sign of the thoroughness of the investigation. Bosch knew that the photos from other rooms of the house would have been a call and request made by the lead investigators. It showed they were not cutting corners.

There were several photos taken in each room of the house and it took Bosch more than a half hour to work his way through them. He saw only the things that looked like the normal trappings of a neatly kept home where there were no children and both husband and wife worked full-time jobs and had active lifestyles. A second bedroom was used as a home gym and a third used as an office. The single-car garage was used to store bikes, surfboards, and camping equipment. There was no room to park a car.

The home office drew Bosch's attention the longest. It looked to him like the room was primarily used by Lexi Parks. The knickknacks and souvenirs on the desk and on the bookcase shelves behind it appeared to have been collected during her duties as a city employee. There was a paperweight from the West Hollywood Rotary Club and framed certificates of appreciation from various gay and lesbian groups in regard to her involvement in the permitting process for the annual gay pride parade that drew participants and watchers from around the world. On the wall beside the desk was a framed diploma from Pepperdine University with the name Alexandra Abbott Parks. Clipped to the sides of the frame were various name tags from functions she had attended as part of her job. Bosch realized there was a large social component to Lexi Parks's work that most likely added a layer of difficulty to the effort of tracking the point where she may have encountered her killer—whether it was Foster or someone else.

His eye held on the diploma frame when he saw a name tag that was unlike the others. It was a red-and-white juror tag that would have been issued by the county and worn by Parks when she was called in for jury service. All that was visible in the photo was a bar code—in keeping with juror anonymity—and no visible indication of when or in which courthouse the juror had served.

More than anything he had seen so far the juror tag bothered him. He had seen nothing in the chrono or other files about this being a branch of the investigation. Though Bosch would freely admit that an investigation was a subjective matter always open to second-guessing—by lawyers, judges, juries, and other investigators—this struck him as something that was either missed or hidden. If Lexi Parks had served on a criminal courts jury, that would have been an important arena for investigators to look into. It would have put her in a building where there was a routine flow of criminals and accused criminals. In a case like this, where the victim appeared to be chosen at random, there is always a crossing point. The place where the predator first encounters his prey. The job of the investigators is to find the crossing, the place where the circle of the victim's life overlaps the circle of the predator.

Now Bosch had to consider whether investigators Lazlo Cornell and Tara Schmidt had missed this possible crossing or whether it was something they purposely left out of discovery to obfuscate the prosecution's case.

He put the thought aside for the time being and went back to the other photographs. The office had two closets. Both were photographed from multiple angles. One was packed with summer dresses and blouses on hangers and shoe boxes on the shelves above. It looked like Parks rotated seasonal clothing. At the time of her death in February temperatures were cooler.

The second closet was used to store boxes from computers, printers, and other household items. On the top shelf Bosch saw a small square box that was made of what looked like brown leather. There was no brand name or logo but Bosch thought it might be a box that a watch would come in. He studied the photo with the magnifying glass. He knew there was no telling whether the box was empty, or whether it was for a woman's or man's watch. Brown leather favored it being a man's watch box.

Bosch heard the front door of the house open. His daughter was home. He had started stacking the second set of photos when he heard her call to him.

"In my room," he called back. "I'll be out in a minute."

He then stacked all the files and photos together on his bureau. He got out his phone and called Mickey Haller. The defense attorney answered right away and Bosch could tell by the background noise that he again was in his car.

"Okay," Bosch said. "I'm ready to talk."

8

They met at the bar at Musso's and both ordered a vodka martini. It was early enough that getting one of the precious stools was not a problem. Bosch didn't want to bring the thick stack of discovery documents in with him and draw attention, so he simply brought the empty file folder on which he had jotted his notes.

Haller was still in a crisp court suit but his tie was long gone. He noticed the empty file that Bosch put down on the old polished wood bar top.

"Well, you're not giving it all back to me," he said. "That's a good sign."

"Not yet, at least," Bosch said.

"So, what do you want to talk about, then?"

"I'm ready to talk to your client. Can you get me in?"

"The easiest and quickest way is for us both to go in tomorrow. Attorney-client visit with an investigator in tow. It cuts through the bullshit. You have a problem with that?"

Bosch thought a moment before answering.

"Do I need to show a PI license? I don't have that. I got one about twelve years ago but it's long expired."

"No need. I'll print out a letter of engagement. It'll say you're working under the aegis of me and Dennis Wojciechowski, a state-licensed private investigator. That'll do it."

"Who the hell is Dennis Woja-whatever-you-just-said?"

"That's Cisco, my investigator."

"Now I know why they call him Cisco."

"And a lot of other things. So I'm clear in the morning and have two things in the CCB after lunch. What's your morning look like?"

"Open."

"Then let's meet at the attorneys' window at nine tomorrow."

Bosch nodded and didn't say anything.

"So, what've you got?" Haller asked.

Bosch pulled the folder over front and center and looked at the few things he had written down during his review of the files.

"Well, these really don't make sense out of context," he said. "There are some things that should have been followed up on. Or maybe they were followed up on and we don't know."

"You mean they've hidden it from us," Haller said, the tone of his voice building to outrage.

"Just hold your horses. We're not in court and you don't have to turn on the outrage. I'm not saying anything's been hidden. I'm saying I saw a few things that bothered me about the investigation. I'm not talking about your client. I'm talking about things I would have followed up on. Maybe they did and maybe they didn't. And maybe…"

"Maybe what?"

"They got lazy. They have a DNA match and maybe they don't think they need to flip all the cards over before going all in. They also have a witness who blows up your client's alibi. Those two things, for most cases that would be enough. Easy."

Haller leaned in close to Bosch.

"Tell me about their alibi wit—is it a woman?"

"No, I think it's a white male because of the name in the report, M. White. I think they're hiding his identity as well as hiding him so they can sandbag you. It's a guy who said he went to Foster's studio that night to see him and he wasn't there. That's why I want to talk to Foster. See if he's lying."

"If he's lying, I'm flying. I tell all my clients that."

Haller poured the rest of his vodka from the shaker into his glass. He swished it around with the olive on the end of a toothpick, then ate the olive.

"Dinner," he said. "You want another one?"

Bosch shook his head.

"I can't stay. Maddie's home tonight and I want to spend some time with her. She's going out of town soon."

"Out of town? Where?"

"They have a seniors' retreat at her school. You know, before graduation. They go camping up at Big Bear, talk about the next step of their lives, stuff like that. I just want to be home as much as I can be when she's there. I also need to get ready for tomorrow. Reread some stuff before I meet the man."

"So have you made the call—guilty as charged?"

"Nope. I think it's more likely than not but, like I said, there were some things they didn't do that I would have done. I don't like coming in and second-guessing but when you see it you see it."

"Can't un-see it."

"Something like that."

"What's the biggest problem with the prosecution's case?"

"Right now?"

"Based on what you read."

Bosch took a drink while he thought of an answer and composed it properly.

"The crossing."

"Meaning?"

"Motive and opportunity. They've got DNA that puts your man in that house and at that crime scene. But how did he get there? Why did he get there? This woman led a fairly public life. City Hall hearings, council meetings, public events, and so on. According to the records, they looked at hundreds of hours of video and they don't have one single frame that has both Lexi Parks and Da'Quan Foster in it."

Haller was nodding, seeing how he could play it.

"Added to that," Bosch continued, "you have the crime scene. They had it profiled and there was all kinds of psychological shit going on in that crime. How does that connect to Foster—a reformed gangbanger from south L.A. with no history of this kind of violence? He may have been a shot caller for the Rollin' 40s but this is a whole different thing."

"I can use this," Haller said. "All of it. I'll tear them a new one."

"Look, these are things that bother me. That doesn't mean they'll bother a jury or a judge. I told you, I think it's more likely your guy did it than not. I'm just reporting what I'm seeing. And I have a question."

"What?"

"Foster's DNA was in the state's data bank because of the rape arrest that didn't stick."

"It didn't stick because it was bullshit."

"Tell me about it."

"What it amounted to was a sweep. The victim was drugged and raped over a couple days in the back room of a drop house. Whoever the bastard was who did it, he also inked her with a 'Property of the Rollin' Forties' tat. So she escapes and that's their clue. They grabbed every guy they had in their Rollin' Forties files and swabbed them all. It never amounted to anything because he didn't do it."

"That's a bad story. Will it come up at trial?"

"Not if I can help it. These are very different circumstances. It's not relevant."

Bosch nodded and again thought about why he was getting involved with this case and this client.

"So we talk to him tomorrow morning," Haller said. "Then what? What do you need from me?"

Bosch finished the last of his drink. He didn't go for the shaker. He wanted no trace of inebriation on him when he got home. His daughter was stricter than a wife about that.

"Let's see if I'm still working it after the interview. If I am, I think you tell the judge you want access to all the video Cornell and Schmidt looked at. They were looking for Da'Quan. But I wonder who else might have been in the places Lexi Parks went."

Haller pointed at him, nodding.

"Alternate theory of the crime. Alternate suspect. Got it. This is good."

"No, it's not good. Not yet, at least. And I should warn you. I'm not going to be nice to your client tomorrow. He's an accused murderer and that's exactly how I'm going to treat him. By the time we're finished, he might not want me working for you or him."

Bosch slid his glass toward the bartender and got off the stool. He saw a woman looking for a spot to sit and signaled her over.

"See you at nine," he said to Haller. "Don't oversleep."

"Don't worry," Haller said. "I'll be there."

9

Ellis and Long watched from a car parked at the curb on Las Palmas west of Musso's rear parking lot. There was an easy silence between them that came from years of sitting in cars and watching people. Long had gone into Musso's earlier and observed from the opposite end of the bar while the lawyer was meeting with another man—a man Long didn't recognize. So when he scanned the parking lot and saw the same mystery man standing under the light at the parking attendant's booth, he sat up straight in the passenger seat.

"That's him," he said. "The guy he was meeting with."

"You sure?" Ellis asked.

He raised a pair of binoculars and studied the mystery man.

"Yeah," Long said. "You should go. In case."

In case the man at the booth had seen Long inside earlier. But they didn't have to finish sentences like that.

Ellis left the binoculars on the dashboard and got out of the car. Long slid over behind the wheel. Just in case. Ellis walked into the lot and ducked between two cars so it would look like he just parked and was walking in. He waited until the man got his keys at the booth and started walking toward his car. Ellis stepped out, hands in his pockets, and started walking down the same driving aisle as the approaching man. Ellis noted he was clean shaven and had a full head of gray hair and a lean build. He guessed he was midfifties but could be one of those lucky fuckers who looked younger than he was.

Just before they passed each other the mystery man turned left between two cars and used his key to unlock the door on an old Jeep Cherokee. Ellis glanced casually at the rear plate and kept going toward the steps that led to the rear entrance at Musso's. He speed-dialed Long. When he answered, Ellis gave his partner the make of the car and the license plate number and told him he was going inside to check on the status of the lawyer.

"Think I should tail the Jeep?" Long asked.

Ellis thought a moment. On principle he didn't like the idea of splitting up. But if this guy was a player, then it could be a missed opportunity.

"I don't know," he said. "What do you think?"

"Go get a beer," Long said. "I'll see where this guy goes."

"He's driving a shit box. He's probably not going far."

"Those old Cherokees? Collectors' items."

"Shit box."

"Go on craigslist, ten grand for a good one, easy. Two hundred thousand miles? Still ten grand."

"Whatever. I'm going in. Haller's in the back bar, right?"

"Yeah, back bar. No names, remember?"

"Right."

Ellis could hear the Cherokee's engine turn over behind him. Then a voice called to him from behind as well.

"Sir, did you park?"

He turned to see the parking attendant in the doorway of the booth.

"No, I'm on the street."

He pointed toward Las Palmas, then turned back and went down the stairs into the hallway behind the restaurant's kitchen. He followed it around past the old wooden phone booths and out into the new dining room. Musso's was almost a hundred years old. There was the new room and the old room but even that distinction was a half century old. He followed an ancient waiter in a red half coat into the old room and then moved into the bar area. It was crowded with a congregation two deep behind the lucky ones sitting on bar stools.

He saw Haller on a stool near the far end. He was engaged in conversation with the woman sitting to his left. It looked like a pickup situation to Ellis but he could tell the woman wasn't having any. The bartender put down fresh martinis in front of them just the same. With sidecar shakers on ice.

Haller wasn't going anywhere soon. Ellis retraced his steps and went into one of the old phone booths in the back entrance hall. There was no longer a pay phone in the booth but the small space could still be used for privacy. He closed the door, pulled out his own phone, and called Long.

"Did you follow him?"

"Yeah, we're going up Highland."

"The plate?"

"There's a law enforcement block on it. Says LAPD."

"He's a cop."

"Yep, or possibly retired. He looked like he could have put in at least twenty-five."

"Either way, what's he doing talking to our guy?"

"No way of telling. Let's see where he goes."

"I'll be here. Looks like our man is working some chick at the bar."

"Talk to you."

Long didn't care what Ellis thought. The blue Cherokee up ahead was a nice ride. Classic squared-off design that was utilitarian and solid. Long wondered why they had changed them. Now they looked like any other SUV. Bloated, like a fat guy whose blubber goes over his belt. His ex-wife called them muffin tops.

The mystery man was now on Cahuenga, still heading north. Long saw the left turn signal on the Cherokee start flashing. The mystery man was going to head up into the hills. This would complicate things for Long.

Long drove by the Cherokee as it waited for an opening in the traffic to turn. He glanced to his left and saw the left turn led to an immediate split. Mulholland Drive to the left, Woodrow Wilson to the right.

He watched the side-view mirror and as soon as he saw the Cherokee make the turn, he hit his emergency lights and made a U-turn right in front of oncoming traffic that had slowed to a stop. He turned off the lights, pegged the accelerator, and got back to the turnoff. There was no sign of the Cherokee's taillights in either direction.

Without hesitation Long chose Mulholland because it was the more popular street and it went farther. He started the winding road up to the crest but pretty soon realized he had chosen wrong. The roadway wound back and forth, edging the mountain. He wasn't that far behind the Cherokee and would have seen its lights on one of the hairpin curves ahead.

Once more he made a U-turn and this time headed back to Woodrow Wilson, pushing the sedan beyond safe limits on the winding road. All he needed was Ellis coming down on him for losing this guy. Fuck the limits.

Woodrow Wilson was a narrow residential road that wound its way up the opposite side of the mountain from Mulholland. After a half dozen switchbacks and hairpins Long finally saw the familiar lights of the Cherokee ahead. He slowed down and maintained distance. Soon he rounded a curve and saw the Cherokee pulling into a lighted carport next to a powder-blue Volkswagen Beetle. He drove by without breaking speed.

Long followed the road around two more bends before pulling over and putting the transmission in park. He checked his phone for texts or missed calls from Ellis. There was nothing. He let three minutes go by and then used the empty carport of a house to turn around. He then killed the lights on his car and coasted past the house where the Cherokee had parked. It was a small cantilevered house with the glowing lights of the city behind it.

Long checked the plates of the Volkswagen as he went by. He also noticed that a city trash bin had been rolled out to the curb.

Haller was striking out with the woman next to him and was chasing defeat with vodka. Ellis watched him in the mirror behind the bar, camouflaged by the crowd. He held a full beer now, as part of blending in, but was not drinking from the bottle. He never ingested alcohol.

The woman Haller was working was at least fifteen years younger and Haller had ignored a key rule when it came to picking up younger women. Avoid reminders of the age difference—especially mirrors behind the bar.

Ellis felt his phone vibrate in his pocket and he retreated to the back hall. He put the beer bottle down on the floor of one of the phone booths and accepted the call from Long as he closed the door for privacy.

"I think he's buttoned up for the night," Long said.

"Where?" Ellis asked.

"House in the hills. Nice on a cop's salary."

"You sure he's staying in?"

"No, but if you want me to sit on it, I'm still in the vicinity. I can go back."

Ellis thought for a moment. A plan was forming. A short-term plan. He needed Long to come back. While he was working it out, Long broke the silence.

"I got his ID."

"How? Who is he?"

"There was another car but I checked it and it's got a law enforcement block on it too. But tomorrow's trash pickup. I grabbed a couple bags out of the bin on the street, then drove away and looked through the shit. I found some mail. The guy's name—not sure how to pronounce it—is Hermonius Bosch or something. All the mail was addressed to him."

"Spell it. First and last."

"H-I-E-R-O-N-Y-M-U-S and B-O-S-C-H."

"Hieronymus, like the painter."

"What painter?"

"Never mind. Just get back here. I have a plan to slow our guy here down."

"Give me fifteen."

"Make it ten. I think he's about to split."

Ellis disconnected, picked up his beer, and went back

to the bar in the old room. Haller was still in place but the woman he had been working was gone and had been replaced by a man in a black leather jacket over a white T-shirt. Haller was holding a silver credit card up and trying to get the bartender's attention with it. He was ready to leave.

Ellis squeezed between two patrons and put his bottle up on the bar. He then went up the steps and out of the restaurant. Walking back out to Las Palmas, he saw a shadowed recess beside the pedestrian entrance of a public parking garage. From there, he would have a line of sight to Musso's parking lot while he waited for Long.

As he moved into the shadows, he nearly tripped over something in the darkness. There was a rustling sound followed by a groan and a complaint.

"What the fuck, man. You're in my space."

Ellis reached into his pocket for his phone. He engaged the screen and turned it so that dim light washed across the concrete floor. There was a man clawing his way out of a dirty sleeping bag, his belongings in plastic bags lined against the wall. Ellis glanced behind him and saw no one in the street and no sign of Haller walking to his car in the lot. He turned back to the homeless man and made a decision. He kicked the man in the ribs as he moved on all fours. Ellis felt the impact of the kick through his whole leg and knew he had broken bone. The man flipped onto his back and released the sound of a wounded animal. Before he could scream Ellis stomped down on the man's throat with all of his weight, crushing the air passage. He then backed off and came right back with a heel to the bridge of the man's nose. The man was silent and unmoving after that.

Ellis returned his phone to his pocket and took a position in the alcove where he could watch for Haller. Soon enough he saw the lawyer emerge from the restaurant's back steps.

"Shit," Ellis whispered.

He noticed that Haller showed no signs of alcohol impairment as he paid the attendant and retrieved his keys. Ellis called Long.

"The fuck are you?"

"Two minutes. Just turned onto Hollywood."

"I'll be at the same spot. Put on the radio."

"Okay. Why?"

Ellis disconnected without answering. He noticed that Haller was talking on his cell phone as he walked to his Lincoln. Ellis reached into another pocket and pulled out a second phone and turned it on. He always carried a burner. While he waited for it to boot up he heard a gurgling sound from behind him. In the enclosed concrete space it echoed. He turned and drove his foot, heel first, into the darkness where he knew the homeless man lay. He connected with solid mass. The gurgling sound stopped.

Once the burner was ready he dialed 911 and pulled the sleeve of his jacket out over his hand to muffle his voice. The call was answered by an operator that Ellis identified as female and black. She sounded calm and efficient.

"Nine-one-one, what is your emergency?"

"There's a man, he's driving drunk, and he's going to kill somebody."

"What is your location, sir?"

"Hollywood Boulevard and Las Palmas. He just pulled right out in front of me on Hollywood."

"Is he traveling eastbound or westbound?"

"Westbound right now."

"And can you describe the vehicle?"

"Black Lincoln Town Car. The license plate is I WALK 'EM."

"Excuse me, sir?"

"It's a personal plate. I-W-A-L-K-E-M. I walk 'em—he must be a lawyer or something."

"Hold a moment, sir."

Ellis knew the operator would now send a hot shot to dispatch. She would then get back to him to request his name and details. He closed the phone, ending the call. He watched as Haller's Lincoln pulled out of the parking lot onto Las Palmas and headed the short distance to Hollywood Boulevard. The Lincoln passed the Challenger that Long was driving.

Ellis stepped out of the alcove and into the street to rendezvous. Just as the Challenger pulled up he bent down and put the burner in front of the back tire so it would be crushed. He opened the door and got into the passenger seat, telling Long to turn the car around. The broadcast on the possible DUI was already going out on the police radio.

"Any Hollywood unit: Citizen reports a DUI driver going westbound on Hollywood Boulevard at Las Palmas. Suspect driving black late-model Lincoln Town Car, California license plate Ida-William-Adam-Lincoln-King-Edward-Mary."

The microphone cord was draped over the rearview mirror, its once tight rubber coils stretched straight by time. Ellis looped it off and brought the microphone to his mouth.

"Six-Victor-fifty-five, we are westbound Hollywood Boulevard and are one minute away from that location."

He took his finger off the send button and turned to Long.

"Go west on Hollywood. He's probably heading home."

Long gunned the engine and proceeded to the end of the block, where he turned around in the intersection and then headed back down to Hollywood Boulevard. Ellis glanced toward the darkened entrance of the parking garage as they went by.

"What are we doing?" Long asked.

"We're going to pull him over and book him for DUI. That ought to slow him down a little bit."

"What if he isn't drunk?"

"Doesn't matter, he's a lawyer. He'll refuse to take the test or a Breathalyzer and we'll get to draw blood. We'll end up booking him. I want to look in his trunk."

Long nodded and drove in silence. They caught up with Haller at a red light at La Brea.

"Now?" Long asked.

"No," Ellis said. "Stay with him. Wait till he crosses La Brea and we're in residential. Less people around. Less cameras."

Ellis raised the microphone to his mouth.

"Six-Victor-fifty-five, show us on a traffic stop Hollywood and Camino Palmero possible DUI driver, license Ida-William-Adam-Lincoln-King-Edward-Mary. Request any A unit for backup."

When the light changed, Long jockeyed back and forth between lanes until he got into position behind the Lincoln. He hit the flashers and Haller pulled to the curb in front of a two-story apartment building.

"Okay, I'll take lead," Ellis said.

He opened the glove box to get out a plastic snap tie. He didn't want to use his cuffs because his intention was to hand off Haller to a patrol unit so he and Long could search the Lincoln.

"He's getting out," Long said.

Ellis looked up and through the windshield. Haller had already gotten out of the Lincoln. He was talking on his cell phone. He finished the call and threw the phone into his car. He hit the lock button and closed the door. He then put his hands on the roof of his car and waited.

"He just locked the car," Long said. "Keys are probably in it."

"Asshole," Ellis said. "He thinks he'll keep us out of it."

He got out and walked between the two cars to get to Haller.

"Hello, Detective," the lawyer said.

"Have you been drinking tonight, sir?" Ellis asked.

"Yes, I have," Haller said. "But not enough to warrant you pulling me over."

"Well, we received a nine-one-one call describing your car down to its vanity plate and reporting erratic, dangerous driving. We were just behind you for about five blocks and you were all over the place."

"That's bullshit. I saw you guys. You were the ones doing the weaving, trying to catch up to me."

"Who were you calling? Do you know it's illegal to talk on a cell phone while driving?"

"The answer to question one is none of your business. And as to question two, I didn't make the call until I pulled to a stop. There's nothing illegal about that. But do what you gotta do, Detective."

"It's Officer, actually. Where are you coming from?"

"Musso and Frank's."

"Did you eat or just drink?"

"I ate some olives, that's for sure."

"Can I see your driver's license, please?"

"Sure thing. May I reach into the front inside pocket of my jacket, *Officer*?"

"Slowly."

Haller retrieved his wallet and handed Ellis his

driver's license. Ellis glanced at it and then put it into his back pocket.

"We're going to step over to the sidewalk and conduct a field sobriety test now," he said.

"Actually, we're not. This is an unwarranted stop and my cooperation ended with me pulling over and giving you my driver's license."

"You understand that not submitting to a field sobriety test or a Breathalyzer exam is cause for arrest and suspension of your driver's license? Then we take you to the hospital and pull your blood anyway."

"I understand that, but like I said, do what you gotta do. I'm not drunk, I'm not impaired, and I gave no cause to be pulled over. This whole thing is bullshit. You have a dash cam on that car?"

"No, sir."

"That's okay. There are plenty of other cameras on Hollywood Boulevard."

"Good luck with that."

"I don't need luck."

"I take it, sir, you are a lawyer."

"That's right. But you already knew that."

Ellis noticed that a patrol car had pulled in behind their unmarked sedan as backup. He took the snap tie out of the pocket of his windbreaker.

"Could you bring your right hand off the car and behind your back, please?"

"Sure thing."

Ellis used the snap tie to bind Haller's hands behind his back. He pulled the plastic strap tight but Haller didn't complain.

After Haller had been taken by the uniforms to the hospital for the drawing of blood, Ellis put on crime scene gloves, then took the air wedge and slim jim out of the trunk of his own car and approached the Lincoln.

Haller thought he was smart locking his keys in his car but Ellis knew he was smarter. He waited for a wave of traffic to go by and then worked the wedge into the crack between the front door's window frame and the body of the car. He started squeezing the hand pump and the wedge slowly expanded, prying open a one-inch space. He slid the metal strip through and punched the electronic unlock button on the door's armrest. He heard the locks pop on all four doors. He knew the alarm was now disengaged and opened the front door. He reached in and popped the trunk. He knew from previous surveillance of Haller that the lawyer worked out of his car and kept his files in the trunk. The uniforms had called the police garage to impound the car. Ellis figured that gave him at least a half hour with those files before the tow truck arrived.

He noticed the lawyer's phone on the car seat. He leaned in and picked it up and engaged the screen but saw it was password protected and useless to him. He was about to toss it back when he saw a call coming in on it. The caller ID said it was from someone named Jennifer Aronson. He didn't recognize the name but put it in his memory bank and threw the phone back on the seat.

He closed the front door and opened the back. Leaning in and looking around, he saw a briefcase on the floor behind the driver's seat. He opened it on the seat and looked through its contents. There were three legal pads with illegible notes on each of them. Different cases got separate legal pads. There was also a stack of business cards bundled with a rubber band. Nothing else of note. Ellis closed the case and put it back down on the floor. He backed out and closed the door.

As he went to the trunk, he checked his partner in the plain-wrap, who was monitoring the police radio. Long gave Ellis a thumbs-up. All was good. Ellis nodded.

In the trunk he saw three long cardboard file boxes sitting side by side. The mother lode. He quickly ticked his latexed finger over the tabs until he reached one marked Foster.

"Bingo," he said.

10

The door to his daughter's room was closed but Bosch saw the light on underneath it. He tapped lightly.

"Hey, I'm home," he said.

"Hi, Dad," she called back.

He waited for an invite. Nothing. He knocked again.

"Can I come in?"

"Sure. It's unlocked."

He opened the door. She was standing by the end of the bed, bent over and shoving a sleeping bag into a large, wheeled duffel bag. The trip wasn't for a few days but she was putting together everything that was on the list they gave her at school.

"Did you eat yet?" he asked. "I brought some stuff from Panera."

"I ate already," she said. "I didn't hear from you, so I made tuna."

"You could have texted."

"You could have texted too."

Bosch decided not to go further into their communication practices. He didn't want to set things off. He pointed at the duffel bag and the array of camping supplies spread on the floor of the room.

"So are you excited?" he asked.

"Not really," she said. "I don't know how to camp."

He wondered if that was a criticism of him. He had never taken her camping. He had never been taken camping, unless his time sleeping in tents and holes in Vietnam counted.

"Well," he said, "you'll learn now. You'll be with friends and it will be fun."

"All people I'll probably never see again after I graduate," she said. "I don't know why we—All I'm saying is this should be an optional camping trip. Not required."

Bosch nodded. She was in a mood that would grow darker with every effort he made to cheer her up. He had been down this path before.

"Well, I've got some reading to do," he said. "Good night, baby."

"Good night, Dad."

He stepped over and kissed her on the top of the head. He then gestured to the huge gray duffel bag on the floor.

"You should probably carry the sleeping bag separate," he said. "It will take up too much room in there."

"No," she said curtly. "They said everything has to be in one duffel bag and this is the biggest one I could find."

"Okay, sorry."

"Dad, how much have you had to drink, anyway?"

"One martini. With your uncle. I left, he didn't."

"You sure?"

"Yes. I left. I have work to do. Look, good night. Okay?"

"Good night."

Bosch closed the door as he left the room. He reminded himself that his daughter was at a point in her life with a lot of stressors. She was learning to deal with them, but he was often the target when she let them out. He couldn't blame her or feel bad. But knowing that was the easy part.

He did feel bad about throwing Uncle Mickey under the bus. He went into the kitchen to eat by himself.

11

At 9 a.m. sharp Bosch approached the attorney check-in window in the lobby of the men's central jail, but Mickey Haller was nowhere to be seen. There was a young woman standing to the side of the window holding an attaché case and she studied Bosch as he approached.

"Mr. Bosch?" she asked.

Bosch paused for a moment and didn't answer. He was still not used to being addressed as "Mr."

"That's me," he finally said.

The woman held out her hand. Bosch had to move the file he was holding to his other hand to shake hers.

"I'm Jennifer Aronson. I work for Mr. Haller."

If Bosch had met her before he didn't remember it.

"He's supposed to be here," he said.

"Yes, I know," she said. "He's tied up at the moment but I will get you in to see Mr. Foster."

"Don't I need an attorney to go with me?"

"I am an attorney, Mr. Bosch. I am associate counsel on this case. I've handled a few filings on your civil case."

Bosch realized he had insulted her, assuming that based on her age — she had to be younger than thirty — she was Haller's secretary instead of his associate.

"I'm sorry about that," he said. "But I expected him to be here. Where exactly is he?"

"Something came up that he had to handle and he was delayed but he will try to join us shortly."

"That's not really good enough. I'm going to call him."

Bosch stepped away from the check-in window to use his phone. Aronson followed him.

"You're not going to reach him," she said. "Why don't we check in and start the interview and Mr. Haller will get here as soon as he can."

Bosch ended the call when Haller's recorded voice picked up and asked him to leave a message. He looked at the woman. He could read that she was lying or holding something back.

"What happened?" he asked.

"Excuse me?" she said.

"Where is he? You're not telling me something."

She looked disappointed in herself for not being able to get past Bosch.

"All right," she said. "He's over at city jail. He was picked up on a trumped-up DUI last night. I've posted his bail and he's waiting to be released."

"I was with him last night," Bosch said. "What time did this happen?"

"Around ten o'clock."

"Why do you say it was trumped up?"

"Because he called me while he was being pulled over and told me. He said they had to have been waiting for him outside Musso's. It happens often. Targeted enforcement. People get set up."

"Well, was he drunk? I left him there at seven-thirty or eight. He stayed another two hours or more."

"He told me no and he's going to be upset that I told you any of this. Please, can we check in now and set up the interview?"

Bosch shook his head once. This whole thing felt like it was slipping sideways and turning tawdry.

"Let's get it over with," he said.

"Here, you'll need this," she said, reaching into her attaché.

She handed him a folded piece of paper.

"It's a letter that says you are an investigator working for Mr. Haller on this case," she said. "Technically, you are working under the license of Dennis Wojciechowski."

It sounded like she pronounced the name Watch-Your-House-Key. Bosch unfolded the letter and quickly read it. It was a point of no return. He knew that if he accepted it and used it to get into the jail, then he would officially be a defense investigator.

"You sure I need this?" he asked.

"If you want to get in to see him you need legal standing," she said.

Bosch put the letter in the pocket inside his jacket.

"Okay," he said. "Let's do it."

Da'Quan Foster was not what Bosch had expected. Because of the brutality of the murder of Lexi Parks, he had expected to see a man of imposing size and musculature. Foster had neither. He was a thin man in jailhouse blues that were two sizes too big. Bosch realized that his wrongful assumption was rooted in his being predisposed to believe Foster was guilty of the crime.

A jail deputy placed Foster in a chair across the table from Bosch and Aronson. He removed the handcuffs from Foster's wrists and then left the small room. Foster had his hair in tight cornrows. He had a lipstick kiss tattooed on the left side of his neck and another tattoo in blue ink on the other side that Bosch could not read against his dark brown skin. Foster looked confused by the two people in front of him. Aronson quickly made introductions.

"Mr. Foster, I'm not sure if you remember me. I'm Jennifer Aronson and I work with Mr. Haller. I was with him at your arraignment and then at the preliminary hearing."

Foster nodded as he remembered her.

"You a lawyer?" he asked.

"Yes, I'm one of your lawyers," she said. "And I want to introduce you to Mr. Bosch, who is working as our investigator on the case. He has some questions for you."

Bosch didn't bother to correct her. He had not officially agreed to come on board yet—despite what the letter said.

"Where Haller at?" Foster said.

"He's tied up on another case at the moment," Aronson said. "But he plans to be here soon—before Mr. Bosch is finished."

Tied up on another case was one way of putting it, Bosch thought.

Foster turned his eyes toward Bosch and apparently didn't like what he saw.

"You look like five-oh to me," he said.

Bosch nodded.

"I was."

"LAPD?"

Bosch nodded again.

"Fuck that," Foster said. "I want somebody else on my case. I ain't want no LAPD on my side."

"Mr. Foster," Aronson said. "First of all, you don't get to choose. And second, Mr. Bosch specializes in homicide investigations and is one of the best in the business."

"I still don't like it," Foster said. "Down south side

the murder cops didn't do shit. Back when I was running with a crew, we lost nine guys in five years and the LAPD didn't make no arrests, no trials, nothin'."

"I didn't work south side," Bosch said.

Foster folded his arms and turned his head to ignore Bosch and look at the wall to his left. Bosch could now clearly see the tattoos on the right side of his neck. There was the standard Crips symbol, a 6 in the center of a six-pointed star created by one triangle with a second inverted triangle over it. Bosch knew the points of the star stood for things that the street gang was supposedly founded on—life, loyalty, love, knowledge, wisdom, and understanding. Next to the symbol was a stylized script tattoo that said *Tookie RIP.* Bosch also knew that this was a reference to Stanley "Tookie" Williams, the well-known cofounder of the gang, who was executed at San Quentin.

Bosch continued.

"You say you didn't commit the murder you are charged with. If that is true, I can help you. If you are lying, I'm going to hurt you. It's as simple as that. You want me to go, I'll go. It's not my ass on the line here."

Foster turned his eyes quickly back to Bosch.

"Fuck you, man. If you're LAPD, then you don't care whether I did it or not. Just as long as you got somebody to pay for it, that's all you people care about. You think if I didn't do this, then I did something else, so what the fuck, same difference."

Bosch looked at Aronson.

"We'll be fine," he said. "Why don't you go see if you can find Mickey and bring him in here?"

"I think I should stay here while we conduct the interview," she said.

"No, we'll be fine. I'm conducting the interview and you can go."

He gave her a hard look and she got the message. She stood up, insulted again, and went to the door and knocked. As soon as the guard opened the door she stepped out. Bosch watched her go and then turned back to Foster.

"Mr. Foster, I'm not here because I want you to be my friend. And you don't need me to be yours. But I'll tell you this. If you are innocent of this crime, then you don't want anybody else but me on it. Because if you're innocent, that means there is somebody else out there, not in jail, who did this. And I'm going to find him."

Bosch opened the file and slid one of the crime scene photos across the table. It was a close-up color shot of Alexandra Parks's brutalized and unrecognizable face. The reports in the murder book said that when her husband found her, a pillow had been placed over her face. In the psychological profile of the crime scene contained in the murder book, it was suggested that the killer did this because he was ashamed of what he had done and was covering it up. If that was the case, Bosch was expecting a reaction from Foster when he saw the horror of the crime.

He got one. Foster glanced down at the photo and then jerked his head back and looked up at the ceiling.

"Oh my lord! Oh my lord!"

Bosch watched him closely, studying his reaction. He believed that in the next few seconds he would decide whether Foster had murdered Alexandra Parks. He was a one-man jury reading the nuances of facial expression before rendering a verdict.

"Take it away," Foster said.

"No, I want you to look at it," Bosch said.

"I can't."

Without bringing his eyes down from the ceiling Foster pointed at the photo on the table.

"I can't believe this. They say I did that, that I would do that to a woman's face."

"That's right."

"My mother will be at the trial and they'll show that?"

"Probably. Unless the judge says it's too prejudicial—good chance of that, I'd say."

Foster made some kind of keening sound from the back of his throat. A wounded animal sound.

"Look at me, Da'Quan," Bosch said. "Look at me."

Foster slowly brought his head and gaze down and looked at Bosch, maintaining an eye-line focus that did not include the photo on the table. Bosch read pain and sympathy in his eyes. He had sat across the table from many murderers in his time as a detective. Most of them, especially the psychopaths, were very good liars. But in the end it was always the eyes that betrayed them. Psychopaths are cold. They can talk sympathy but they can't show it in their eyes. Bosch always looked at their eyes.

"Did you do this, Da'Quan?" Bosch asked.

"I didn't," Foster said.

What Bosch believed he saw in Da'Quan Foster's eyes now was the truth. He reached over and flipped the photograph over so it was no longer a threat.

"Okay, you can relax about it now," Bosch said.

Foster's shoulders were slumped and he looked wrung out. It was dawning on him, possibly for the first time, that he stood accused of the worst kind of crime.

"I think I believe you, Da'Quan. That's a good thing. What is bad is that your DNA was found *in* the victim and we need to explain that."

"It wadn't mine."

"That's just a denial and that doesn't work as an explanation. The science is against you so far. The DNA makes this a slam-dunk case for the prosecution, Da'Quan. You're a dead man walking unless we can explain it."

"I can't explain it. I know it wasn't from me. That's it."

"Then how did it get there, Da'Quan?"

"I don't know! It's like planted evidence."

"Planted by who?"

"I don't know!"

"The cops?"

"Somebody."

"Were you there that night? In this lady's house?"

"Hell, no!"

"Then where were you?"

"At the studio. I was painting."

"No, you weren't. That's bullshit. The Sheriff's Department has a witness. He says he went by the studio. You weren't there."

"Yes, I was."

"Their witness is going to get on the stand at your trial and testify that he went to the studio to see you but you weren't there. You add that to the DNA and you're done. All over. You understand?"

Bosch pointed to the overturned photo.

"A crime like that, no judge and no jury's going to have a second thought about giving you the death penalty. You'll go the way Tookie went."

He let that sink in for a moment before continuing in a softer voice.

"You want me to help you, Da'Quan? I need to know everything. Good and bad. You can lie to your lawyer but you can't lie to me. I can read it. So one more time, where were you? You don't tell me and I'm out of here. What's it going to be?"

Foster lowered his eyes to the table. Bosch waited

him out. He could tell Foster was about to break and tell the story.

"All right," he said. "This is the deal. I was up there in Hollywood. And I was with someone, not my wife."

"Okay," Bosch said. "Who is she?"

"Not a she," Foster said.

12

Haller missed the entire session with Foster. He was either a celebrity lawyer or a notorious lawyer, depending on how you looked at it. He had received the ultimate imprimatur of L.A. acceptance — a movie about one of his cases starring no less than Matthew McConaughey. He had also run for district attorney in the last election cycle and lost the race because of a scandal that erupted when a client he had previously cleared of a DUI charge killed two people and himself while driving drunk. So either way he was news, and the officers at city jail helpfully stalled his release until the media could be fully notified of his arrest, his mug shot could be uploaded to the Internet, and an assemblage of reporters, photographers, and videographers could muster outside the jail's release door to document his walk of shame.

Bosch accompanied Jennifer Aronson, acting as Haller's lawyer, into the jail to warn him about what awaited outside. She had a plan that involved Bosch pulling up to the door in his Cherokee and allowing Haller to step out quickly and jump in the back. Bosch would then speed away. But Haller said he wanted no part in such a cowardly exit. Once he collected his personal property, he pulled the tie out of his suit pocket and clipped it on. He smoothed it down on his chest and then stepped through the release door with his chin held high. He walked directly to the media cluster, waited a beat until all lenses were focused and microphones positioned, and then started speaking.

"I just want to say that I have been the target of law enforcement intimidation practices," he began. "But I am not intimidated. I was set up and taken down. I was not driving while intoxicated and there is no evidence that I was. I'll be fighting these charges and will ultimately be proven innocent. They will not deter me from the work I do defending the underdogs of our society. Thank you."

There was a clamor of voices as questions were hurled at him. Bosch heard one woman's deep voice drown out the others.

"Why are they trying to intimidate you?"

"I don't know yet," Haller said. "I have a number of cases in which I plan to put the police on trial in defense of my client. They know that. This could have come from any quarter, as far as I'm concerned."

The same woman yelled a follow-up.

"Could it have anything to do with the Lexi Parks case?"

"I don't know," Haller said. "I just know that what was done to me was not right. And it will be corrected."

Another reporter called out. Bosch recognized him from the *Times* but couldn't remember his name. But he had sources in the police department and usually had valid information.

"Your blood was drawn at Queen of Angels," he said. "The blood-alcohol content was measured at point-one-one, according to the LAPD. That is beyond the legal limit."

Haller nodded as though he knew what was coming and relished the chance to attack the accusation.

"The measurement was point-oh-six—check your source on that, Tyler," he said. "The LAPD then used a faulty B-A-C extrapolation formula to push it past to the point-oh-eight threshold at the time of arrest. This formula will not bear the scrutiny of the courts and I will be exonerated."

Bosch needed to go get the car and bring it around but he wanted to watch Haller work. He had such ease and control with the crowd of reporters. Unintimidated, undaunted. Bosch marveled at it. No wonder he was a killer in front of a jury.

"But you have been arrested for DUI in the past, isn't that so?"

It was a question from a different reporter. Haller shook his head.

"This isn't about the past," he said. "This is about right now and the question of whether we want our police department to be targeting law-abiding citizens. The intrusion of the government into our lives is pervasive. Where do we make a stand? I'm making mine right here."

The questions started getting repetitive or bizarrely far afield. It was pretty clear the reporters weren't going to run out of things to ask until Haller ran out of responses. The assemblage was a mixture of legitimate local news media and softer entertainment reporters. Haller was one of those rare people with a foot in both camps. The last question Bosch heard before turning a corner to head toward the parking garage was someone asking Haller if he had been in touch with Matthew McConaughey and if there would be a sequel to *The Lincoln Lawyer* film.

Haller said he didn't know.

13

Haller was starved, having passed on the baloney sandwich and apple offered at the jail for breakfast. But he wanted to get his car and cell phone back before eating.

Aronson split off to go back to work on her own courthouse caseload and Bosch drove Haller to the Official Police Garage in Hollywood to reclaim his Lincoln Town Car. Along the way Haller told him about the arrest and how he was sure the plainclothes officers who popped him had been lying in wait. Nothing Bosch heard in the story supported that and it appeared to him to be a pure case of paranoia. He did think it was curious that he had been pulled over by officers in plain clothes. He wondered if Haller had strayed into a vice operation.

The OPG contract belonged to Hollywood Tow on Mansfield Avenue. Haller paid the impound fees without dispute and the attendant handed him his car keys. Haller stared at them in his hand and then looked at the attendant.

"Did you people break into my car?" he asked.

The man looked at the document Haller had just signed.

"No, sir, we didn't," the man said. "No broken locks, it says the vehicle was OOA—open on arrival. We track that sort of stuff, sir. You want to challenge that or make a complaint, I can give you the paperwork to fill out."

"Really? I bet they'd jump right on it. Tell you what, just tell me where the car is."

"Space twenty-three. Down the main aisle and on your left."

Bosch followed Haller to the car. The first thing he did was grab his phone off the front seat and check to see if it had been tampered with. It was password locked and appeared to have been untouched. He then popped the trunk and looked through three side-by-side file boxes, ticking the tabs with his finger as if to make sure all the files were there. He then went to the backseat and grabbed his briefcase. He opened it on the roof of the car and checked its contents.

"They had plenty of time to copy anything they wanted," he said.

"They?" Bosch asked. "Who?"

"Whoever. The cops that pulled me over. Whoever sent them."

"You sure you want to play it this way?"

"How else should I play it?"

"I think you're being a little paranoid. You were in there drinking for three hours by my count."

"I was pacing myself and I wasn't inebriated and certainly wasn't impaired. When they pulled me over I got out and locked the car. With the keys inside it. Now the guy in there tells me it was unlocked when the tow truck arrived. Explain that."

Bosch said nothing. Haller snapped the briefcase closed and looked at him.

"Welcome to the other side of the aisle, Harry. Let's go eat. I'm fucking starved."

He stepped over and closed the trunk. Bosch saw that the license plate said IWALKEM.

He reminded himself that he never wanted to be seen riding in the car with Haller.

They drove separately to Pink's on La Brea and grabbed one of the tables in the back room after getting their food. It was early for lunch and the line was manageable. While Haller ravenously ate his foot-long, Bosch told him about his visit with Da'Quan Foster and what Foster had said about his broken alibi. Haller didn't bother to wipe the mustard off his mouth until he had finished the hot dog.

"Hard to believe he'd be willing to go to prison over a secret like that," Bosch said.

"He's a proud guy and he's got standing in the community. Plus the wife and kids. He didn't want to see all of that undone. Besides, I think when you're innocent, you always think deep down that you'll be saved, that the truth will set you free and all of that bullshit. Even an old gangbanger like him believes the fantasy."

Bosch pushed his untouched hot dog across the table to Haller and shook his head.

"Bullshit."

"I know it is."

"No, I'm not talking about the truth setting you free. I'm talking about your bullshit."

"Me? What bullshit?"

"Come on. This whole thing was a setup. You set me up."

"I'm not seeing that."

"You led me down the path, Mick. Put the scent in my nose and knew I'd eventually follow it to county and talk to Da'Quan. You knew they have a witness who knocks down his alibi. But you already knew the real story. You knew it all along."

Haller paused after a bite of the second hot dog. He

tried to smile with his mouth full. Then he swallowed and wiped the mustard off his mouth with a napkin.

"How 'bout next time you give me your hot dog you don't put so much mustard on it?"

"I'll remember that. Don't change the subject. What I don't understand is, if Da'Quan told you the truth about his alibi, why'd he start out lying to me about it?"

"Maybe he didn't trust you at first. Maybe he was taking your measure."

"That's just more bullshit. But it does make me wonder about you not telling me either. You had to take my measure, too?"

"No, no, nothing like that. I did it because I had to get you invested."

"Invested? Bullshit. You used me."

"Maybe. But maybe I saved you."

"Saved me from what?"

"You're a homicide investigator. The Los Angeles Police Department decided it didn't need you anymore. There are places—people—that still do."

Bosch shook his head and brought his hands up on the table.

"Why didn't you just lay it out for me as it is, then let me make a choice?"

"What, you mean lay out for you that I had a guy accused of the most heinous murder this town's seen since Nicole Simpson got butchered and that his DNA just happens to be inside the victim and he just happened to lie about his alibi because his real alibi was that he was shacked up in a motel room with a transvestite who goes by the name Sindy as in S-I-N Sindy? Yeah, I guess that would've worked if I'd played it that way."

Bosch didn't say anything because he sensed there was more. He was right.

"And here's the kicker. That alibi, as crazy as it is,

is impossible to prove now, because Sindy got himself murdered in an alley in Hollywood before I could get to him."

Bosch leaned forward as his body tensed. Foster hadn't told him that piece of information.

"When was this?" he asked.

"Back in March," Haller said.

"Before or after Foster was arrested for Parks?"

"After."

"How long after?"

"A few days, I think."

Bosch thought about that for a moment before asking the next question.

"Anybody picked up for it?"

"I don't know. Not as of the last time I checked. This is why I need an investigator, Harry. A homicide investigator. Cisco was just getting into it when he laid his bike down and fucked himself up."

"You should've told me all of this."

"I just did."

"I should have known earlier."

"Well, you know it all now. So are you in, or are you out?"

14

Bosch thought he would die soon. There was no physical or health threat that caused him to think this. He was actually in good shape for a man his age. He had worked a case years before in which a murder involved the theft of radioactive material. He had been exposed and treated, the twice-annual chest X-rays had been cut to annual checks in recent years and each time the film came back clear. It wasn't that or anything else from the job he'd held for more than three decades.

It was his daughter who made him think this way. Bosch had been a step-in father. He didn't know he had a child until she was almost four, and she didn't come to live with him until she was thirteen. It had only been five years since then but he had come to believe that parents see their children not only as they are but as they hope they will be in the future. Happy, fulfilled, not afraid. When Maddie first came to live with him Bosch didn't have this vision right away, but soon enough he earned it. When he closed his eyes at night, he saw her older: beautiful and confident, happy and healed. Not scared of anything.

Time had passed and his daughter had gotten to the age of that young woman in his vision. But the vision went no further. It didn't grow older, and he believed this was because one of them would not be around to see it. He didn't want it to be her so he believed it was he who would not be there.

When Bosch got home that evening he decided he had to tell his daughter what he was doing. Her bedroom door was closed. He texted her and asked her to come out for a few minutes to talk.

When she emerged from the room, she was already in her sleeping clothes.

"Are you all right?" he asked.

"Of course," she said. "Why?"

"I don't know. It looks like you're going to bed."

"I just got ready. I want to go to bed early to stock up on my sleep."

"What do you mean?"

"You know, like hibernating. I doubt I'm going to get any sleep when we go camping."

"You finish packing yet?"

"I have a few things left. So what's up?"

"Are you going to eat dinner?"

"No, I'm trying to be healthy."

Bosch knew this meant she had probably looked at herself in the mirror and, seeing something no one else could see, determined she had to lose weight.

"Skipping meals is not healthy, Maddie," Bosch said.

"You should talk," she said. "What about all the times on cases you didn't eat?"

"That was because I couldn't get food or didn't have time. You could eat dinner and be healthy about it."

She made her end-of-conversation face.

"Dad, let me do this. Is that all you wanted?"

Bosch frowned.

"Well, no," he said. "I was going to tell you something about what I'm doing but I can tell you later."

"No, tell me," she said, eager to move on from discussing her eating habits.

Bosch nodded.

"Okay," he said. "Well, remember a while ago when we were talking about my work and how I thought what I did—the homicide work—was like a calling and how I could never work for a defense lawyer like your uncle?"

"Yeah, sure," she said. "Why?"

Bosch hesitated and then decided to just get it over with.

"Well, I wanted to tell you that Mickey came to me with a case," he said. "A murder case. A case where he felt sure that the client was innocent and that he had been framed."

He held there but she didn't say anything.

"He asked me to look into the case," he continued. "You know, to see if there was evidence that he was framed. And so…I've agreed to do that."

Maddie stared at him for a long moment and then finally spoke.

"Who was murdered?" she asked.

"A woman," Bosch said. "It was very brutal, awful."

"You said you could never do this."

"I know what I said. But with this case, I thought, if there is a possibility that this man didn't do it, then somebody is still out there who did. And that bothers me—that somebody like this could be still out there in the world with you and everybody else. So I told Mickey today I would look into it. And I just thought you should know."

She nodded and dropped her eyes from Bosch's. That hurt him more than what she said next.

"Is he in jail?" she asked.

"Yes," Bosch said. "Two months now."

"So the opposite of what you're saying is that you may be working to put a very bad person back out into the world with me and everybody else."

"No, Mads, I wouldn't do that. I'll stop before that happens."

"But how can you know for sure?"

"I guess nothing can be known for sure."

She shook her head at that response.

"I'm going to bed," she said.

She turned from him and rounded the corner into the hallway.

"Come on, Mads. Don't be like that. Let's talk about it."

He heard her bedroom door close and lock. He stood still and considered her response. He expected news of what he was doing to bring a large backlash from those he knew in law enforcement. But he hadn't expected it from his daughter.

He decided that he, too, had no appetite for dinner.

15

Bosch got up early to review his notes and the reports in the murder book. He waited to call Lucia Soto at precisely twenty minutes after eight. He knew that if she had not deviated from her routine since she had served as his partner in the last few months of his LAPD career, then she would be walking to the Starbucks on First Street, a block from the PAB.

She answered right away.

"Soto."

"Lucia."

"Harry, what's up?"

Bosch had the caller ID on his phone blocked, so she still recognized his voice or remembered that he was the only one who called her Lucia. Everybody else called her Lucy or Lucky or Lucky Lucy, none of which she cared for.

"You going to get coffee?"

"You know me. It's good to hear from you. How's retired life?"

"Not so retiring, it turns out. I was wondering if you might do me a favor when you get back to the squad with your latte."

"Sure, Harry, what do you need?"

"Before I tell you, I want to be up front with you. I am looking into a case for my half brother."

"The defense lawyer."

"Yeah, the defense lawyer."

"And he's also the guy you're using to sue the department."

"That's right."

Bosch waited and there was a long pause before Soto responded.

"Okay. So what do you need?"

Bosch smiled. He knew he could count on her.

"I don't need your help on the specific case I'm working but there is another case that I heard about that might be related in some way. I just need to get a line on it, find out what it is."

He paused to give her a chance to shut it down but she said nothing. So far so good, Bosch thought. He'd had no doubt that she would do the favor for him but he didn't want her to feel compromised or fear that he might put her in any departmental crosshairs. They had only talked a few times since he had walked out the door of the Open-Unsolved Unit the year before, never to return. When he had checked in with her after the first of the year to see how she was doing, he learned that she had already been hit with some of the blowback from his departure.

The captain of the unit had partnered her with a veteran detective named Stanley O'Shaughnessy. Known as Stanley the Steamer by most of the other detectives in the Robbery-Homicide Division, O'Shaughnessy was the worst kind of partner to be saddled with. He didn't work hard at solving murders but was very active when it came to discussing what was wrong with the department and filing complaints against other detectives and supervisors who he felt had slighted him. He was a man who let his frustrations and disappointments with his life and career paralyze him. Consequently, his partners never stayed with him for long unless they had no choice in the matter. Soto, being the low man on the totem pole in RHD, would probably be stuck with Stanley the Steamer until the next round of promotions brought new blood into the division, and that was only if a new detective coming in had less seniority than her. Since Soto had been on the job less than eight years, the chances of that were almost nonexistent. She was stuck and she knew it. She spent her days largely working cases on her own and only bringing in O'Shaughnessy when department policy required two partners on an excursion.

All of this had been accorded her because she had been Harry Bosch's partner for the last four months of his career and had refused to rat him out in an Internal Affairs investigation prompted by the same captain who handed out the partner assignments. When she had told Bosch how she had landed, all he could do was encourage her to leave O'Shaughnessy behind and go out and work cases, knock on doors. She did that and called Bosch a few times to tap into his experience and ask his advice. He had been happy to give it. It had been a one-way road like that until now.

"Do you know the murder journals in the captain's office?" he asked.

"Sure," she said.

"I'm looking for a case. I don't have a name or an exact date, only that it was in Hollywood and probably took place within a week after March nineteenth this year."

"Okay, but why don't I just look it up on CTS and do it real quick?"

CTS was the LAPD's internal Crime Tracking System, which she could access from her computer. But to access it she would have to sign in with her user key.

"No, don't go on CTS," Bosch said. "I have no idea where this will go, so just to be safe, don't leave any digital fingerprints."

"Okay, got it. Anything else?"

"I don't know if it will be in the journal but the victim was a prostitute. Might be listed as a dragon or a tranny or something like that. The street name was Sindy, spelled S-I-N-D-Y, and that's all I got."

In the age of electronic data compilation and storage, the LAPD still kept a tradition of logging every murder in a leather-bound journal. The journals had been religiously kept since September 9, 1899, when a man named Simon Christenson was found dead on a downtown railroad bridge—the first recorded murder in the LAPD's history. Detectives at the time believed Christenson had been beaten to death and then placed on the tracks so a train would hit his body and the killing would look like a suicide. It was a misdirection that didn't work, yet no one was ever charged with the murder.

Bosch had read through the journals regularly when he worked in RHD. It was a hobby of sorts, to read the paragraph or two written about every murder that had been recorded. He had committed Christenson's name to memory. Not because it was the first murder, but because it was the first *and* it was never solved. It always bothered Bosch that there had been no justice for Simon Christenson.

"What do I tell the captain?" Soto asked. "He'll probably ask me why I'm looking at that case."

Bosch had anticipated the question before he made the call to her.

"Don't tell him you're looking at a specific case," he said. "Pull the latest journal and tell him you're just trying to keep up with what's going on out there. A lot of guys check those books out. I read through every one of them at least once."

"Okay, got it. Let me get my coffee now, and then I'll go back up and do it first thing."

"Thanks, Lucia."

Bosch disconnected and thought about next steps. If Lucia came through, then he'd have a starting point on the Sindy case. He might be able to determine if there was any link to Lexi Parks and whether Da'Quan Foster's alibi was for real.

While Bosch waited for the callback from Soto, his daughter emerged from her bedroom dressed for school, her backpack slung over a shoulder.

"Hey," she said. "I'm late."

She grabbed her car keys off the table by the front door. Bosch got up from the table to follow her.

"Not going to eat again?" he asked.

"No time," she said, moving toward the door.

"Maddie, I'm starting to get worried about this."

"Don't. Just worry about that killer guy you're working for."

"Oh, come on, Mads. Don't be so dramatic. If the guy's a killer he won't be going anywhere. Trust me, okay?"

"Okay. Bye."

She went through the front door, letting it bang loudly behind her. Bosch just stood there.

After an hour of waiting for Soto to call, Bosch started to worry that something had gone wrong with the captain when she went into his office to look at the murder journal. He started pacing, wondering if he should call to check on her but knowing that an ill-timed call from him—if she was in a jam with the captain—might make matters worse. Besides, if she was in a jam, there was nothing he could do about it. He was an outsider now.

Finally, after another twenty minutes, his phone buzzed and he saw on the screen that she was calling from her desk phone. He'd expected that when she called, it would be on her cell and from outside the building, or at least from a stall in the women's room.

"Lucia?"

"Hi, Harry. I got you some information."

"You're at your desk. Where's the Steamer?"

"Oh, he's probably off filing a complaint or something. He came in and then mysteriously left without saying anything. He does that a lot."

"Well, at least that means he's out of your hair. So you got a look at the journal?"

Bosch sat down at the dining room table and opened his notebook. He took out a pen and got ready to write.

"I did and I'm pretty sure I found your case."

"No problem with the captain?"

"No, I said what you told me to say and he sort of waved me off, told me to have at it. No problem. To make it look good I took a couple of the other journals, too. The first one goes back to eighteen ninety-nine."

"Simon Christenson."

"God, how do you remember that?"

"I don't really know. I just do. Killed on a bridge and nobody ever charged."

"Not a good start for LAPD homicide, huh?"

"No, not good. So, what did you find for me?"

"March twenty-first, the body of James Allen, white male, age twenty-six, was found in an alley running parallel to Santa Monica Boulevard at El Centro. It was behind an auto repair shop. Victim was a prostitute with multiple hits for solicitation, drug possession, the usual stuff. That's all it says in the journal other than that the case was assigned to RHD and detectives Stotter and Karim."

Bosch stopped writing. Robbery-Homicide Division comprised the elite detective squads that worked out of the PAB and usually handled cases that were politically or media sensitive or considered too complex for divisional detective squads because of the time commitment needed. Mike Stotter and Ali Karim were assigned to Homicide Special, the elite of the elite. To Bosch it seemed unusual for the murder of a Hollywood prostitute to be assigned to RHD. In a perfect world all murder victims would be treated equally. Everybody counts or nobody counts. But it wasn't a perfect world and some murders were big and some were small.

"RHD?" Bosch asked.

"Yeah, I thought that was strange, too," Soto said. "So I wandered over to that side of the room and Ali was at his desk and so I asked him what was with that. He—"

"Lucia, you shouldn't have done that. You can't let anybody know you have any interest in this case or it might come back to bite you on the ass if I end up making waves with it. Ali's going to know I sent you to him."

"Harry, relax, I'm not that stupid. Give me a little credit here, okay? I didn't go blundering over to Homicide Special and start asking questions about the case. Besides Ali and I are pals. He was called out the night of my thing in Rampart and handled the scene till the shooting team got there. He was very nice to me that night, calmed me down, coached me on how to deal with the shooting team. And when I got here after that, he was one of the few people who didn't look down their nose at me, you know what I mean? In fact, it was just Ali and you, to be exact."

She was talking about her path to RHD and the Open-Unsolved Unit. Less than two years earlier she was a slick sleeve assigned to patrol in Rampart Division. But her bravery and deadly calm in surviving a shoot-out with four armed robbers that left her partner dead catapulted her into the media spotlight. She was dubbed Lucky Lucy in a profile published by the *Times,* and the department quickly took advantage of the rare bit of positive attention she was drawing. The chief of police offered her a promotion and told her she could pick her spot. She chose the RHD's Open-Unsolved Unit and was elevated to homicide detective before she had logged five years on the job.

The media loved it but it didn't go over so well with those in the department who had been waiting years and even decades for a slot on a homicide squad anywhere, let alone the elite Robbery-Homicide Division. Soto came in with that kind of enmity in her backpack and had to deal with a squad room where more than half of her colleagues didn't think she belonged there or had earned it. While the media called her Lucky Lucy, some in RHD referred to her as FasTrak, after the electronic pass that allows motorists to use express lanes to blow by traffic on the city's crowded freeways.

"I finessed it, Harry," Soto said. "I stopped by his cube to shoot the shit and, sure enough, he had the murder book right on his desk. I asked what he was working on and he spilled. I also asked what was so special about it that made it a Homicide Special assignment and he said the case got kicked to him and Mike because everybody in West Bureau was tied up on a training day the morning the body was found."

Bosch nodded. It made sense. The murder rate in the city had fallen so much in recent years that many of the divisional homicide teams were consolidated. Hollywood Homicide was gone and the few murders that occurred in the area were now assigned to a squad that worked out of the West Bureau. This created a higher likelihood for cases to get kicked over to RHD because of backups and other conflicts. Satisfied that the case had not drawn any unusual attention from the department, Bosch now wanted to know what Soto had learned.

"So you asked him about it?"

"Yeah, I asked him, and you know Ali, he's a storyteller. He told me the whole thing. The victim was a transvestite who usually worked out of a room at the Haven House near Gower. There's a whole book on him at Hollywood Vice."

"Did he say what room?"

"He didn't but I saw the photos. Room six, bottom floor."

"So what's their theory?"

"Ali said they figure the odds just caught up to him and some john he picked up probably did him in. They've got no suspects but they think it might be a serial."

"Did he say why they think that?"

"Yeah, because fifteen months before, another pro got offed and left in the same alley."

"How similar are the cases?"

"I didn't really ask."

"You ask about cause of death?"

"Didn't have to. Like I said, Ali showed me the pictures. The guy was strangled from behind with a wire. One thin line across the front of the neck. It broke the skin. Ali said that when they checked out his room at the motel they found a framed picture of Marilyn Monroe on the floor, leaning against the wall. They saw there was a nail in the wall but when they checked the back of the picture, the wire for hanging it was gone. They think that's what the killer used."

"Was that where he was killed? The room?"

"That's the theory. Ali said no signs of a struggle in the room but the picture frame missing the wire is kind of a marker, you know? He thinks that the john met the victim there and things went sideways and he got killed. The body was moved to a car and then taken to the alley and dumped. Because of the one fourteen months before, they got a profile from Behavioral and it says the killer was probably some guy with a wife and kids at home and he somehow blamed the victim for his crossing the line into that kind of activity. So he killed Allen, dumped him, and went back to his normal life in the Valley or wherever. Pure psychopath."

Bosch didn't correct her but he didn't think there was enough information in the profile or case summary to declare the suspect a pure psychopath. It was a young detective's easy response. But based on the facts known to him, the murder looked spontaneous. The killer had not brought a weapon and there was no other evidence of prior planning. The possibility that the killing of Allen was connected to a prior murder was the only real indication of psychopathy.

"So have they officially connected this one and the one fourteen months before?" he asked.

"Not yet," Soto said. "West Bureau still has the first one. Ali said there's a bit of a tug-of-war but that there are elements of the cases that don't match."

It was not unusual for the divisional detective squads to fight against having to turn over investigations to the big shots downtown. People who worked homicide were not timid people. They were confident investigators who believed they could crack any case, given enough time and support.

"Did Ali say whether they got DNA off the body?" he asked.

"No, no DNA directly on the body. The victim was into safe sex—I saw photos of the room and the guy had a big ol' industrial-size container of condoms. Like what they used to put licorice and candy in in the clinic waiting room. But they swept the room and got what you'd expect from a room like that, a ton of hair and fiber. None of it has led to anything."

Bosch thought for a moment about what else he could ask. He felt there was something he had missed, maybe a follow-up on the information she had just given him. It didn't come to him and he decided to leave it at that. She had helped enough.

"Thanks, Lucia," he finally said. "I owe you one."

"Not at all," she said. "Did it help?"

Bosch nodded even though she could not see this.

"I think so."

"Then call me for lunch sometime."

"I don't know if you want to be seen with me. I'm persona non grata, remember?"

"Fuck 'em, Harry. Just call me."

Bosch laughed.

"Will do."

16

Bosch read the notes he had taken during the phone call and tried to put things in context. Two days after Da'Quan Foster was arrested for killing Lexi Parks in West Hollywood, the man he would claim was his alibi for the time of that murder was himself murdered in Hollywood, possibly by a serial killer. There was no evidence or even suggestion that this was anything other than a grim coincidence — Allen's profession put him at a higher probability of becoming a murder victim than most. But Bosch only accepted coincidence grudgingly.

From victim profile to crime scene to method of murder the two killings were different, at least as far as Bosch had seen from photos of one and a verbal description of the other. Still, the possible connection bore further scrutiny. Bosch considered what Lucia had told him about the investigation of the Allen case. The motel room had been processed by a forensic team. Bosch wondered, What were the chances that hair and fiber left behind six weeks earlier by Foster could have been collected during the sweep of the room. What about DNA? What about fingerprints?

Regardless, he knew that the six-week time difference between Allen's death and the night of Lexi Parks's murder would render any such evidence inconclusive in terms of the law. It would not be viable in establishing an alibi, and no judge would allow it into court. There would be no way of establishing when the evidence was put in the motel room. But Bosch was not a court of law. He worked on instinct. If Da'Quan Foster had left any microscopic trace in Allen's motel room, it would go a long way toward assuring Bosch that Foster's account of his whereabouts on the night Lexi Parks died was true.

Bosch got up from the table and went out to the back deck. As he slid open the glass door he was greeted by the ever-present sound of the freeway at the bottom of the Cahuenga Pass. He put his elbows on the wood railing and looked down, not really seeing the spectacle of the crowded freeway below. He was thinking. Lucia had said that Mike Stotter and Ali Karim had had the case profiled. He wanted to read the profile to compare it with the Parks profile and see if there were any psychological links between the two killings. The problem was he couldn't go to Stotter and Karim without revealing what he was up to and he knew that he could not go back to Soto. Asking her to do anything further might put her in jeopardy.

In his mind Bosch pulled up a visual of the massive RHD squad room and moved across the rows of cubicles, remembering who sat where, trying to conjure a face of somebody he could reach out to and ask for help. Suddenly he realized he was looking in the wrong place. He went back inside to the table where he had left his phone.

He scrolled through his contacts list until he came to the name he wanted and made the call. He was expecting to have to leave a message and was surprised when the call was picked up live.

"Dr. Hinojos."

"Doctor, it's Harry Bosch."

"Well, Harry…how are you? How is retirement?"

"Uh, retirement's not so bad. How are you doing?"

"I'm okay, but you know I'm mad at you."

"Me? What for?"

"I didn't get an invite to your retirement dinner. I thought for sure you would have—"

"Doc, nobody got invited to my retirement dinner. I didn't have one."

"What? Why not? Every detective has a retirement party."

"And at every one of them people stand around telling stories everybody else has heard a hundred times before. I didn't want that. Besides I went out under a cloud, you know? I didn't want to put anybody on the spot by asking them to come to my retirement party."

"I'm sure they all would have come. How is your daughter?"

"She's good. She's actually the reason I'm calling."

Bosch and Hinojos had known each other twenty years. She was head of the Behavioral Science Unit now, but when they had first met, she was a department shrink charged with determining whether Bosch was fit to return to duty after a suspension incurred when he had pushed a supervisor through a glass window for interfering with Bosch's interview of a murder suspect. It wouldn't be the last time she would have to make the return-to-duty call with him.

Their relationship continued in a new way five years earlier when Maddie had come to Los Angeles to live with Bosch and to try to get over the grief that engulfed her after her mother's murder. Hinojos had volunteered her services free of charge and it was those therapy sessions that helped Maddie to eventually get through the trauma. Bosch was indebted to Hinojos on many levels and now was going to try to use her in an underhanded way. It made him feel guilty before he had even started.

"Does she want to come in and talk?" Hinojos asked. "I'll open my calendar."

"Actually, no, she doesn't really need to talk," Bosch said. "She's going to college in September down at Chapman in Orange."

"Good school. What's she going to study?"

"Psychology. She wants to be like you, a profiler."

"Well, with me that's only been part of the job, but I have to say I'm flattered."

Bosch hadn't lied so far. And what he was about to ask he could defend to a certain degree. He would do what he said—if Hinojos came through.

"So I was thinking," he said, "most of what she knows about it is from watching TV and reading books but she's never actually seen a profile of a real case, you know? That's why I'm calling. I was wondering if you had a few profiles of recent cases that you could give me to show her. You know, you could redact the names or whatever you needed to do. I'd just like her to actually see one of these things so she has a better idea of what the job's about."

Hinojos took a few moments to answer.

"Well," she finally said, "I think I might be able to pull something together. But are you sure she's ready for this, Harry? As you know, these profiles are very detailed and they don't shy away from describing the most heinous aspects of these cases. The sexual assaults in particular. It's not gratuitously graphic but the details are important."

"I know that," he said. "I'm just concerned that she may not really understand what it's about. The kid's binge-watched sixteen seasons of *SVU* and other stuff like that and now wants to be a profiler. I want her to get a good read on it and not think it's like a TV show."

Bosch waited.

"Let me see what I can put together," Hinojos said. "Give me till the end of the day. It's actually been kind of slow in the profiling department but we had a few cases so far this year. And I could look in the archives, too. Maybe it would be better to pull them out of closed cases."

Bosch didn't want that.

"Whatever way you want to do it, Doctor," he said. "But I think the more recent, the better. You know, it would show how it's done and put together right now. But I'll leave it to you and she'll be very thankful for whatever I can get for her. I'll make sure she calls you to tell you what she thinks."

"I hope it makes her more certain of her choice," Hinojos said.

"Should I call you later?"

"That will be fine, Harry."

17

Bosch was late for his appointment when he pulled to the curb in front of the house on Orlando. He was supposed to meet the real estate agent who was selling the house where Lexi Parks was murdered but didn't see a car in the driveway or anyone waiting near the front door. He thought maybe she had come and gone after he was not on time.

Bosch got out of the car and called the number on the for sale sign below the agent's name. She answered right away.

"Taylor Mitchell."

"Ms. Mitchell? It's Harry Bosch. I'm at the house on Orlando and think I may have just missed you. I'm sorry I'm so late. I got caught up with…"

Bosch didn't really have a valid excuse and had not taken the time to think of one. He went with the old reliable.

"…traffic this morning."

"Oh, don't worry about it," she said cheerily. "And you didn't miss me. I'm here in the house waiting for you."

Bosch crossed the street toward the house.

"Oh, okay," he said. "I'm here, too, and I didn't see a car or anybody around. Thought I missed you."

"I live in the neighborhood and just walked over. I'll meet you at the door."

"See you soon."

Bosch disconnected and walked through the archway cut into the tall hedge that surrounded the house. As he went up the three steps of the porch the front door opened and a young woman with reddish blond hair was standing behind it. She was attractive with a sincere smile. She held out her hand to him and invited him in.

"Thanks for getting me in on short notice," Bosch said.

"Not a problem," she said. "Like I said, I live nearby. I work most days from home and it's easy with a listing like this to just walk over."

Bosch turned and took in what he could see of the house from the entry area.

"Let me walk you through," Mitchell said.

They started in the living room and worked their way toward the bedrooms in the back of the house. The house was furnished but looked unlived in. None of the signs of daily habitation were visible. There were no photos on the fireplace mantel, no shopping list held on the refrigerator with a magnet. Bosch wondered if Lexi Parks's husband, Vincent Harrick, had moved out.

Eventually Mitchell moved the tour down the hallway to the bedrooms. They first stepped into the room that had been converted to an office. Appearing to be interested in how much storage space the room offered, Bosch opened the folding doors of the closet to check it out. The closet looked like it had not been disturbed since the crime scene photos were taken. Most notably, the brown leather watch box was still up on the top shelf. As Bosch stepped away, he left the closet doors open in case he got the opportunity to break away from Mitchell and check its contents.

As he circled the room, acting like he was getting a

feel for it as a potential buyer, he came to the framed diploma hung on the wall next to the desk. He acted like he was casually reading the details of the degree bestowed on Alexandra Parks but he was really looking at the juror ID tag, trying to see if there were any identifiers on it.

As he looked closer he realized the tag was not real. It was a photocopy of a real juror tag that had been used in a gag or maybe a work presentation or play and Parks had held on to it as a keepsake. In faded pencil not picked up in the crime scene photo someone had printed:

ALEXANDRA PARKS
JUDGE *AND* JURY

Bosch wasn't sure what the tag had been used for but he now dismissed it as an avenue of investigation. He also realized he owed Cornell and Schmidt, the Sheriff's investigators, a mental apology for questioning their competency when he was reviewing the crime scene photos.

The next stop was the guest bedroom and here Bosch saw signs of life. The bed was made but it looked a bit haphazard, as if it had been done quickly, and Bosch saw a pair of shower sandals peeking out from beneath it. On the bureau, there was a hairbrush and some change in a dish. Bosch guessed that Harrick might be using the guest room, since the murder had taken place in the master.

He checked the size of the closet in this room as well, even though he was not as interested in its contents.

As they moved back into the hallway Mitchell finally spoke of what had occurred in the room at the end of the hall.

"I have to make a disclosure to you about this next room," she said. "There was a crime—a woman died in this room."

They stepped into the room Bosch had seen in crime scene photos. But it was completely empty. Every piece of furniture had been removed and the twin closet doors were open, revealing that space to be empty as well. Bosch was disappointed. His purpose in visiting the crime scene was to absorb it and put together his own spatial orientation of things. It would be difficult now because he was standing in an empty room.

"Really?" he said. "A crime? What happened?"

"Well, the woman who lived here was sleeping and a man came in and killed her," Mitchell said. "But he was caught and he's in jail, so there is nothing to worry about in that regard."

Bosch noticed the smell of fresh paint in the room. The blood spatter tracks on the wall behind the bed and the ceiling had been covered over.

"Did he know her?" he asked. "Who was he?"

"No, it was like a random thing. It was like a gang member from downtown or something. Still, we understand that something random like that is disconcerting. That's why the price point on the property is where it is. It would be unethical to not disclose the history."

"How long ago was this?"

"It was earlier this year."

"Wow, recent. Did you know her? You being in the neighborhood and all."

"I did. I sold this house to her and her husband four years ago. Lexi was a great person and it's awful what happened. Just horrible. It could have been me! I live one block over."

"Yeah, calling it random violence doesn't necessarily make one feel better about it."

"No, I guess not. But I can assure you, this has always been a very safe neighborhood. My kids play with their friends on the front lawn. What happened here was really an aberration."

"I understand."

"Do you want to see the back porch? There is a built-in barbecue you will love."

"In a bit. I want to get the dimensions of the bedrooms. To see if they fit everything I have."

Bosch moved into the space where he knew the bed had been located. Working off his memory of the crime scene photos, he stood in the place where the victim had been found on the right side of the bed. He scanned the room, looking at what Lexi Parks would have seen. There were two windows on the opposite wall and they offered views of the side yard and the hedge. He closed his eyes for a moment to concentrate and absorb.

"Mr. Bosch, are you all right?"

Bosch opened his eyes. She was staring at him.

"Sure. Do you have a tape measure by any chance?"

"I might in my trunk—oh, that's right, I didn't drive here. Sorry. But I do have the dimensions on the listing sheet. There's a stack in the kitchen."

"That'll have to do then."

She headed toward the door and extended her arm to signal him to leave the room ahead of her. Bosch walked into the hallway and started back toward the kitchen. When he got to the door to the office, he paused and let her pass.

"I just want to look at this room again," he said. "I have two daughters, and if one gets a bigger room than the other, I'm going to have a problem."

"Of course," she said. "I'll go get the listing sheet."

She continued up the hallway and he stepped into the office. He quickly went to the open closet and reached up to the watch box. He realized he would look like a thief if Mitchell came back and found him holding it. He tried to quickly open it but the fine crafting of the box made it a puzzle to open. He finally realized the front panel opened like a drawer.

He heard Mitchell's voice from the kitchen. She was talking excitedly to someone. Bosch thought it was a phone call but then he heard the low bass sound of a male's voice in reply. Someone else was now in the house with them.

As soon as he pulled the box open he determined there was no watch in it. There was a brown velvet cushion on which the watch should be set when not being worn. But it was empty. There was an instruction booklet in the box and a small square envelope marked in handwritten ink:

RECEIPT. DON'T LOOK! (UNLESS YOU ARE RETURNING IT. 🙁)

Bosch quickly put the box under his arm and opened the envelope. He removed the receipt and unfolded it. The watch had been manufactured by Audemars Piguet and purchased at a jewelry store on Sunset Boulevard called Nelson Grant & Sons. The watch was called a Royal Oak Offshore and had cost $6,322 when purchased in December 2014. The name of the buyer on the receipt was Vincent Harrick.

Bosch assumed that the watch had been purchased by Harrick as a Christmas gift to his wife. He wondered briefly how a Sheriff's deputy could afford such an expensive watch but the question did not rise to the level of suspicion. People made all kinds of concessions to love—money choices being the least of them.

He quickly put the receipt back into the envelope and returned it to the box. He closed it, having to push the front panel in and hearing the air whoosh out. He placed it back in its spot on the shelf and stepped away. He was in the middle of the room when Mitchell walked in, carrying the listing sheet.

"This says both guest rooms are fourteen by twelve," she said. "This room probably just feels smaller because of the bookcase."

Bosch looked at the shelves behind the desk and nodded.

"Oh, okay," he said. "That makes sense."

She handed him the listing sheet. He looked at it as if he were genuinely interested.

"Do you want to check out the barbecue now?" she asked.

"Sure," he said. "But is someone here? I heard you talking."

"It was the owner. He thought we would be finished by now but I told him we got a late start."

"Oh, I can leave."

"No, it's fine. And he's fine. Let's go out on the deck."

Bosch followed her through the house to the sliding door off the kitchen. He did not see Harrick anywhere. They stepped onto a planked deck with a vine-covered latticework sun cover and a built-in barbecue station. It was all in good shape but didn't look like it had been used in a long time. The yard beyond was tiny but private. The front hedge ran along the sides and turned to continue along the property lines of the back, giving the yard and the back of the house complete privacy.

"There is probably just enough room for a hot tub, if you were interested," Mitchell said.

"Yeah, but I wonder how they'd get it in here," Bosch said. "Take down the hedge, I guess."

"No, they would crane it over. They do it all the time."

Behind him Bosch heard the glass door roll open.

"Taylor?" a man said. "Can I talk to you for a second?"

"Of course," Mitchell responded.

Bosch turned to see Vincent Harrick standing in the open door. Bosch nodded and he nodded back.

"Sorry. I won't keep her long," Harrick said.

"I'll be fine," Bosch said.

Mitchell went through the door and Harrick shut it behind her so Bosch would not hear their conversation. Bosch felt sweat start to pop on his scalp as he wondered if he had put the watch box in the wrong position or had somehow been seen.

Before he could worry further about it, the sliding door came open and Mitchell stepped back out.

"So, what do you think?" she asked.

Bosch nodded.

"It's nice," he said. "Very nice. I'll have to think about it and talk to my girls."

He looked through the glass into the kitchen as he spoke but didn't see Harrick.

"I'll call you tomorrow," he added.

"Just let me know if they would like to take a look for themselves," she said cheerily. "I'm only a block away and can make that happen pretty quickly."

"Great."

Bosch headed toward the door. He was still holding the listing sheet, which he folded lengthwise and put into the inside pocket of his sport coat. He hesitated before going back into the house.

"You think I should just go around the house so I don't intrude on the owner?" he asked.

"Oh, he left," Mitchell said. "When I told him we

weren't finished, he said he was going to run up the street to get something at Gelson's."

She came up next to Bosch and opened the slider. He stepped in and walked through the house to the front door. He then thanked Mitchell again and left.

As Bosch passed through the archway cut into the hedge and walked out to the sidewalk he saw a man leaning against the front of his Cherokee across the street. It was Harrick and he was waiting for Bosch, his arms folded across his chest.

Bosch crossed the street toward his car, unsure how he was going to handle what might be about to turn ugly.

"It's Bosch, right?" Harrick said.

"That's right," Bosch said. "Sorry we took so long in—"

"Save your bullshit."

Bosch stopped in front of him. There wasn't much sense in continuing the play since Harrick wasn't buying it. Bosch held his hands out as if to signal *you got me*.

"I thought you were a fucking reporter," Harrick said. "Piece-of-shit car like this, you can't afford a house like that. So I run your plate and it's got an LAPD block on it. I make a couple calls and I get the story. Retired cop. Retired *homicide* cop. So tell me, Detective Bosch, what the fuck are you doing in my house?"

Bosch knew that the situation could quickly go sideways. He was acting as an extension of Haller's defense of Da'Quan Foster. A complaint that brought the ethics of his scam with Taylor Mitchell before a judge could cause blowback for Haller. He had to salvage this somehow.

"Look, I'll be honest with you," he said. "I've been asked to look into the case privately by someone who has reason to believe Da'Quan Foster was set up and that he didn't kill your wife."

Harrick's eyes disappeared in the creases of his squint. His ruddy complexion turned a darker shade.

"What the fuck are you talking about?" he said. "Who has reason to believe that?"

"I can't tell you that," Bosch said. "It's a matter of client confidentiality. I agreed to look into the case and I wanted to see the crime scene. I apologize. I didn't expect you to be here and to be confronted by this. It was a mistake."

Before Harrick could respond, Mitchell called from across the street while on her walk back to her house.

"Do you need me for anything, gentlemen?"

Both Bosch and Harrick turned to her.

"We're fine, Taylor," Harrick called back. "Thank you."

He added a wave to keep her going. She was one house from the corner. As soon as she got there she turned left and disappeared from sight.

"Put your hands on the hood," Harrick said.

"Excuse me?" Bosch asked.

"On the hood. Assume the position."

"No, I'm not going to do that."

"You want to go to jail, Bosch?"

"You can take me to jail but I don't think I'll be staying there long. I haven't committed any crime."

"You've got a choice here. Put your hands on the hood so I can check for weapons. Or go to jail."

He took a phone out of his pocket and got ready to make a call.

"I'm unarmed," Bosch said and he stepped forward, put his hands on the front hood, and spread his feet.

Harrick quickly frisked him and found no weapons. Bosch didn't like the way this was heading. He had to change the course.

"What happened to her watch?" he asked.

Harrick's hands froze for a moment as he was patting down Bosch's front pants pockets. He then stood straight up, put a hand on Bosch's arm, and turned him away from the hood of the car.

"What did you say?" Harrick asked.

"Her watch," Bosch said calmly. "The one you gave her. The Audemars Piguet—if I am saying that right. It wasn't on her wrist and it wasn't on any property report from the crime scene. It didn't turn up in the search of Da'Quan Foster's house, studio, or van. It's not in its box either. So, what happened to it?"

Harrick took a half step back as he considered what Bosch had just said. Bosch recognized it as a move to create space between them and a potential prelude to a punch. He braced himself to block but Harrick managed to control his rage and the swing never came.

"Just go," Harrick said. "You don't know what you're talking about. Get out of here."

Bosch reached in his pocket for his keys and stepped around the front of the car. When he got to the driver's-side door, he looked back at Harrick, who had not moved.

"It doesn't matter who I'm working for if I'm trying to find the truth," he said. "If Foster didn't do it, somebody else did. And he's still out there. Think about that."

Harrick shook his head.

"Who are you, fucking Batman?" he said. "You don't know what you're talking about. The watch was broken. It was being fixed. It's got nothing to do with anything."

"Then, where is it? Did you get it back?"

Harrick opened his mouth to say something, then paused and shook his head.

"I'm not talking to you."

He turned, checked for traffic, and then crossed the street toward his house.

Bosch watched him disappear through the archway, then got in the Cherokee and drove off. He angrily banged his palm on the steering wheel. He knew that his anonymity on the case had just come to an end. Harrick didn't know who Bosch worked for but he would soon enough find out. A complaint might follow. Whether it did or it didn't, Bosch needed to get ready for the onslaught of anger that would come his way.

18

The Haven House was an aging two-story motel with neon promises of free HBO and Wi-Fi. It was the kind of place that probably looked shabby on the day it opened in the 1940s and had only gone downhill from there. The kind that served as a last-stop shelter before the car became primary domicile. Bosch pulled into the parking lot off Santa Monica and cruised slowly. The motel was situated on what was known as a flag lot. A narrow fronting on Santa Monica led into a bigger, wider piece of property in the rear that ran behind other businesses. This afforded the rear parking lot and motel rooms significant privacy. It was no wonder that it had become a place favored by people engaged in illicit sexual transactions.

He saw a door with a 6 painted on it and parked in the spot in front of it. He realized it was the same sort of move he would make when he worked cold cases. Visit the scene of the crime long after the crime had been committed. He called it looking for ghosts. He believed every murder left a trace on the environment, no matter how old.

In this case only a few months had passed but that still made it a cold case.

Bosch got out and looked around. There were a few cars parked in the lot and it was surrounded by the

windowless rear side of the businesses fronting Santa
Monica on one side and an L-shaped apartment building on two others. There was a row of tall and mature
cypress trees buffering the line between the parking lot
and the apartment building. The fourth side was lined
by wood fencing that ran along the backyard of a private residence.

Bosch thought about Lucia Soto's report on the
James Allen case. The supposition was that Allen had
been murdered in room 6 and then his body was removed and dumped in the alley off El Centro. Putting
aside the question of why the body was moved, Bosch
now saw that it could have been accomplished without
great risk. In the middle of the night the parking lot
would have been deserted and unseen from the outside.
He looked around for any cameras and saw none. It
wasn't the kind of place where customers wanted to be
photographed.

Bosch walked back around the corner to the office
at the front of the building. The office was not open
to the public. The door had a shelf below a sliding window. There was a push-button bell there and
Bosch used his palm to ring it three quick times. He
waited and was about to hit it again when an Asian
man slid the glass window open and looked at Bosch
through watery eyes.

"I need a room," Bosch said. "I want number six."

"Check-in at three," the man said.

That would be in four hours. Bosch looked back at
the parking lot and saw a total of six cars including his
own. He looked back at the man.

"I need it now. How much?"

"Check-in three, check-out twelve noon. Rules."

"How about I check in yesterday at three, check out
today at noon?"

The man studied him. Bosch didn't look like his usual clientele.

"You cop?"

Bosch shook his head.

"No, no cop. I just want to look at room six. How much? I'll be out by twelve. Less than an hour."

"Forty dollar."

"Deal."

Bosch pulled out his cash.

"Sixty," the man said.

Bosch looked up from his money at him and silently communicated the message that the man was fucking with the wrong guy.

"Okay, forty," the man said.

Bosch put two twenties down on the window's counter. The man slid out a 3 x 5 registration card but didn't ask for any formal identification confirming the information Bosch quickly wrote on it.

The man then slid out a key attached to a diamond-shaped piece of plastic with the number 6 on it.

"One hour," he said.

Bosch nodded and took the key.

"You betcha," he said.

He walked back around the corner of the building and used the key to open room 6. He stepped in and closed the door behind him. He stood there, taking the whole room in. The first thing he noticed was the rectangular discoloration on the wall where the picture of Marilyn Monroe had obviously hung. It was gone now, most likely taken as evidence.

He turned his head and slowly swept the room, looking for anything unusual about it but committing its well-worn furnishings and drab curtains to memory. Anything that had belonged to James Allen was long gone. It was just a threadbare room with its aging furnishings. It was depressing to think someone had lived here. Even more so to think someone may have died here.

His phone buzzed and he saw that it was Haller.

"Yeah."

"Where are we?"

"We? We are in a shabby-as-shit room in a hot-sheet motel in Hollywood. The place Da'Quan claims he was at when Lexi Parks was murdered."

"And?"

"And nothing. A big fat nothing. Mighta helped if he'd scratched his initials into the bed table or put some gang graffiti on the shower curtain. You know, to show he was here."

"I meant, 'and what are you doing there?'"

"My job. Covering all the bases. Absorbing, thinking. Looking for ghosts."

Bosch's words were clipped. He didn't like the interruption. He was in the middle of an established process. He was also annoyed with himself for what he had to say next.

"Look, I may have messed up."

"How so?"

"I posed as a real-estate buyer and got inside the victim's house. I wanted to look around."

"And look for ghosts? What happened?"

"Her husband, the deputy sheriff, came by and ran my plate because he thought I was a reporter or something. Instead, he found out I was a retired cop and I was working on the case."

"That's not a mess-up. That's a full-fledged fuckup. You know if the guy makes a complaint, it goes on me with the judge, right?"

"I know. I messed up—I fucked up. I just wanted to see—"

"You sure did. But nothing we can do about it now. What's next? Why are you at the motel?"

"Same reason."

"Ghosts. Really?"

"When I investigate a murder, I want to be where that murder took place, or where it may have taken place."

There was a pause before Haller responded.

"Then I guess I'll leave you to it," he said.

"Talk to you later," Bosch said.

Bosch clicked off the call and continued to stare at the room until he finally stepped toward the bed.

Thirty minutes later he left the room with no more than he had when he entered. If anything had remained to prove Da'Quan Foster was there the night of the Lexi Parks murder, it had been swept up by the LAPD forensics team. As he walked to his car he wondered if something more than forensics had been left behind that could help Foster. James Allen was a prostitute, after all. And many prostitutes kept records. In these digital times a prostitute's little black book would more likely be his little black cell phone. After her conversation with Ali Karim, Soto had mentioned nothing about the recovery of a cell phone either from the body or from room six.

Bosch diverted and walked back to the office window. He rang the bell again and the same man slid the window open. Bosch put the room key down on the counter.

"I'm out," he said. "You don't even have to make the bed."

"Okay, very fine, thank you," the man said.

He started to slide the window closed but Bosch blocked it with his hand.

"Hold on a second," he said. "The man who had that room back in March got murdered, you remember that?"

"Nobody get murder here."

"Not here. Or maybe not here. His body was found down the street in an alley. But he had room six here, and the police came to investigate. James Allen. You remember now?"

"No, not here."

"Yes, here. Look, I'm just trying to figure out what happened to all his belongings. His property. The police took things, I know that. Did they take everything?"

"No, his friends come. They take clothes and things."

"Friends? Did you get any names?"

"No, no names here."

"Do they do what he did? Do they stay here?"

"Sometimes they stay."

"Any of them here now?"

"No, not now. Nobody here."

Bosch pulled out his notebook and wrote his name and number down. He tore the page out and handed it through the window.

"If any of his friends come back, you call me and I'll pay you."

"How much you pay?"

"Fifty bucks."

"You pay now."

"No, I'll pay when you tell me they're here."

Bosch rapped his knuckles on the shelf under the window and turned back toward the parking lot. He walked around the corner of the building and got in his car. Before starting the engine, he called Haller, who answered right away.

"We need to talk."

"That's funny, because I called you about a half hour ago and it was pretty clear you didn't want to talk to me."

"That was then. We need to talk about next moves. This is your show and I don't want to do something that hurts things down the line in court."

"You mean like get caught sneaking into the victim's house?"

"I told you that was a mistake. It won't happen again. That's why I'm calling."

"Did you find something?"

"No, nothing. I still need to check the street, but so far nothing. I'm talking about other things. The next move—whether you make it in court or I make it out here."

"Sounds mysterious. Where are you? I can come now."

"On Santa Monica near Gower. I need to work the street here a little bit."

"I'll head that way. You in the Cherokee? The one you claim is a classic?"

"I am, and it is."

Bosch disconnected and started the car. He drove to the motel's parking lot exit on Santa Monica and paused there while he looked right and then left at the small businesses that lined the four-lane boulevard. They were a mixture of industrial and commercial businesses. Several of the big studios were nearby—he could see Paramount's water tower rising behind the shops fronting Santa Monica. This meant that there were also all manner of feeder companies in the neighborhood that lived off the scraps of the behemoths—prop houses, costume shops, camera equipment renters—interspersed with a routine variety of fast-food dreck. There was a do-it-yourself car wash and across the street and down a half block was the entrance to Hollywood Forever—the onetime cemetery to the stars.

Bosch nodded. The cemetery was his best lead. He knew Rudolph Valentino was buried there as well as many other long-ago Hollywood greats and pioneers, like Douglas Fairbanks Jr., Cecil B. DeMille, and John Huston. Many years back Bosch had worked a suicide at Hollywood Forever. The victim was a woman who had laid herself out on top of Tyrone Power's crypt and then cut her wrists. Before she died she managed to write her name in blood beneath his name on the memorial stone. Bosch did the math on the dead woman and determined she was not even born until five years after Power died. The case seemed to underline what many in homicide work knew; you can't explain crazy.

Bosch knew that in any town in the country the local cemetery was a draw for a certain class of odd people. In Hollywood, that draw was amped exponentially because there were graves with famous names carved on them. That meant there would be security. And that meant cameras. The woman who killed herself on Tyrone Power's crypt had done it under a camera. The problem was, no one was watching, and she bled out.

When the traffic momentarily cleared, Bosch turned left out of the parking lot and drove down to Hollywood Forever. The cemetery was surrounded by an eight-foot stone wall interrupted only by entrance and exit lanes. As Bosch pulled in he readily saw cameras affixed to the walls and focused on the auto lanes. Bosch couldn't tell by his cursory glance whether they were in position to also record activities a half block down Santa Monica Boulevard. But he recognized that the cameras were placed in obviously public positions, thereby acting as a deterrent as well as a recording device. He was interested in them but he was also interested in the cameras nobody could see.

Once past the wall, he saw a parking area and a complex that included the cemetery office as well as a chapel and a casket-and-stone showroom. It was a full-service operation. Beyond this, the cemetery lay spread out and was sectioned by various driving lanes and other, smaller parking areas. Rising above the back wall Bosch could see the giant stages of Paramount Studios and the water tower. He saw cameras on the tower.

There were a number of cars parked in various sections of the cemetery and pedestrians moving among the stones. It was a busy day. Bosch could also see a Hollywood tour van moving slowly next to one of the larger monuments. It was garishly painted with the roof cut off for open-air viewing from the six rows of seats behind the driver. The van was packed with tourists. Bosch lowered his window and could hear the tour guide's amplified voice echoing off the mausoleums and carrying across the rows of stones.

"Mickey Rooney is the latest Hollywood great to join the others here at Hollywood Forever, the resting place of the stars…"

Bosch put his window back up and got out of the car. On the way into the office he called Haller and told him where he would be.

The man in charge of security at Hollywood Forever was named Oscar Gascon. He was ex-LAPD but had retired so long ago that there was no point in trading names to see who knew whom. Bosch was just happy to make the ex-cop connection and hoped it would give him an edge. He got right to the point.

"I'm working a case, trying to establish an alibi of someone accused of a crime."

"What, here?"

"No, actually down the street at the Haven House."

"That dump? They should tear that place down."

"I wouldn't argue with that."

"So then how does HoFo fit in?"

It took Bosch a moment to translate HoFo into Holly-wood Forever. They were in Gascon's tiny office, sitting on either side of a small table that passed for his desk. There was a stack of pamphlets displaying headstones and statues and Bosch got the idea that Gascon wasn't only security director at the place. He was also in sales.

"Well, it doesn't really fit in, but I am interested in your cameras," Bosch said. "I'm wondering if any of them capture the front of Haven House down the street."

Gascon whistled as if Bosch had just asked for the moon and stars in a box with a ribbon on it.

"What date are we talking about?" he asked.

"February ninth," Bosch said. "Do you keep video going back that long?"

Gascon nodded and tapped the screen of an ancient computer on a second table to his side.

"Yeah, we're backed up on the cloud," he said. "In-surance makes us keep everything a year. But I don't know. That's a whole block away. I doubt anything would be in focus that far off."

He stopped there and waited. Bosch knew what he was doing. Harry picked up one of the pamphlets and glanced at it.

"You sell these, too?" he asked.

"Yeah, on the side," Gascon said.

"What do you get for one of these—as a salesman?"

"Depends on the stone. I made a grand on the Johnny Ramone statue. That had to be designed and special ordered."

Bosch put the pamphlet back down.

"Tell you what," he said. "My employer is on his way here to meet me. He would be willing to buy a stone if there is something on the cameras we can use."

The men studied each other. Gascon looked very interested in the prospect of making money.

"Do you have access to the camera on the Paramount tower?" Bosch asked. "It looked like it was pointed over here."

"Yeah, that's ours," Gascon said. "We needed an overview perspective. We have a joint agreement with them. They have access to it, too."

Bosch nodded.

"So, should we take a look?" he asked.

"Yeah, sure," Gascon said. "Why not? Nothing's going on around here. I mean, it's pretty dead."

Bosch said nothing.

"Get it?" Gascon asked.

Bosch nodded. He was sure Gascon used that line whenever he could.

"Yeah, I get it," he said.

Gascon turned to the computer and went to work. As he was typing commands, Bosch adopted a gossipy, casual tone when he asked his next question.

"Did you know there was a murder over there at the Haven House in March?"

"Maybe there was," Gascon said. "The cops that came in here said they weren't sure where it went down but that the guy that got himself killed was living there. They said he was a dragon."

It was old LAPD slang for drag queen. That was the catchall for the whole slew of different classifications running the gamut from transvestite to transgender. It even often used to go on reports, something that nowadays would draw protest. Gascon's mention of it made Bosch remember that official police reports often abbreviated the term "drag queen" to DQ. He now wondered if that was known to Da'Quan Foster and a reason for his nickname.

"So they came in to look at video, too?" Bosch asked.

"Yeah, they were here," Gascon said. "But just like you're gonna find out, there's not much to see of that place on our cameras."

Bosch waited for Haller in the parking lot. He wanted to talk to him before they went back in and talked to Gascon and played the video again.

When the Lincoln finally pulled in Bosch saw that Haller was in the backseat. He got out with his brief-case.

"You've got a driver now," Bosch said.

"Had to," Haller said. "Got my license suspended because of that little stunt the cops pulled on me the other night. Why are we meeting at a cemetery?"

Bosch pointed across the expanse of the cemetery to the back wall. The Paramount Studios water tower was the highest profile structure behind the wall.

"Cameras," he said. "They've got a reciprocal security agreement with Paramount here. You watch my back, I'll watch yours. There is a camera up on that tower. Takes in the whole cemetery and then some."

They headed toward the office door.

"This guy, you're going to have to buy a headstone," Bosch whispered.

Haller stopped in his tracks.

"What?"

"To get him to cooperate. I don't have a badge any-more, you know. He sells gravestones on the side and I told him if he cooperated, you'd buy a stone."

"First of all, why would I want a headstone? Whose name do I put on it? And secondly, and most importantly, we can't be paying potential witnesses. You know how that will look in court?"

"He doesn't matter. His video is what matters."

"But I might need him to introduce it in court. To authenticate it. You see? And I don't want the prosecutor asking him how much we paid him. It looks bad to a jury."

"Look, if you don't want a headstone, don't buy a headstone, but this guy needs to be compensated for his cooperation. What he's got is important. It changes things."

Five minutes later Bosch and Haller were standing behind a seated Gascon as he manipulated the video playback from the Paramount water tank camera.

On the screen was the entire cemetery. It was a macro security image. The confines of the picture extended out to Santa Monica Boulevard. At the very top left corner was the Santa Monica entrance to the Haven House motel. The frame cut off the view of the actual motel and its rear parking lot. But it did show vehicular ingress and egress from that entrance. A code along the bottom frame showed the time as 9:44 p.m. on February 9, 2015.

"Okay, what am I looking at?" Haller asked.

Bosch pointed out the particulars.

"This is Santa Monica Boulevard and this is the entrance to Haven House—where DQ says he was on the night of the ninth."

"Okay."

"The Haven House is on a flag lot. You know what that is?"

"Yes."

"Okay, so this is the only ingress and egress point.

You go in and drive by the office and the parking is in the back by the rooms. Very private."

"Got it."

"Okay, now watch this van. Go ahead, Oscar."

Gascon started the video moving. Bosch reached over his shoulder to point out the white van moving in a westerly direction on Santa Monica. It was crossing in front of the cemetery. He added commentary.

"The reports you gave me said the Sheriff's impounded and searched Foster's nineteen ninety-three white Ford Econoline, turning up no evidence in the case. That on the screen is a white Ford Econoline. I can tell by the lights. I don't know the year at this point but it's no spring chicken. It turns into Haven House at nine forty-five p.m. February ninth."

"Okay, this is good."

"Oscar, jump it."

Gascon put the playback on fast-forward and they watched traffic on Santa Monica speed by and the minutes on the time counter move like seconds until Gascon slowed things down at the 11:40 mark.

"Now watch," Bosch said.

At 11:43 the van came back into the picture, waiting to turn left out of the motel lot. Eventually traffic opened up and the van exited the motel lot and proceeded east on Santa Monica, back the way it had come.

"If your client was coming up from his studio, he would take the one-ten to the one-oh-one and then exit on Santa Monica," Bosch said. "He'd drive west to the motel, then he'd drive east on his way back."

"Does the Sheriff's Department have this?" Haller asked.

"Not yet," Bosch said.

"We need to confirm that it's Foster's van," Haller said.

"Oscar, can you make a copy of this? Mickey, you will need to have someone enhance it and work on that."

"I've got a person."

"What about me?" Oscar asked without taking his eyes off the screen.

"What about you, Oscar?" Haller said. "Mr. Bosch spoke too quickly. I don't want to buy a headstone. Don't have much use for one. But I've got a thumb drive on my keychain and if you can put the video on it, I will pay for your time. And I will pay well."

Bosch nodded. That was the best way to do it.

"Sure, I think that should work," Gascon said.

Haller looked at Bosch as he pulled his keys.

"I'll wait outside while you two talk business," Bosch said.

19

Bosch was standing at the edge of one of the cemetery lawns, looking at the grave of Mel Blanc, the voice artist behind a thousand or more cartoons. On the stone it said, "That's all, Folks!"

He turned as Haller approached after leaving the office.

"Good stuff," Haller said.

"How much did you pay?" Bosch asked.

"A couple hundred bucks. A bargain if only I had a paying client."

"Maybe you should have offered him a painting."

"Gascon didn't look like a patron of the arts to me."

They started walking through the cemetery with no clear direction other than trying to stay between the graves if possible.

"The coroner's report puts time of death at between ten and midnight," Haller said. "They'll argue it's an inexact window and there was still time for Foster to get in under the wire."

"And a jury will know they're stretching it," Bosch said. "Besides, if he was shacked up with the prostitute for two hours, where's the motivation for jumping in a van and hurrying over to West Hollywood to rape and kill Lexi Parks? On top of that, he heads the wrong way—away from West Hollywood—when he pulls out."

"I know, I know. I'm just looking at all the arguments the prosecution has. A lot of cars go in and out of that place on the video. They'll say he could have jumped in another car and gone out to do the deed."

Bosch didn't argue back. He thought he had made a significant find with the video. Now the excitement was dissipating.

"I'm just saying we need to be ready for anything," Haller said. "I'd still rather have this video than not have it."

Bosch nodded.

"How long will your video person take to analyze it?"

"I don't know but I'll get her right on it."

"Good."

They walked silently for a bit. Bosch was reading the names on tombstones but not really comprehending.

"So, what are you thinking?" Haller asked.

"I'm doing a lot of thinking," Bosch said. "A lot of possibilities, a lot of scenarios. I need to see the James Allen file."

Haller nodded.

"They vacuumed the room," he said. "Hair and fiber, fingerprints. They might have evidence that puts Da'Quan in that room."

"Right. And with the van on the video, you can pin it to that day—February ninth."

"Very good. This is why I came to you, Harry."

"I think you came to me because you knew I would work for free."

"Bullshit. You'll get paid. You're a patron of the arts."

"Yeah, bullshit's bullshit. Your investigator would have gotten to the same point eventually."

"Maybe."

"So, how do you want to do this? If you go into court and ask for access to the forensics on the Allen case, you'll be showing your hand to the prosecution. You cool with that?"

"I'm never cool with showing anything to the prosecution. Let's see what my video gal comes up with on the van before we take that next step and advertise what we're doing."

Bosch nodded.

"Your call. I'm thinking it's probably a long shot anyway—especially on prints. If Allen was killed in that room, then the killer might have wiped it down. In fact, he probably did. If there were prints in that room that matched Foster, they would have gone to see him in county to ask what he knew about Allen."

"Or they checked with the Sheriff's first and decided not to step in it. No way it could have been DQ, since he was in jail."

"Spoken like a true defense attorney. Always looking for the conspiracy."

"Might serve you to start thinking that way."

"Maybe."

That seemed to end the conversation but they kept walking. They passed a monument with a kneeling angel on top of it. Its wings were broken and jagged from previously being toppled over—by vandals or earthquakes.

Bosch finally spoke. "For now, I can try to back-channel it and get a look at the murder book on Allen. Try to keep it quiet."

"Okay. Step carefully."

"There's something else you should do, I think."

"What?"

"The company doing your DNA analysis. See if they can check the sample for CTE."

"What is CTE?"

"Condom trace evidence."

"I'm not following you."

"If the science is solid and your lab confirms the state's match, then you need to explain how Foster's DNA got to the crime scene, right? You need to explain the setup. If your client is innocent, how was his DNA taken from him and how was it transported?"

Haller stopped walking as he considered this.

"Holy shit," he said. "I like it. I might be able to do great things with that in court, Bosch. I really like it."

"Well, don't start loving it just yet," Bosch said. "It's missing parts. A lot of parts. But I'm working on it."

"Wouldn't the Sheriff's crime lab check for this CTE?"

"No, they don't. The LAPD and the Sheriff's labs are in the same building. I know for a fact that it's not part of the DNA protocol for either one. It costs too much money. So it's done only on request and even then it's farmed out. The only time I ever had a case where we needed to check for CTE, the sample was sent down to a lab in San Diego to the expert in the field. A guy named Blackledge. But last I heard he was retired."

"A lot of guys who retire from the public sector end up working in the private sector."

"Maybe that's what he's doing."

Haller nodded. He had the scent in his nose and would follow it.

"Where do you go from here?" he asked. "You going to check out the alley where Allen was left?"

Bosch shook his head. He noticed that a peacock was following them through the graveyard.

"Not without seeing the crime scene photos," he said. "No use going there until I know the layout of the scene. But you don't have to worry, I'm keeping busy. There is still a lot on Parks for me to be doing."

He momentarily thought about the empty watch box. The explanation from Harrick bothered him. If the watch was broken and being fixed, why was the empty box still at the house?

"I'm not worried," Haller said.

Haller looked down at a memorial plaque in the grass where he had stopped.

"Look at that," he said. "Carl Switzer. Alfalfa from *Our Gang.* I used to watch the reruns when I was a kid."

"Yeah, me too," Bosch said.

Haller pointed at the dates with the toe of his polished shoe.

"He died young. Thirty-one years old."

"He got shot during a fight over a dog up in the Valley."

Haller looked from the gravestone to Bosch.

"You're kidding, right?"

"No, that's what happened. And nobody was ever charged—ruled justifiable."

"No, I mean, how the hell do you know that?"

"It's in the murder journals they keep at the PAB. I used to read them—when I was waiting for cases."

"You're saying you just read the murder journals and remembered the details of a killing from nineteen fifty-nine?"

"I don't remember all of them but some I do. You gotta remember it when it's Alfalfa."

"Man, Bosch, I'm not sure this retirement thing is going to work out for you."

"Yeah, we'll see."

They turned and headed back to their cars.

20

Ellis and Long watched the cemetery from a parking spot on the north side of Santa Monica Boulevard. Long was texting someone on his cell phone but Ellis kept the watch. He had the binoculars in his lap and every now and then he brought them up for a close look at Bosch and Haller.

Ellis was fascinated by Bosch and what he was doing. They had researched the man and learned he had been a near legend in the department. Now look at him. Working cases for a douche-bag defense attorney. There was no loyalty anymore. Nobody with a moral compass.

"What do you think they're doing?" Long asked without looking up from his cell's screen.

"Talking about whatever they found in the office," Ellis said.

"Which is?"

"My guess is video. There's a camera up there on the Paramount water tower."

That got Long's attention and he looked up from his phone.

"Fuck. You think —"

"I don't know. There's no way to know unless we go in there and ask the same questions they did. But we can't do that. So we're watching."

"Fuck, I'm totally not into this."

"No kidding."

"They're leaving."

"I got eyes."

"We staying with the painter?"

Long had taken to referring to Bosch as the painter because of his name. This annoyed Ellis.

"We're staying with Bosch," he said.

"I bet I know where he's going," Long said.

"Where?"

"The alley. It's the logical next step."

"Maybe. This guy's different."

"When are we going to talk about taking him out?"

"We're not. We took out the first guy. We take out two investigators on the same case and it doesn't look like coincidence. We need to figure out something else."

Long was wrong. Bosch pulled out of the cemetery and turned east on Santa Monica. Ellis had their undercover car pointing the opposite way and had to maneuver to turn around and follow.

They tailed Bosch east on Santa Monica until he turned onto Normandie and headed south. Traffic was terrible as usual and they didn't speak for twenty minutes—until Bosch turned right on Wilshire and almost immediately into the parking garage of a nondescript office building in Koreatown.

"What the fuck?" Long said.

"He's going up to Behavioral," Ellis said.

"Yeah, but he's retired."

"Probably some kind of retirement aftercare. He killed a lot of people. Over the years."

"The reigning champ till he hung it up."

"Officially, at least."

They both smiled at the same time. Ellis drove past

Bosch's car and then pulled to a stop at a red curb about half a block farther down the street. He started positioning the mirrors so he could keep an eye on Bosch's car.

"You want me to go in?" Long asked.

"No, sit tight," Ellis said. "This will be fast."

"How do you know?"

"He didn't put money in the meter. He's a citizen now and has to pony up. So he must be going in to pick up a prescription or something."

"Viagra."

Ellis felt his work phone vibrating. He checked the screen. It was Lieutenant Gonzalez.

"It's Gonzo," he said, signaling Long to be quiet.

He shut the car down and then answered.

"Hey L-T."

"Where you at, Ellis?"

"Watching the suspect location. As instructed."

"Anything?"

"Not yet."

"Are they even home? Don't they work days up in the Valley?"

"Haven't determined that, L-T. The complaint uses the phrase 'night and day.' I was thinking if we don't see some sign of life soon, we'll think of something and door-knock 'em."

"Look, I don't want you guys fucking around. If it's not there, we need to move on to the next one. I'm thinking one more day on it and then you throw a scare at 'em, move 'em to West Hollywood, and let the Sheriff's deal with it."

"Yes, sir. Sounds like a plan."

"And check in from time to time, Ellis. I shouldn't have to hunt you guys down."

"Yes, sir. Absolutely."

"And tell your partner to wipe the shit-eating grin off his face."

Gonzalez disconnected. Ellis lowered the phone and looked at Long and saw that he was indeed smiling.

"Gonzo's got you pegged, partner. You better be careful about that."

"Absolutely."

Long laughed as Ellis shook his head. Ellis then saw Bosch come out through the glass doors of the elevator alcove.

"He's back," he said.

He watched in the rearview mirror as Bosch got back in his car.

"He was carrying a file," he said. "Not a prescription."

"What color?" Long asked.

"Plain."

"What's plain?"

"Manila."

"Not a psych file then. They put those in blue."

As Ellis watched, Bosch's car pulled away from the curb, made a U-turn on Hill, and headed back toward the freeway. Ellis started the engine.

After following Bosch to Woodrow Wilson Drive, they peeled off in order to avoid detection. They didn't need to stay on him all the time because they had LoJacked his Cherokee the evening before. Long had slid underneath on a dolly and hooked on a GPS tracker. He had set the app on his phone to alert him if the vehicle moved.

They guessed that Bosch would be in his home for a few hours and this would give them the opportunity to go down to the Crescent Arms, where they were supposed to be on a surveillance post.

*   *   *

Ellis and Long referred to the objects of their supposed surveillance as the Bobbsey Twins. This was because of the way their heads bobbed in unison during a performance of side-by-side fellatio in one of the videos they had put on the Internet. They were two porno girls who had moved into a two-bedroom apartment at the Crescent Arms two months earlier. Previously they had put a variety of short videos up on free porn sites across the Internet. These served to establish their credentials and draw viewers to their website, which included pay windows that allowed fans to make direct contact. There was a personal vetting process at that point designed to weed out inquiries from law enforcement, and, eventually, invitations were made and the most intrepid fans could finally pay for a face-to-face meeting with either performer or both and all the sexual abandon that would come with it. Some customers had flown in from as far as Japan to cavort with the girls. Most of them never knew that they were secretly videoed from the moment they entered the apartment to the moment they left.

The problem with the setup was that business was always good and invariably too many men would be coming in and out of the apartment at all hours of day and night. Within days, this traffic was noticed by other tenants in the apartment complex. Within weeks, there were complaints to management, and by the one-month mark, the problem reached the attention of the LAPD. It was a constant cycle. The porno girls, stage-named Ashley Juggs and Annie Minx, had moved house on average every eight weeks in the last year. Finding new places to set up the operation had become a never-ending task for Ellis and Long. Making sure that they were the ones who handled the complaints when they were forwarded to the Vice Unit was also taxing. But the operation was too profitable to discontinue.

The Crescent Arms was a two-story courtyard-style apartment building with exterior stairs and walkways. When Ellis and Long got to apartment 2B, Ellis used a key to open the door without knocking. One of the Bobbsey Twins was sitting on the couch watching the Home Shopping Network on the flat-screen. She didn't appear surprised to see them. She kept glancing at the screen, where there was a sale countdown on a high-powered blender that could be bought in three easy payments.

"Where's Ashley?" Ellis asked.

"I'm Ashley," the woman said.

"Sorry. Where's Annie?"

"Her bedroom."

"Does she have a date? I didn't see the bear."

The arrangement was that a small teddy bear was put in the window next to the door when the apartment was a no-fly zone because of a customer visit.

"No, I think she's just sleeping or something," Ashley said.

"Well, go get her," Ellis said.

"Chop-chop," Long said.

Ashley got up off the couch. She was wearing only a hot pink T-shirt that was barely long enough to cover her hairless crotch. It said "Porn Star" on it, the letters stretched by her unnaturally large breasts. She quickly disappeared into a hallway that led to the back bedrooms. Ellis and Long didn't talk while they waited. Ellis stepped over to the IKEA table in front of the couch and turned off the television with the remote. He then went to the coat closet next to the front door, unlocked it, and opened it, revealing the video surveillance equipment stacked on a steel rack. There was a nine-inch screen on top and he was able to rewind and play back surveillance video from the twins' most recent dates. Each of their bedrooms was outfitted with two pinhole cameras—one in a ceiling fan, the other in the fake thermostat on the wall by the door. There were two more cameras hidden in the living room.

Ellis put the playback on fast-forward so he could quickly speed through all the sex scenes. At intervals he stopped the playback and froze the image so he could get a look at the customer. He usually did this while they were still clothed so he could make judgments on their wealth and possibly gain hints about their professions. All that went out the window when guys got naked. Usually the rich guys were fat and ugly. Ellis needed to see them with their clothes and confidence still on. He'd also look for wedding rings or the indentations on fingers where the wedding rings had recently been.

Long came and looked over his shoulder but said nothing. Ellis scanned through five separate dates. Two singles for each of the twins and then a threesome on the couch in the living room. None of the johns looked like good candidates to Ellis.

"Anything?" Long asked.

"Doesn't look like it," Ellis said.

He set the equipment back up for recording and closed and locked the door. When he turned around, Ashley and Annie were sitting together on the couch. Annie wore neon pink panties and a black bra. It was like they were sharing parts of one outfit. They were both bottle blondes with breast enlargements and spray-on tans. Their lips were distended beyond natural bounds. There wasn't a thing about them that looked real and lately there had been some buyer's remorse. The videos on the free porn sites were about five years old now and filmed before the girls had made some of the supposed enhancements to their bodies. Putting up fresh videos wouldn't solve the problem, because in porn, five years was a lifetime. It was a young woman's game. In this case, honesty in advertising would backfire.

"It's time to move again," Ellis said. "So, tomorrow morning get out your suitcases and pack your shit. We'll come by to move you at two."

"Where are we going?" Annie asked in a whiny voice.

"A place off of Beverly by the Farmer's Market. It's big, there's a lot of units, and maybe we'll get to stay longer this time. There's a Starbucks over there that you can walk to."

He paused to see if they would complain. They didn't. They knew better.

"Okay, then," he said. "What's on the schedule today?"

"We've got a double at ten tonight," Annie said. "So far that's it."

"How much?"

"Two."

Ellis showed his disappointment with his silence. The threshold for a double was supposed to be three grand.

"Better than nothing," Long said.

Ellis glared at him. He had just ruined the chance for Ellis to make it a teachable moment.

"Let's go," he said instead.

He walked to the door. Before opening it he turned back to the twins. "Remember, tomorrow at two," he said.

21

Dr. Hinojos had put three different profiles into a file for Bosch. All were redacted in very minor ways—primarily with the names of victims and witnesses blotted out with a black marker and no crime scene photos attached.

The second profile in the folder came from the James Allen case. This was obvious to Bosch because Haven House was named in the summary and because of the date of the murder. Bosch put the other two aside and dove in. He had always found a similarity in all the profiles he encountered as a detective—whether they came from inside the department's Behavioral Science Unit or the FBI's profilers in Quantico. There were only so many ways to describe a psychopath and the unstopped urges of a sexual predator. But after reading the profile on the Allen murder, he reread the Sheriff's Department profile on the killer of Lexi Parks—done before DNA found in and on the victim was matched to Da'Quan Foster. These profiles carried some basic similarities but their conclusions about the killer from each case were distinctly different.

The summary on the Parks case had pegged the killer as a nascent sexual predator who had likely stalked Parks and meticulously planned the deadly attack, only to be disorganized in carrying it out and to make several mistakes, chief of which was leaving his DNA behind. The culmination of his plan in murder left the killer feeling guilty enough to attempt to psychologically cover up his crime by placing the pillow over the victim's face. This was indicative of a sexual predator who was new at killing, who had moved up the ladder from other lesser sex crimes to murder—possibly for the first time.

The profile of the murderer of James Allen was different. Because of the victim's occupation, it was concluded that the killing came out of a prostitution arrangement and was not motivated by a compulsive psychosexual urge. But as with the Parks killing, there was evidence of guilt being a motivating factor, this time with transference—blaming and punishing the victim for the killer's own actions. The profile suggested that Allen's killer was likely a closeted homosexual male who hid his sexual orientation behind the front of a heterosexual lifestyle. It was further surmised that the killer was probably married with children and a career, all of which he would consider threatened by a sexual liaison with Allen. The feeling of threat was turned into rage and then directed at Allen for "exploiting the suspect's weakness." The killer blamed Allen and sought to end the threat to his family and livelihood by eliminating him. Discarding the body in the alley underlined the suspect's dismissal of Allen as nothing more than detritus. He was human trash left in the alley for pickup.

It was also suggested that this killer could have acted in such a way before. Details of the prior murder that Ali had mentioned to Soto were contained in the profile but also redacted. The victim's name was not given, but a summary of the facts of the case showed both eerie similarities and stark differences.

The main similarities were that the victims were both male prostitutes who were murdered elsewhere and then "displayed" in the alley in roughly the same spot and same pose. The differences were in victim type. Beyond both being prostitutes, one was a diminutive white man and the other a heavyset black man. The profile said their "penetrative" roles were different, with Allen being a bottom and the other victim being a top. These roles indicated different client bases and therefore different killers.

Investigators in the first case had not found the murder scene. The victim lived in a shared apartment in East Hollywood but was not killed there, indicating an unknown rendezvous point with his killer, whereas in the Allen case, evidence indicated that he was murdered in his motel room and then taken to the alley and dumped.

The profiler—Dr. Hinojos—concluded that the two killings were the work of two separate suspects. She further posited that Allen's killer might have had knowledge of the first killing through the media or street gossip or possibly law enforcement sources and attempted to copy aspects of the crime to throw off the investigation.

The profile noted several other aspects of the crime for consideration by investigators. No DNA evidence was collected from Allen's body and no evidence of either sexual assault or consensual sex was found during autopsy. This seemed to suggest that the murderous rage erupted before there was a sex act. The profile also discounted any suggestion that the sex act had occurred much earlier and that the killer had returned to the hotel room to murder Allen. The use of the picture-frame wire to strangle the victim indicated that the killer had not come prepared to commit murder but that the killing was a spur-of-the-moment decision made while the killer was in the room. While Allen was in the bathroom or otherwise distracted or incapacitated, the wire was removed from the picture frame and then used to strangle him.

Bosch put the two profiles in the folder Hinojos had given him. He got up and started pacing the living room as he thought about what he had read and what he knew. It was time to walk himself through the cases and establish clear lines of theory.

Two murders, two different killers. The profiles suggested two different kinds of psychological motivation. Da'Quan Foster was charged with the murder of Lexi Parks but the forensic profile drawn up before the DNA connection was made did not match him on psychological or evidentiary levels. Meantime, the irony was that aspects of his life did fit the profile on the James Allen case, for which he had an ironclad alibi— he was in jail.

Bosch paused in his pacing at the sliding door to look out into the canyon. But what he saw was his own dark reflection in the glass. He shook his head at the thought of the complicated trail he had delineated between the two cases. Allen was Foster's alibi for the Parks killing and with Allen's death much of Foster's defense died.

And then there was the DNA. If at the time of Parks's murder Foster was with Allen, as he reluctantly revealed and as the video from Hollywood Forever inched toward confirming, then the DNA was planted on Parks in an effort to misdirect investigators and possibly frame Foster.

Bosch stepped back from the glass and started moving around the room again. He felt his energy building. He sensed he was getting close to something but wasn't sure what it was. He was still far outside the case and needed better access, but he was homing in just the same. He believed that Lexi Parks still held the secret to both cases. Why was she killed? Answer that and Bosch knew everything would unravel.

Loose ends and unexplained details always bothered Bosch. Unanswered questions. They were the bane of the homicide detective's life. Sometimes they were big questions, sometimes not, but they were always a pebble in the shoe. The missing watch still bothered him. The husband's explanation only answered one question with another. Why had she not turned the watch in for repair in its box? Had she simply dropped off the expensive watch at the jeweler's?

That didn't completely make sense to Bosch and so he could not put the watch aside.

He was also anxious about the Allen case and the need to keep moving forward. When a case stalled, it was often difficult to get momentum back. Sometimes it was like trying to start a car with a dead battery.

He called Lucia Soto's cell.

"You still at the PAB?"

"Yep. About to move the red magnet."

Bosch remembered the board the captain had put up in the squad room. Each detective slid a red magnet to the off-duty square when checking out for the day. A stupid little device to give the captain a sense of control. He had probably gotten the idea from a book on corporate management. When he was with the department Bosch had always made it his practice to ignore the magnets. He felt like he was always on duty.

"You feel like that drink tonight?" he asked.

"Tonight? Uh—"

"I want to pick your brain about what you saw in the Allen file."

"Uh, well, yeah, I guess I could meet. When?"

"Whenever, wherever you want."

"Really? You'll come to my turf?" She sounded impressed.

"Your turf is my turf. Name the time and place."

"Okay, how about eight? I'll be at my local in Boyle Heights."

"Which is?"

"Eastside Luv on First, a couple blocks from Hollenbeck Station."

Bosch heard the carport door to the kitchen open and knew his daughter was home. He had been so consumed with the phone call that he had not heard her car pull in.

"Okay, I'll be there," he said into the phone.

"Cool," Soto said. "See you then."

He disconnected the call. He heard Maddie stop at the refrigerator before emerging from the kitchen, a juice bottle in hand, backpack over her shoulder.

"Hey, Dad."

"Hey, Mads."

"What are you doing?"

"Just finished a call. How was school?"

"Fine."

"Homework?"

"Lots."

"Sorry. Listen, I'm going to need to go out for a couple hours in a little while. You okay making dinner or ordering in?"

"No problem."

"You will eat something, right?"

"Yes, I promise."

"Okay."

He was thankful for that and thankful that so far she hadn't brought up anything about his work on the defense case for Mickey Haller.

"Who are you going out with, Virginia?"

"No, I'm meeting my old partner for a drink."

"Which old partner?"

"Lucia."

"All right, cool."

"Hey, there's something I should probably tell you about Virginia. We're not going out anymore."

"Really? What happened?"

"Uh, um, I don't know, we just hadn't really been seeing each other a lot and…"

"She dumped you."

Bosch hated that word.

"It's not that simple. We talked the other night at dinner and just sort of decided to let things go for now."

"She dumped you."

"Uh, yes, I guess so."

"Are you okay?"

"Yeah, I'm good. I saw it coming. Kind of relieved."

"If you're sure. I'm going to get to work."

"I'm okay. I'm sure."

"Okay. I'm sorry, Dad."

"Don't be. I'm not."

"Okay."

Bosch was glad to get the awkward conversation over with. She turned toward the hallway. She always disappeared into her room to do her homework. He then remembered something.

"Oh, wait. Take a look at this."

Bosch went to the table and picked up the folder containing the profiles.

"You remember Dr. Hinojos? I happened to see her today and I asked if she had any case profiles that she could let me have to show you. I told her you wanted to study psychology and go in that direction. You know, profiling."

"Dad, don't tell people that."

Her tone implied that he had deeply humiliated her. He didn't understand his misstep.

"What do you mean? I thought that's what you wanted to do."

"It is, but you don't have to go telling people."

"So then it's a secret? I don't—"

"It's not a secret but I don't like everybody knowing my business."

"Well, I haven't told everybody. I told a profiler who might be pretty helpful to you down the road."

"Whatever."

Bosch held out the folder. He had given up trying to understand the way Maddie thought and trying to identify and read her stressors. He invariably failed and said the wrong word or celebrated the wrong achievement or complimented the wrong thing.

She took the file without saying thank you and headed toward the hallway leading to her room. A heavy backpack was slung over her shoulder. In the age of laptops and iPads and all manner of digital media, she still carried a big load of books wherever she went.

It was another thing Bosch didn't understand.

"Why were you talking to Hinojos?" she said without looking back. "Was it about that creep you're trying to get off for murder?"

Bosch watched her go. He didn't answer and she didn't pause to hear a reply.

22

Eastside Luv was a corner bar with a mural on the outside wall showing an old mariachi with white whiskers and a wide-brim hat. Bosch had driven by it hundreds of times over the years but never stopped in once. It was an upscale hangout for the Chicano hipsters who were reinventing Boyle Heights block by block.

The bar that was the centerpiece of the establishment was crowded two and three deep and most of those people turned to check out Bosch as he entered through the front door. Los Lobos was blasting from the sound system, a song about a wicked rain coming down. Bosch moved his eyes across the space and found Soto sitting by herself at a table in the back corner. Bosch made his way to her and pulled out the chair opposite.

"I didn't take you for a Chipster," he said. "I thought you might be more of a Las Palomas girl."

Las Palomas was the next bar down, a working-class watering hole with harsh lighting and harsher drinks. Bosch had been in there several times over the years looking for people.

Soto laughed at his comment.

"Sometimes I end up there, but not too often."

She had already ordered two bottles of Modelo. They picked them up and clinked glasses.

"Thanks for seeing me," he yelled just as the music stopped.

That brought another round of attention to him, and both he and Soto laughed.

Soto looked like she was doing well. Her hair was down and she was wearing a sleeveless black shirt and faded jeans. Her smooth brown arms showed off the tattoos she wasn't allowed to show on the job. There was an RIP list on the inside of her left forearm containing the names of lost friends from when she was growing up in Westlake, and a tat on the right arm that was a string of Spanish words wrapping her biceps in a font that looked like barbed wire.

"Hard to park around here," Bosch said. "I didn't see your car in the back."

"I didn't drive," she said. "I Ubered it. A DUI would get me washed out of detectives and back on patrol."

They toasted that and drank more beer.

"Uber—that's that taxi thing, right?" Bosch asked.

"Yes, it's an app, Harry," she said. "You should try it."

"Sure. What's an app?"

She smiled, knowing he knew what an app was but also knowing he would never try Uber or any other one.

"So, you want to pick my brain, huh?"

"Yeah, I just have more questions about—"

"You don't have to. You can just look at the book."

From the empty seat next to her she raised a red tote bag up onto the table and then peeled it down around a thick blue binder. Bosch recognized it as an LAPD murder book but he couldn't comprehend how and why she had it.

"Is that the Allen case?" he asked.

"It is," she said. "I sort of borrowed it off of Ali's desk after he left for the day."

Bosch was stunned. It was an infraction far worse

than what had gotten him suspended and pushed out of the department.

"Lucia, you can't do this," he said. "The last thing I want you to do for me is something that could sink your whole career worse than a DUI. You—"

"Harry, relax," she said. "He's never going to know. You can look at it right now and I'll take it back tonight. Besides, he broke the rules. It's supposed to be locked in the closet at night."

"I don't care about him. You're going to waltz in there after a few beers and just put it back on his desk?"

"Yeah, why not?"

"You are taking a big risk, Lucia. I don't want it on my head if it goes sideways. What you already did was enough. I was just going to ask you some follow-ups, that's all."

She nodded like his daughter always did when he spoke sternly to her. Soto was ten years older than Maddie but sometimes it was hard to tell. This was a foolish stunt.

"Look, Harry, last year you took a big risk for me when we were partners," she said. "I owe you this and I'm happy to be able to do it. So why don't we stop talking about it and you look for what you need. I trust you. I know you're working for a lawyer but I believe you when you say you're looking for the truth, no matter how it falls."

Now it was Bosch's turn to nod. He reached across the table and slowly pulled the binder across. The music had started up loud again, this time a song in Spanish with horns playing sharply in the background.

"How about we go sit in my car?" he asked. "It's so loud in here I can't think straight."

She smiled and shook her head.

"Such an old man," she said. "Let's go."

Bosch took one last pull on his bottle of beer and stood up.

23

Bosch looked at the crime scene photos first. It was the closest he could come to being called to the scene, observing the details, and conducting the on-site investigation.

James Allen's body was found fully clothed and propped against the back wall of an auto-repair and sales garage in an alley at Santa Monica Boulevard and El Centro. The alley was like most any other alley in a city where the infrastructure was crumbling, in a state where the infrastructure was crumbling. It was a patchwork of asphalt spot repairs and loose gravel over a crumbling base of decades-old concrete.

Environmental shots of the spot where the body was discovered showed this part of the alley to be hidden well by the garage on one side and the back side of an apartment building on the other. The only windows on the apartment building that would give a view of the alley were glazed bathroom windows. Just another fifty feet up the alley going in from El Centro it opened wider to accommodate a large parking lot behind a four-floor brick loft building. The immediate impression Bosch got from viewing the photos was that the killer who left Allen's body there knew the alley and knew he could dump the body at the end behind the car shop without being seen. It was possible he also knew that the body would be discovered the following morning when workers in the loft building entered the alley to reach their parking lot.

Next Bosch studied the close-up shots of the body. The victim was clothed in a pair of gray running shorts and a pink collared shirt. No shoes, but on the feet were the kind of shoe liners worn by women to protect against blisters when wearing shoes without socks or stockings. On his head was a stocking cap that would have been worn under a wig. The shirt collar helped hide the braided wire that was cinched around the neck. The wire had been pulled so tight that it had cut into the skin. Bleeding was minimal because the heart had stopped pumping shortly after the wire cut the skin.

The victim's hairless legs were stretched out into the alley and his hands were lying in his lap. Close-up shots of the hands revealed no broken fingernails or blood. It made Bosch wonder if Allen had been somehow prevented from fighting against the wire as it was pulled tight around his neck.

"What is it?" Soto asked.

She was sitting in the passenger seat next to him and had been silent as Bosch went through the photos. She had smuggled her beer out of the bar and had been sipping it as she watched Bosch study the book.

"What do you mean?" Bosch asked.

"I've watched you look through a murder book before," she said. "I can tell when you see something that doesn't add up."

Bosch nodded.

"Well, there is no trauma to the hands. No blood, no broken fingernails. Somebody pulls a wire around your neck and you'd think your hands would go to your neck and start fighting the wire."

"So what is that telling you?"

"Well, either that he wasn't conscious when he was choked out or something or someone was holding his hands down. There's no sign of binding marks on the wrists, so…"

He didn't finish.

"What? No sign of binding means what?"

"That maybe there were two."

"Two killers?"

"One to hold him down and control his hands, one to work the wire. There are other things, too."

"I don't think Karim and Stotter have tumbled to that. What other things?"

Bosch shrugged.

"Guy's feet. No shoes but he's wearing these liner socks."

"They're called Peds."

"Okay, Peds. I don't see any abrasions on the legs or anywhere else on the body from it being dragged."

Soto leaned across the center console to look closer at the photo Bosch was looking at.

"Okay," she said.

"The body is propped against the wall," he said. "Presumably it was removed from a car and put there. It was carried. The victim's not a big guy. Sure, it could've been done by one person, but still. One person carrying him from a vehicle to that spot? I don't know. It gives me pause, Lucia."

Soto just nodded after leaning back into her seat and taking another pull on her bottle.

The photos were contained in plastic sleeves with three holes that allowed them to be secured by the three rings of the binder. Bosch flipped back and forth between photos, double-checking his statements. He then took his phone out and took a picture of one of the photos—a midrange shot that showed the body in its entirety slumped against the graffiti-covered rear wall of the car shop.

"Harry, you can't," Soto said.

He knew what she meant. If a photo of a crime scene photo turned up in court or anywhere else, it would be obvious that Bosch had had access to the murder book. That could spawn an investigation that would lead back to Soto.

"I know," Bosch said. "I'm just taking it to place the body on the wall. So I'll know when I check out the alley. I want to get the location right, and this graffiti will help. After I go by there and check things out, I will destroy the photo. How's that?"

"Okay, I guess."

Bosch moved on to the next set of photos. These were taken inside room 6 at the Haven House. This was when the room was still crowded with James Allen's belongings. There were clothes in the closet, several pairs of shoes and high heels on the floor. Two wigs— one blond, one brunette—on stands on the bureau. There were several candles in the room—on the bureau, on both bed tables, and on the shelf above the headboard of the bed. Also on the shelf was a large clear plastic container half full of condoms. The brand label on the container was Rainbow Pride. The label advertised that the container held three hundred lubricated condoms in six different colors. Bosch took out his notebook and wrote down the details to give to Haller later. He noted that Soto's observation when reporting on the photos the day before was correct. The condom container was similar to the candy containers he remembered seeing in doctors' offices and at convenience store cash registers.

Bosch closely scanned the photos of the motel room

for any sign of a cell phone but didn't see one. He knew there had to be one somewhere, because Da'Quan Foster had told Bosch during the interview at county jail that he had called Allen to arrange to meet him the night of the Lexi Parks killing.

Bosch flipped over to section five of the murder book, which he knew would contain the property report. He studied the lists of items retrieved by investigators at both crime scenes—the alley and the motel room where Allen lived. There was no mention of a phone on either list.

The conclusion: The killer had taken Allen's phone because the phone contained a record of contact with him.

Bosch quickly went through the book to see if Karim and Stotter had subpoenaed any phone records. There were none and no record that a subpoena had been written or filed, and this led Bosch to believe that Allen either used a legit phone that was registered to someone else or used a throwaway that would be impossible to procure records for without either the phone or its number and service provider in hand.

Bosch made a note about going back to Da'Quan Foster and getting the number he used to contact Allen. That would be a start in tracing Allen's phone activities.

"Sorry," Bosch said.

"What are you talking about?" Soto said.

"I'm sure you weren't planning on spending your evening sitting in my car."

"It's okay. Things don't really get going in there until later. That's when people start dancing on the bar and taking off their clothes."

"Right."

"I'm serious."

"Oh, then I'll hurry up here so you don't miss that."

"Maybe you should stay so you don't miss it. Maybe loosen you up some, Harry."

Bosch glanced at her and then back at the book. He was looking for the autopsy report.

"You think I'm too stiff, huh?"

"Well, around me. I think you always thought I was too fragile for the work. Deep down, I think you think it's men's work."

"No, not true. For a long time my daughter wanted to do what you do. What I did. I didn't discourage it."

"But now she wants to be a profiler, right?"

"I think, but you never know."

"She probably got the same message I got from you. 'You are not suited for this.'"

"Yeah, well, maybe I'm old-fashioned. I kind of hate the idea of women seeing the evil men do. Something like that."

He found the autopsy. He had read a thousand autopsy reports in his time. He knew the form of the document by heart and that form had barely changed in the last four decades. He quickly paged through to the measurements of the body. He didn't need any of the conclusions. He just wanted to know what the victim weighed.

"Here it is," he said. "Guy weighed a buck and a half. That's not a lot but I'm thinking a lone killer drags a hundred fifty pounds. He doesn't carry it."

"I'll tell Ali and Mike," Soto said.

"No, you can't. You never had this conversation."

"Right, right."

Bosch checked his watch. They had already been in the car an hour. He would have liked nothing more than to spend several hours scouring the murder book. He had yet to look at any records from the earlier murder, in which the victim was left in the same alley. But he knew he had to let Soto go soon. She had already gone above and beyond the call of duty to a former partner. Especially one who was no longer a cop.

"Let me just take a quick run through the rest of this and then I'll get you out of here," he said.

"It's okay, Harry," Soto said. "You know, after you walked out the door of the squad, I thought I'd never get a chance to see you work again. I like this. I learn from you."

"What, just sitting there watching me read a murder book?"

"Yes. I learn what you think is important, how you put things together, make conclusions. You remember you told me once that all the answers are usually in the murder book. We just don't see them."

Bosch nodded.

"Yeah, I remember."

He was looking at James Allen's lengthy arrest record. It was six pages in the book. He scanned them quickly because they were routinely repetitive with several prostitution and loitering arrests plus a few drug possession busts spanning the last seven years. It was a very common rap sheet for a prostitute. Several of the arrests were suspended or not prosecuted as Allen was initially diverted into pre-trial sex-worker and drug-rehab programs. Once that string was played out, his arrests started resulting in convictions and jail time. Never anything in a state correctional facility, always short stints in county jail. Thirty days here, forty-five there, the jail becoming not so much a deterrent as a revolving door—the sad norm for a recidivist sex worker.

The only unusual thing about Allen's rap sheet was his last arrest—a loitering-with-intent-to-commit-prostitution bust. What caught Bosch's eye was that the arrest came fourteen months prior to his death and had resulted in a nolle pros—meaning no charges were ever filed against him. Allen was simply released.

"Wait a minute," Bosch said.

He flipped to the front of the murder book and scanned the crime report and then the first summary filed by Karim and Stotter.

"What is it?" Soto asked.

"This guy hadn't been arrested in over a year," Bosch said as he was reading.

"So?"

"Well, he was sort of camped out there on Santa Monica…"

"So?"

Bosch flipped back to the rap sheet and turned the book so she could see it. He started flipping through the pages.

"This guy gets busted three or four times a year for five years and then nothing for the last fourteen months before he gets killed," he said. "That makes me think he had a guardian angel."

"What do you mean, someone in the LAPD watching out for him?"

"Yeah, that he was working for somebody. But there's nothing in here about him being a snitch. No CI number, no report."

There were protocols for dealing with confidential informants, including in the event that an informant was murdered. But there was nothing in the murder book that clearly indicated that James Allen was an informant.

"Maybe he just got lucky and avoided arrest in that last year," Soto said. "I mean, arrests have been down across the board the last year. All these shootings with cops and Ferguson and Baltimore and all of that, the uniforms are doing the minimum required. Nobody's proactive anymore."

"Do the math," Bosch said. "These fourteen months go back way before Baltimore, way before Ferguson."

Bosch shook his head. He had now counted seventeen arrests in five years for Allen on the rap sheet, then more than a year of clean living.

"I think he was working for somebody," he said. "Off book."

It was a violation of department policy for an officer to work a snitch without registering the individual with a supervisor and entering the name in the CI Tracking System database. But Bosch knew it regularly occurred. Snitches were procured over time and often used in test situations. Still, fourteen months seemed like a long time to test whether Allen would be a reliable informant.

Stotter and Karim had pulled all of the arrest reports and Bosch started going through these. The names of arresting officers were not on the abbreviated summaries but their unit call signs were listed. He noted that one number was the same on three of Allen's last five arrests before the fourteen months of non-activity. It was 6-Victor-55. Hollywood Division was denoted by the 6, Victor meant Vice, and 55 indicated it was a two-officer undercover team. He wrote it down on a page of his notebook, then wrote it again on the next page. He tore the second page out and handed it to Soto.

"I think these are probably the guys that were working him," he said. "Next time you're on the company computer, see if you can get me their names out of Hollywood Vice. I want to talk to them."

She looked at the number, then folded the piece of paper and put it into the pocket of her jeans.

"Sure."

Bosch closed the murder book and handed it to her. She returned it to the red tote bag.

"You sure you can get that back without causing a stir?" he asked.

"They'll never know," she said.

"That's good. And thanks, Lucia. It's going to help a lot."

"Anytime. You want to go back in and get another beer?"

Bosch thought for a moment and then shook his head.

"Nah, I got the vibe on this thing. I should stay with it."

"Big Mo, huh?"

"Yeah, I got momentum back—thanks to you."

"Okay, Harry, roll with it. Stay safe."

"You, too."

She opened the door and got out. Bosch started the engine but didn't move the car until he watched her walk safely through the back door of the bar.

24

Bosch pulled into the alley off El Centro and checked his watch. It was 10:40 p.m. and he knew that he was inside the window of time during which it was estimated that James Allen was murdered and left propped against the wall behind the car repair shop on the night of March 21. Though time of death in the autopsy was estimated to have been anywhere from 10 p.m. to 1 a.m., he knew he would be encountering the same general environmental conditions as on the night of the murder. Evening temperatures in L.A. did not fluctuate much between March and May. But beyond climate, Bosch was interested in ambient light and its sources, a sense of how sound carried in the alley, and any other factors that might have been in play the night James Allen's body was left behind.

Bosch drove past the repair shop and stopped in the parking lot behind the loft building. The lot was deserted. He killed the engine, took a flashlight out of the glove box, and got out of the car.

Walking back toward the repair shop, he stopped once to take a wide shot of the alley and the scene of the crime with his phone. He then proceeded to the rear wall of the repair shop. To his disappointment, he found that the graffiti on the wall had been painted over since the night James Allen's body had been left in the alley. There was only one tag so far on the fresh paint, a depiction of a snake that formed the number 18—the mark of the notorious 18th Street gang out of Rampart that had sets all over the city, including Hollywood.

He pulled up the photo of the wall that he had copied from the murder book earlier and using a portion of the crumbled asphalt in the picture was still able to place the spot where James Allen's body had been propped up.

He stepped over to the spot and put his back to the wall. He looked up and down the alley, then up at the apartment building across from him. One of the small bathroom windows on the second floor had a light on. It was cracked open a few inches. Bosch grew annoyed with himself. He had been so concerned about not robbing Soto of her whole evening that he had not taken the proper time—or at least as much time as she would have allowed—to read through all sections of the murder book. He had not seen a report on the canvass of the neighborhood following the discovery of the body. Now he was looking at a lighted and open window that conceivably had a view of the crime scene. Had the resident there been questioned by police? Probably, but Bosch didn't know for sure.

He considered calling Soto and asking her to look in the book for him but decided he had already asked too much of her. With each call and request, he was putting her in more danger of being found consorting with the enemy. He thought about the sign he used to hang on the partition in his cubicle when he had worn a badge: *Get Off Your Ass and Knock On Doors.*

Bosch pushed off the wall and walked out of the alley onto El Centro. The apartment building that backed the alley was a pink stucco affair built quickly and cheaply during a boom in the eighties. Its architectural flourishes were few, unless the filigreed design of the gated entrance counted. Bosch had to step back and look up at the two-story structure to try to figure out which apartment the lighted bathroom might belong to and then what number that unit would be.

The directory next to the gate's phone listed eight units—101 through 104 and 201 through 204. He went with the twos and decided on unit 203 first. He picked up the phone and followed the prompts and the call went unanswered. He tried 204 next and this time got a response.

"*Qué?*"

"*Hola,*" Bosch said haltingly. "*Policía. Abierto por favor.*"

He realized that he only had his policeman's Spanish. He didn't know how to say that he was a private investigator.

The person on the other end of the line—a woman—said something too quickly to understand. He responded with the old standby said more sternly.

"*Policía. Abierto.*"

The lock on the metal door buzzed and he pulled it open. He stepped in. There were stairs on either end of the building. He took the set on the right and they delivered him to a walkway leading to two apartment doors on the side of the building that backed up to the alley. Though it had been the person in 204 who had let him through the gate, Bosch now could confirm that unit 203 was the one with the open window and light on in the bathroom. He went to that door first and knocked. While he waited for a response, the door to 204 opened and an old woman stuck her head out to look at him. Bosch knocked again, louder this time, on the door to 203 but then walked over to the woman in the open doorway.

"Do you speak English?" he asked.

"*Poquito,*" she said.

"The murder in the alley? Two months ago? El asasinato?"

"*Sí.*"

Bosch pointed to his ear and then his eye.

"Did you hear anything? Did you see anything?"

"Oh, no. They very quiet. I hear nothing."

"They?"

"*Los matadores.*"

Bosch now held up two fingers.

"*Matadores?* Two?"

The old lady shrugged.

"I don't know."

"Why did you say 'they?'"

She pointed to the door that Bosch had just knocked on.

"She say."

Bosch looked at the unanswered door and then back at the old woman.

"Where is she?"

"She work now."

"Do you know where?"

The woman brought her arms together in a rocking motion.

"Babysitting?" Bosch asked. "Child care?"

"*Sí, sí, sí.*"

"Do you know when she comes home?"

The woman looked at him and he could tell she didn't understand.

"Uh, *finito?*"

He walked two fingers across the palm of his hand and pointed at the door to unit 203. The woman shook her head. She either didn't know or she still didn't understand. Bosch nodded. It was the best he could do for now.

"Gracias."

He headed back to the stairs and went down. Before he got to the gate, he heard a voice from behind.

"Hey, *policía.*"

Bosch turned. There was a man standing in the alcove by the door to apartment 103. He was smoking a cigarette under the light above the door. Bosch walked back to him.

"Are you police?" the man asked.

Up close Bosch could see the Latino man was about thirty with a strong build. He wore a white T-shirt that had been bleached so many times it glowed under the light. He had no visible tattoos, which made Bosch think he wasn't a gang member.

"A detective," Bosch said. "I'm working on the murder that happened in the alley in March. Do you know anything about it?"

"Just that some faggot whore got his throat cut or some shit," the man said.

"Were you home that night?"

"Sure."

"Did you see anything?"

"Nah, man, I didn't see nothing. I was in bed."

"Hear anything?"

"Well, yeah, I heard 'em but I didn't think it was anything so I didn't get up to look."

"What did you hear?"

"I heard them dump the guy out."

"What's that sound like?"

"Well, I heard a trunk. You know, like a trunk closing. It came from the alley."

"A trunk."

"Yeah, a trunk. You know how you can tell the difference between the sound of a car door and a trunk? It was a trunk."

"Did you also hear a car door?"

"Yeah, I heard that. I heard the trunk, then I heard the doors close."

"Doors?"

"Yeah, two doors."

"You heard two car doors close? You sure?"

The man shrugged.

"I hear all kinds of stuff from that alley. All night some nights."

"Okay. Did you tell what you just told me to the police?"

"Nope."

"Why not?"

"I don't know, they left a card one day in my door, asking me to call. I never got around to calling. I stay busy, you know what I mean?"

"You mean a business card? Do you still have it?"

"Yeah, on the fridge. I guess I could still call but I'm talkin' to you, right?"

"Right. Can I see it? I want to get the name."

"Yeah, sure. Hold on."

The man opened his door and went in. He left the door open and Bosch saw a living room that was sparsely furnished. There was a crucifix on the wall and a couch with Mexican blankets draped over it. No expense had been spared on the large flat-screen television on the wall. It was showing a soccer game somewhere.

The man came from the kitchen and closed the door as he stepped back out. He handed Bosch a standard-issue LAPD business card with the name Edward Montez on it. On the flip side a handwritten note in two languages. The English said, "Please call."

Bosch knew the name Montez but not the man. He and his partner must have been charged by Stotter and Karim with handling the neighborhood canvas. Montez had done a poor job if he left cards in doors and never followed up. It was not surprising, however. So few people in minority neighborhoods wished to get involved as witnesses in cases that most efforts of investigators were focused on looking for non-human witnesses—cameras.

"So you've never talked to the police about that night," Bosch said.

"No, man. Nobody came that night and I work during the day. That's when they left the card."

"Do you know, did anybody in this building talk to the police?"

"Mrs. Jiminez did. She lives upstairs. But she didn't see shit and she can't hear too good."

"What else did you hear besides the sound of the trunk and then the doors?"

"Nothing, man, that was it."

"You didn't look through a window to see what it was about?"

"No, man, I was tired. I didn't want to get up. Besides…"

"Besides what?"

"You stick your nose into stuff like that, you might get a problem."

"You mean a gang problem?"

"Yeah, like that."

Bosch nodded. The 18th Street gang was not known for its peaceful coexistence in the neighborhoods it claimed as its turf. He could not second-guess someone for not rushing to his window to check out the activity in an alley.

"You remember what time it was when you heard the trunk and the doors?"

"Not really, not anymore. But it was definitely the night of the murder because the next morning all the police were in the alley. I saw them when I left for work."

"Where do you work?"

"LAX."

"TSA?"

He laughed like Bosch had made a joke.

"No, man, baggage. I work for Delta."

Bosch nodded.

"Okay. What's your name?"

"Ricardo."

"Last name?"

"You're not a cop, are you?"

"I used to be."

"Used to be? What's that mean?"

"I'm not sure."

"Just Ricardo, okay?"

"Sure. Thanks, Ricardo."

Ricardo dropped his cigarette to the concrete, crushed it with his foot, and then kicked it into a nearby flower bed.

"Good night, Mr. I-Used-To-Be-A-Cop."

"Yeah, good night."

Bosch left through the gate and stopped to look at the directory. He confirmed the name Jiminez on unit 203 and saw the name R. Benitez on the line next to 103. He headed back into the alley where his car was waiting.

Once he was behind the wheel, he put the key in the ignition but didn't turn it. He sat for a moment looking through the windshield at the spot where James Allen's body was left and thinking about what Ricardo Benitez had just told him. He heard a car trunk being closed followed by two car doors. Bosch envisioned a car coming into the alley with its lights off. Two people get out, leave their doors open, and go to the trunk. They remove the body, prop it against the wall, then go back to the car. One closes the trunk as he goes around the back of the car. They get in, close their doors, and the car takes off. In and out in — what? — thirty seconds tops?

Bosch nodded.

Two people, he thought.

He turned the key and started the engine.

25

There was a line of light under the door of his daughter's room when Bosch got home. He hesitated in the hallway for a moment and then lightly knocked. He expected there would be no reply because she usually had her earbuds in and was listening to music. But he was surprised.

"You can come in," she called.

Bosch opened the door and stepped in. Maddie was under the bedcovers with her laptop open in front of her. She had her earbuds in.

"Hey, I'm home," he said.

She pulled out the buds.

"I know."

"So what are you doing?"

"Just music."

Bosch came over and sat on the edge of her bed, trying not to show any frustration with her one- and two-word answers.

"What music?"

"Death Cab."

"That the song or the band?"

"The band is Death Cab for Cutie. The song I like is 'Black Sun.'"

"Sounds uplifting."

"It's a great song, Dad. It reminds me of you."

"How come?"

"I don't know. It just does."

"Did you look at those profiles?"

"I did."

"And?"

"Well, first of all, they were amazingly repetitive. Like you could apply the same stuff to every case even though they were different cases and different kinds of murders."

"Well, they say it's an inexact science."

She folded her arms across her chest.

"What's that supposed to mean?" she asked.

"I don't know, that they try to cover all the bases," he said. "So that when someone gets caught, they're covered by the generics."

"Let me ask you something, Dad. Did a profile of a killer or a crime scene ever help you solve a case? Tell the truth."

Bosch had to think for a moment because there wasn't a ready answer.

"I guess that answers my question," Maddie said.

"No, wait," Bosch said. "I was just thinking. I haven't had a case where I got a profile and it was so dead-on that it pointed me right to the killer. But they've been helpful to me a lot of times. Your mother..."

She waited but he didn't go on.

"My mother what?"

"No, I was just going to say that she wasn't really a profiler but she was still the best profiler I ever knew. She could read people. I think her life experiences helped make her empathic. She always had a good feel for a crime scene and for the killer's motivations. I'd show her pictures from my cases and she'd tell me what she thought."

"She never told me that."

"Well, you know, you were young. She didn't want to talk about murder with you, I think."

Bosch was silent for a moment as he realized he had

not thought about Eleanor Wish in a long time. It made him feel bad.

"You know, she had this theory," he said quietly. "She always said that the motivation for all murders could be dialed back to shame."

"Just shame, that's it?" Maddie asked.

"Yeah, just shame. People covering up shame and finding any kind of way to do it. I don't know, I think it was pretty smart."

Maddie nodded.

"I miss her," she said.

Bosch nodded.

"Yeah," he said. "I get that. It will probably always be that way."

"I wonder what it would be like, you know, if she were still around," she said. "Like when I have to decide things, I wish she was here."

"You can always talk to me," Bosch said. "You know that, right?"

"I'm talking about girl things."

"Right."

Bosch wasn't sure what to say. He was happy that Maddie was opening up for the first time in a long time but he felt ill equipped to seize the moment. It underlined his failings as a father.

"Is it school?" he asked. "Are you worried about anything?"

"No, school is school. It's like all the girls talk about how their mothers are dumb or about how they want to control them and everything about graduation and college and all of that. I kind of wish I had that sometimes, you know. A mother to tell me stuff."

Bosch nodded.

"I should talk," she said. "You didn't have a mother *or* a father."

"It was a little different, I think," Bosch said. "I think a girl really needs a mother."

"Oh, well. I lost my chance."

Bosch leaned over and kissed the top of her head. For the first time in a long time he picked up no vibe of resistance from her. He stood up from the bed and saw her big gray duffel bag on the floor, all packed and ready to go. He realized that she was leaving from school for the camping trip the very next day.

"Shit," he said.

"What?" she said.

"I forgot tomorrow's the day you leave. I shouldn't have gone out."

"It's okay. I had to finish packing. I'll only be gone three nights."

Bosch sat back down on the bed.

"I'm sorry," he said.

"Don't be," she said.

"I hope you have some fun up there."

"I doubt it."

"Well, try. Okay?"

"Okay."

"And text me."

"They told us the service is really bad."

"Okay, well, if you get a signal, let me know everything's all right."

He leaned over and kissed the top of her head again, mindful this time not to breathe out and reveal he had beer on his breath.

He stood up and headed toward the door.

"I love you, kid," he said. "I'll see you in the morning before you go."

"Love you, Dad," she said.

He believed she meant it.

26

The next morning Maddie grudgingly allowed him to lug her duffel bag to her car. She then went off to school and her required camping trip, telling Bosch that a bus would pick the campers up from the school and take them to the mountains.

He watched her drive down the street and felt sad that she would not be in the house for the next three nights. He went back inside, brewed a pot of coffee, and settled down with a cup at the dining-room-table-turned-worktable. He did what he always did when he had worked with a badge. He went back to the book.

To Bosch the murder book was an evolving tool. It was true that in this case he had only a copy of the book and would not be adding to it with his own investigation. No matter how many times he looked at it, the page count would not change and every word would stay the same. But that didn't matter. The meaning of things changed as investigations progressed. The simple fact was that Bosch knew more about the case now than he had when he last looked through the Lexi Parks murder book. That meant that the significance of things could change as he filtered them through the net of his growing knowledge of the case.

He started rereading the documents from page one

and eventually got to the phone logs. The investigators on the case had begun examining the call logs from the victim's personal and business phones for the three months prior to her murder. They were in the process of identifying and questioning the parties involved in those calls with Lexi Parks when the results of the DNA analysis came back from the lab matching Da'Quan Foster to the murder scene. That turned everything in a new direction and it appeared to Bosch that the study of the call lists was then dropped as Foster became the intensive and sole focus of the investigation. Still, much of the work was already done on the lists, with most numbers on a spreadsheet explained in a sentence or two or dismissed as "NS"—short for not suspicious.

Bosch had checked the spreadsheet before, but this time when he scanned it a name caught in his filters. Four days before her murder Alexandra Parks had called Nelson Grant & Sons Jewelers. The call had been given an NS designation by the investigators.

It seemed obvious that the call was about her broken watch and it had drawn no suspicion from the Sheriff's investigators. But the watch was on Bosch's radar because of the empty box on the shelf in her home. He wondered if Parks had been calling to inquire if her watch had been repaired. He scanned the rest of the call list and jumped to the list of numbers called from her office line. He saw no other calls to the jewelry store.

The office line spreadsheet was incomplete. Parks had made hundreds of calls from the line in the months before her death, and the project was daunting. Cornell and Schmidt were probably happy to leave it behind once the DNA match came through, hanging the case on Da'Quan Foster. All they had to do at that point was check the call lists to see if there had been any contact between the victim and suspect. There had not been, and the call list analysis had been discontinued. It was a subtle form of tunnel vision. They now had the bird in hand—Foster—so there was no need to finish going through hundreds of phone calls and numbers that did not have any direct ties to their suspect.

Bosch opened his laptop and looked up Nelson Grant & Sons Jewelers. With Google maps he located its Sunset Boulevard address in the upscale Sunset Plaza shopping district and learned that the store opened at ten o'clock each morning.

He decided to visit the store as soon as it opened, but that wouldn't be for nearly an hour. He opened the business's website and determined that the shop dealt in many lines of jewelry and watches as well as handled estate sales. But he could not find any references to Audemars Piguet watches.

He then Googled the watchmaker and found several online dealers. He clicked on one of these and soon was looking at an array of watches manufactured by the Swiss company. He further refined his search to the Royal Oak Offshore model and soon was looking at a watch with a $14,000 price tag.

Bosch whistled. The discrepancy between what Harrick paid a year ago for the same model and the current online retail price was nearly ten thousand dollars.

He went back to the manufacturer's website and clicked on the list of certified Audemars Piguet dealers. There were only three shops and service centers in the United States and the closest to L.A. was in Las Vegas. Bosch pulled up two numbers for the service center and then went back to the phone logs from the murder book. Scanning the call logs for matches was easy and quick because of the 702 area code for Las Vegas. Bosch found two calls connected to the service center. On

Thursday, February 5—the same day Lexi Parks called Nelson Grant & Sons—a call had been placed from her office line to the Audemars Piguet service center. The call lasted almost six minutes. Then there was a return call from the service center to Parks's office four hours later. That call lasted two minutes.

Bosch assumed that all the calls were regarding her watch and its repair. He pulled his own phone out and was about to call the first number, when he decided to wait. He needed to gather more information before blindly making the call.

On the inside cover of the folder he wrote out a timeline involving the calls Parks had made and received. The first call was to the service center in Vegas. He assumed this was a call in which Parks asked about getting her watch repaired.

But then only fourteen minutes later she called Nelson Grant & Sons, the store where her husband had bought the watch. This call lasted only seventy-seven seconds.

Then four hours later, someone at the service center in Las Vegas called Parks on her office line. That call lasted two minutes and two seconds.

Bosch had no idea what any of this meant and whether it was germane to the murder that would follow four days later. But it was a case anomaly and he would not be able to let it go until he understood it. The watch had not even come up on the radar with the Sheriff's investigators. They were too far into the tunnel. That left it to Bosch. He decided he would start at the jewelry store where the victim's husband had bought the watch at what appeared to be a very deep discount. From there he would go to the manufacturer's service center.

He gathered all the reports back up into a single pile,

squared the edges, and weighted the stack down on the table with his laptop. In the kitchen he poured another dose of coffee into his travel mug and grabbed his keys. He was about to go through the kitchen door into the carport when he heard the chime from the front door. He put the coffee down on the counter and went to answer it.

A man and woman stood at the door. Both had stocky builds and wore suits, the man with a tie. They didn't smile and there was a coldness in their eyes that allowed Bosch to peg them as cops before they identified themselves.

"Mr. Bosch?" the man asked.

"That's me," Bosch said. "What can I do for you?"

"We're investigators with the Sheriff's Department. This is Detective Schmidt and I'm Cornell. We'd like to talk to you if you have the time."

"Sure. I've got some time."

There was an awkward pause as Bosch made no move to invite them into the house.

"Do you want to do this right here at the door?" Cornell asked.

"Might as well," Bosch said. "I'm assuming this will be quick. It's about me going by the house yesterday, right?"

"Are you working for the defense in the Parks case?"

"I am."

"Are you a licensed private investigator, sir?"

"I was one about a dozen years ago but the license lapsed. So I am working for a state-licensed private investigator while I apply for my own to be reinstated. I have a letter of engagement from him that explains this and makes it clear—and legal."

"Can we take a look at that letter, Mr. Bosch?"

"Sure. I'll be right back."

Bosch closed the door and left them there. He went and got the letter Haller had provided and came back to the door with it. Schmidt, who hadn't said anything so far, took it and read it while her partner lectured Bosch.

"That was uncool, what you did yesterday," Cornell said.

"What was that?" Bosch asked.

"You know what it was. You presented yourself in a false light to gain access to a crime scene."

"I don't know what you're talking about. I went to look at a house that's for sale. I've been thinking about selling this place. I've got a kid with four years of college coming up and I could use the equity I've got in it."

"Look, Bosch, I'm not going to fuck around with you. You cross the line again and there will be consequences. I'm giving you a break here. We checked you out and you used to be legit. Used to be. Now not so much."

"Fuck off, Cornell. I've seen your work on this. It's weak."

Schmidt handed the letter back to Bosch but Cornell snatched it out of her hand before Bosch reached for it.

"This is what I think of your letter," he said.

He reached inside his suit jacket and around the back of his pants. He pantomimed wiping his ass with the letter, then held it out to Bosch. He didn't take it.

"Nice," Bosch said. "Classy and clever."

Bosch took a step back so he could close the door on them. Cornell quickly used two hands to crunch the letter in a ball and then threw it at Bosch as he was closing the door. It bounced off his chest and fell to the floor.

Bosch stood at the door, listening to the steps as Cornell and Schmidt walked away. He could feel his face burning red with humiliation. If they had checked him out, it meant that everybody in the LAPD would know he had crossed to the dark side. It would not matter to them that Bosch actually believed there was a good chance that the man accused of the crime was innocent. The bottom line would be that Bosch was now a defense investigator.

He leaned his forehead against the door. A week ago he was a retired LAPD detective. He now seemed to have a whole new identity. He heard their car start out at the curb. He waited, head against the door, for it to drive away, and then he left, too.

27

Bosch was parked at the curb in front of Nelson Grant & Sons before it opened. He saw lights go on first and then at 10:05 he watched a young Asian man inside the shop come to the front glass door and stoop down to unlock it at the bottom. He then stepped outside with a folding sign that advertised Estate Sales, positioned it on the sidewalk, and returned to the shop. Nelson Grant & Sons was open for business. Bosch took the last drink of his coffee and got out of the Cherokee. It was midmorning and traffic was thick on Sunset but the sidewalks and shops of Sunset Plaza were deserted. It was a shopping and eating destination largely favored by European visitors, and things usually didn't start stirring until lunchtime and later.

There appeared to be no one in the store when Bosch entered, setting off a low chime somewhere in the back. A few seconds later the man he had seen before stepped out from a back room, his mouth full and chewing. He took a position behind the center segment of the U-shaped glass display counter and held up a finger, asking for a moment. He finally swallowed whatever he was eating and smiled and asked Bosch if he could help him.

"I hope so," Bosch said, stepping to the counter directly across from the man. "Do you sell watches by Audemars Piguet?"

"Audemars Piguet," the man said, pronouncing it quite differently than Bosch had. "We are not a dealer. But on occasion we sell AP watches through estate sales. We had two last year but they sold. They're collector's items and they go quickly when we get them."

"So they would have been used."

"We prefer to say estate owned."

"Got it. Estate owned. You know, now that you mention it, I think I was in here last year and saw one. It was a ladies' watch? Was that back in December when you had it?"

"Uh, yes, I believe so. That was the last one we had."

"A Royal Oak, right?"

"Actually, the model was a Royal Oak Offshore. Are you a collector, sir?"

"A collector? In a way, yeah. So I have a friend. Vincent Harrick? You know him? He was the one who bought that AP watch back in December, right?"

The man looked suspicious and confused at the same time.

"I'm not at liberty to discuss our clients, sir. Is there a watch here that we do have that I can show you?"

He gestured with his arm across the glass top of the counter. Bosch looked at him without answering. There was something off. As soon as Bosch mentioned Harrick and the watch bought in December, the man seemed to grow nervous. He had made a furtive glance behind him at the door to the back room.

Bosch decided to push things a bit and to gauge the man's reactions.

"So who died?" he asked.

"What are you talking about?" the man replied, his voice almost shrill.

"To have an estate sale, somebody's gotta die, right?"

"No, that is not always the case. We have people who

decide for whatever reason to sell their jewelry collections. Their watches. These are considered estates."

He turned slightly and looked back at the door again.

"Is Mr. Grant back there?" Bosch asked.

"Who?"

"Nelson Grant. Is he back there?"

"There is no Nelson Grant. It's just a name on a sign. My father made it up when he opened the store. People would have trouble pronouncing our name."

"Is your father back there?"

"No, no one is back there and my father retired long ago. My brother and I run the shop. What exactly is this all about?"

"It's about a murder. What is your name, sir?"

"I don't have to give you my name. I'm going to have to ask you to leave now, sir, if you are not interested in making a purchase."

Bosch smiled.

"Really?"

"Yes, really. Please go."

Bosch saw a plastic business card holder on the glass top of the case to his right. He calmly walked over to it and picked off the top card in the stack. There were two names on it. The brothers. He read them out loud.

"Peter and Paul Nguyen. Did I pronounce that right? Like you can't *win* 'em all?"

"Yes. Please leave now."

"I can see why the old man went with Grant. Are you Peter or Paul?"

"Why do you need to know this?"

"Well, because I'm conducting an investigation."

Bosch pulled his wallet out and produced his LAPD identification card. When he held it up to the man, he kept it clipped between his fingers, with the finger on the front strategically placed over the word RETIRED. He had practiced this move in front of the mirror over the bureau in his bedroom.

"Okay, what about a badge?" the man said. "Don't you have a badge?"

"I don't need a badge to ask you a few simple questions—if you are willing to cooperate."

"Whatever will get this over with the quickest."

"Good. Okay, so which is it, Peter or Paul?"

"Peter."

"Okay, Peter, take a look at this."

Bosch opened the photo archive on his phone. He quickly pulled up the photo of Lexi Parks he had taken from one of the *Times* stories on the murder. He held it up to Nguyen.

"Do you recognize this woman? Had she been in this store in the early part of this year?"

Nguyen shook his head as if totally lost.

"Do you know how many people have been in this store since the beginning of the year?" he asked. "And I'm not even here every minute of every day. My brother and I have employees. Your question is impossible to answer."

"She was murdered."

"I'm sorry, but it doesn't have anything to do with the store."

"She called here four days before she was murdered. Back in February."

The man seemed to freeze and his mouth formed an O as he remembered something.

"What?" Bosch asked.

"I remember now," the man said. "The Sheriff's Department called about that. A detective called and she asked about that woman who was killed and the phone call."

"Was her name Schmidt? What did you tell her?"

"I can't remember the caller's name. I had to check with my brother, who was on duty here the day they were talking about. He said the woman who called asked about how to get her watch fixed and he told her to look up the brand online and make contact with them. We don't do watch repairs. We strictly just sell."

Bosch stared at him. He thought he was either lying or had been lied to by his brother. The call to the shop came after Lexi Parks had called the Audemars Piguet repair center in Las Vegas. It seemed unlikely that she would call to ask about how to get her watch repaired. She called for another reason and this guy and his brother were hiding it.

"Where's your brother?" he asked. "I need to talk to him."

"He's on vacation," the counter man said.

"Till when?"

"Until he comes back. Look, we did nothing wrong here. Paul answered the phone and told her what to do."

"That's a lie, Peter, and we both know it. When I figure out why you're lying I'll be back. That is, unless you want to save yourself some trouble and tell me the whole story now."

Nguyen looked at him without answering. Bosch tried another tack.

"And if I have to drag your father into it, I will."

"My father is dead. When he died, this business was shit. My brother and I, we built this."

He made a sweeping move with his arm as if to encompass all the display cases and the glittering jewelry they held. Just then another customer stepped in through the glass door and casually moved to the display cases on the right. He was wearing a wide-brimmed hat. He started bending down over the glass so he could see the jewelry pieces better.

Bosch glanced at him and then back at Nguyen.

"I have a customer," Nguyen said. "You must go now."

Bosch reached into his pocket for a card. It was an old business card from when he was still with the LAPD. He had scratched out the number for the Open-Unsolved Unit and written in his cell number. He had also scribbled the word "retired" in barely legible script on the card in case it fell into the wrong hands and was used against him.

He put it down on the counter in front of Nguyen.

"Think about it," he said "Have your brother call me before it gets too late."

Bosch walked back to his car. He had gathered no reliable information inside the jewelry store but felt he had rattled a cage and gathered something possibly more important. Suspicion. He felt he was getting closer to the crossing, the place where Lexi Parks had tripped a wire that resulted in her death.

He sat behind the wheel without turning the ignition and thought about next moves. He picked up his coffee cup but then remembered he had finished it. For the first time he realized how free he was to follow his instincts and cast his net in whatever direction he wanted. With the department he had certainly employed his instincts. But there was always a lieutenant and sometimes a captain to be briefed and an approval needed. There were rules of procedure and rules of evidence. There was a partner and a division of labor. There was a budget and there was the constant, never abating knowledge that every move he made, every word he typed would be reviewed and possibly turned against him.

Bosch didn't carry those burdens now and for the first time he understood and felt the change. His inner voice told him that that watch with a brand name he could not even pronounce correctly was at the center of the mystery here. Nguyen had acted so shifty in the jewelry store—his own turf and comfort zone—that the watch lead could not be ignored. Bosch considered waiting until his customer left and going back into the store to press Nguyen further, or possibly sitting on the street and watching to see if the other brother showed up. But then he decided to use the freedom he had to follow his instincts without permission or approval.

He started the Cherokee and pulled away from the curb.

28

Long got back into the car and surveyed Sunset Boulevard.

"Where'd he go?" he asked.

From behind the wheel Ellis pointed east.

"Probably back home," he said. "What did Nguyen say?"

"Bosch asked about the watch and he asked about the phone call Parks made. Nguyen played dumb, said his brother dealt with it. But Bosch will definitely be back. This is getting serious, partner. He's getting close."

Ellis considered that. He still hadn't started the car.

"What else?" he asked.

"He says that's all," Long said. "He was scared of me. If there was more, he would've given it up."

Ellis was reaching to the ignition but let his hand drop.

"Where the fuck is his brother?"

"He says he doesn't know. Thinks Mexico."

"What did you hear when you got in there?"

"I just got the tail end. Bosch wasn't buying what he was selling, that's for sure. I'm thinking we need to close this thing down. Zip it up. This isn't like the motorcycle guy—a precautionary move. Bosch is zeroing in."

"We'd have to wait until the brothers are together. That Mexico story is bullshit."

"What I was thinking. You want to wait?"

Silence filled the car when Ellis didn't speak. Eventually Long pushed it.

"So, then when?"

"Check your phone. Where'd Bosch just go to?"

"You said probably back home."

"Yeah, well, make sure."

Long opened the app on his phone. It took him a few moments to locate Bosch.

"Actually, he's going down La Cienega toward the ten."

"He could be going anywhere."

Ellis turned the key and started the car.

"So, what do we do about him?" Long asked. "We take him out, we end the problem."

Ellis shook his head.

"Not that easy," he said. "He has friends. And if Haller loses his second investigator on this, there'll be questions. We don't want that kind of heat."

Ellis checked his mirror and was about to pull away from the curb.

"It's going to come to a point," Long said, "where we don't have a choice."

"Maybe," Ellis said. "But we're not there yet."

He saw a familiar figure cross Sunset in the mirror.

"Good things come to those who wait," he said. "There's the brother."

"Where?" Long asked.

"Behind us. Coming up to the shop. I knew it was a lie."

Ellis turned off the ignition. Both brothers together changed things.

29

Bosch took La Cienega south from Sunset toward I-10. Along the way he stopped to gas up the Cherokee and soon after was fighting his way east on the freeway toward the glass-and-stone towers of downtown. He didn't break free until he cleared the city's center and got out to I-15, where he started heading north on a clear shot to Las Vegas. He had decided to follow the watch trail directly rather than by phone. Badge or no badge, he knew that the best way to get information was to ask for it in person. It's easy to hang up a phone, much harder to close a door in someone's face.

Besides that, he needed to think and to grind things down. He knew that the wide-open spaces of the desert between Los Angeles and Las Vegas would help him open his mind to the nuances and possibilities of the investigation. This was why he always preferred driving over flying to the gambling mecca in the Nevada desert.

Halfway across, he decided to call Haller. He had not seen or heard from him since their walk among the tombstones. The call went to message and Bosch reported that he was on his way to Vegas and had time to talk.

Twenty minutes later Haller called back, saying he had just gotten out of a hearing on an unrelated case.

"Vegas?" he said. "What's in Vegas?"

"Not sure," Bosch said. "Sort of following a flier. If it amounts to anything, you'll be the first I let know."

"Couldn't you just call over there? That's a four-hour drive."

"You can always just call—if you know who to call. But sometimes your gut tells you to drive."

"Very Zen, Harry."

"No, more like Homicide one-oh-one."

Bosch was passing through Primm at the Nevada border. He'd be at his destination in an hour.

"So what's happening with the video from the cemetery?" he asked.

"Got a pro working on it today," Haller said. "Anything I get, you get."

"Okay."

"Your little do-si-do at the murder house has landed. The sheriffs complained to the DA, and the DA complained to the judge on this thing. I gotta go see him in chambers today to explain my actions."

"Shit. Sorry about that. You want me there? I'll turn around."

"I don't want you anywhere near there. In fact, I'm glad you'll be in Vegas. There's my excuse. I'll be able to handle it. I know the judge. Former defense lawyer, so he'll be sympathetic to my plight. I'll tell him I just can't get good help these days."

Bosch smiled. He was sure Haller was smiling, too.

"Yeah, tell him I didn't know what I was doing, that I'm new at this."

"Definitely."

They went off case then and talked about their daughters and graduation. Haller proposed giving the girls a joint gift, a cruise up the west coast of Canada to Alaska, where they could dogsled on glaciers while getting to know each other better before rooming together at Chapman in the fall. Bosch felt blindsided because he had not even been thinking about a graduation gift. He hadn't realized there should be one.

He ultimately agreed to the cruise idea and Haller said he would handle it. He had a travel agent he worked with. They signed off then and Bosch went back to thoughts about the case and prepping for his destination.

It had been a long time since Bosch had come to Vegas on a case and he found that once again the city had redefined itself with new casinos, traffic patterns, and shopping meccas. The Audemars Piguet shop and service center was located in a new shopping center on the strip. It was part of a massive glass complex of casinos and hotels and commercial and residential structures that dwarfed everything around it. The whole thing had been built since the last time Bosch had been in the city. He circled the project twice—a journey of fifteen minutes because of traffic—before finding an entrance to a parking garage. Soon afterward he was walking through a mall lined with the most upscale collection of shops he had ever seen in one location, including Rodeo Drive in Beverly Hills.

The Audemars Piguet shop was all dark-wood-and-glass cases where watches were displayed on individual pedestals. There was a security man, complete with Secret Service–style earbud, posted at the entrance. He wore a suit nicer than anything Bosch had ever owned. A woman who looked like she was dressed for the opera sat behind a reception desk and welcomed Bosch with a sincere smile. She knew better than to judge Bosch by his blue jeans and corduroy sport jacket. Vegas gamblers often chose to hide wealth behind a rumpled facade. Bosch had the facade, at least. He felt lucky that the cuff of his jacket was just long enough to hide that he wore a Timex on his right wrist.

"Is there a different entrance for the service center?" Bosch asked.

"No, this is our showroom as well as our service center," the woman said cheerfully. "Are you here to pick up a watch?"

"Not exactly. I'm wondering, is there a service manager I could speak to? I need to ask about a watch that came here for repairs earlier this year."

The woman's eyebrows rose at forty-five-degree angles as she frowned.

"Let me get Mr. Gerard for you," she said.

She stood up and disappeared through a doorway behind her station. Bosch spent the waiting time looking at the various displays, all the while feeling the eyes of the security guy on the back of his neck.

"Sir?"

Bosch turned and saw a man standing by one of the counters. He wore a suit and tie and had a full beard— maybe to make up for the loss of hair on top—and glasses with a pull-down magnifier over the left lens.

"Can I help you?" he asked.

"Yes," Bosch said. "I want to make an inquiry about a watch I believe was sent to you for repair earlier this year."

"I'm not sure I understand. Are you the owner?"

He spoke with an accent Bosch could not readily identify. Something European. Maybe Swiss, maybe German.

"No, I'm not the owner. I'm an investigator from Los Angeles and I am trying to locate the watch and find out the details surrounding it."

"This is very unusual. Are you the police?"

"I just retired from the Los Angeles police. I have been asked to look into this matter. It involves a murder."

The last word seemed to crowd the man's face with suspicion.

"A murder."

"Yes. I was a homicide detective. If you are concerned about talking with me, I can provide you with names and numbers of people in the LAPD who can verify and vouch for me."

"Can you show me your identification?"

"Of course."

Bosch pulled his wallet and removed his LAPD ID. There was no need to try to cover up the retired demarcation this time.

"What watch are you speaking about?" the man asked as he handed back the ID card.

"You're Mr. Gerard?" Bosch asked.

"Yes, Bertrand Gerard. I am the manager of sales and service here. Who was murdered?"

"A woman named Alexandra Parks. Back in February. Did you hear about that over here?"

The man shook his head like he was not sure what he had heard. It did not appear to Bosch that Parks's name was known to him.

"It's a pretty big case back in L.A.," Bosch said. "But she may have used her husband's last name in her dealings regarding the watch. That name is Harrick."

Now Bosch got a reaction. Not an alert of any kind, but a recognition for sure.

"You know her?" Bosch asked.

"Yes, I know this name," Gerard answered. "But I didn't know what happened. Her phone number was disconnected and the original owner didn't want the watch back. So...we still have it here."

Bosch paused. Gerard had just revealed something Bosch didn't already know or understand. He wanted to keep the man talking but didn't want to make a misstep that could spoil cooperation.

"The original owner," he said tentatively. "Why didn't she want the watch back?"

"Technically, it was not a she," Gerard said. "The buyer was a man, though he did purchase it for his wife. Who asked you to look into this matter?"

There was the misstep. Bosch looked around. He had to change things.

"Mr. Gerard, do you have an office or somewhere we can talk privately?"

Now Gerard paused, probably deciding how much further he wanted to be involved in this.

"Yes, follow me, please," he finally said.

Gerard nodded to the security man, a signal that all was well, as he brought Bosch through the door behind the displays.

Gerard had a small private office located off a larger back room where a workbench stood with various small tools on a rack. Against the back wall Bosch saw a floor-to-ceiling safe where inventory was probably housed. There was no one in the back room. That and the magnifier attached to his glasses made it clear that Gerard ran the shop and was also the technician who made the repairs and adjustments to the watches.

Gerard took a seat behind a perfectly clean desk and flipped open an At-A-Glance calendar book. He paged back through it until he saw a name or notation, then opened a drawer and removed a corresponding file with a watch attached to it in a padded pouch. He unclipped the pouch, removed the watch, and put it carefully down on his desk, then opened the file.

"The watch was sent to us for repair by Alexandra

Harrick," he said. "She sent it from West Hollywood, California, but you already know that."

"Yes," Bosch said.

With Gerard talking, Bosch said as little as possible, not wanting to mention anything that would put the brakes on his revealing information.

"Our website provides precise details on how one should proceed to have a watch serviced or repaired."

"What was wrong with the watch?" Bosch asked, immediately regretting that he had said anything.

Gerard picked up the watch and used a finger to circle its face.

"The crystal was fractured," he said. "No explanation given. But it was a simple repair. The only issue was the replacement crystal. I had to order it from Switzerland and that took about ten days."

Gerard looked up from the watch to Bosch, waiting for the next question. Bosch had blown the momentum of the conversation and had to try to get it back.

"When was the watch sent here?" he asked.

Gerard consulted notes written on the file.

"Received on February second," he said. "Sent by FedEx."

Bosch noted the date—one week before the murder of Alexandra Parks.

"That was when it was received—we document that," Gerard said. "But I didn't actually open the box and examine its contents until three days later—on the fifth."

"What happened then?" Bosch asked.

"Well, all of our pieces are registered upon purchase," Gerard said. "In the case of a resale, they can be reregistered by the new purchaser, after which they can enjoy the benefits of customer service. What happened here was that this watch was not registered in the name Harrick. It still carried the original owner's registration."

"It was bought used as a gift," Bosch said. "An estate sale."

"The problem was that I happened to know about this specific watch," Gerard said. "Because I had sold it originally."

He said nothing else and Bosch was unsure what to ask next. The story of the watch, whatever it was, obviously had puzzled or bothered Gerard in some way that was unsaid. Bosch needed to get it said.

"You sold it originally and had not heard about it being resold?"

"Exactly."

"Who did you sell it to originally?"

"I can't tell you that. We have a privacy policy and we can't reveal client names. People who buy these watches expect and get a high level of confidentiality."

"All right, so what did you do?"

"The original purchaser had bought two watches from me in the past three years. He was a collector of fine timepieces and bought for himself and his wife. And as far as I knew, he still had them both, but then this watch came in from someone else. So I took the initiative to call his home to verify that the repurchase was legitimate."

Gerard was now following a pattern of letting the story stall and needing to be prompted. In Bosch's experience it was a sign of reluctance. It happened often when people—completely innocent or uninvolved people—were questioned about things related to a murder.

"What did he tell you?"

"I didn't talk to him at first. His wife answered the phone. I asked for the husband but he was not home."

"So you talked to her."

"I didn't feel I should raise an alarm with her if it wasn't necessary. I identified myself and said I was just calling as a follow-up to see if they remained happy with their timepieces and if there was anything I could do. We offer a free service and cleaning to our clients. They pay only for shipping and insurance."

"That was a smart way to handle it. What did she say?"

"She told me that both of the watches purchased through me had been stolen."

"Stolen."

"Yes, there was a burglary. She was in Paris and never traveled with her watch for fear of robbery. It was at home, and her husband had stayed home because he had to work. There was a break-in one day at the house while he was out and all of their jewelry was taken."

"Did she say when this was?"

"Just a few months before. I didn't get an exact date."

"Do they live here in Las Vegas?"

Gerard hesitated but then decided he could reveal his client's place of residence without violating company policy.

"They live in Beverly Hills," he said.

"Okay," Bosch said. "Did you tell the wife that you had her stolen watch in your shop?"

Gerard hesitated again and Bosch thought he saw where the man's discomfort might be centered.

"Not exactly," he said. "I wanted to talk to the husband, you see. Technically he was the client. I asked her to have him call me. And I told her that I may have located one of the watches."

"That's how you said it?" Bosch said.

"Yes. I did not say I had it in hand."

"And did the husband call you?"

"Yes, that same afternoon. He told me a completely different story. He said the watches were not stolen. That was what he had told his wife because he had actually sold the watches and the jewelry without her knowing. He was nervous and embarrassed, but he admitted that he'd had a cash-flow problem and had sold the watches to cover some gambling losses that he didn't want his wife to know about."

"So he made up the story about the burglary."

"Exactly."

"Was he known to you as a gambler?"

"I didn't know him outside of this store, but he lives in Beverly Hills and we are in Las Vegas. He paid cash for his purchases. I always assumed that he came here to do more than buy watches."

"What does he do for a living?"

"He's a doctor but I don't know what kind."

Bosch thought about this. If the story was true, his pursuit of this loose end to the Parks case was tied up now and seemingly unrelated to her murder. It was just an odd side story that he had wasted time on. He wondered if he looked disappointed.

"Did he say where he sold the watches or to whom?"

"No, I didn't ask. The conversation was short. He just wanted to make sure that I knew the information his wife had given me wasn't accurate. He asked if I had called the police and I said no, that I had wanted to talk to him first."

Bosch nodded and studied Gerard. The man still looked uncomfortable, as though telling the story had not exorcised whatever it was that was bothering him.

"Is there more, Mr. Gerard?" he asked.

"More?"

"More to the story. Did you leave something out?"

"Well, no, that's all he said."

"Had you called the police?"

"No, of course not. I didn't lie about that."

"What about Mrs. Harrick? Did you ever talk to her about any of this?"

Gerard averted his eyes, looking down at his hands on the desk, and Bosch knew he was zeroing in on something.

"You talked to her," he said.

Gerard said nothing.

"Did you tell her you thought her watch had been purchased stolen?" Bosch asked.

Gerard nodded without looking up.

"She happened to call between the time I talked to the original purchaser's wife and when he—the doctor—called me back. Mrs. Harrick called because she wanted to know if the watch had been repaired yet. I told her that it had been received and that I had ordered the replacement crystal. I then asked her where it was purchased. She told me the name of a jewelry store in Los Angeles and said it had been part of an estate sale."

"Nelson Grant and Sons?"

"I don't recall the name."

"So, what did you tell her?"

"I was honest. I told her the repair would be easy once the crystal arrived but that I was not sure I could work on the piece because there was a question about its ownership."

"What was her reaction?"

"Well, she was a bit shocked. She said it was a legitimate purchase, that her husband had bought the watch and that he was a policeman. She said she would never buy stolen property, that she could lose her job and her reputation, and she got very upset with me for implying such a thing. I tried to calm her down. I apologized and told her that I was waiting for additional information and to please call me back in a day or two when I would know more."

Gerard finally looked up at Bosch, his eyes filled with regret over the phone call.

"And then the doctor called you," Bosch said.

"Yes, the doctor called and told me his story and said he had sold the watch in question."

Gerard shook his head at the memory of the mess he had created.

"Did you call Mrs. Harrick back and tell her?" Bosch asked.

"Yes, I called her and, of course, she was very angry, but there was nothing I could do. Some people can't be mollified. Being in retail, I know this."

Bosch nodded. This seemed like a dead end to him. He pointed at the watch on the desk and asked his last question.

"Why do you still have the watch?"

Gerard picked it up and looked at it. When he did so, Bosch saw a scribble on a yellow Post-it note attached to the file. He could clearly read a name, though it was upside down. Dr. Schubert. There was also a phone number with a 310 area code, which Bosch knew encompassed Beverly Hills.

"She did not provide a method of payment for the repair," Gerard said. "After the crystal came in and I installed it, I tried to contact her on the number she provided with the shipment but the number was disconnected. So I kept the watch here and waited for her to call. Then, quite frankly, I forgot about it. I had other work and I forgot. Now you tell me that she is dead, murdered."

Bosch nodded. Parks had provided her cell with the packaging of the watch for shipment. By the time Gerard had called it, Harrick had already canceled the number following his wife's death.

"This is very bad," Gerard said.

"Yes, very bad," Bosch said.

Gerard nodded and then spoke timidly as he placed the watch down on the desk.

"Is this watch the reason for her murder?"

He asked as though dreading the answer.

"I don't think so," Bosch said.

Gerard picked up the watch again and started to return it to its padded pouch. Bosch noticed something on the back of the watch.

"May I see the watch for a minute?"

Gerard handed it to him. Harry turned it over and looked at an inscription.

Vince and Lexi
Forever and a Day

Bosch wrapped the watch back up and put it down on the desk.

"I have one last question," he said. "Then I'll get out of your hair."

"Yes, please," Gerard said.

"Why do you think she sent it to you like that—in the padded pouch? How come she didn't send it in its box?"

Gerard shrugged. "Was there a box?" he asked.

Bosch nodded.

"Yes, in her closet. With the receipt from where her husband bought it. It was right there but she didn't send it to you in the box."

Gerard shrugged again.

"The box is bulky," he offered. "Perhaps it was easier to wrap it and send it in a FedEx box instead. I remember that was how we received it. But it's not unusual for our customers to ship items this way."

There could have been multiple reasons, Bosch knew. The question had no answer since the only person who really knew it was dead.

"What about the price?" he asked. "The husband got it for six thousand dollars used. Was that a good deal?"

Gerard frowned.

"Our pieces are collected around the world," he said. "They hold value and some models even go up. Yes, that was a good deal. A very good deal. A deal to quickly initiate a sale."

Bosch nodded.

"Thank you, Mr. Gerard."

30

Kamasi Washington's tenor sax was coming from the stereo, the sun-scoured desert was hurtling by on either side of the freeway, and Bosch was grinding the case down as he made his way back to L.A.

He loved these solitary moments of concentration and case thought. He always broke his thoughts into three distinct channels of logic: the things he knew, the things he could assume, and the things he wanted to know. The last channel was always the widest.

The trip to Las Vegas to run down the missing watch appeared on surface to be a bust. The watch was accounted for and the explanation of events from Bertrand Gerard was plausible. But Bosch wasn't quite ready to drop the watch from his investigation. The call Parks made to Nelson Grant & Sons still chafed simply because Peter Nguyen had been evasive and uncooperative with Bosch. Harry decided that he would take another run at Nguyen—and his brother, if possible—and he would also talk to Dr. Schubert to measure his version of the story against Gerard's. It was a basic elimination strategy. It was covering all the bases.

As he cleared the Las Vegas strip and got onto the open road, Bosch's thoughts came back to the victim. Alexandra Parks was a public official. Among her duties was running West Hollywood's consumer protection unit. It would have been highly embarrassing and even job threatening should it turn out that she wore a stolen watch. Bosch wondered what she did in the hours between when Gerard planted the suggestion that she had been doing just that, and the second call when he told her it was a false alarm. He knew she called Nelson Grant & Sons. But who else did she call? Her husband, the Sheriff's deputy, the man who gave her the watch?

Bosch planned to take a second look at the phone records in the murder book when he got back to Los Angeles. Before he dismissed the watch from having any significance to the case, he still had work to do.

As he was cruising through Primm, the last stop for gambling before the California border, Bosch got a call. It was marked *Unknown Caller* on his screen but he took it because this most likely meant it was a cop.

"Harry, say it ain't so."

"Who is this?"

"Tim Marcia. The word around here today is that you've crossed over."

Marcia had been in the Open-Unsolved Unit with Bosch. He was still fighting the good fight and if anyone deserved an explanation from Bosch it was him.

"Only temporarily," Bosch said. "And it's a Sheriff's case, not LAPD."

"Well, I'm not sure that's going to make a lot of difference around here," Marcia said. "But that's all right with me. Especially the temporary part."

"Thanks, Tim. So who's putting out the word?"

"What I heard was that the Sheriff's Department was checking you out. Somebody over there put in a call to the captain and then he was more than happy to spread the word that you were working for the other side."

"No surprise there. Look, like I said, this is temporary. And for the record, I think the Sheriff's may have blown this case and gotten the wrong guy."

"I hear ya. Just keep your head down, brother."

"Yeah, will do."

Bosch disconnected and went back to grinding the case but was soon interrupted by another call from an unknown caller. He took this one and didn't recognize the male voice.

"This is Kim."

"Okay. What's up, Kim?"

Bosch couldn't think of who he knew named Kim.

"I have phone number of dead guy's friend," Kim said.

Bosch realized he was talking to the manager of Haven House.

"That's good," he said. "But I'm on a freeway and can't write. Can I call you back as soon as I can?"

"You buy number," Kim said. "Fifty dollar."

Bosch remembered the bounty he had offered Kim for connecting him to any friends or associates of James Allen.

"Okay, I owe you fifty," Bosch said.

"You pay me now first," said Kim.

"Okay, okay. I'm out of town right now. As soon as I get back I will come see you, okay?"

"You pay me. I give you number."

"That's a deal."

Another hour went by and he soon realized he had fueled himself on nothing but coffee and adrenaline through the day and had to stop to eat. He took the Route 66 exit into Victorville and ordered a hamburger at a roadside diner.

The hamburger came between two slices of sourdough toast. It hit the spot and he was soon heading back to the 15. At a truck stop by the freeway entrance, he was gassing up the Cherokee when his phone buzzed and the ID once again said *Unknown Caller.* He took the call and did not recognize the voice that cursed him.

"You asshole, Bosch. You ever come up against me on a case and I'll kick your ass."

"Who is this?"

"It's your fucking conscience. You know you're betraying a lot of people around here. You—"

"Fuck off."

Bosch disconnected. He knew not every one of his former brothers and sisters in blue were going to be as understanding as Tim Marcia and Lucia Soto. He finished gassing up and walked around the Cherokee to eye check the tires, a long-held habit. He then got back out on the road.

Five minutes after he merged onto the freeway, his phone buzzed with yet another call from an unknown caller. Bosch decided he didn't need the aggravation and distraction. He didn't take the call and was surprised when the message alert sounded. Leaving a recording of a threatening nature was not smart. Curious about who would make such a bad move, he played the message.

"Harry Bosch, this is Dick Sutton with the Sheriff's Department. I need you to call me as soon as you get this message. We have a situation here and it's urgent."

Sutton left his cell number and before ending the message once again urged Bosch to call back quickly.

Bosch did not immediately return the call. He thought about things first. He knew Dick Sutton. Bosch had worked with him on a few interagency task forces, and though they never got closer than that, Bosch had formed a good opinion of the man. Sutton was a plain-spoken Oklahoman who didn't play games. He was a senior investigator in the Sheriff's Homicide Unit and Bosch wondered if he was now somehow involved in the Lexi Parks case.

Harry listened to the message one more time to memorize the number, then made the call back. Sutton answered immediately.

"It's Harry Bosch."

"Good, Harry, where are you?"

"The fifteen freeway coming back from Vegas."

"You were in Vegas today?"

"That's right. What's up?"

"Harry, we need you to come in and talk to us. How far out are you?"

"Depending on traffic, two hours max. What do I need to talk to you about, Dick?"

"There was a double-homicide today in West Hollywood. Two guys who run a jewelry store in Sunset Plaza. A place called Nelson Grant and Sons. You know it?"

"You know I do, Dick. You found my business card, right?"

"Uh, yeah, that's right. When were you in there?"

"This morning, when one of them unlocked the door and opened up."

There was a long pause before Sutton responded.

"Well, Harry," he said. "You got lucky."

"Tell me about it."

"I will when you get here. Come straightaway, okay?"

"No problem. But let me ask you something, Dick. Am I a suspect?"

"Harry, come on, you and I, we go way back. You're not a suspect. We need your help. We don't have anything going on this and can use all the help we can get."

"You at the scene?"

"I am now but I'll be leaving soon for the West Hollywood substation to start talking to people."

Bosch knew this meant that others had been brought in to be interviewed.

"You know where it is, right?" Sutton asked.

"On San Vicente," Bosch said.

"That's the one."

"I'll see you there."

After disconnecting, Bosch thought about what Sutton had said about him not being a suspect. It was counter to the other thing he said about not having anything going on the investigation. The rule was that when you were drawing blanks on a case, then everybody was a suspect.

Bosch liked and respected Sutton but he had to recognize the situation he was in. He was on the other side of the aisle now, the so-called dark side, and Sutton would certainly view him differently than he did when they were fellow homicide investigators working out of different law enforcement agencies.

Bosch decided to call Mickey Haller to tell him what was going on. There was no answer, so he left a message.

"It's Bosch. At seven o'clock tonight I'm going to need you to meet me in front of the Sheriff's West Hollywood substation. I'm going in to see a homicide investigator named Dick Sutton and I think I might need a lawyer."

Bosch almost disconnected at that point but then added one more thing.

"And Haller, be careful. I don't know what's going on but…just watch your back."

31

Haller was waiting for Bosch on the front steps of the Sheriff's substation on San Vicente Boulevard by the Pacific Design Center. Before going in, Bosch filled him in on what he knew and what he guessed was about to go down. Haller said he would protect Bosch from making any misstep but that he also wanted Bosch to think about what best served their client before he answered every question.

"Remember, you don't carry a badge anymore," Haller said as he opened the front door of the substation.

Dick Sutton was waiting for Bosch in the detective bureau. As a well-known defense attorney and former candidate for district attorney, Haller was immediately recognized by Sutton.

"Oh, come on, we're old friends here," he said. "A defense attorney, Harry? Really? There's no need for extreme measures."

"I don't think that protecting oneself legally is an extreme measure," Haller said.

"Sorry, Dick," Bosch said. "But I've got a kid and no wife and I need to make sure I get home tonight."

He didn't bother to mention that his kid was out in Big Bear for the next three nights.

"Well, I've got a double homicide and I think you

might be the only man who can help me make sense of it," Sutton responded. "Let's go into the meeting room and put our cards on the table."

He escorted Bosch and Haller into a large meeting room with a wide oval table big enough to seat the board of directors of a midsize company. It was a smooth move on Sutton's part, not putting Bosch into a regular interrogation room. That would have iced things over. Instead, he was trying to make Bosch feel like he was part of the investigation, not the subject of it.

Waiting and already seated were Cornell and Schmidt, whom Bosch had just met that morning, and another man he didn't recognize but assumed was Sutton's partner.

"I understand you already know Detectives Cornell and Schmidt," Sutton said. "And this is Gil Contreras, who puts up with me."

Sutton pointed to the visitors and introduced Bosch and his lawyer. A mild grumbling about the lawyer followed, and Haller attempted to quell it by holding his hands up as if in surrender.

"I'm just here to protect my client and facilitate an exchange of information I hope will be beneficial to us all," he said.

Haller and Bosch pulled out chairs next to each other and sat down. Sutton moved around the table and sat next to his partner and directly across the table from Bosch.

"Isn't that some kind of a conflict of interest?" Schmidt said.

Haller calmly clasped his hands together on the table and leaned forward so he could see past Bosch and down the table to Schmidt.

"How so, Detective?" he asked.

"He's your investigator on the Parks case and now you say he's your client," she said.

"I don't see it," Haller said. "But if you want to postpone this meeting until we can find a lawyer for Mr. Bosch that passes your conflict test, then we can do that. Not a problem."

"We don't want to do that," Sutton interjected quickly. "Let's just have a talk among friends here."

He threw Schmidt a look that said, *Stand down.*

"Then, where do we start?" Haller said.

Sutton nodded, appearing to be happy to get by the potential roadblock Schmidt had blundered into. He opened a file that was on the table in front of him. Bosch could see several notes written on a piece of paper clipped to the left side. On the right side was a plastic sleeve used to protect documents that had evidentiary value in an investigation.

"Let's start with this," Sutton said.

He picked up the sleeve and slid it across the table to a spot where both Bosch and Haller could see it. It contained what Bosch assumed was the same business card he had given Peter Nguyen that morning in the jewelry store.

"Is that your card, Harry?" Sutton asked.

"Looks like it," Bosch said.

Haller put his hand on Bosch's arm, a warning about answering questions before he had legally vetted them. Bosch had called Haller but that was for the larger picture. He was not going to engage in games with Sutton for the sake of games. Harry had been across the table from that kind of guy before and it was the last person he wanted to be.

"Can you tell us who you gave it to?" Sutton asked.

"We're going to step outside," Haller said quickly. "It'll just be a quick minute."

"These are basic questions," Sutton said, protest in his voice.

"Just a quick conference," Haller said.

He got up and Bosch reluctantly followed, embarrassed that he was acting the way he had seen so many suspects act with their attorneys over his years as a detective.

They stepped into the hallway and Haller pulled the door closed. Bosch spoke first.

"Look, I need to tell them what I know," he said. "This may actually help Foster. I didn't call you out so you could object to every—"

"It's not Foster that I'm worried about," Haller said. "If you think they're not looking at you for this, then you are not as smart as I thought you were, Bosch."

"They have nothing. When you have nothing, everybody's a suspect. I get that. They'll see pretty quick that I'm not the guy."

Bosch made a move toward the door.

"Then, why am I here?" Haller asked.

Bosch paused with his hand on the doorknob. He looked back at Haller.

"Don't worry, I'm going to need you," he said. "But not until we get this basic stuff out of the way."

"Let me try one thing when we go back in," Haller said. "Just a quick thing. Let me talk first."

"What?"

"You'll see."

Bosch frowned but opened the door and they went back to their seats.

"Detectives, let's make this a fair playing field," Haller said. "Let's make it a fair trade of information."

"We're not trading information on a double homicide," Sutton said. "We ask questions, Harry answers them. That's how it goes."

"How about we ask a question for every question you ask?" Haller insisted. "For example, what are Cornell and Schmidt doing here? Is this double homicide you're investigating related to the Parks case?"

Sutton looked annoyed and Bosch knew why. The one lawyer in the room was trying to hijack the interview.

"We don't know what this case is related to," he said impatiently. "Harry's card was found at the crime scene and it so happened that I heard these two talking about Bosch earlier today. So I called them out. Does that answer your question? Can I ask mine now?"

"Please," Haller said. "It's a two-way street."

Sutton turned his attention to Bosch.

"Harry, this card was found in the coat pocket of one of two men shot to death late this morning in the rear room of the Nelson Grant and Sons jewelry store. Can you tell me about it?"

"I'm assuming it was in the pocket of Peter Nguyen," Bosch said. "I gave it to him this morning when I was in the store."

"Exactly what time was that?"

"I was there as soon as he unlocked the door at ten. I was gone by ten-fifteen tops. Who was the other victim?"

Sutton hesitated before answering but not for too long.

"His brother, Paul."

"I don't think he was there when I was but he might have been expected. Peter kept checking the door to the back room like he was waiting for somebody to come through. When did this go down?"

"We're not sure yet. They were found by a customer about noon. They were on the floor in the back room. The coroner will narrow it down later."

"No video?"

Cornell raised his hands in frustration.

"He's asking all of the questions," he said. "Just ask him what the fuck he was doing in there."

Sutton held Cornell with his eyes, silently communicating the rebuke for the interruption and the language. Sutton's glare reminded Cornell and Schmidt that they were observers. This was Sutton and his partner's case.

"No, no video," Sutton said. "Whoever killed them took the disc out of the recorder. It's an old system with no backup to the cloud. The shopkeeper next door thought she saw two men go in that back door off the rear parking lot about ten forty-five. They were wearing white overalls. She thought they were window washers. She didn't hear any shots."

"Two men…"

"Yes, two men. We're looking for cameras in the area but so far no luck with that. So what were you doing in there, Harry?"

Bosch felt a sense of dread crowd into his chest. He couldn't help but feel responsible for the killing of the Nguyen brothers. All of his instincts told him he had led the killers there, or at the very least created the need for the Nguyen brothers to be killed.

"What was taken?" he asked.

"Harry, your lawyer said this is a two-way street," Sutton said. "You're giving me nothing and you're asking all the questions."

"Just answer one last question. Was it a robbery or an execution?"

Sutton shook his head. He had let the interview get away from him. Bosch had seized control.

"It was certainly either a robbery or made to look like a robbery," he said. "One of the display cases was cleaned out."

"Only one?" Bosch asked. "Which one?"

"The case on the right when you walk in the front door."

"That was the estate stuff, right?"

Sutton shook his head.

"That's it, Harry. No more. You answer questions now. Why did you go in there this morning?"

Haller leaned in close to Bosch and whispered.

"Let me remind you that you are working for me and the protection of confidentiality that my client enjoys extends from me to you," he said. "So you be careful here."

Bosch looked at Sutton.

"I have a confidentiality issue here," he said. "I am working as a defense investigator and I can't talk to you about things pertaining to that case without my client or his attorney's approval."

"And you're not going to get that," Haller added.

Bosch backed him off with his hand and continued.

"Suffice it to say I don't know who killed the Nguyen brothers," he said. "If I did, I would tell you, client or no client."

"What were you doing there?" Sutton asked.

Bosch looked directly at Cornell while he answered.

"I was asking about a watch they sold about six months ago to the husband of an Alexandra Parks. As you know, she was murdered. Her watch was unaccounted for in the investigative file. I don't like loose ends like that and was trying to tie it up."

"Was Peter Nguyen helpful?"

"No, he was not."

"Was that where the watch was bought?"

"I believe so."

"And what makes you believe that?"

Haller answered before Bosch could.

"He's not going to answer that," Haller said. "I think we need to cut this off here, Detectives."

Cornell muttered something under his breath again and Haller jumped on it.

"What's that? You have a problem with Harry Bosch doing your job for you?"

"Fuck you, lawyer," Cornell said. "This is all just smoke and mirrors—trying to muddy the waters your client is drowning in. He's still going down."

"You keep thinking that," Haller said. "And we might go out and solve this thing for you. I mean really solve it, not pin it on somebody."

"I'm truly frightened of that."

Haller shook off the sarcasm with a killer smile aimed at Cornell and then slowly turned toward Sutton.

"What do you say, Detective? Anything else?"

"Not for now," Sutton said.

"Then we won't trouble you any further."

Haller got up and Bosch followed. They didn't speak until they were standing on the sidewalk outside the building. Bosch was upset. He felt as though he had betrayed someone—maybe himself.

"Look, I don't like doing it this way," he said. "I should be telling them everything I know."

"Really?" Haller said. "What exactly do you know? The truth is, you don't know anything. *We* don't know anything. Not yet."

"I know that I probably led those two killers to the two brothers in that store."

"Really? How? You're saying that the two brothers weren't involved in this and they got whacked because you talked to them?"

"No, I…Look, less than an hour after I was in that store, they get hit. You're saying that's a coincidence?"

"What I'm saying is we don't know enough to go around telling the cops anything, not when we have a client in county who is looking at the rest of his life in prison."

Haller pointed in the direction of downtown even though it was miles from where they stood.

"That is where our allegiance lies," he said. "Not to those assholes in that room."

"I used to be one of those assholes," Bosch said.

"Look, all I'm saying is we're still pulling in the nets, Harry. Let's finish pulling them in and then see what we got. Then we decide what we tell and who we tell it to and, most important of all, where we tell it. We've got a trial in five weeks and we need to know the whole story by then."

Bosch broke away from him and walked out to the curb. He realized he had made a terrible mistake crossing to the other side of the aisle. Haller came up behind him and spoke to his back.

"Anything we tell them now, we give them the opportunity to turn it against us and our client. *Our* client, Harry. You have to remember that."

Bosch shook his head and looked off down the street.

"What did those two brothers know?" Haller asked. "Why were they killed?"

Bosch turned and looked at Haller.

"I don't know yet. But I will."

"All right, then. What's next?"

"I picked up a name in Vegas. A guy in Beverly Hills who may know the secret behind this watch. Behind everything. He's next."

"All right. Keep me informed."

"Yeah, will do. And listen, if they followed me to the jewelry store, they might also be following you."

"I haven't seen any sign of that."

"That's the point. You wouldn't. You have anyone who can check your car? I'm going to check mine."

"I'll get it done."

"Good. Like I said before, be careful. Watch your back."

"You, too."

32

Bosch drove directly home from the substation and came in from the carport to an empty house. He called out his daughter's name and got no answer. Fear stabbed at him until he remembered that she was on the camping trip. His mind had been so cramped with thoughts about the jewelry store murders that he had forgotten. Relieved, he texted her to see if she had made it to the mountain without problem. Her response was succinct as usual.

Made it. Bus ride was bouncy.

Bosch changed clothes, getting into an old set of coveralls he used to wear at crime scenes. He grabbed a flashlight out of a kitchen cabinet and went out into the carport. Before turning on the light he studied the street in front of his house and the driveways of his neighbors. He was looking for any vehicle that was occupied or seemingly didn't fit in. He was sure he was being watched in some way—the killing of the Nguyen brothers told him this. But he needed to determine to what extent. Was there physical and electronic surveillance? Was there any window of opportunity for him to make a move without being watched?

He saw no vehicles in the street that drew his suspicion. He next studied the utility poles and trees for a reflection of light that might come off a camera lens. He saw nothing and, emboldened, stepped down the short inclined driveway to the street to further extend the sweep of his visual search. He covered what he was doing by going to the mailbox and retrieving the day's delivery.

Bosch saw no indication of surveillance in either direction on the street. He walked back up the driveway and into the carport, flipping a light switch and tossing the mail onto the workbench. He walked to the front of the Cherokee and then crouched down in front of its grill. He flicked on the flashlight and began a search of the front end, looking in all places where a GPS transmitter could be attached.

Soon he was under the car, the engine compartment close to his face and still hot. He felt as though he was getting slow-roasted from above but pursued the search, even after a searing drop of engine oil streaked down his cheek and he cursed out loud.

He found the GPS tag in the front left wheel well behind one of the suspension struts, where it would not be in danger of getting hit and knocked off by any road debris kicked up by the tire. It was in a plastic case held to the internal cowling with two heavy-duty magnets. The case snapped open to reveal the transmitter and the power source consisting of two AA batteries. The device would send an uninterrupted signal to a cellular receiver, allowing its holder to track the movement of the Cherokee in real time on a laptop map. The fact that the device was battery operated and not hardwired to an electrical line in the car indicated to Bosch that this was most likely considered a short-term surveillance by those watching his moves.

Bosch snapped off the flashlight and lay unmoving

under the Cherokee for a few minutes as he thought about whether to remove the tracker — and thereby reveal to his followers that he had found it — or leave it in place and fold it into his investigative strategy moving forward.

He decided to leave the tracker in place for now. He climbed out from beneath his car, turned off the light, and stepped out to the end of the carport. He looked around once more and saw no one.

Bosch went back into the house and locked the door behind him. He changed back into his regular clothes and then made a call to Lucia Soto. She answered right away.

"Harry."

"Hey, how's it going?"

"All right. I was going to call you. The secret's out and everybody knows you're doing defense work."

"Yeah, I've been getting the calls."

"Well, it wasn't me, if that's why you're calling. I didn't tell a soul."

"No, I know it wasn't you."

"So then what's up?"

"Uh, my daughter's not around and she usually helps me with the phone stuff. You mentioned Uber last night. How do I go about getting that?"

"That's easy. First put your phone on speaker so you can hear me while I walk you through it."

"How do I do that?"

"Are you kidding me?"

"Yeah. You're on speaker."

Soto talked him through the setup. The operation took less than ten minutes.

"Okay, you're ready to rock," Soto said.

"Cool," Bosch said. "So I can just order a car now?"

"That's right."

"Great."

"It's late. Where are you going?"

"I don't know. Just for a ride. I want to check out a place."

"What place?"

Bosch worked the screen and successfully ordered a car.

"Just some guy's place. Says the car will be here in six minutes. The driver's name is Marko and he's driving a black Tesla."

"Well done."

"It's asking my destination."

"You can put it in or leave it blank. They'll still come. That way they don't program an address and you can tell them what way to go."

Bosch left it blank because he wasn't sure of his destination yet.

"Thanks, Lucia."

"I'm gonna go now."

"Oh, wait. One question. Is this like a cab? Can you make the driver wait, like if you have to go into a store or a house or something?"

"Yeah, you just tell them what you want and it goes on your credit card. I think there's like a charge for every fifteen minutes of waiting time."

"Okay, cool. Thanks, and good night."

"Good night."

Bosch waited out in front of his house so that he could get a read on whether his Uber driver was followed up the hill. Marko was now supposed to arrive in three minutes, according to the app.

While he waited, Bosch went on his phone's search engine and plugged in "Schubert MD, Beverly Hills." He got a hit for a plastic surgeon named George Schubert with offices at something called the Center for Cosmetic Creation on Third Street near the Cedars-Sinai Medical Center. The address was actually in West Hollywood. Nothing else came up, and there was no listing for a residential address.

Bosch clicked over and made a call back to Lucia Soto, hoping she hadn't gone to sleep or out to Eastside Luv again.

"Now what, Harry? You want to know about the phone dating app?"

"No. You mean there is one?"

"There's an app for everything. What's up? I have to get to bed. Last night I stayed at it way too long."

"You dance on the bar at Eastside Luv?"

"Matter of fact I did. But I kept my clothes on. What's up?"

Bosch could see headlights coming around the bend. His ride was arriving.

"You got your laptop home with you?"

"What do you need?"

"I was wondering if you could use your tracker software to run a name for me. A doctor in Beverly Hills."

When they had been partners, Soto was the one who was computer adept and had subscribed to a number of Internet services and software that helped track addresses through financial, property, and utility records. These methods were often quicker and more reliable than established law enforcement data banks. What Bosch was asking her to do broke no rules because she was using her own laptop and software.

"No problem."

Bosch gave her Schubert's name and she said she would call him back as soon as she had something. He thanked her and disconnected. A car had now cleared the bend and was approaching with its high beams on. Bosch felt lit up and vulnerable in the darkness.

The near-silent Tesla came to a stop in front of him. Bosch checked the clock on his phone. Marko was right on time. Being new to Uber, Bosch didn't know if he was supposed to get in the front or the back but opted for opening the front door.

"Marko?"

"Yes, sir."

A deep eastern European accent.

"Where do I sit?"

"Right in front is very good."

Bosch got in.

"Which way?" Marko asked. "You did not put in destination."

"I thought that was an option," Bosch said. "I want you to go up the hill. When we get to the top at Mulholland we'll turn around and come back down."

"That's it?"

"No, then we're going to go down into Beverly Hills, I think."

"Do you have address? I plug it in."

"Not yet. But I'll get it before we get there."

"Whatever you say."

The car took off up the hill. There was no engine sound. It reminded Bosch of amusement park bumper cars.

"It's quiet," he said. "You could sneak up on people."

"Yes, I drive Tesla," Marko said. "The people out here like the electric car. The Hollywood people. I get the repeat business, you see. Besides this, I am Serb. From Smiljan."

Bosch nodded like he understood the connection between Hollywood and Smiljan.

"Tesla," Marko explained. "A great man who came from my hometown."

"The car? It's his company?"

"No, he worked with Edison to make electricity. Long time ago. The car, it is name for him."

"Right. I forgot."

Bosch noted that based on his singular experience, Uber drivers seemed to talk way more than taxi drivers. The ride was as much a social outing as it was getting from point A to point B. When they got up to the stop sign at Mulholland, Bosch told Marko to turn the car around and go back down Woodrow Wilson past his house.

Bosch saw nothing suspicious on the ride back through his neighborhood. No out-of-place cars, no pedestrians who didn't belong, no glowing cigarettes in the dark recesses between houses. He felt confident that the GPS tracker on his car was the key to the surveillance. He could work with that—drive the Cherokee when he needed to go to insignificant locations, just to show movement, then use Uber or rent a car for when he needed to go places he didn't want the followers to know about. Just to be sure, Bosch turned and looked back through the rear window to see if a car was trailing in their wake.

He saw nothing.

Soto called him back just as they got to the bottom of the hill and had turned south on Cahuenga toward Hollywood. She had come up with a residential address for Schubert on Elevado in the flats of Beverly Hills.

"It comes up the same on three different search-wares, so I think it's legit and current," she said.

"Excellent," Bosch said. "Thank you."

"Glad to help, Harry. Anything else?"

"Uh, actually one other thing. Did you ever get the names on that Vice Unit I gave you the call sign for? The guys that might've been working James Allen off book as an informant?"

"Yeah, I thought I sent that to you," Soto said.

"You mean an e-mail? I haven't checked. I'll do it as soon—"

"Just hold on. I have it right here."

Bosch waited and listened as he heard her flip through the pages of a notebook. In the short period they had been partners, she had adopted Bosch's habit of carrying a small notebook with her at all times.

"Okay," she finally said. "That was six-Victor-fifty-five and that belongs to Don Ellis and Kevin Long. Do you know them?"

Bosch thought for a moment. The names meant nothing to him. It had been more than ten years since he worked out of Hollywood Division. The personnel there were probably 95 percent different now.

"No, I don't know them," he said.

"How are you going to check that?" she asked. "If they were working an informant off book, they're not going to just tell you about it."

"I don't know yet."

He thanked her again and told her to get some sleep. He disconnected and then told Marko to work his way down to Sunset and head west toward Beverly Hills.

"You sure?" Marko said. "Sunset Strip will be very slow this time of the night. I think Santa Monica better."

"Santa Monica is better but I want to take Sunset," Bosch said. "There's something I want to see."

"Okay, you be the boss."

Marko drove as instructed and was dead-on about the traffic on Sunset. Late-evening cruisers slowed movement to a crawl on the Strip. Bosch saw black-clad crowds lining up outside the clubs, tourist vans on nighttime celebrity patrols, minimum-wage hustlers waving flashlights toward overpriced parking lots,

Sheriff's patrol cars flashing blues to keep people moving along. He gazed out past the neon reflected on the windshield of the Tesla but was deep in reflective thought, the colors not penetrating his dark eyes.

He was thinking about Vin Scully, the Los Angeles Dodgers broadcaster. He had been calling games for more than sixty years—more than ten thousand games in all. There was no voice that was as iconic or as synonymous with Los Angeles as his. He had called so many games and yet never lost his love of the game or the city of his team. And he was always and repeatedly tickled when the vagaries of coincidence produced a running line of twos on the scoreboard. *The deuces are wild,* he would announce before a pitch. Two balls, two strikes, two out, two on, and two to two in the bottom of the second.

Bosch could hear Scully's voice in his head as he considered that the deuces were now wild in his own game. Two murders possibly connected and followed by two brothers killed in the back room of a jewelry store. Two possible killers at the jewelry store. Two car doors heard in the alley where James Allen's body was left propped against a wall. Two watches said to be stolen and then not. Two vice cops who pull over Mickey Haller on a DUI and two vice cops who may have worked James Allen as an informant. Coincidence? Bosch had a feeling Vin Scully wouldn't think so, and he didn't either.

The deuces were wild all right and Bosch was on the case. He called Haller and woke him up.

"What's wrong?" the lawyer said.

"Nothing," Bosch said. "Got a question. Your DUI. You said you were pulled over by a couple of plainclothes guys."

"That's right. They were lying in wait for me. What's the question?"

"Were they vice cops?"

"Could have been."

"What were their names?"

"I don't know. They passed me off to the backup team. A couple of patrol cops."

"Aren't their names on the arrest report?"

"Maybe but I haven't gotten it yet."

"Shit."

"Why are you calling me up at this hour, asking about those bastards?"

"Not sure. When I know more I'll call you back."

"Make sure it's tomorrow. I'm going back to sleep."

Bosch disconnected and bounced the phone a couple times off his chin as he thought about what he could do to answer the question he had just posed to Haller. He knew he could go back to Lucia Soto but he also knew that a records search for an arrest report would leave digital fingerprints. He couldn't put her in that kind of danger. He had to find another way of getting there.

When they drove by Nelson Grant & Sons in Sunset Plaza the media trucks were gathered along the curb in front of the jewelry store. Bosch saw television reporters and videographers claiming spots and setting up for live reports at eleven. Looking past them Bosch could see mobile lights set up in the store's showroom. The crime scene was still being processed twelve hours after the murders. Two Sheriff's deputies were stationed outside the door for security.

"Something bad happen there," Marko said.

"Yeah," Bosch said. "Something really bad."

Once into Beverly Hills they made a left on Camden and dropped down into the flats, a square mile or so of residences between Sunset and Santa Monica Boulevard that comprised one of the wealthiest neighborhoods in all of California. It was a cool, crisp night with wind rippling through the fronds of the palm trees that lined the streets. The Tesla took one more turn and then came to a silent stop against the curb on El-evado. The house where George Schubert lived was a mansion of Spanish design that sprawled across two lots and stood tall behind a wide and deep lawn displayed beneath lights attached to the palm trees. The lawn's edges were cut razor sharp and it seemingly was un-touched by the ravages of the California drought. In Beverly Hills the lawns always somehow managed to stay green even in times of water restriction.

Bosch made no move to get out. He just studied the home through the car's window. Finally, Marko spoke.

"You get out here?" Marko asked.

"No, I'm just looking," Bosch said.

"What you look for?"

"Nothing. Nobody. Just looking."

Several lights were on behind the windows of the house and as he lowered his window Bosch thought he could hear music coming from within. He made no move to get out of the car. Music and lights aside, he saw no movement behind the windows. He checked his watch—it was 11 o'clock—and knew it was too late to brace Schubert at his door.

"So, are you pie?" Marko asked.

Bosch turned his eyes from the house to look at him.

"Excuse me?" he asked.

"You know, pie," Marko said. "You watch people and investigate?"

Bosch understood.

"You mean a PI. Private investigator. Yeah, I'm a PI."

"PI. Very cool, yes?"

Bosch shrugged and turned back to look at the house. He thought that the lighting configuration had changed. Bosch was sure a light had been turned out behind one of the windows but he couldn't remember which one had been lit.

"So," Marko said. "We stay?"

Bosch didn't look back at him this time. He kept his eyes on the house.

"You still get paid for sitting here, right?" he asked.

"Yes, I make pay," Marko said.

"Okay, then let's sit here for a little while, see what happens."

"Is it dangerous, this work? If so, I should get extra pay."

"No, it's not dangerous. We're just sitting here watching a house."

"How much you get paid to watch house?"

"As a matter of fact, nothing."

"This then is not very good job for you."

"No kidding."

Bosch grasped the door's handle but still hesitated. Not because it was late, but because he hated the idea of knocking on a door and not knowing what exactly to ask—especially with a new witness. Sometimes you only got one shot at a witness, and being unprepared could cripple you. He went back to his first decision to wait.

"Okay, Marko, we can go," he said.

"Where to now?" Marko asked.

"The airport."

"You have no suitcase."

"I just need to pick up a car."

"No car. I, Marko, will drive you."

"Not where I have to go."

33

Bosch pulled to the curb on Wilcox south of Hollywood Station. It was quiet on the street. The neon glow from the bail bonds office across from the station entrance cast a red tint on the night. Bosch watched the gate to the parking lot that hugged the south side of the two-story station. He was sitting in a black Chrysler 300 he had rented at Hertz. It was the closest approximation to a plain-wrap detective car he could get on such short notice.

He was counting on the lateness of the hour working in his favor. They would be shorthanded on the midnight shift in the watch office. He doubted anybody would be watching the lot monitors. Getting by the gate was the first and easiest step to his plan.

Almost ten minutes went by before he saw the glow of headlights coming up on the other side of the five-foot metal gate. A car was coming out. Bosch dropped the 300 into drive and waited until he saw the gate start to roll open on its track. He then pulled away from the curb, put on his turn signal, and headed toward the opening.

He timed it perfectly. A black-and-white was moving out through the gate with speed just as Bosch came cruising up. The gate was still on its opening circuit, just crossing the entrance lane. Bosch barely touched the brake pedal as he turned in, putting his hand out the window in the traditional smooth-waves signal to the officers in the emerging car. The Chrysler hit the gate's metal track a little hard and loud but Bosch was in. He checked the rearview and saw no brake lights on the patrol car as it turned north on Wilcox.

Bosch drove into the lot and down the parking lane that would give him a view of the back door to the station. He found an open spot and pulled in. He checked the door and immediately saw that he had an opportunity. There was a patrol car parked in one of the two booking stalls next to the door, and two officers were unloading two custodies. The station's rear entrance had an electronic lock requiring a key card. It would be the last hurdle.

Bosch gathered himself for a moment and got out. He had worked in the Hollywood Division for several years as both a patrol officer and, later, as a detective. He knew the layout of the place like he knew his own house, and he had a good sense of the ebb and flow of personnel in the station. Inside it would be a skeleton staff on duty, concentrated primarily in the watch office, front desk, report room, and the jail.

All of these locations were in the front of the station at the end of a hallway entered through the rear door of the station. There was a second hallway that ran along the back of the building and led to the detective unit, the station commander's suite of offices, and the stairs leading up to the Vice Unit offices, the roll-call room, and the break room.

Bosch knew that all of these areas would likely be deserted unless the Vice Unit was working a late-night operation or patrol officers were in the break room or detective room, writing reports. Those were the risks he would have to take.

Bosch walked slowly through the lot until he saw the two officers heading toward the back door with their handcuffed charges. He then picked up speed to catch up. He knew that if he acted like he belonged, then chances were good that he would be taken as such. The department had more than a thousand detectives and they rotated in and out of squads all over the city all the time. There was no way anyone could know everyone. He was counting on that. Playing a detective would be the easiest role of his life.

He got to the back door just as one of the patrol officers used his key card to unlock it. As the officer started to pull the door open, Bosch moved around behind him.

"I got it," he said.

He grabbed the door by the steel handle and pulled it all the way open. He then stood back to allow the officers to walk in the two disheveled men in handcuffs.

"Welcome, gentlemen," he said, sweeping his hand toward the opening. "Please enter."

"Thank you, sir," one of the patrol cops said.

"Fuck you, sir," one of the disheveled men said.

Bosch took that as another test passed. The foursome entered the station and started down the hallway toward the booking room and jail. Bosch entered right behind them and then immediately split off to the right to the rear hallway. It was empty and he quickly moved down to the end and glanced into the detective squad room. It was deserted and only two of the four room-length rows of overhead lights were on, casting the vast room in a dim glow.

Bosch backed away and then went to the stairs. He stood at the first step and leaned forward, straining to hear any noise from the second level. If there were people in vice or the roll-call or break rooms, he would be able to hear the murmur of conversation, but he heard nothing. He then turned to the entrance to the suite of command staff offices. These included private offices for two captains and then an open area containing three desks for secretaries and adjutants. This was Bosch's destination. On a corkboard that covered one wall of this area was the division's personnel pyramid, complete with photos and names of every officer assigned to the station, from captain to rookie. The photo display was often referred to by the division's personnel as the "lineup board" because it was often used to identify officers when citizens came to the front desk of the station to complain about an officer's conduct but didn't have the officer's name. The complainant was taken to the board and asked to find the offending officer.

The bottom two rows of the pyramid were dedicated to the various patrol shifts. Above these rungs were the members of the detective squads and the Special Services Unit, which Bosch knew was the designation for specialized groups, including vice. He looked at these photos and immediately came upon the face shots of Don Ellis and Kevin Long. Both were white, both had the practiced dead-eyed stare of veteran street warriors—cops who have seen it all three times over. Ellis was the older of the two and something about the way he stared coldly at the camera told Bosch he was the alpha of this street team.

The photos were pinned to the board. Personnel shifted too often to make a permanent installation of anyone on the pyramid. Bosch unpinned the photos of Ellis and Long and took them over to the color copier next to the desk of the station commander's secretary. He put them side by side on the glass and made two copies, blowing them up larger than the original face shots. When he reached down to the tray for them and saw the enlarged photos, he was struck with a familiarity about Ellis. He straightened up and looked at the photocopy for a moment and tried to place where he had seen or known him before. The vice cop looked like he was in his early forties and probably had twenty years in with the department. It could easily be the case that he and Bosch had crossed paths somewhere. A crime scene, a police station, a retirement party. There were myriad possibilities.

Suddenly Bosch heard approaching voices in the back hallway. He reached for the knob on the commander's office door but it was locked. He then quickly moved to the wall of file cabinets that separated one secretary's desk from another. He crouched down but knew that if the voices were coming this way, he would be found. He waited and listened and realized the discussion was about how to word the probable-cause statement on a search warrant. It had to be two detectives heading to the squad room at the end of the rear hallway.

Bosch folded the photocopies and put them in the inside pocket of his sport coat. He waited and heard the voices go by the opening to the command suite. As soon as he judged it was clear, he stood up and headed out of the suite into the back hallway, maintaining his pose of familiarity and belonging.

There was no one in the hallway. He had a clear shot to the exit. He moved quickly but not like a man trying to escape. He turned the last corner and pushed through the heavy steel door and out into the night. The drive-up/drop-off alley was clear but out in the lot were two patrol officers closing shop—that is, finishing their shift and taking the shotgun and personal equipment out of their car. They were too busy with the process of going off shift to pay any attention to Bosch as he crossed the lot to his rental car.

The parking lot gate automatically opened for cars approaching from the inside. Bosch didn't breathe easy until the Chrysler rolled through the gate and out onto Wilcox. He turned north toward Sunset Boulevard. When he caught the light at Sunset, he pulled out his phone and called Haller once again.

"Twice in one night, Bosch?" he protested. "Are you kidding me? It's after midnight."

"Put on your bathrobe," Bosch said. "I'm coming by."

He disconnected the call before Haller could protest further.

34

Haller was indeed wearing a white terry-cloth robe when he opened his front door. Bosch could see the words *Ritz Carlton* in gold over the breast pocket. Haller's hair was unkempt and he was wearing black-framed glasses. Bosch realized for the first time that he must wear contact lenses during normal waking hours.

"What is so important that it can't wait for the morning?" Haller asked. "I've got an eight-o'clock motions hearing tomorrow and I would like to get some sleep so I am fully functioning."

"Motions on Foster?" Bosch asked.

"No, another case. Unrelated. But it doesn't matter, I still need to—"

"Just take a look at these."

Bosch pulled the photocopies out of his pocket, unfolded the sheets, and handed one to Haller. He refolded the other and put it back in his pocket.

"Are those the guys?" he asked.

"What guys?" Haller asked.

"The cops who pulled you over on the deuce."

Bosch said it in a tone that implied that he was frustrated by Haller's inability to follow Bosch's own logic.

"Why do you care who pulled me over that night?" Haller said. "It's not your con—"

"Just look at the pictures," Bosch commanded. "Are those the guys?"

Haller held the photocopy at arm's length. Bosch guessed that his glasses carried an old prescription.

"Well, one guy stayed in the car and I didn't really see him," Haller said. "The other...this one on the right... this guy could've been...yes, it's him. This is the one that came up to the car."

Haller flipped the page over so Bosch could see his choice. It was Ellis, the one Bosch thought had looked familiar.

"So, what's going on, Harry?" Haller asked. "Why are we standing here in the middle of the night with this?"

"Those guys pulled you over," Bosch said. "They also arrested James Allen several times, and I think they were using him as an informant."

Haller nodded but showed no excitement.

"Okay," he said. "They're Hollywood vice cops. It's not surprising that they would have popped Allen a few times or that they used him as an informant. And as far as my thing goes, they picked off the radio broadcast because they were in the area. That area being Hollywood, where they work."

It sounded like a different tune from Haller. Outside the jail after he was bailed out, he was spinning tales of conspiracy and lying-in-wait to the media. Now he was giving reasons for why the conspiracy Bosch was beginning to see was perfectly explainable.

"I've got a witness who heard two car doors close in the alley the night Allen's body was dumped there," Bosch said. "And you heard Dick Sutton a few hours ago. They think it might have been two guys who went in there and killed the Nguyen brothers. The deuces are wild on this, Mick. I think we're looking for two people."

They were still standing in the entryway of Haller's house. Mickey looked down at the photocopy.

"You drink bourbon?" he asked.

"On occasion," Bosch said.

"Let's sit down and work this through some Woodford Reserve."

He stepped back and let Bosch enter the living room.

"Have a seat," Haller said. "I'll get a couple of glasses. You take it with ice?"

"A couple cubes is all," Bosch said.

He took a seat on a couch that gave him a view through the picture window to the lights of the city. Haller's house sat on the shoulder of Laurel Canyon and offered unobstructed views of the city to the west and out toward Catalina.

Haller was back soon with two glasses with amber liquid and easy on the ice. He put them down on the coffee table along with the photocopy but didn't sit down.

"I gotta go put in my contacts," he said. "These things give me a headache."

He disappeared down a hallway toward the back of the house. Bosch took a sip of the Woodford and felt it burn on the way down. It was good stuff, a better bottle of bourbon than he ever kept on hand at his house for unscheduled visitors.

He took another sip and then studied the photos of the two vice cops. He wondered if they had put the GPS locator on his Cherokee. Thinking about the Cherokee in regard to the two men brought a focus, and Bosch suddenly realized where he had seen Don Ellis. It was in the parking lot behind Musso's. Bosch had passed him when he had left the bar the night Haller would get pulled over on the DUI. It meant Haller was right. The DUI was a setup. Ellis and Long had been lying in wait for him.

When Haller came back, the glasses and the bathrobe were gone. He was in blue jeans and a maroon Chapman T-shirt. He took the chair across the table from Bosch with no view of the city. He took a healthy pull from his glass of fine bourbon and followed it with his best impression of Jack Nicholson drinking whiskey and flapping an arm like a chicken wing in *Easy Rider*. He then settled back in his chair and looked at Bosch.

"So," he said. "What do we do?"

"A couple things first," Bosch said. "Tomorrow morning, after your driver drops you at court? Have your driver or somebody you trust get your car checked for a GPS tag. There's one on my car and I think these two guys put it there."

He pointed toward the photocopy on the coffee table.

"It was already on my to-do list," Haller said.

"Well, get it done," Bosch said. "And if something's found under there, don't remove it. Don't let them know we're onto them. We can possibly use this to our advantage. I rented a car tonight. I'll use that for when I don't want them to know where I'm going."

"Okay," Haller said. "First thing."

"I also want to talk to your investigator."

"Cisco? Why?"

Bosch reached down, grabbed his glass, and took a large gulp. It burned all his breathing passages and brought tears to his eyes.

"Easy, boy," Haller said. "This is sipping bourbon."

"Right," Bosch said. "Look, you need to see the big picture here. Your man, Cisco, was working on this case and he gets sent into oncoming traffic and taken out. You're on the case and you get pulled over on a setup DUI. The Nguyen brothers get whacked for reasons we don't yet know—less than an hour after I talk to them. We can believe it's all coincidence or we can look at it in its entirety and see a bigger picture. I want to ask Cisco what he was working on the day somebody knocked him out of the game."

Haller nodded.

"He has physical therapy every morning at the Veterans in Westwood."

"Good," Bosch said. "I'll see him there."

"What else?"

Pointing to Ellis and Long, Bosch said, "One of us should talk to DQ and see if he's ever had any interaction with these two guys. Just to be sure."

"I can do it," Haller said. "I need to see him about some pre-trial stuff and get his measurements for a trial suit. Hope I got something that fits in my client closet."

He pointed to the photocopy on the table.

"Can I take that, show it to him?" he asked.

"I've got another," Bosch said.

Bosch remembered something.

"When you see him, ask him if he remembers James Allen's phone number. Cops never found Allen's phone. If I can get the number we might be able to pull records that will show the two of them in contact."

"And bolster the alibi. Good one. What about you?"

"I still think the watch is the key to all of this. I need to get to the original buyer."

"The guy in Beverly Hills?"

"Yeah. I went by his house tonight. Nice spread. He's got money. I need to corner him and see where the connections are."

"Good luck with that."

"Thanks."

They sat there for the next few minutes without talking. They sipped bourbon and worked their own thoughts. Finally, it was Haller who spoke.

"This is good stuff," he said.

Bosch looked at his glass and rolled the ice around the bottom of it.

"Better than I got at home," he said.

"Well, don't get me wrong, the bourbon is good, but I'm talking about everything you've pulled together these last few days. There's a lot here. A lot I can work with. We're going to be able to mount an actual alternate-theory defense. This stuff goes beyond reasonable doubt."

Bosch finished the remaining bourbon in his glass. He realized that he and Haller would always have a fundamental difference in how they looked at evidence and the other nuances of an investigation. Haller had to put things in the context of trial and how it might be used to knock down the prosecution's case. Bosch only had to look at the evidence as a bridge to the truth. This is why he knew he had not really crossed to the dark side. He could never work a case from Haller's angle.

"I don't really care about alternate theories or reasonable doubt," he said. "To me it's a simple equation. If your client didn't do it, then I'm going to find out who did. That's the person or persons I want."

Haller nodded and raised his glass to Bosch. He then finished off his drink.

"That works for me," he said.

35

The Vice Unit's weekly all-hands meeting was the usual waste of time. It finally ended and Ellis crossed the hall to the break room so he could refill his cup with black coffee. He was unused to coming in so early and he needed to double down on the caffeine.

But he had to wait his turn behind Janet, the captain's secretary, who looked like she was putting together an order of coffees for the whole command staff downstairs. Janet was a wide body and Ellis could not get to the coffee urn until she was finished adding cream and various sweeteners to the five cups in front of her. This annoyed Ellis because he just wanted to top off his cup with the straight black stuff and then get back over to the unit.

"Sorry," Janet said, sensing someone behind her.

"No problem," Ellis said. "Take your time."

Recognition of his voice made Janet glance back and confirm it was Ellis.

"Oh, Don, I wanted to ask you something."

"Fire away."

"Were you in the office this morning or last night?"

"What office?"

"I'm sorry. I mean downstairs. The command offices."

Ellis shook his head, confused.

"No, what do you mean?"

"Well, it's just funny. I came in today and I had to make copies of the overnight log for both captains. It's the first thing I do every day."

She turned back to finishing her work on the array of coffee cups on the counter in front of her.

"Okay."

"And when I went to the copier, I found your and Kevin's photos already in the machine. Like they had been left there by accident."

Ellis wanted to grab her and turn her around.

"I don't understand," he said. "Our photos? What were we doing in the photos?"

Janet laughed at his confusion.

"No, no, you weren't doing anything. It was your photo from the station personnel chart. The one on the wall down there. Somebody unpinned your photos, took them over to the copy machine, and then I guess made copies. Then forgot to put them back on the wall. They were under the flap on the glass this morning when I went to make copies of the overnight log."

She was weaving her fingers through the handles of five coffee mugs now. Ellis threw his cup into a trash can and moved in next to her at the counter.

"Let me help you," he said. "You'll burn yourself."

She laughed that possibility off.

"I do this every morning and every afternoon," she said. "I've never burned myself once."

"I'll help you anyway," Ellis said. "Did you ask in the office if anybody was making the copies? The captain, maybe?"

"Yes, and that's the mystery. Nobody did it. I asked everybody, including both captains. Somebody must have come in after hours to do it and then forgot to put the photos back up. I thought you might want to know. In case somebody's pulling a prank."

"Thanks, I do. And I think you're right about somebody working up a prank."

Janet laughed.

"Some people have too much time on their hands, that's for sure."

There was a long tradition of pranking in every station in the LAPD. Photos were often used in the commission of such efforts. Ellis was thinking that something else might be in play but was happy to allow Janet to think otherwise.

He followed her down the steps, across the back hallway, and into the command-office suite. He put the two cups of coffee he was carrying down on her desk for her to deliver, then scanned the room and looked at the personnel pyramid on the opposite wall. His photo was in place next to Long's on the line containing the undercover units. All was how it should be.

"Thank you, Don," Janet said.

"Glad to," he said. "Thanks for the heads-up on the prank."

"I wonder what they're up to."

"Like you said, some people have too much time on their hands."

Ellis and Long shared a cubicle in the corner of the Vice Unit. It afforded them the most privacy available in the room and they got it because of Ellis's seniority. Ellis now came back to the cubicle and signaled his partner to roll his chair over so they could huddle and speak privately.

"What's up?" Long asked.

"Not sure," Ellis said. "You checked on our guy today?"

"He was still at home. I get a text if he goes anywhere."

"What about last night?"

"He stayed in."

"According to your phone?"

"Well, yeah."

"Well, maybe just his car stayed in. I want you to go up there, confirm that he's there."

"What, now?"

"Yes, now. I'll cover for you here. Go."

"What happened? What's going on?"

"What's going on is that your phone says his car didn't move, but last night somebody was in the station making copies of our photos off the wall in the captain's office."

"What the fuck?"

Ellis checked the rest of the squad room to make sure Long's outburst had not drawn unwanted attention. He then looked back at Long.

"Exactly," he said. "I think Bosch is up to something and I want to know what. It starts with you going up there and trying to figure out if he's even there. Not just his fucking car."

"Okay, okay. I'm going. But maybe we have to rethink things and figure out a way to remove the threat, you know?"

"Yeah, and look where doing that has gotten us. It's like fucking dominoes. One thing we do leads to the next thing. Where does it stop?"

"I'm just saying."

"Yeah, I'm just saying go up the hill and find out if Bosch is there or if he's fucking with us."

36

Long drove by the house twice. The Cherokee was in the carport but there wasn't any other sign that anyone was home. The Volkswagen was gone and he guessed that the girl had school. He drove down the hill and around the next bend in the road. He had seen an opening where a house had been cleared off a cantilevered pad to make way for a rebuild. It would give him a good look at the rear windows and deck of Bosch's house.

He parked in front of someone's garage and got out of the car with the binoculars. He hurried across the street and ducked under the yellow DANGER/PELIGRO tape strung between two stakes at the front of the pad. He walked out and immediately realized how out in the open he was. He first posed with the binoculars as if he were looking toward Universal City or the mountains beyond. But then he turned slightly to his left and focused the binoculars on Bosch's house. He saw no activity behind any of the glass. The deck was empty and its sliding glass door closed.

He lowered the binoculars and acted once again as though he were just taking in the sights. He glanced once more at Bosch's house and saw no movement. He turned and started walking off the pad, wondering what move he should make next to confirm Bosch's absence.

When he got back to the yellow tape there was a man standing there waiting for him.

"You're trespassing," he said.

"No, I'm not," Long said. "I have permission."

"Really? From whom? Give me a name."

"No, I don't need to do that."

Long ducked under the yellow tape and crossed the street toward his car.

"I have your license plate," the man said. "You're up to something."

Long turned and walked right back toward the man, pulling his badge, which was on a neck chain under his shirt.

"Mister, you are impeding a police investigation," he said. "Go back to your house and mind your own business or you'll find yourself in a cell."

The man stepped back, looking almost scared of Long now. Long turned to his car.

"It's called Neighborhood Watch," the man called after regaining his courage. "We watch out for one another up here."

"Whatever," Long said as he opened his car door.

Long drove away and at the first chance turned the car around and headed back up the hill. He passed the busybody still standing in the street in front of the cantilevered pad. Driving around the bend, he once more came to Bosch's house and stopped directly in front. He studied the house, thought about what to do, and grew frustrated.

"Fuck it," he said.

He honked the horn three times like he was there to pick someone up. He kept the car in drive and watched the front door. If Bosch or anyone else opened the door, he would take off. The windows on the car were smoked dark enough that he felt he would not be identified.

Nobody opened the door.

Long honked once more and waited and watched. Nobody answered.

"Fuck it," he said again.

Long pulled away, drove up to Mulholland, and then turned around. When he drove back down Woodrow Wilson and past Bosch's house, he honked impotently once more without stopping. He then called Ellis.

"He fucked us," he reported. "His car's here but he's not. He must know we LoJacked it."

"Are you heading back now?" Ellis asked calmly.

"On my way."

"Good. He doesn't know that we know. We may be able to use that."

"Exactly what I was thinking. What do you think he's up to?"

"Who knows?"

"How do we find him?"

Ellis didn't respond right away.

"We go where we think he'll show up, and wait."

"Yeah, where's that?"

"Just get back here and we'll figure it out."

Ellis disconnected without saying another word.

37

Bosch was familiar with the sprawling Veterans Hospital in Westwood from many years of visiting doctors and once rehabbing there from a gunshot wound. The complex was divided by Wilshire Boulevard and Bosch knew that the rehab centers were on the south side. He parked in a lot that told much about the clientele that the medical center served. Mostly old, taped-up cars, live-in vans, and pickups with camper shells, all of them pasted with bumper stickers proudly proclaiming their service to their country, their specific branch of the military, fighting unit, and politics. The message was clear. It didn't matter what war was fought, coming back home was another battle altogether.

He went in through a glass door printed with the motto SERVING THOSE WHO SERVED and checked the sign-in list at the front counter of the physical therapy center. There was a receptionist there but she didn't look up from her computer screen. Bosch saw that Dennis Wojciechowski, aka Cisco, had checked in forty minutes before. Bosch figured he would almost be through with his session. He took a seat in the waiting room where he could see the door and would be able to spot Cisco as he was leaving.

Bosch noted that the magazines spread across the

table in front of the couch were all several months old. Instead of picking one up, he opened his e-mail on his phone for the first time in several days. He saw the one from Lucia Soto providing the names of Ellis and Long. Most of the other e-mails were spam and he deleted them. There were two from former colleagues, containing messages of disappointment over the news that Bosch was now working in criminal defense. Bosch started typing out a return e-mail to the first one but halfway through realized he could never explain himself or win back the loyalty of the men and women still in the LAPD. He stopped writing and deleted the message.

The thought of his predicament was depressing. He decided he would not check his e-mail going forward because it was likely that he would be receiving more of the same kind of messages. He was putting his phone back into his pocket when it buzzed in his hand. He checked the screen before answering it and saw the name Francis Albert. He didn't recognize the name but took the call, getting up and walking out through the door to abide by the signs that said no cell phone calls in the waiting room.

"Harry Bosch."

He stepped into an alcove to the right.

"Detective Bosch, this is Francis Albert, your neighbor on Woodrow Wilson."

Bosch still couldn't place the name or come up with a face. And he didn't know if Francis Albert was the full name or a two-part first name, maybe in homage to Francis Albert Sinatra.

"Yes. How are you?"

"I'm fine. You might not remember me, but I hosted the Neighborhood Watch meeting a couple months ago that you were kind enough to attend."

Now Bosch had him. Old man, stooped shoulders, no family, and too much free time on his hands. Bosch, newly retired and with too much time on his own hands, had agreed to attend the meeting back in March. Francis Albert probably wanted him to come back and address the troops again.

"Of course I remember you," Bosch said. "But I'm kind of in the middle of something right now. Can I call you back later?"

"Sure, that's fine. But I just thought you'd want to know that somebody was watching your house this morning. He claimed he was a cop but I have my doubts."

Suddenly Bosch wasn't in such a hurry to end the call.

"What do you mean 'watching my house'?" he asked.

"Well, you know the Robinson's property across the street from me?" Francis Albert responded. "Where they knocked the house down but left the pad there to build on?"

"Right, I know it."

"I go out this morning to pick up the paper, and first thing I see is some schmuck's parked in front of my garage. And then I see the guy. He went under the tape and is out on the pad with a pair of binoculars. And he's looking right at your house, Detective Bosch."

"Call me Harry. I'm not a detective anymore. Are you sure he was looking at my house?"

"Definitely looked that way to me. And you call me Frank."

"How long did he stay there, Frank?"

"Till I hassled him and he took off. That's why I don't think he was a legit cop—even though he showed me a badge."

"You hassled him?"

"Yeah, I went out and asked him what he was doing. He got all nervous and left. That's when he showed me this cockamamie badge he had around his neck."

Bosch reached into his jacket and pulled out the remaining photocopy of the photos of Ellis and Long. He unfolded it and stared at the two vice cops.

"What did he look like?" he asked.

There was a long pause before Albert answered.

"I don't know, he was normal," he finally said.

"Normal?" Bosch asked. "Was he white, black, brown?"

"White."

"How old?"

"Uh, forties. I think. Maybe thirties."

Bosch looked at the two photos.

"Did he have a mustache?"

"Yeah, he had a mustache. You know him?"

Long had a mustache. Ellis didn't.

"I don't know. Are you going to be around later? I have a couple photos I'd like to show you."

"Sure, I'm here all the time."

"Thanks, Frank."

"Just watching out for the neighborhood. That's what we do."

Bosch disconnected and looked at the photos of the two vice cops. He didn't think he needed to go by Frank's to confirm what he knew in his gut. It had been Long with the binoculars. It seemed odd to Bosch that he was snooping around so soon. It was only nine-thirty. Why had he already gotten suspicious about the Cherokee not moving?

Bosch decided that there must be something else that had sent Long up the hill. He folded the photocopy and put it back into his jacket pocket. While he was doing it, he saw a man he believed was Wojciechowski walk-ing out through the front door of the rehab center.

The man had a noticeable limp and was walking with the aid of a cane—black with flames painted on it. He wore blue jeans, a black T-shirt, and a leather vest with the Harley-Davidson insignia on the back. The traditional wings of the logo were broken. Bosch knew this was to indicate the rider had gone down, gotten hurt, and had survived.

"Cisco?" Bosch called.

The man stopped and turned back to see who had called out. Bosch caught up to him.

"You're Cisco, right?"

"Maybe. Who are you?"

"Harry Bosch. Mickey Haller's—"

"Investigator. Yeah, you took my job."

"I was going to say brother. I didn't take your job. I don't want your job, and it will be there for you as soon as you're ready to go back. I'm just working this one case for him and that's it."

Cisco put both hands on the cane. Bosch could tell that standing and walking weren't his favorite pastimes at the moment. There were several benches lining the walkway, places for people to wait for those in rehab.

"Can we sit down for a minute?" Bosch asked.

He pointed to one of the benches. Cisco headed that way and seemed relieved to take his weight off his knee. He was a big man with massive arms and a power-ful V-shaped torso, an inverted pyramid unsteady on its points of support.

"So this isn't a coincidence?" he asked. "Mick told me you were in the Army, too."

"I was in the Army and I've been in this place before, but this isn't a coincidence," Bosch said. "I came looking for you. I need to ask you a few questions."

"About what?"

"Well, let's start with your accident. Mickey told—"

"It was no accident."

"Well, that's what I want to know. Tell me what happened."

"I don't get it. Why?"

"You heard that Mickey got popped for a DUI, right?"

"Yeah. Your old pals the LAPD."

"It was a setup. I think it was to hinder his efforts on the Foster case. I think the same thing might've happened with you. So what happened?"

Bosch could see a coldness set in Cisco's eyes.

"It was fucking April Fools' Day. I was on Ventura Boulevard in Studio City, heading down toward Hollywood. The guy in the lane next to me pushes over and I had no choice; let him knock me down and go under his wheels or take my chances in the oncoming lanes. I almost made it."

"What makes you think it was intentional?"

"I don't think it. I know it. Two things. Number one, the guy didn't stop. I mean, he didn't even slow down. And number two, he knew what he was doing. Hell, I reached out and kicked the side of his car and he still kept coming. Steel-toe boot, man. He heard it. He knew I was there."

"You saw the driver?"

Bosch started taking the photocopy back out of his coat pocket.

"No, I didn't see him," Cisco said. "The windows on the car were tinted too dark. Way beyond legal."

Bosch left the photocopy in his pocket.

He knew that a favored tactic of the UC units in the LAPD was to smoke the windows of their cars beyond legal limits.

"What kind of car was it?"

"A Camaro. Burnt orange with black rims and yellow calipers. I got a good look at the wheels, you could say. Real up close and personal."

"But I take it you didn't get the plate."

"Too busy trying to stay alive by that point. What's in your pocket anyway? What were you going to show me?"

Bosch pulled out the photocopy.

"These are the two guys who pulled over Haller. I thought maybe you'd recognize one of them—if you had seen the driver."

Cisco unfolded the page and looked at the two faces. They were just head shots, but in both, the top collars of police uniforms were evident.

"So you're saying two cops might be behind all of this?" he said.

Bosch nodded.

"It's beginning to look that way."

"Jesus Christ. Rogue cops. What'll they think of next?"

"I'm going to need you to keep all of this to yourself. Haller's okay, but nobody else. It might fuck things up if it leaks."

"You didn't have to say that."

"Right, sorry. So your accident, it occurred—"

"I told you, it was no accident."

"Right, sorry, wrong word. So this attack occurred right after Haller got the Foster case. Had you started working the case yet?"

"Not in a big way. We had the case and we were gearing up for it, but the discovery hadn't come in yet and so we were sort of waiting on the D.A. to cough up the murder book."

Bosch nodded.

"So you really hadn't begun."

"Not really. Just sort of grasping at straws until we got our hands on those records. That's where it all starts, you know?"

"Yeah, I get that. So 'grasping at straws'—what does that mean?"

"Well, you always get your client's side of the story and you can pursue that. Our guy said he had an alibi, so I looked into that and found we were a day late and a dollar short. The pro he said he was with got himself murdered."

"James Allen."

"That was the guy."

"How deep did you go into that?"

"Not that deep. The guy was dead and we couldn't talk to him, end of story. I had a couple calls into the LAPD guys on it but—big surprise—hadn't heard anything back."

"Do you think you did anything on the investigation that could have brought about the attack with the Camaro? Anything come to mind at all?"

Cisco thought for a moment and then shook his head.

"I really don't, or else I would have already jumped on it, you know?"

"Yeah."

Bosch realized that if there was a connection between Cisco being sent into oncoming traffic and Ellis and Long, then he was going to have to find it through other means.

"Sorry I'm not much help," Cisco said.

"You gave me a solid description of the car. That'll help."

"I wish I knew something, but I don't know what I did that would have brought them on. Mickey I get. But I had barely started on the case."

"Well, you did something or they thought you were about to do something. Maybe they just wanted to put Haller in the hole by knocking out his investigator. Maybe we'll never know."

"Maybe."

"Did you report the incident to the police?"

"Sure, but that was a waste of time."

"Why do you say that?"

"Come on, man, look at me. The cops take one look at me and say 'biker.' They think whoever ran me off the road was doing the public a solid. I called them and they didn't give a shit. The report went straight into the circular file. All it got me was my insurance payout, but the cops I never heard from again."

There was a time when Bosch might have defended the LAPD against those kind of accusations. But he wasn't in the fold anymore. He just nodded in an understanding way. The men exchanged cell numbers and then Bosch headed off, leaving Cisco on the bench. He said he was going to rest the knee a little longer before getting up and going to the parking lot.

38

It wasn't that Bosch had expected Cisco to identify one of his attackers as Ellis or Long, but he had hoped for further confirmation of his belief that the two vice cops were behind everything that had happened involving the case.

Still, he was undaunted and knew of other ways to close in on the proof. First stop on that path was the Hollywood Athletic Club. He went directly from Westwood and along the way called Haller, who picked up right away.

"Good morning," he said cheerily. "I was just about to call you."

"I was going to leave a message," Bosch said. "Last night you said you had court."

"I did, but I'm done."

"You sound happy. Let me guess, you got another case dismissed and another drug dealer goes free."

"I'm happy but not because of another case. I have news. But you go first. You called me."

"All right, well, I just came from talking to Cisco. He never got a look at whoever ran him off the road. But he did describe the car—right down to the yellow brake calipers. It was a burnt-orange Camaro with black rims. I was calling to see if it rings any bells with you."

There was a moment before Haller answered.

"No," he finally said. "Should it?"

"What about the car that pulled you over on the DUI?" Bosch asked.

"No, it wasn't a Camaro. It was a Dodge. A Challenger or a Charger. I didn't look all that closely but definitely not a Camaro."

"You sure?"

"Hey, I'm the Lincoln Lawyer. I know cars. Plus it wasn't burnt orange. It was jet-black. Like the souls of those two fuckers who were riding in it."

"Okay, well, that's all I had. Strike two. First Cisco, now you. Lift my spirits. What's your news?"

"Got our DNA back today."

"And Foster isn't a match."

"No, not quite. He's a match, all right."

"And that's what's making you so happy?"

"No, the condom trace evidence is what's doing that. You were right. They found it in the sample."

Bosch thought about that. It was a moment of vindication. The finding supported the case theory that semen from Da'Quan Foster could have been transported to the murder scene and planted in and on the body of Alexandra Parks.

"Next, they have to try to match it to a specific brand," Haller said. "Allen's brand. We get that, and they won't be able to wriggle out of this by claiming he had a condom all along and it just broke."

"Okay," Bosch said.

"You know, usually I feel like I'm shooting at the state's case with a damn BB gun. I'm beginning to think we got ourselves a shotgun on this one. Double-barrel. We are going to blow big holes in their case. Big fucking holes."

Haller sounded almost giddy about the DNA analysis. But for Bosch the upcoming trial was still too far distant. Long and Ellis were running around loose and five weeks was too long to wait to get something done.

"All you think about is the trial," Bosch snapped.

"Because that's my job," Haller said. "Our job. What's going on, Harry? I thought this would be good news for you. You're on the right track, man."

"What's going on is Ellis and Long are out there doing what they do. They're watching my house, they know about my kid. I can't prove it yet but I think they took out Cisco because somehow he threatened them, and now I'm threatening them. The trial is more than a month away and we have to be thinking about the right now. You get Foster off at trial and so what? The prosecution will spin it, call it smoke and mirrors, and not do anything about these two guys. What happens then?"

Haller took some time to compose his response.

"Harry, you spent all those years chasing killers and I know that's your natural instinct, to do it here," he said. "But I keep telling you, we are working this from a different angle. It's not what you're used to, but our responsibility above all is to the client. We can't do anything that may hurt the possibility of a successful defense at trial. Now, I know it's going to take some getting used to but—"

"Don't worry about it," Bosch interrupted. "I don't want to get used to it. After this, I'm done."

"Well, suit yourself. We'll talk about it down the line."

"What about us going into LAPD and showing what we got? I can make the case that they need to take these two off the street. At the very least, they'll put eyeballs on them."

"Not going to happen," Haller said emphatically. "We do that and we are giving the prosecution five

weeks to prepare for what they'll know we are bringing."

"Maybe there won't even be a trial. They bring these
two in, play them against each other, and one guy
coughs up the other — oldest trick in the book. End of
case."

"Too risky. I'm not going to do it. And you aren't either."

Bosch was silent. He had to consider Haller's motives. Was he really protecting his client's chances at a
not-guilty verdict or preserving his own shot at glory
at trial? A murder case provided the biggest stage in
the courthouse. If Haller won at trial, he'd be the hero
and prospective clients would start lining up. If the case
never made it to trial, somebody else would get the ap-
plause.

"You still there?" Haller asked.

"Yeah," Bosch said. "We're not done talking about
this."

"All right, all right. Tell you what, let's meet tomorrow morning. Breakfast at Du-Par's. How's eight
o'clock sound? You make your case to me. I'll listen."

"Which Du-Par's?"

"Farmer's Market."

"I'll be there."

"Where are you headed now?"

"Hollywood. To check something out."

Haller waited for more but Bosch wasn't giving. He
tried to shake off his upset and refocus.

"I'll let you know if it pans out," he finally said.

"Okay," Haller said. "See you tomorrow."

Bosch disconnected, pulled the earbud out, and
dropped the phone into one of the cup holders in the
center console. He regretted his outburst with Haller
but there was nothing to do about it now. He focused

on his driving as he took Fairfax up from Santa Monica to Sunset.

A few years earlier it was discovered that members of an Armenian street gang had rented an office suite in the twelve-story building located at Sunset and Wilcox. The office was on the seventh floor and at the back of the building, where its windows overlooked the LAPD Hollywood Station with a full view of its rear door and adjoining parking lots. By posting someone behind a telescope in the office twenty-four hours a day the gang was able to gather intelligence on the undercover Narcotics and Vice Units as well as the gang-suppression teams. They learned the times when the various units were on duty, when they were out on the streets, and the general direction they went after mounting up in the parking lot and heading through the gate.

At some point an informant revealed the existence of the spy post to a DEA handler and it was shut down in an FBI raid that thoroughly embarrassed the department. The FBI seized surveillance logbooks that had individual code names for various members of the Hollywood Station units, describing both their personal cars and their undercover vehicles. It was also discovered that the Armenian gang had been selling the fruits of their intelligence gathering to other gangs and criminal enterprises operating in Hollywood.

The department instituted several procedural changes designed to prevent such embarrassment from happening again. Among them was moving the undercover car pool from the station lot to an off-site lot where space was donated by a supportive local business—the Hollywood Athletic Club. As with most secrets within the department, the location of the undercover lot was not so secret. The spy post scandal had occurred after Bosch moved to the Open-Unsolved

Unit in the downtown PAB, but even he had heard where they had moved the UC car lot to.

The HAC was on Sunset and only a few blocks from the Hollywood Station. Its parking lot was behind it and was surrounded by buildings on three sides and a fence on the fourth that ran along Selma. There was no parking attendant on-site but a key card was required to enter through the gate.

Bosch didn't have a key card but he didn't need to enter the lot. He parked at the curb on Selma, got out, and walked to the fence. He knew it was a good time to inventory the UC cars, because almost all of them would be in the lot. It was only 10 a.m. and the vice, drug, and gang teams that used the cars kept the same hours as their prey. That is, they started operations in the afternoons and worked into the nights. The mornings were for sleeping late.

The pool cars used by the undercover teams were changed out or swapped with other divisions at least once a year to avoid familiarity on the street. Some were pulled out of circulation for a month here and there as well. Some were traded with other divisions so each would have fresh cars. It had been two months since Cisco Wojciechowski had been run into oncoming traffic and so there was a possibility that the burnt-orange Camaro that Bosch was looking for would be gone already. The fact that Ellis and Long were using a different UC car when they bagged Haller on the DUI seemed to indicate that the car had been changed over. On the other hand, Bosch thought, if they had committed a crime in the Camaro, they might trade it in right away for a different car. A jet-black Dodge, for example.

Either way Bosch had to make sure, and his diligence paid off. He spotted the familiar front lights of a

Camaro that was backed into a parking spot against the rear wall of the lot. It had a heavy layer of smog dust on its windshield and obviously had not been driven for quite a while. He had to move down the fence a few paces to get a side angle on it and confirm its color: burnt orange.

He used his phone to take a photo of the car. He then texted it to the number Cisco had given him earlier with a question: Is this the car?

Bosch walked back to his rental. Cisco answered as he was opening the door: I think so. Looks like it.

Bosch got into the car. He felt the spark ignite in his bloodstream. Seeing the Camaro confirmed only a small part of his theory and was proof of nothing, but the charge of adrenaline came nonetheless. He was putting pieces of the puzzle together, and there was always a charge when even the smallest pieces fit. The Camaro was important. If Ellis and Long were using it when they ran Cisco off the road, they may have been using it a few weeks earlier when James Allen's body was transported to the alley off of El Centro.

He got back in the Chrysler and worked his way down to Santa Monica and then over to the Hollywood Forever cemetery. He parked in front of the office, went in, and found Oscar Gascon behind the desk in his little office. He recognized Bosch from the prior visit.

"Detective, you're back," he said.

"I am," Bosch said. "How's business?"

"Still dead. You need to look at my cameras again?"

"That's right. But I've got a different date for you. When I was here before, you said the LAPD guys came by to look at tape for the night of that murder down at the Haven House."

"That's right."

"All right if I take a look at the same night?"

Gascon studied Bosch for a moment like he was trying to figure out his angle. Finally, he shrugged.

"Don't see why not."

It took Gascon five minutes to retrieve the video from the cloud of the night James Allen was murdered. He put it on fast play and Bosch watched the entrance of the motel property.

"What are we looking for?" Gascon asked.

Bosch answered without taking his eyes off the screen.

"A burnt-orange Camaro," he said.

They watched silently for the next ten minutes. Cars moved up and down Santa Monica with an unnatural speed. Bosch decided that if they got through the night without seeing the Camaro, he would ask to watch it again on a slower speed. Gascon might object to that but Bosch would push for it.

"There," Gascon suddenly said. "Was that a Camaro?"

"Slow it," Bosch said.

The playback went to normal speed and they watched wordlessly. The car they had seen enter the Haven House parking lot did not come back out. Bosch realized that there was no reason to think the car would reemerge quickly.

"Let's back it up and see that again," he said.

Gascon did as instructed. Then on his own he put the playback on slow motion. They waited and an orange car came into the screen from the left side and turned left toward the motel entrance.

"Freeze it," Bosch ordered.

Gascon froze the image as the car was crossing the westbound lanes of Santa Monica. It was directly sideways to the camera but the image was grainy and undefined. The general lines of the car appeared to match those of a Camaro. A two-door coupe design with a sleek, low profile roof.

"What do you think?" Gascon asked.

Bosch didn't answer. He was studying the dark band of windows on the car and the matching dark wheels. It was close but Bosch couldn't call it. He wondered if Haller's video-enhancement person could improve the image.

"Go ahead and play it," he said. "Speed it up."

He noted the time on the bottom of the screen. The orange car entered the motel lot at 11:09 p.m. Gascon went back to triple speed and they sat and watched silently for several minutes. Several cars went in and out. It was a busy night at the motel. Finally, the orange car appeared and disappeared. Gascon reversed the video and they watched again on slow speed. The car pulled out of the motel without stopping, turned right, and went west on Santa Monica and out of the frame.

"He's in a hurry now," Gascon said.

Bosch looked at the time counter. The orange car left at 11:32 p.m., just twenty-three minutes after entering. Bosch wondered if that was enough time for them to go into Allen's room and extricate him, alive or dead.

"When the LAPD guys were here, did they key on this car?" Bosch asked.

"Uh, no, not really," Gascon said. "They watched for a while and seemed like they thought it was kind of useless. They took a copy to give to the Video Tech Unit for enhancement. I never heard from them after that."

Bosch kept his eyes on the playback while they talked. From the right side of the screen he now saw an orange car moving west on Santa Monica toward the Haven House. It crossed the screen and turned into the entryway before disappearing.

"He's back," he said.

Gascon looked at the screen but the car was already gone.

"Back it up," Bosch instructed. "He comes in from the east this time. Freeze it when he gets to the center."

Gascon quickly executed and Bosch leaned in close to the screen. There was a head visible in the car as it crossed directly in front of the cemetery. The image was still small and grainy but it was more defined because the car was closer to the camera. Bosch had no doubt now that it was a Camaro. From this angle, he could even see a few yellow pixels in the center of the black wheels—the yellow brake calipers that Cisco Wojciechowski had described.

But the distance from the camera and the dark-tinted windows made it impossible for Bosch to get a bead on the driver.

"Okay, play it," he said. "Let's see how long they stay this time."

Bosch noted that the time on the video was now 11:41 p.m. They watched the Camaro turn into the motel entrance again. Gascon then sped the playback and they watched and waited. Bosch thought about why there had been two visits to the motel. He guessed that the first time, Ellis and Long may have been casing the motel and Allen's room. Another possibility was that the rear parking lot was too busy with people coming and going. A third possibility was that Allen was with a client.

This time the Camaro did not emerge for fifty-one minutes. Once again it left quickly, turning right without stopping as it emerged and then going west and out of the picture. Bosch considered the time that had elapsed, and his instincts told him that James Allen was dead and in the trunk of the Camaro when it drove out of the frame.

"What do you think?" Gascon asked.

"I think I need a copy of that," he said.

"Got a drive?"

"Nope."

"How about two hundred beans, like I got before?"

"I have that."

"Then let me see if I can find somebody around here with a drive."

39

On his way back to his house, Bosch parked his rental behind the Poquito Mas on Cahuenga. He went into the restaurant and ordered a chile pasilla plate to go. He then used his Uber app to call for a car. Both the car and his food order arrived at the same time. He took the car up to his house, checking along the drive for indications of surveillance from Ellis and Long. There was no sign of the vice cops and no conversation with the driver this time. Bosch decided it had something to do with sitting in the backseat.

Once inside the house Bosch grabbed the discovery file out of his bedroom and dropped it on the dining room table. Before beginning his work he opened the sliders to let in some fresh air. He stepped out on the deck for a moment and looked around. To his right he could see across a cut in the canyon to the cantilevered deck from which Long had been watching that morning. He wondered if they had figured out that he was not home and not using the Cherokee.

He went back inside to the table and pulled a legal pad over front and center. He started using the discovery file and his own notes and memory to construct a timeline that would allow him to see and contemplate the case as a whole, beginning it far before the murder of Alexandra Parks. He first posted the murders on the timeline and then added the other relevant events around them.

He was fifteen minutes into the project when the doorbell rang. He got up quietly and approached the door. Through the peephole he saw the top of a bald head with a scattershot spread of sun spots on it. He stepped back and opened the door. It was his neighbor Francis Albert.

"Detective Bosch, I saw you out on the deck a little bit ago. Were you going to show me any pictures?"

"Totally forgot, Frank. Hold on a second."

It was rude but Bosch left him standing on the front stoop. He didn't want Albert coming inside because it might then be difficult to get him back out. Bosch returned to the table where he had left his coat draped over a chair. He pulled the photos of Ellis and Long out of the pocket and went back to the door. He handed the photocopy containing both headshots to Albert.

"Was the guy you saw this morning one of them?" he asked.

Albert didn't take very long to draw a conclusion. He nodded.

"Yeah, this guy, he was the clown," he said.

He turned the photo of Long toward Bosch. Bosch nodded.

"Yeah, I thought it might be," he said. "Thanks, Frank."

There was an awkward pause as Frank didn't move and waited for more.

"Will you give me a call if you see him again?" Bosch asked.

"Sure," Albert said. "Do you think he's really a cop?"

Bosch paused for a moment and thought about the question and what he should tell Albert.

"Not really," he said.

He went back to the table after closing the door and repeatedly went through the timeline, adding nuances of detail as he went. After another half hour he finally had a document he believed detailed the case and his investigation in its entirety.

Unknown Date 2013—watch bought by Dr. Schubert

Unknown Date 2014—watch stolen or sold by Schubert

Dec. 11—watch bought by Harrick at Grant & Sons

Dec. 25—watch given to Alexandra Parks

Unknown Date—watch's crystal is broken

Feb. 2—watch arrives by FedEx to Las Vegas

Feb. 5—Gerard examines watch—still registered to Schubert

Feb. 5—Gerard calls Mrs. Schubert (watch stolen)

Feb. 5—Parks calls Gerard, learns her watch may have been stolen

Feb. 5—Parks calls Grant & Sons (conversation unknown)

Feb. 5—Dr. Schubert calls Gerard—watch not stolen, paid gambling debt

Feb. 5—Gerard calls Parks (watch not stolen)

Feb. 9—Alexandra Parks murdered

Mar. 19—Da'Quan Foster arrested—DNA match

Mar. 21–22—James Allen murdered—orange Camaro in Haven House lot—two car doors in alley—two killers?

Apr. 1—Cisco crashes—orange Camaro

May 5—Haller arrested—Ellis and Long

May 7—Nguyen brothers questioned by

Bosch—Nguyen brothers murdered—two killers?

Bosch finally put the pen down and studied the dates and events on each line. Deconstructing the case to a simple timeline helped him see how everything was connected and how the events fell like dominoes, one leading to the next. And through all of it was the watch. Could four murders actually be linked by the changing ownership of a watch?

Bosch knew that it was time to meet Dr. Schubert and finish the puzzle. He sat back and considered how to best do this. He drew certain conclusions about the man he had never met or even seen before—conclusions based on what he did for a living and where and how he lived.

He decided that the best approach would be to scare Schubert and gain his cooperation through fear. And in this case, he wasn't going to have to fake it.

Bosch got up from the table and headed down the hallway to his bedroom. It was time to change into real detective clothes.

40

Ellis was in the new apartment with the twins. He was reviewing the last day's recordings, looking for the next project to work. Long called him on the burner.

"You were right," he said. "He just showed up. I think you need to get over here."

One of the girls was sitting on the couch, painting her fingernails. The other was taking a nap because the night before had been so busy. Ellis moved into the kitchen so he would have some privacy. He spoke in a low voice to Long.

"What's he doing?" he asked.

"Well, he's wearing a suit and tie for one thing," Long said.

"Trying to look like a detective. That'll be his play. What else?"

"He's holding a file."

"Where exactly is he?"

"The garage, leaning against a car that looks like a plain-wrap. You should get over here. Something is going to go down, I think."

"He'll want to get him away by himself. Someplace private."

Ellis had to think about this. What would be the best opportunity for their own play?

"You still there?" Long asked.

"I'm here," Ellis said. "Can you tell, is he carrying?"

"Uh...yeah, he's carrying. Left hip. I see the jacket riding up on it."

"We'll have to remember that. And you're sure he didn't see you."

"No, man, he drove in right by me."

"In the Cherokee?"

"No, he's got a Chrysler. Looks like a rental."

Ellis considered this. Bosch knew that they had tagged the Cherokee. Did he know they were watching Schubert?

"You coming or not?" Long asked.

"Soon."

He disconnected and walked into the living room.

41

The Center for Cosmetic Creation was located in a two-story structure a block from Cedars-Sinai in West Hollywood. The entire first level served as a parking garage with the medical facilities just a short elevator ride up. Bosch found Schubert's car easily in the parking garage—he had a reserved spot with his name stenciled on the wall in front of it. There was a sleek-looking silver Mercedes-Benz sitting in the space. Bosch drove past it and found an open space nearby. He parked and waited. As he did so, he looked through the file of reports and photos he had put together, and worked on his pitch. That was what it was going to be. A pitch to Schubert. An offer to save his life.

While Bosch waited he saw a few patients of the cosmetic surgery center come out of the elevator and leave after being discharged from whatever treatment they had elected. They were wheeled out by nurses and then helped into waiting Town Cars. Bosch noticed that the Lincolns all had license plate frames from the same car service and he got the idea that the ride was part of the surgery package. All but one of the patients had bandages on her face. Bosch guessed that the one who didn't had gone in for breast enhancement or liposuction. She carried herself gingerly when she stood from the wheelchair and climbed slowly into the back of the waiting car.

All of the patients Bosch saw leaving were women. All of them middle-aged or older. All of them by themselves. All of them probably trying to hold on to an image of youth, pushing back that moment when they feared men would stop looking at them.

It was a rough and tough world out there. It made Bosch think about his daughter and how soon she would be leaving home and going out on her own. He hoped that she would never have a destination like this place. He pulled out his phone and fired off a text to her, even though she had told him it was unlikely they would be camping in a place with cellular service. He sent the text anyway, more for himself than for her.

Hey, hope you're having fun. I miss ya!

Bosch was looking at the phone's screen, hoping for a reply, when he heard the chirp of a car being unlocked. He looked up and saw two women in patterned nursing scrubs heading toward their cars. The medical offices were probably closing for the day. Moments behind them came a man who Bosch guessed was possibly a doctor. He was heading toward the Mercedes in the parking spot marked for Schubert but he walked by it to the car right next to it. After the man pulled out of the spot, Bosch started his car and moved it over to the open space next to Schubert's. He got out with the file and walked around to Schubert's Mercedes. Leaning against the back of the car, he put the file down on the trunk lid and folded his arms across his chest.

For the next twenty minutes nurses and staff members continued to sporadically emerge from the elevator and enter the garage, but no one approached Schubert's

Mercedes. A few gave Bosch an inquisitive look but no one asked him why he was there or what he was doing. It was Friday afternoon, the end of the week, and they wanted to get out of there. Bosch used his phone to search Google images for an online photo of the plastic surgeon. He found only one and it was from a 2003 article in a Beverly Hills society paper. The photo depicted the doctor and his wife, Gail, attending a charity event at the Beverly Hilton. It looked to Bosch as though the wife had made a visit or two to her husband's office for professional reasons. There was a chiseled look to her chin and the ridge of her eyebrows.

A text from Maddie popped up on his phone screen.

Really cold at night. See you Sunday!

It was like her to keep it succinct and deliver the real message outside the words—the message being that she would be holding off on communicating until she got back home. Bosch opened up a window to tap out a return message but was unsure what to say.

"Excuse me."

Bosch looked up. A man was approaching and Bosch recognized him from the twelve-year-old photo he had just pulled up on his phone. Schubert gestured toward the Mercedes that Bosch was leaning against.

"My car, if you don't mind," he said.

He wore green pants and a light-blue button-down shirt and gray tie. He wore no sport coat, most likely because he wore a doctor's white coat inside the center. Bosch pushed off the trunk of the car and adjusted his jacket, being sure to flip it enough to show off the gun holstered on his hip. He saw Schubert's eyes hold on it.

"What is this?" Schubert said.

"Dr. Schubert, my name's Bosch and I'm here to save

your life," Bosch said. "Is there a place we can talk privately?"

"What?" the doctor exclaimed. "Is this some kind of a joke? Who the hell are you?"

Schubert gave Bosch a wide berth as he moved toward the driver's-side door of his car. He pulled a key from his pocket and clicked it, unlocking the doors.

"I wouldn't do that if I were you," Bosch said.

Schubert stopped, his hand in midreach to the door, as if Bosch were warning him that he might trigger a bomb should he pull the handle. Bosch came around the back of the car, sliding the file off the trunk as he approached.

"Look, who are you?" Schubert said.

"I told you who I am," Bosch said. "I'm the guy trying to keep you breathing."

He handed the file to Schubert, who reluctantly took it. So far, things were going according to the pitch Bosch had worked out. The next ten seconds would determine if it stayed that way.

"Look at it," Bosch said. "I'm investigating a series of murders, Dr. Schubert. And I have reason to believe you—and possibly your wife—could be next in line."

Schubert reacted as if the file were red hot. Bosch was studying him. It was more a reaction of fear than surprise.

"Open it," Bosch commanded.

"This is not how you do this," the doctor protested. "You don't—"

He stopped short when he saw the image clipped to the inside of the file. The close-up of Alexandra Parks's horribly damaged face. His eyes widened and Bosch assumed that the plastic man had never seen a face like that in all his years of work.

Schubert's eyes scanned the other side of the file.

Bosch had clipped the incident report to the right side, not for its content but because it was a copy of an official document and he knew the imprimatur of the Los Angeles County Sheriff's Department printed at the top would further his legitimacy in Schubert's eyes. Harry wanted him thinking he was a real cop for as long as possible. The charade would be over if Schubert asked to see a badge. To keep that from happening, Bosch's plan was to keep him off balance and play on his fears.

Schubert closed the file and looked stricken. He tried to hand it back but Bosch did not take it.

"Look, what is this about?" he pleaded. "What does it have to do with me?"

"It all started with you, Doctor," Bosch said. "With you and Ellis and Long."

The recognition was unmistakable in Schubert's face. Recognition and dread, as if he had expected all along that his business with Ellis and Long—whatever it was—was not done.

Bosch stepped forward and finally took the file away.

"Now," he said. "Where can we go to talk?"

42

Schubert used a key to unlock the elevator. The steel box rose slowly, and neither he nor Bosch spoke. Once the doors opened, the two men moved through a high-luxury reception area and waiting room with plush seating and a coffee bar. The spaces were empty and unmanned. It appeared that everyone had gone home for the day. They moved down a hallway and into Schubert's private office. He flipped on the light switch as they entered a large room with an informal seating arrangement of couch and chairs on one side and a desk and computer station on the other side. The two areas were separated by a folding partition of Japanese design. Schubert sat down heavily in the high-backed leather chair positioned behind the desk. He shook his head like a man who suddenly understands that the trappings of his life that were so perfectly put in place are now changing.

"I just can't believe this," he said.

He gestured toward Bosch as though he were responsible for it all. Bosch sat down in a chair in front of the desk and put the file down on the ultra-modern brushed-aluminum desktop.

"Relax, Doctor," Bosch said. "We'll work this out. The woman in the photo you don't want to look at was Alexandra Parks. Does that name ring a bell with you?"

Schubert started to shake his head in a reflex response but then his mind snagged on the name.

"The woman from West Hollywood?" he asked. "The one who worked for the city? I thought they caught somebody for that. A black gang member."

Bosch thought it interesting that Schubert had described the suspect by race, like there was a causal relationship to the crime. It gave Bosch a small insight into the man he had to convince in the next five minutes to open up and talk.

"Yeah, well, we got the wrong guy," Bosch said. "And the right guys are still out there."

"You mean those two men? The two L.A. cops?"

"That's right. And I need to know what you know about them so that we can stop them."

"I don't know anything about this."

"Yes, you do."

"I can't get involved. In my business, reputation is everything. I—"

"Your reputation won't mean much if you're dead, and we have good reason to believe you are on their list."

"That's impossible. I paid and I'll pay again by the end of next month. They know that. Why would they—"

Schubert realized that in his panic and fear he had already revealed himself.

Bosch nodded.

"That's why we need to talk," he said. "Help us end this thing. We'll do it quietly and safely. As much as possible I will keep you out of it. I need your information, not you."

Now Schubert nodded, not so much to Bosch but to acknowledge that a moment he had been dreading for a long time was finally here and had to be dealt with.

"Okay, good," Bosch said. "But before we start, I need to check in with my partner and tell him where I'm at. It's a safety thing."

"I thought you were supposed to be with a partner at all times."

Bosch took out his phone and typed in the password.

"In a perfect world," he said. "But with an investigation like this, we cover more ground if we split up. We keep momentum."

Bosch checked his watch and acted like he was making a call. Instead, he had opened the memo app and started a recording. He then held the phone up to his ear as though he had made the call and was waiting for an answer. He waited several seconds and then left a message.

"Hey, it's Harry. It's five forty-five and I'm with Dr. Schubert at his office and I'll conduct the interview here. He wants to cooperate. I'll let you know if anything comes up I can't handle. Talk to you later."

Finished with his message, he pantomimed disconnecting the call and put the phone down on the file on the desktop. At the same time, he leaned forward to pull his notebook out of his back pocket. He then patted the pockets of his jacket, looking for a pen. Not finding one, he reached over to a cup on the desk that was filled with pens and pencils.

"All right if I borrow one of these and take some notes?" he asked.

"Look, I didn't exactly say I wanted to cooperate," Schubert said. "You are forcing me. You tell someone they're going to get murdered, and sure they want to talk to you and find out what it's about."

"So is that an okay on the notes?"

"Whatever."

Bosch looked at the file that had been placed on the desk and then up at Schubert.

"Why don't we start with the watch?" he said.

"What watch?" Schubert asked. "What are we talking about?"

"Dr. Schubert, you know what watch I'm talking about. The Audemars Piguet that you bought in Las Vegas two years ago. The ladies' Royal Oak Offshore model. The one your wife said was stolen but then you said was sold to pay a gambling debt."

Schubert seemed stunned by Bosch's knowledge.

"But that was a lie, wasn't it?" Bosch said. "I can't help you unless you start talking and telling the truth. Four people are dead, Doctor. Four. What connects them is that watch. You want to protect yourself, then tell me the real story."

Schubert closed his eyes as if this could help ward off the terrible predicament he was in.

"This can't go anywhere," he said. "I have clients. I have…"

He faltered.

"A reputation, yes, you said that," Bosch said. "I get that. I can't promise you anything but I'll do my best for you. If you tell the truth."

"My wife doesn't know," Schubert said. "I love her and it would hurt her very, very badly."

He said it more to himself, and Bosch elected to hold back, to wait and let him work through it. Finally a resolve seemed to come to him and Schubert opened his eyes and looked at Bosch.

"I made one mistake," he said. "One awful mistake and…"

He trailed off again.

"What mistake, Doctor?" Bosch asked.

Considering the other players involved, he had an idea where this was going. Ellis and Long were vice cops and they worked in the dark corridors of the sex trade. That was how they had crossed paths with James Allen. There was no reason to think that Schubert was going in a different direction.

"I had a relationship with a patient," Schubert said. "She happened to work in the adult entertainment business. Over the years, there were several surgeries. Every enhancement you can think of—lips, breasts, buttocks. We did Botox regularly. There was labiaplasty, face-lift, arm-lift…everything to keep her career going."

Bosch had no idea what a labiaplasty was but didn't want to ask for fear it would depress him to depths beyond the level to which the rest of the list had sent him.

"This of course was over a number of years," Schubert said. "Almost a decade."

He stopped there as if he had laid out enough for Bosch to figure out the rest. Bosch knew he probably could do just that but he needed Schubert to tell the story.

"When you say 'relationship,' what are we talking about?" Bosch asked.

"A doctor-patient relationship," Schubert said curtly. "It was professional."

"Okay. So what happened that brought vice officers Ellis and Long into your life?"

Schubert cast his eyes down for a moment and came to grips with what he must do.

"I want your promise that you won't put this in any police reports that are not held as strictly confidential," he said.

Bosch nodded.

"You have my promise. I won't put any of this into any police reports."

Schubert studied him for a long moment as if taking measure of his truthfulness. He then nodded, more to himself than to Bosch.

"I crossed a line," Schubert said. "I slept with her. I slept with my patient. Only one time but I have regretted it every moment since."

Bosch nodded as though he believed him.

"When did this crossing of the line happen?" he asked.

"Last year," Schubert said. "Right before Thanksgiving. It was a setup. A trap."

"What is her name?"

"Deborah Stovall. She uses a different name as a performer. I think it's Ashley Juggs or something like that."

"You said it was a setup. How?"

"She called the office and asked for me. I do my phone consults at the end of the day. So I called and she said she was having an allergic reaction to a Botox injection received at our offices. I told her to come in first thing the next day and I'd take a look, but she said she couldn't go out in public because of the swelling of her face. She wanted me to come to her."

"So you went."

"Against my better judgment, I did. At the end of my schedule that day, I packed a medical bag and went to her apartment. That part was not unusual. I occasionally make house calls, depending on who the client is. In fact, she was the second of two calls I was scheduled to make that day. But I should have known with her—because of what she does for a living—where this might lead."

"Where was her place?"

"Over on Fountain near Crescent Heights. An apartment. I can't remember the exact address. It's in her medical file."

"What happened when you got there?"

"Well, she wasn't exhibiting any symptoms of infection or allergic reaction. She told me that the problem had cleared up during the day and the swelling she had experienced was gone now. I don't think there ever actually was a problem."

"Okay, so you went there," Bosch said. "Then what happened?"

"She had a roommate who was there," Schubert said. "And this girl just wasn't wearing any clothes. And one thing—"

"What was the roommate's name?"

"It was Annie but I don't know if that was her real name or not."

"Was she in the adult entertainment world as well?"

"Yes, of course."

"Okay. So what, you had sex with one or both of them?"

Schubert dropped his chin and made a noise from his throat that Bosch thought was intended to be interpreted as a choking back of tears.

"Yes...I did. I was weak."

Bosch left him hanging without a sympathetic reaction.

"So I'm assuming there were cameras but you didn't see them," he said.

"Yes, there were cameras," Schubert said quietly. "Hidden cameras."

"Who did you hear from, the women or Ellis and Long?"

"Ellis and Long. They came here, sat in front of the desk like you are now, and showed me the video on a phone. Then they told me how things were going to be. I was going to do what they told me and pay them what they wanted or they would disseminate the video on the Internet. They would make sure it was seen by my wife and they would make Deborah file a complaint with the California Medical Ethics Board. They would ruin me."

Bosch nodded, the closest he could come to a sign of sympathy.

"How much did they want?" he asked.

"A hundred thousand dollars starting out," Schubert said. "And then another fifty thousand every six months."

Bosch was beginning to get a hook on why Ellis and Long had taken such extreme measures in killing anyone perceived as a threat to their operation. Schubert was a goose laying golden eggs—an annual income stream for them as long as the plastic man wished to cover up his indiscretion.

"So you paid them the first hundred."

"I paid them."

"How exactly?"

Schubert had now turned in his desk chair and was no longer looking at Bosch. To his right was a large poster covering one wall that showed an outline of a woman's body. It was clinical, not erotic, and it detailed outside the lines of the body the many different procedures that could be performed on various parts. It appeared to Bosch that he was addressing the woman on the poster as he answered.

"I told them I couldn't pay in cash," he said. "My money—I never see my money. I have a firm that manages the center here, and what comes to me goes to direct deposit and into the control of accountants and money managers. All of this is monitored by my wife. I had an addiction disease that required that we do it this way."

"A gambling addiction?" Bosch asked.

Schubert turned and glanced at Bosch as if just remembering that he was in the room. He then turned back to the poster.

"Yes, gambling," he said. "It had gotten out of control and I lost a lot, so they took my money from me. Controlled it. It was the only way to save my marriage. But it means I can't just go to the bank or write a check that size without a cosigner."

"So you gave jewelry instead," Bosch said. "Your wife's watch."

"Yes, exactly. She was away on a holiday. Out of town. I gave them the jewelry. Her watch, my watch, several diamond pieces. It was their idea to make it look like a burglary. When she came home, I told her there had been a break-in and the police were on it. They were investigating. Ellis broke a window in the French doors at the back of the house so it would look like that's how the robbers got in."

Bosch reached over to the desk for the file. He slid it out from beneath the phone.

"Let me take a look at something here," he said.

He opened the file and flipped through the reports clipped to the right side until he found the timeline he had put together that morning.

Schubert's story fit with the facts Bosch had accumulated. He gives the jewelry to Ellis and Long as an extortion payoff. They then strike a deal with the Nguyen brothers to sell it as estate property at Nelson Grant & Sons. The jewelry starts to sell—Harrick buys the ladies' watch for his wife as a Christmas present. Ellis and Long start to get their money and the Nguyen brothers get a cut for selling it without delving into its provenance.

Things go wrong when Alexandra Parks breaks the crystal on her watch and sends it for repair to the shop in Las Vegas. When she learns there may be a problem with the watch's ownership, Parks, head of the consumer protection unit and married to a law officer, quietly tries to look into the watch's history. She calls Nelson Grant & Sons to make inquiries. Maybe she tells them her husband is a Sheriff's deputy, maybe they knew that from when he bought the watch in the first place. Whatever was said, her call worries the Nguyen brothers to the point that they contact Ellis and Long and say, "We might have a problem here."

Ellis and Long decide on an extreme response: take out Parks before she investigates further and pulls the thread on their extortion operation. Bosch had to assume that Schubert wasn't the only victim in the scheme and that there was a bigger moneymaking machine afoot, using the women to entice men into performing before the hidden cameras.

Ellis and Long concoct a scheme to murder Parks and make it look like a sexually motivated crime. They use James Allen, a snitch they controlled and may have used in similar extortion schemes, to procure a condom containing semen that could be planted at the crime scene to send investigators in the wrong direction toward the wrong man.

That theory left James Allen and the question of why he was in turn murdered. To tie up loose ends? Or had he threatened the vice cops in some way? The murder of Lexi Parks had splashed big in the media. Allen could have caught the story, then put two and two together after his customer Da'Quan Foster was arrested based on DNA evidence. If he made a move against Ellis and Long, asked for money or threatened them in any way, it could have cost him his life. He was murdered, and his body was staged in a way that might send investigators off in the wrong direction. Ellis and Long would have been aware of the earlier murder, the body left in the alley off El Centro. They may have even been responsible for it.

The misdirection, Bosch thought. There was a pattern in it. A repeating pattern. First Alexandra Parks, then James Allen.

43

Ellis joined Long in the Charger.

"'Bout time," Long said.

"Quit whining," Ellis said. "I was taking care of business with the girls. What's the status here?"

"Schubert came out and Bosch confronted him. Then they went inside. That was thirty-five minutes ago."

Ellis nodded and thought about things. Schubert had been inside with Bosch long enough that it should be assumed that he was spilling his guts. That signaled the endgame to Ellis. It was time to close down the operation. Time to close down all operations.

He didn't know about Long but he had certainly planned for this day. He pulled out his phone and opened the weather app. He had several cities tabbed just in case his phone ever fell into the wrong hands. But only one mattered. It was seventy-six degrees in Placencia, Belize. What could be more perfect?

He put his phone away.

"This is it," he said.

"What is it?" Long asked.

"This. Right here. This is the end of the line. We have a choice to make."

"What choice?"

"You take this car, I go back to my car, and we split. We grab our stashes and we split. For good."

"No, no, we can't just—"

"It's over. Over."

"What's the other choice?"

Long's voice was off. It had gone up a notch or two as panic began to take hold of his vocal cords.

"We go in," Ellis said. "And we finish it. Leave no one to tell the story."

"That's it?" Long asked. "That's your big plan?"

"It's not a plan. It just might buy us more time. We go in, take care of business, and it might be tomorrow morning before anyone finds them. By then, you're in Mexico and I'm halfway to wherever."

Long drummed the fingers of both hands on his thighs.

"There's gotta be another way, another plan," he said.

"There's nothing," Ellis said. "I told you. Dominoes. It's come to this. Make the call."

"What about the girls? We could take—"

"Forget the girls. I'll take care of them as soon as I leave here."

Long looked sharply at him.

"What the fuck, man?" he said.

"I told you," Ellis said. "Dominoes."

Now Long was rubbing his jaw with one hand while gripping the wheel with the other.

"Make the call," Ellis repeated.

44

Bosch studied the timeline and saw how it all worked, how the dominoes all fell in a way pointing directly to Ellis and Long.

"When was the last time you saw Ellis and Long?" he asked.

Schubert had dropped into a quiet reverie while Bosch looked at the timeline. Now he straightened up at the question.

"Seen them? I haven't seen them in months. But they've called me a lot. They called me two days ago to ask if anybody had been snooping around. I guess they were talking about you."

Bosch nodded.

"Do you have their number?" he asked.

"No, they always call me," Schubert said. "The number is always blocked."

"What about Deborah? You have a number for her?"

"In the files."

"I need to get that. And her address."

"I think it's illegal for me to share information from a medical file."

"Yes, but we're well beyond that now, right?"

"Right, I guess. What happens now?"

"Uh...I have some work to do getting independent

confirmation of some of this. And I'm going to pay a visit to Deborah and her roommate. I'm going to need a list of all the jewelry you gave Long and Ellis in addition to the watches."

"I have a list. My wife made it."

"Good. Where did you physically hand over all of the stuff to them?"

Schubert looked down when he answered.

"They came to my house and looked through what we had," he said. "My wife was in Europe. I stood there while they went through her things. They took what they wanted and left the rest. They knew what was valuable and what wasn't. What they could and couldn't sell."

"They take anything besides jewelry?"

"One of them—Ellis—knew his wine. He went through our storage rack and took my two bottles of 'eighty-two Lafite."

"Maybe he just took the old stuff because it looked valuable."

"No, he took the 'eighty-two Lafite and left the nineteen eighty. The 'eighty-two is worth fifty times what the 'eighty is worth and will taste fifty times as good. He knew that."

Bosch nodded. He realized the wine might be more important to the case than the jewelry. If Ellis had kept it for himself, there might still be a bottle somewhere in his possession, and it could link him to the case and be a verifiable point should Schubert's story be challenged in court or elsewhere.

"You said it was their idea to make it look like a burglary?"

"When I told them I couldn't pay them cash without my wife knowing, they said we could make it look like a burglary, only I wouldn't report it. I would only tell my wife I had reported it when she came back from her trip. They even mocked up a burglary report that I could show her. It had phony names, phony everything."

"Do you still have it?"

"Yes. At the house."

"We're going to need that. Did you make an insurance claim on everything that was taken?"

If Schubert had also engaged in insurance fraud, it could undercut his strength as a witness.

"No, I didn't," Schubert said. "That was their rule. They didn't want the stuff reported stolen because it would make it hard for them to sell it and get their money. They told me if they found out I'd made a claim, they would come back and kill my wife and me."

"So didn't your wife wonder about that? The insurance, I mean."

"I told her we were negotiating with them and then I went out and made some cash calls, slowly got the money together, and made it look like it had come from the insurance company."

"'Cash calls'?"

"Like I said before, I do house calls on occasion. There are people out there, Detective, who have money and are willing to pay for privacy. They don't use medical insurance. They pay cash for procedures so there is no record and no one will ever know. I get requests like that— mostly I'm talking about Botox injections and other minor things but it sometimes goes to full surgeries."

This wasn't news to Bosch. The rich and famous in Los Angeles had such power. Michael Jackson came to mind. The megastar singer had died while at home and under the care of a private doctor. In a place where image often counted more than anything else, a plastic man who made cash calls could do well.

"Is that how you planned to get the money to pay them fifty grand every six months?"

"That was the plan. There is a payment at the end of June and I'm almost ready for it."

Bosch nodded. He wanted to tell Schubert that he wouldn't have to make that payment but he held off. There was no telling for sure how long the investigation would wind out. He brought the interview back on point.

"Did they take anything else in this phony burglary?"

"A piece of artwork. It wasn't worth much. It was just special to me. I think it's why they took it. They said they owned me and could take whatever they wanted."

Schubert was slouched with his elbows on the arms of his seat. He closed his eyes and massaged the bridge of his nose with two fingers.

"This is all going to come out now, isn't it?" he said.

"We'll do our best to keep you away from it," Bosch said. "Everything that has happened occurred after this anyway. It was all triggered by Alexandra Parks sending the watch out to be fixed."

"Then, what makes you so sure that I'm in danger?"

"Because these two guys are cops and they know how the system works. If there are no witnesses, then there is no threat to them. They haven't come back to you because they don't know yet that everything has been traced back to that watch. When they do, they'll come—and it won't be just to collect the next fifty grand."

"Well, don't you have enough to arrest them now? You seem to know everything."

"I think with confirmation of parts of your story, there will be more than enough evidence to do that."

"Are you Internal Affairs?"

"No, I'm not."

"Then—"

There was a noise from outside the office. It sounded like the thump of a door closing.

"Is there anybody else still here?" Bosch asked.

"Uh, maybe one of the girls," Schubert said.

Bosch stood up.

"I didn't see anybody when we walked in," he said quietly.

He walked to the door, thought about opening it and looking into the hallway, but then thought better of it. He leaned his head toward the jamb and listened. He heard nothing at first but then clearly heard a whispered voice from out in the hallway say, "Clear."

It was a man. He knew then that Ellis and Long were in the building and were coming for them.

45

Bosch quickly pushed the button on the doorknob, locking it, then reached over and flicked off the office's overhead light. He moved quickly back toward the desk, pulling his weapon out of the holster on his hip.

Schubert stood up from his chair and his eyes grew wider with every step Bosch took toward him.

"They're here," Bosch whispered. "They must've followed me or they were watching you and waiting."

"For what?"

"For me to make the connection."

Bosch pointed to a door to the left of the desk.

"Where does that go?" he asked.

"It's just a bathroom," Schubert said.

"Is there a window?"

"Yes, but it's small and it's a twenty-foot drop."

"Shit."

Bosch turned around and surveyed the room, trying to come up with a plan. He knew that going out into the hall would be a mistake. They'd be open targets. They were going to have to make their stand right where they were.

He turned back and grabbed the corded phone off the desk. He knew calling on the landline would automatically deliver the building's address to the 911 operator. It would speed the response.

"How do I get an outside line?" he asked quickly.

Schubert reached over and hit a button on the bottom of the phone base. Bosch heard the dial tone and punched in 9-1-1. He then pointed toward the office window.

"Close the curtain, make it dark."

The call to 911 started ringing. Schubert did as instructed, hitting a button on the wall next to the window. A curtain started automatically moving across the ceiling track. Bosch kept his eyes on the office door.

"Come on, come on, come on, pick up," he said.

Once the curtain closed off direct light, the room dropped into shadow. Bosch then pointed at the bathroom door.

"Go in there," he commanded. "Lock the door and stay low."

Schubert didn't move.

"You dialed nine-one-one," he said. "Can't you just call for backup?"

"No, I can't."

"Why not?"

"Because I'm not a cop. Now go in there."

Schubert looked puzzled.

"I thought—"

"I said GO!"

There was nothing whispered about the command this time. It propelled Schubert backward toward the bathroom door. He went inside and closed the door. Bosch heard the click of the lock. He knew it wouldn't stop Ellis and Long if it came to that. But it might buy a few more seconds.

The 911 operator finally answered and Bosch spoke in a loud and exaggeratedly panicked voice. He wanted Ellis and Long to know he was calling for help. They were probably in the hallway outside at that moment

and Bosch thought there was a chance they would retreat if they heard him making the call.

"Yes, hello, I need help. There are two armed men
in my office and they're going to kill everybody," he
said loudly. "Their names are Ellis and Long, Ellis and
Long, and they came here to kill us."

"Hold on, sir," the operator said. "Your location is
fifteen-fifteen West Third Street?"

"Yes, that's it. Hurry!"

"What is your name, sir?"

"What does that matter? Just send help."

"I need your name, sir."

"Harry Bosch."

"Okay, sir, we are sending help. Please stay on the
line for me."

Bosch moved directly behind the desk. He put the
phone in the crook of his neck and used his thigh and
his free hand to lift the edge of the desk and tip it over
on its side, its aluminum top now a barricade facing
the door. Everything on the desk, including the desk
phone, his own phone, and the cup full of pens slid off
and loudly crashed to the floor. The phone's handset
was yanked from his neck when the cord reached its
maximum extension. Bosch knew there was no time to
go back around to retrieve it. He had to hope the call
wasn't disconnected and that the operator didn't decide
it was a prank.

Bosch crouched down behind the barricade. He
knocked a fist on the underside of the desktop and felt
and heard wood. The double layer of wood and metal
might actually stop bullets—if he was lucky.

He squatted down further behind the blind and
pointed his Glock at the door. He had brought the gun
as part of the show to trick Schubert into believing he
was a cop. Now it might be the only thing that kept

them alive. The gun was maxed with thirteen rounds in the magazine and one in the chamber. He hoped it would be enough.

He heard a slight metallic sound from the far side of the room and knew Ellis and Long were outside the door and trying the knob. They were about to come in. Bosch realized at that very moment that he was in the wrong spot. He was positioned dead center in the room exactly where they would expect him to be.

46

Ellis signaled to Long that the door was locked and that he should kick it in. Long tossed him the flashlight and then backed off a few feet. He raised his leg, aiming his heel at a spot just above the doorknob. He had done this a lot over the years and was good at it.

The door flew open and slammed back on the inside wall of the office, revealing a darkened room lit only by the dim light leaking around the edges of a window curtain on the far wall. Long was left in a vulnerable position as the momentum from his kick carried him into the office. Ellis moved in behind him, following his left flank and holding his gun and the flashlight in the standard crossed-wrists configuration.

"Police!" he called out. "Nobody move!"

The light fell on a desk that had been tipped onto its side to create a barricade. He put the aim of his weapon on the top edge of the desk, ready for Bosch or Schubert to show himself.

"Wait!"

The voice called out from behind the door to the left of the desk. Ellis recalibrated the aim of both his light and gun.

"It's me!" Schubert called. "He told me he was a cop!"

The door opened and there stood Schubert, his hands raised.

"Don't shoot. I thought he—"

Ellis opened fire, sending three quick shots toward Schubert. In his peripheral vision he saw Long on his right, turning and raising his gun to fire as well.

"No!"

The shout came from behind him and to the right. Ellis turned and saw Bosch moving laterally out from behind a folding partition that split the room. He had a gun up and opened fire as Ellis realized the overturned desk had been a decoy and Bosch had the superior position.

Ellis lurched forward to put Long's larger body between Bosch and himself. He saw his partner react as the bullets struck him. The impacts redirected Long's momentum into a spin. He was going to go down. Ellis shifted his weight and drove his shoulder into Long's upper body, holding his partner up and swinging his own gun hand around his torso at the same time. Ellis fired wildly, shooting blindly in the direction he had last seen Bosch. He then reversed his footing and started back toward the door, dragging Long with him as a shield.

There was more gunfire, and Ellis felt the impacts through his partner's body. At the doorway he dropped Long and fired two more shots in the direction of where Bosch's fire had come from. He backed into the hallway and then turned and ran toward a door marked with an exit sign.

As he raced down the stairway to the garage, Ellis had one question bouncing through the impulses of his brain.

Fight or flight?

Was it all over or was there still a chance he could

contain this, somehow turn it all on Bosch? Tell them Bosch was the one. Bosch opened fire. Bosch had some kind of crazy vendetta going. Bosch—

He knew he was kidding himself. It couldn't work. If Bosch was still alive up there, then it wouldn't work.

Ellis ran across the garage to his car. He could hear an approaching siren—Sheriff's deputies responding to Bosch's 911 call. He judged it to be two or three blocks away. He had to get out before they got here. That was priority one. After that, he knew it was time to fly.

He was prepared. He had known it might someday come to this and he had planned for it.

47

His gun braced in two hands, Bosch moved in on Long, who was collapsed in the doorway. He was writhing in pain and gasping for breath. Bosch saw the last two bullets he had fired embedded in Long's shirt, held in place by the bulletproof vest underneath. Bosch yanked the gun out of Long's hand and slid it across the floor behind him. He put his weight down on Long and leaned forward to cautiously look into the hallway and make sure Ellis wasn't waiting out there.

Satisfied that Ellis was gone, Bosch pulled back into the room and turned Long over onto his chest. He took the vice cop's cuffs off his belt and used them to bind his wrists behind his back. He then saw the blood on Long's right side. One of Bosch's shots had found skin below the vest. Long was bleeding from a wound just above his right hip. Bosch knew that a .45 slug fired from ten feet was going to do major internal damage. Long might be mortally wounded.

"You motherfucker," Long finally managed to get out. "You're going to die."

"Everybody dies, Long," Bosch said. "Tell me something I don't know."

Bosch heard multiple sirens now and wondered if the Sheriff's had gotten Ellis on his way out.

"Your partner abandoned you, Long," he said.

"First, he uses you as a human shield and then he drops you like a bag of oranges. That's some partner."

Bosch patted him on the back and then moved away. He went to the other doorway to check on Schubert. The doctor was lying on his back, his head under the bathroom sink and his left leg folded awkwardly underneath his body. There were two impact wounds in his upper chest and one in the center of his neck. One of them had clipped his spine, causing him to drop the way he had. His eyes were open and he wasn't breathing. There was nothing Bosch could do. He couldn't fathom why Schubert thought that if he gave himself up to Ellis and Long, he would be spared. He wondered if he should feel remorse for leading him on, convincing him he was a cop on a case.

He didn't.

As Bosch knelt next to Schubert, he became aware of a pulsing tone from the desk phone on the floor behind him. It had disconnected from the call to the Sheriff's communication center when Bosch had tipped over the desk. He turned from the body, found the handset, and reunited it with the base, leaving it on the floor. He also saw a shattered frame that had fallen from the desk. It contained a photo of Schubert and his wife sitting in the cockpit of a sailboat and smiling at the camera.

The desk phone started to ring, one of the buttons flashing. Bosch picked up the handset and pushed the button.

"Harry Bosch."

"This is Sheriff's Deputy Maywood, who am I speaking with?"

"I just told you, Harry Bosch."

"We are outside the Center for Cosmetic Creation. What is the situation in there?"

"We've got one dead and one wounded. And then

me—I made the nine-one-one call. One gunman escaped. Did you get him?"

Maywood ignored Bosch's question.

"Okay, sir, I want you to listen closely. I need you and the wounded man to come out of the building with your hands behind your head, fingers laced. If you have any weapons, leave them inside the building."

"I don't think the wounded man's going to be walking anytime soon."

"Is he armed?"

"Not anymore."

"Okay, then, sir, I need you to come out now— hands laced behind your head. Leave all weapons inside."

"You got it."

"If we see a weapon, we will consider it a provocative action. Are we clear, sir?"

"Crystal. I'm coming down in the elevator."

"We'll be waiting."

Bosch disconnected and stood up. He looked around for a place to leave his Glock and saw Long's gun on the floor next to the right side of the desk. He went over and picked it up, careful not to touch the trigger and obliterate a fingerprint with his own. He put both weapons on top of a glass display cabinet that contained a collection of antique surgical instruments.

Before leaving the office, Bosch looked around in the debris on the floor for his phone. It had slid across the floor when he had tipped over the desk. He picked it up and looked at the screen. It was still recording. He turned it off and named the file "Schubert." He then texted it to Mickey Haller and put the phone in his pocket.

He started toward the doorway but thought about something. He had no idea how long he would be held and questioned by the Sheriff's Department. He had no idea if news of the shooting would reach the mountains outside the city. But just in case, he made a call to his daughter. He knew she had spotty cell service but he left her a message.

"Maddie, it's me. Just wanted you to know I'm okay. Whatever you hear, I'm okay. If you call and can't reach me, call Uncle Mickey. He'll fill you in."

Bosch pulled the phone away and was about to disconnect, when he had a second thought and raised the phone again.

"I love you, Mads, and I'll see you soon."

He ended the call.

As he left the office, Bosch had to step around Long in the doorway. The vice cop was not moving. His breathing was shallow now and his face was very pale and dotted with sweat. There was also a growing stain of blood on the floor next to him.

"Get me an ambulance," Long managed to say, his voice a hoarse whisper. "I'm dying."

"I'll tell them that," Bosch said. "Anything else you want to tell me before I go? Maybe something about Ellis? Like where he would run from here?"

"Yeah, I'll tell you something. How 'bout fuck you."

"Good one, Long."

Bosch stepped into the hall and started to retrace his path to the elevator. But two steps into it, he realized that there was a possibility that Ellis was still in the building. He could have been too late with his escape and seen Sheriff's deputies responding. It was possible he had retreated and was hiding.

Bosch quickly returned to the office and retrieved his Glock. He then moved back into the hallway and toward the elevator, moving in a combat stance with the gun up and braced.

He got to the elevator without seeing any sign of Ellis. He pushed the button and the doors opened immediately. The stainless steel box was empty and he stepped in. He pushed the button for the ground floor and the doors closed. As the elevator dropped, Bosch quickly took the magazine out of the Glock and ejected the round in the chamber. He loaded the loose bullet into the magazine and put it and the weapon down on the floor in the back corner of the elevator. He then turned to the doors, raised his hands, and laced his fingers together behind his head.

When the doors opened a moment later, Bosch saw a Sheriff's patrol car parked sideways across the elevator entry area with two deputies using it as cover, their weapons drawn and aimed at him. One man had his two-handed grip extended over the front hood, the other was similarly positioned across the rear trunk.

"Step out of the elevator," the front man called out. "Keep your hands behind your head."

Bosch started to step out as instructed.

"My gun is on the floor of the elevator," Bosch called out. "It is unloaded."

The moment Bosch cleared the elevator, he saw the men on the car raise their weapons. That gave him a split-second notice that he was about to be taken to the ground. Deputies came from either side of the elevator and grabbed him. He was taken down face-first on the tiled floor, then his arms were yanked behind his back and he was handcuffed.

Pain shot through Bosch's jaw. He had turned his face at the last moment during the takedown but still took the full impact along the left side of his face and jaw.

He felt hands roughly going through his pockets and removing his phone, wallet, and keys. He saw a pair of polished black patrol boots take a position in front of his face. The deputy squatted down and Bosch could see the lower half of his face if he turned his eyes up toward him. He saw sergeant stripes on the sleeves of the uniform. The man was looking at Bosch's retired officer ID card. He then squatted down to look at Bosch.

"Mr. Bosch, I'm Sergeant Cotilla. Who else is inside the building?"

"Like I said on the phone, you got one dead and one wounded," Bosch answered. "That's all I know for sure. There was a third man but he ran. He could possibly be hiding in there but I don't know for sure. The wounded man will be dead soon if you don't get a medical team to him. He's an LAPD vice officer named Kevin Long. As near as I could tell, he was hit once in the side, above the right hip."

"Okay, we have paramedics en route. And the dead man is who?"

"Dr. Schubert, the guy who owns this place."

"And you are former LAPD."

"Retired this year. I'm now a private detective. I'm also the one who shot Long—before he could shoot me."

There was a long silence as Cotilla digested that last piece of information. Like a smart street cop, he decided that Bosch's statement was for others to respond to.

"We're going to put you in a car, Mr. Bosch," he said. "The detectives will want to talk to you about all of that."

"Can you make a call out to Detective Sutton?" Bosch asked. "This is related to the two-bagger yesterday in the Sunset Plaza jewelry store. I'm pretty sure it's going to be his case."

48

This time they didn't put him in the boardroom at the West Hollywood substation. He was placed in a gray-walled interrogation room, the eye of a camera watching him from above. They kept him handcuffed and didn't give him back his phone, wallet, or keys.

The Glock was as good as gone, too.

At the two-hour mark Bosch's hands were numb and he was growing increasingly restless from the wait. He knew full well that the investigators—whether led by Dick Sutton or not—would be at the crime scene, supervising the collection and documentation of physical evidence. But what frustrated Bosch was that no one had even conducted a five-minute preliminary interview with him. For all he knew, the information he had given Sergeant Cotilla had not been forwarded to the investigators and there wasn't even a Wanted alert out yet on Don Ellis. Bosch figured that he could be across the Mexican border before the Sheriff's Department finally put out the alert.

At the 150-minute mark he got up and walked to the door of the box. He turned his back to it and used his hands to try to turn the knob. As he expected, the door was locked. Angrily he started kicking backwards toward the door, driving his heel into the kick panel. It created a loud noise that Bosch expected would bring a response—if not directly to the box, then to the cameras.

He looked up, certain that his actions were now being monitored by the camera gazers.

"Hey!" he yelled up. "I want to talk. Send somebody in to talk to me. Now!"

Twenty more minutes went by. Bosch was considering whether to start breaking the furniture. The table was old and scarred and looked as though it had withstood the assaults of many. But the chairs were different. They were newer and the support struts were thin enough that Bosch knew he could break them with his feet.

He looked up at the camera.

"I know you can hear me," he called out. "Get somebody in here now. I have important information. Dick Sutton, Lazlo Cornell, Sheriff Martin himself. I don't care, a killer is getting away."

He waited a beat and was about to start another rant when he heard the door being unlocked. It opened and in stepped Dick Sutton. He acted like he had no idea what Bosch had been through for the last three hours.

"Harry, sorry to hold you up in here," he began. "I've been working the crime scene and am just now getting back over here to talk to you and see what we've got."

"Well," Bosch said, "you just saved the station having to replace the furniture in here, because I was about to start busting the place up. I can't feel my hands, Dick."

"Oh, Jesus, they shouldn't have done that. Turn around and let me get those."

Bosch turned his back to Sutton and soon felt the relief of blood circulating in his hands again.

"Sit down," Sutton said. "Let's talk."

Bosch was rubbing his hands together, trying to get rid of the pins and needles sensation. He kicked out a chair and sat down.

"Why was the door locked, Dick?" he asked.

"Precaution," Sutton said. "We had to see what we had first."

"And?"

"And it's a complicated scene. You told the sergeant out there that a fourth man was involved and that he got away."

"That's right, Don Ellis. He's Long's partner, though he threw him under the bus back there."

"How so?"

"Used him as a shield when the shooting started. Then left him behind. Speaking of Long, did he make it?"

"Yeah, he made it. Just a few blocks from Cedars—that was lucky. My partner's over there now, hoping to get in a room with him and hear his story."

"I wish I could be there for that. The guy's going to lie his ass off and put everything on me, or if he's smart, he'll put it on Ellis."

"We'll worry about Long later. I want to hear your story, Harry. You told the sergeant that these are the two guys who took down the jewelry store yesterday?"

"That and Lexi Parks and a male pro in Hollywood a couple months ago. They've been busy."

"All right, we'll get to all of that, but tell me what happened up in that office today."

"I can tell you but you could also hear it for yourself."

This gave Sutton great pause. Bosch nodded.

"Bring me my phone," Bosch said. "I recorded my whole interview with Schubert on my phone. It was still taping when Ellis and Long showed up."

"You're saying you have the shooting on tape?" Sutton said.

"That's right. But you can't access it without a warrant. You want to hear it now, bring me the phone. I'll play it for you. Bring Cornell and Schmidt in here. I want them to hear it, too."

Bosch considered in that moment whether he should ask for Haller to be called in as well, but he let the thought go. The last time he had called Haller in, things had not gone well. Bosch had been in a thousand interview rooms before, and there was no move a detective could make that he wouldn't see coming. He felt he could protect himself as well as Haller could protect him.

Sutton got up and moved toward the door.

"Dick, one other thing," Bosch said.

Sutton paused, hand on the doorknob.

"What's that?" he asked.

"Heads-up on the recording," Bosch said. "My coaching tip is to make sure it is handled right. It can't disappear or get buried. You're not the only one who has it."

"Haller?"

"That's right."

"So you took the time to send it to him before you surrendered out there?"

Bosch nodded.

"I'm not stupid, Dick," he said. "The LAPD isn't going to like the way this case falls out and I don't think the Sheriff's Department is going to like the outcome much either. You've got a guy in county for a killing Long and Ellis did. So, yeah, I took the time to get it to my lawyer."

Sutton opened the door and left.

49

Bosch had to be moved back to the boardroom for the playing of the recording from his phone. This was to accommodate the crowd of investigators and brass who needed to listen to the forty-two-minute audio accounting of what happened in Dr. Schubert's office. There was Sutton, of course, and Schmidt and Cornell, as well as two detectives from the LAPD's Officer Involved Shooting team and one from the Internal Affairs Division.

The IAD investigator was Nancy Mendenhall and Bosch knew her from a case when he was still with the department. His experience with her had been good and fair. Seeing her in the group gathered around the oval table put a positive spin on things for Bosch. He knew she would listen and do the right thing—as far as she was allowed. Also in the room was Captain Ron Ellington, commander of LAPD's Professional Standards Bureau, which included Internal Affairs. He was Mendenhall's boss and was there because it would be his report on the exploits of Ellis and Long that would land on the desks of the chief of police and the Police Commission.

Even though the shooting had occurred on Sheriff's Department turf, the investigation was now a joint-department affair because of the involvement of Ellis and Long. Sutton explained this after the group was seated around the table. He also announced that there was a recording of the shooting and that he wanted the group to hear it first. He invited Bosch to offer commentary where needed as it played.

The phone was then placed on speaker mode and the recording played, with Bosch stopping the playback from time to time to describe things visually or to explain how Schubert's responses to questions fit with the investigation of the murder of Alexandra Parks and the murders that followed. Only Mendenhall took notes. The others just listened and sometimes cut off Bosch's explanations as if they didn't want him to interpret the meaning of things said in Schubert's office.

Halfway into the playback, the recording was interrupted when Mickey Haller's name popped up on the screen. He was calling Bosch's phone.

"It's my lawyer," Bosch said. "All right if I take this?"

"Fine," Sutton said. "Make it quick."

Bosch stood up and took the phone out of the room and into the hallway so he could have some privacy.

"I've listened to the recording. Thank Christ you're okay, brother," Haller said.

"Yeah, it was a close one," Bosch said. "I've just been playing it to a room full of cops—Sheriff's and LAPD."

There was a pause as Haller digested that.

"I'm not sure that was the right move," he finally said.

"It's the only move," Bosch said. "It's the only way I'm going to get out of here tonight. Besides, there are at least two in there I trust to do the right thing. One from each team."

"Well, no doubt the recording is the Holy Grail. I wanna go in with a nine-nine-five as soon as we can.

DQ's going to walk right out of county after this. You did it, man. I was so fucking right about you."

"Yeah, well, we'll see."

Bosch knew that a 995 motion in this case was essentially a petition to the court to change its mind based on new evidence. It would be filed before the judge who had held Da'Quan Foster over for trial at the preliminary hearing.

"Where are you, Whittier or West Hollywood?" Haller asked.

"West Hollywood substation," Bosch said. "The same gang as before with a few more from the LAPD in the mix now."

"I bet they're not happy."

"No, doesn't look like it. Ellis and Long are their guys."

Sutton stuck his head out from the boardroom and twirled a finger, signaling Bosch to wrap up the call and get back to the meeting and the playback. Bosch nodded and held up a finger. One minute.

"You need me to come over and kick some ass?" Haller asked.

"No, not yet," Bosch said. "Let's see how it goes. I'll call you if I need you."

"Okay, but remember what I told you last time. They're not your friends anymore, Harry, and they certainly aren't Da'Quan Foster's friends. Watch yourself."

"Got it."

Bosch disconnected and went back in.

The playback continued, and at the thirty-four-minute mark, the intensity in the boardroom palpably heightened when on the recording Bosch said, "Is there anybody else here?"

Where Bosch had mostly kept quiet during the playback of the interview with Schubert, he now felt compelled to offer descriptions of what was happening in the office to supplement what was captured on the recording. The recording was clear to a zone of about six feet. Sounds and voices more distant were fuzzy and lacking clarity. Bosch tried to be brief with his descriptions so as not to overlap what was coming from the phone.

"We heard a noise, like a door closing out in the hall...."

"I was listening at the door to the office and I heard one of them say, 'Clear.' I knew they were out there searching for us...."

"I tipped the desk over because my first plan was to make a barricade...."

"The first three were Ellis shooting Schubert. The doctor had his hands up and posed no threat. He shot him three times. Then that was me yelling there and firing. Four shots, I think, at first. Then two more when Ellis was backing out, using Long as a shield."

The recording ended with Bosch's announcement to the deputy on the office phone that he was coming out. There was a gulf of silence from the investigators gathered around the table. Bosch then noticed Cornell shake his head and lean back in his chair in a dismissive manner.

"What?" Bosch said. "You're going to stick with Foster as your guy?"

Cornell pointed at the phone that still sat in the middle of the table.

"You know what that is?" he asked. "It's just a bunch of words. You've got nothing—no evidence—that directly links these two to Parks. And let's not forget, you're a guy suing your own department and you'll do anything to embarrass it."

Now Bosch shook his head dismissively and looked at Sutton, who was still in the posture he had adopted while listening to the playback, leaning forward, hands clasped on the table. He now extended a finger and pointed at Bosch's phone.

"I need you to send me that," he said.

"Me, too," Mendenhall said.

Bosch nodded and picked up his phone. He moved a file containing a copy of the recording into an e-mail and then handed his phone to Sutton so he could type in his e-mail address. The process was then repeated with Mendenhall.

"Now what?" Bosch asked.

"You can go," Sutton said.

Cornell made another gesture of dissatisfaction, tossing a hand up in the air. Sutton ignored it.

"Do us a favor, Harry," Sutton said. "We've got a bunch of TV reporters outside the station, doing their stand-ups for the eleven-o'clock news. Don't talk to them about any of this, huh? That won't help anybody."

Bosch stood up, putting his phone away.

"No worries," he said. "What about the rest of my stuff? Wallet, gun, car?"

Sutton frowned.

"Uh, we'll get you your wallet," he said. "The car and gun we're going to need to hang on to for the moment. We're going to put together a full ballistics package and we'll need the weapon for that. And that whole building is taped off and considered a crime scene right now. We'll be working it for a few more hours. All right if we wait on the car until tomorrow morning?"

"No problem. I've got another at home."

He knew he had another gun at home as well, but he didn't mention that.

Standing up, Mendenhall put her notebook away in a leather satchel that doubled as purse and briefcase and probably contained her service weapon as well.

"I can give you a ride," she said.

50

Mendenhall drove her company car toward Hollywood. Bosch judged that there had been a purpose beyond courtesy to her offering to give him a ride. After telling her he lived in the Cahuenga Pass, he got down to business, turning in his seat to look at her. She was a brunette with dark eyes and smooth skin. Bosch put her at late forties. Looking at her hands on the wheel, he saw no rings. He remembered that from Modesto. No rings.

"So, how come you ended up with this mess?" he asked.

"I would say it's because of my familiarity with you. Your last interaction with IA is in litigation, so that created a conflict of interest with O'Dell. I was next on the list because of Modesto."

Bosch's lawsuit against the department for unfair labor practices named IAD investigator Martin O'Dell as a defendant along with several others involved in his being forced to retire. A few years before, Bosch had worked a case in which Mendenhall had trailed him to Modesto on suspicion that he was acting outside the policies of the department. She ended up helping him escape from captors who intended to kill him and clearing him of any departmental wrongdoing. The episode left Bosch with something he had never known before—respect for an Internal Affairs investigator. There had been a connection between them in Modesto. But because at the time he was the subject of an investigation being conducted by her, Bosch never did anything about it.

"Let me ask you something," he said.

"You can ask me anything, Harry," she said. "But I'm not promising to answer. Some things I can't talk about. But just like before, you be straight with me, I'll be straight with you."

"Fair enough."

"Which way should I go, Laurel Canyon up to Mulholland or down to Highland and then up?"

"Uh, I'd take Laurel Canyon."

His suggested route would take longer than the other choice. He hoped to be able to use the extra time to draw more information out of her.

"So, did Ellington tell you ahead of time to give me a ride? Maybe get me to talk outside the room?"

"No, it was just spur of the moment. You needed a ride. I offered. If you want to tell more, I'll certainly listen."

"There is something more, but let me ask a few questions first. Let's start with Ellis and Long. Big surprise today in IAD, or were they a known quantity?"

"Well, you really don't beat around the bush, do you?"

"They're bad cops. You guys go after bad cops. I'm just wondering if they were already on the radar."

"I can't go into specifics, but, yes, they were on the radar. The thing is, we're not even remotely talking about the level of action we are looking at today. It involved use of time complaints, insubordination. But usually when you have those things happening, they're indicators of bigger problems."

"So no external complaints. All department bred."

"No, none."

"What about Long? Is he going to make it?"

"He'll recover."

"Is he talking?"

"Last I heard, not yet."

"And nobody's got a line on Ellis?"

"Not yet, but not for lack of trying. It's a Sheriff's Department op, but we're all over it. RHD, Major Crimes, Fugitives—they don't want this to blow up into another Dorner. They want a quick end to it."

Christopher Dorner was an ex-LAPD cop who went on a killing rampage a couple years before. A massive manhunt ended at a cabin near Big Bear where he killed himself during a firefight with officers who had surrounded the location. His notoriety was such that within the department his last name had become a noun applied to any officer controversy or scandal involving crazy and deadly behavior.

"So, the big question," Bosch said, "is whether there's a case? Are they going to be charged?"

"That's actually two big questions," Mendenhall said. "The answers, as far as I'm concerned, are yes and yes. But it's a Sheriff's case. You never know. We will be looking into anything on our turf, which includes James Allen and whatever else those two had going."

Bosch nodded and let some more asphalt go under the car before responding.

"So you want my coaching tip on Allen?" he asked.

"Of course," she said.

"Check out the UC car lot behind the Hollywood Athletic Club. On the back row against the wall is a burnt-orange Camaro that's been taken out of circulation."

"Okay."

"I'm pretty sure Ellis and Long were using it back in March when Allen got dumped in that alley."

"The trunk?"

Bosch nodded.

"I'll order a full forensic workup," she said.

"You get something, send a copy of the report to that asshole Cornell."

Bosch could see Mendenhall smile in the glow from the dash lights. They drove in silence for a while. She made the turn onto Mulholland and started east. When she spoke, it had nothing to do with the case at hand.

"Harry, I'm curious. Why didn't you call me after Modesto?"

Bosch was caught off guard.

"That's a curve ball," he managed to say while trying to formulate an answer.

"Sorry, I was just thinking out loud," she said. "It's just that I thought we had a connection when we were up there. Modesto. I thought you might call."

"Well, I just thought…you know, that with you being in IAD and me being investigated, it would have been uncool to follow up on anything. That could end up with you being the one investigated."

She nodded but didn't say anything. Bosch looked over at her and couldn't read her reaction.

"Forget it," she said. "I shouldn't have asked that. Very unprofessional. Keep asking your questions."

Bosch nodded.

"Okay," he said. "Well, what is the current thinking on Ellis and his whereabouts?"

"The current thinking is Mexico," she said. "He probably had a getaway package ready to go. Car, money, probably multiple IDs. He lived alone and it looks like he never went back after he left Schubert's office."

"He's in the wind."

She nodded.

"He could be anywhere."

51

Ellis waited in darkness, his face a dim shade of blue cast by the light of a phone screen. He waited to take care of the last detail before his exit. His final touch and statement on this place that had changed him in so many ways.

He checked his news feed and reread the story. It contained the slimmest grouping of facts and had not been updated in at least two hours. He knew it was all that would be released tonight. The press conference had been scheduled for the morning, when the sheriff and chief of police would share a podium and address the media together. Ellis considered sticking around to watch it live on local TV, to see how the chief tried to spin it. But his survival instinct overrode that desire. He knew that the hours in between would be best used to put distance between himself and the city. This ugly city that hollows people, corrodes them from the inside out.

Besides, he would get everything on the news feed. The story would no doubt break big and national. Especially after they found Bosch. And after they found the twins.

He thought about the twins. They had not been watching the news. They knew nothing and expected nothing but the usual from him. Even when they saw the weapon in his hand, they believed he was there to protect them from some outside threat. They died thinking that.

He opened the photo app on the phone and went to the archives. He had taken three shots of the twins in final repose. But he realized it was impossible to tell that they were dead in these photos. Their faces had been so sculpted and stretched and reshaped by surgeries as to look frozen in both life and death.

After a while he went back to the news feed once more. Still nothing new on the events in Schubert's office. There wasn't even an update on Long's medical status. All that had been reported so far was that he was alive and being treated at Cedars, where he was listed in critical condition.

Long's name had not been put out publicly. The stories just said he was an LAPD vice officer who was off duty at the time of the shooting. No explanation was offered for what he was doing at the plastic surgery center where the events occurred.

There was no mention of Ellis either. No word that they were looking for him or that he had even been at the site. All of that would come in the morning when the chief of police stood before the media and tried to put the spin on another story of cops gone wrong.

Ellis wondered how much time he would have before Long started talking. He had no doubt that it would happen eventually. Long was the weak one. He could be manipulated. That was why Ellis had chosen him. But now the others would manipulate him. The investigators. The interrogators. The attorneys. They would squeeze him, break him down, and then finally give him a glimpse of light, and he would go for it. It would be a false light but he would not know that.

Once more Ellis reviewed his situation. Had he ever

made any mention to Long about his exit strategy? The getaway plan was only as good as its self-containment. It only worked if just one person knew the plan, and once more Ellis reassured himself that Long knew nothing. He was safe.

52

After being dropped off in front of his house, Bosch went into the carport to the Cherokee. Sutton had kept the keys to Bosch's rental car but not the ring that had his house and personal car keys on it. He quietly unlocked the Jeep's front door and leaned in behind the wheel. He reached under the driver's seat and then up into the springs. His hand found the grip of the Kimber Ultra Carry. He brought it out and checked the action and the magazine. It had served as his backup gun for the last decade of his LAPD career. He put a bullet into the chamber and was good to go.

From a low crouch he unlocked the kitchen door and pushed it open. As it swung into the house, he raised his weapon but was greeted with only a still darkness. He reached up and in and flicked the double switches on the inside wall. The lights in the galley kitchen as well as the hallway beyond came on.

Bosch advanced through the kitchen and flicked the same lights off when he got to the opposite end. He didn't want to be illuminated as he stepped into the hallway and farther into the house.

Bosch moved slowly and cautiously through his home, lighting rooms as he searched them. There was no sign of Ellis. When he got to the last room—his daughter's bedroom—he turned around and cleared every room and closet again.

Satisfied that his hunch that Ellis might make a move against him was wrong, Bosch started to relax. He turned on the lights in the living room and went to the stereo. He hit the power button and put the needle down on the album already on the turntable. He didn't even look to see what it was.

He put his gun down on the stereo receiver and, stripping his jacket off, tossed it over to the couch. He was dead tired from the long and strenuous day but too keyed up for sleep. The first strains of trumpet rose from the speakers and Bosch knew it was Wynton Marsalis playing "The Majesty of the Blues," an old one he had picked up recently on vinyl. The song seemed appropriate to the moment. He opened the slider and stepped out onto the back deck.

He went to the railing and exhaled deeply. The night air was crisp and carried the scent of eucalyptus. Bosch checked his watch and decided it was too late to call Haller and update him. He'd make contact in the morning, probably after seeing how the LAPD and Sheriff's Department played things out at the press conference that was sure to be scheduled. What the sheriff and chief of police said would surely dictate Haller's strategy.

He leaned down, put his elbows on the railing, and looked at the freeway at the bottom of the pass. It was after midnight and yet the traffic persisted in both directions. It was always that way. Bosch was unsure that he would ever be able to sleep comfortably in a house without the background sound of the freeway from below.

He realized that he should have entered the house the way his daughter always did after school. That is, immediately stopping at the refrigerator upon entering through the kitchen door. In his case a nice cold beer would have tasted perfect right about now.

He heard the voice behind him before he heard anything else.

"Bosch."

He turned slowly, and there was a figure shrouded in the darkness of the back corner of the deck, where even the faint moonlight was blocked by the roof's eave. Bosch realized he had walked right past him when he stepped onto the deck. The shadows in the corner were too deep to see a face but he knew the voice.

"Ellis," Bosch said. "What are you doing here? What do you want?"

The figure stepped forward. First the pointed gun entered the dim moonlight, then Ellis. Bosch looked past him into the living room where he could see the Kimber left on the stereo receiver. It would do him no good now.

"What do you think I want?" Ellis said. "Did you think I would just run without paying you a visit?"

"I didn't think you were that stupid," Bosch said. "I thought you were the smart one."

"Stupid? I'm not the one who came home alone."

"You should have gone to Mexico while you had the head start."

"Mexico is so obvious, Bosch. I have other plans. Just have to finish up a little bit of business here."

"That's right, you're a no-loose-ends sort of guy."

"I couldn't risk that you wouldn't give it up. We checked you out, Bosch. Retired and relentless are two things that don't mesh together very well. I couldn't risk that you'd keep looking for me. The department will give it up. Bringing me back for trial is not something that's going to make anybody's priority list at the PAB. But you...I figured I needed to end it right here before going."

Ellis took another step toward Bosch, closing the distance for the shot. He fully emerged from the darkness. Bosch could see his face. The skin was drawn tight around eyes that had a wet glint at their black center. Bosch realized it might be the last face he ever saw.

"Going where?" he asked.

Harry raised his hands slowly, out to his sides, as if to underscore his vulnerability. To let Ellis know he had won and allow him the moment.

There was a pause and then Ellis answered.

"Belize. There's a beach there. And a place I can't be traced to."

Bosch knew then that he had a chance. Ellis wanted to talk, to gloat, even.

"Tell me about Alexandra Parks," he said.

Ellis smirked. He knew Bosch's play.

"I don't think I want to give you that," he said. "You need to take that one with you."

Ellis calibrated the aim of his weapon, bringing the muzzle up in case Bosch was wearing a vest. From this close he couldn't miss with a face shot.

Bosch looked over his killer's shoulder once more into the living room and at the gun he had left behind. A fatal mistake.

Then he saw movement in the house. Mendenhall was in the living room, moving toward the open door of the deck. Between the music inside and the freeway outside, Ellis would not hear her. She was closing on him, gun raised in a two-handed grip and ready.

Bosch looked at Ellis.

"Then let me ask you something else," he said. "You and Long watched me. You know about my daughter. What would have happened if she were here tonight when you came?"

Bosch could see a smile form in the shadows of his killer's face.

"What would have happened is she would have been dead before you got here," Ellis said. "I would've let you find her."

Bosch held his eyes. He thought of the crime scene photos of Alexandra Parks. The brutality inflicted on her. He wanted to make a move toward Ellis, to go for his throat. But he would be expecting that.

Instead, he stood still. He saw that Mendenhall was on the threshold between the house and the deck. He knew that as soon as she stepped onto one of the wooden planks, Ellis would know she was there. Bosch slightly changed his stance to try to cover her advance.

"Why don't you just do it now?" he said.

Mendenhall took the last two steps up behind Ellis and then, without pause, there was the sharp sound of a shot that seemed to echo right through Bosch's chest.

Ellis dropped to the deck without firing a shot. Bosch felt a fine mist of blood hit him full in the face.

For a moment he and Mendenhall stood there facing each other. Then Mendenhall dropped to her knees next to Ellis and quickly cuffed his hands behind his back, following policy and procedure even though it was clear he was not a threat to anyone. She then took out her phone and hit a speed-dial number. While she waited for the call to go through, she looked up at Bosch, who had not moved more than an inch since Ellis had pointed the gun at him.

"You okay?" she asked. "I was worried about a through-and-through shot hitting you."

Bosch bent over for a moment, putting his hands on his knees.

"I'm good," Bosch said. "That was close. I was seeing the end of things, you know what I mean?"

"I think so," Mendenhall said.

"What do you want me to do?"

"Uh, how about you go in and find a seat. Let's keep the deck clear. I'm calling everybody out."

Just then her call was answered and she identified herself and gave the house's address. In a voice as calm as the one she'd use to order a pizza, she asked for a rescue ambulance and a supervisor. She stressed that the scene was secured and then disconnected. Bosch knew she had been talking to the communications center and had been circumspect in the details she offered because she didn't want to draw the media. There were police scanners in every newsroom in the city.

Mendenhall next made a call to her boss, Ellington, and informed him in more detail of what had just occurred. When she was finished with that call she came inside the house to where Bosch was sitting on the couch in the living room.

"You turned off the music," she said.

"Yeah, I thought I should," he said.

"What was that?"

"Wynton Marsalis. 'The Majesty of the Blues.'"

"It covered me, you know. Ellis didn't hear me come up on him."

"If I ever meet Wynton, I'll thank him. That's twice now, you know."

"What's twice?"

"That you've saved my life."

She shrugged.

"To protect and serve—you know the deal."

"It's more than that. What made you come back?"

"Your tip about the burnt-orange Camaro. There's one parked around the bend. I go by it on my way down the hill and think, *That's him, he's waiting for Bosch.* So I came back."

"And the door? I'm pretty sure I locked it."

"Internal Affairs one-oh-one. I've planted a lot of

bugs in my time. I know my way around a lock with a pick."

"Impressive, Mendenhall. But you know you'll probably pay for this—in the department. Doesn't matter that he was bent. You killed a cop."

"I had no choice," she said. "It was a good shooting and I'm not worried."

"It was right as rain but there still will be blowback."

Bosch knew that department policy held that deadly force was justified if it was used to prevent imminent death or great bodily harm to an officer or a citizen. Mendenhall was not required to identify herself or give Ellis the opportunity to drop his weapon. Her coming up behind him and putting a round into his brain was within policy. She would be quickly cleared by the internal-shooting review board and then the District Attorney's Office. It would be in the opinion of her peers and the innuendo and gossip that would follow her in the department that she might not fare so well.

Mendenhall looked out the open door at the body and Bosch saw her trying to control a momentary tremor within her own body. It was a response that often came after a shooting.

"You okay?" he asked.

"I'm good," she said. "Just sort of…I just killed a man, you know?"

Bosch nodded.

"And you saved one," he said. "Remember that."

"I will," she said. "What was he saying? At the end. I couldn't hear anything when I was coming up behind him. The music covered that, too."

Bosch paused before answering. He realized he had an opportunity here. Mendenhall had heard nothing. There was no witness to what Ellis said to him on the deck. What Bosch said now would be considered contemporaneous recall by the courts and given the weight of truth when repeated from the witness stand. He knew that he could guarantee Da'Quan Foster's freedom by saying that Ellis had gloated that he and Long had murdered Alexandra Parks, that he had admitted everything.

Bosch thought about all the invisible lines he had crossed in the week he had worked the case. An image came to mind; a man with an umbrella struggling for balance on a tightrope. That man was Bosch.

He decided this was one line he couldn't cross.

"He didn't say much other than that he was going to Belize," he said. "He just wanted to make sure I was dead before he split."

Mendenhall nodded.

"Big mistake," she said.

53

Bosch was soon haunted by his decision not to lie and say Ellis had admitted he and Long killed Alexandra Parks. In the days following the vice cop's death, the charges in the Parks murder remained lodged against Da'Quan Foster as the Sheriff's Department dragged its feet on the investigation. Long was charged with a variety of crimes, including the murder of Dr. George Schubert under the felony-murder law that held him responsible for his co-conspirator's actions. But the official stand on the Parks case remained unchanged. The Sheriff's Department refused to acknowledge that the murder charge against Foster was the result of a complex frame-up orchestrated by Ellis and Long.

Bureaucracy, politics, and the inability of public institutions to humbly acknowledge mistakes were all to blame. The two law enforcement agencies were biding their time, refusing comment on what they termed an ongoing joint investigation into the relationship between the murders of Alexandra Parks, James Allen, Peter and Paul Nguyen, and George Schubert. The slayings of Deborah Stovall and Josette Leroux, professionally known on the porno circuit as Ashley Juggs and Annie Minx, were also folded in as part of the joint investigation. All the while, Foster remained in the L.A. County Jail on a no-bail hold.

The law enforcement agencies might have been engulfed by inertia, but Foster's attorney was a blur of forward motion. When charges against his client were not immediately dropped in the aftermath of Ellis's death and the charging of Long with murder, Mickey Haller filed an emergency 995 motion to overturn the findings of the preliminary hearing based on new evidence—a lot of new evidence. A week later, on a Thursday morning when the temperature in downtown had already ticked past 80 degrees by the 8 a.m. call to order, Mickey Haller stood before Judge Joseph Sackville in Department 114 of the Criminal Courts Building.

One thing that was different from the last time Bosch had seen Haller perform in court was that Bosch was now a participant rather than an observer. Haller would call Bosch as his only witness and use him to introduce the recording taken during the interview and then shoot-out in Schubert's office. He would also ask him to detail the steps of his investigation of the Parks murder and its connection to the murder of James Allen.

Foster would not be called to the witness stand. It was too risky a move. Any misstep in his testimony could be used against him later at trial should Haller be unsuccessful in his bid to overturn the judge's ruling at the preliminary hearing. The details of his alibi could be covered in Bosch's summary of his investigation. Bosch's experience testifying in trials for more than three decades made him the easy choice over Foster.

Bosch's testimony had been carefully choreographed by Haller in a two-day run-up to the hearing. Haller made sure Bosch's testimony thoroughly covered the defense theory that Foster was framed with his own

DNA, obtained by Ellis and Long through James Allen. Ellis and Allen were dead and Long was not cooperating. The burden was all on Bosch.

A large audience filled the courtroom. The case had grown to involve seven murders plus the justifiable killing of LAPD Officer Don Ellis. Eight deaths in all made it the biggest thing going in the courthouse or anywhere else in the city, and it was drawing maximum exposure in the media. Local, national, and international reporters crowded the benches in the courtroom gallery. They were supplemented by lawyers and investigators with tangential parts of the case, and various other casual observers. Bosch's daughter was in the front row behind the defense table, having taken off one of her last remaining days of high school to attend. She was sitting next to Mendenhall, who also had a vested interest in the outcome of the hearing. Noticeably absent from the courtroom was Foster's own family. He had told Haller not to invite or tell his wife about the hearing for fear she would hear testimony about her husband's lifestyle choices that would jeopardize their marriage. It would probably be impossible to keep it from her but at least she wouldn't be on display in a crowded courtroom when the details were aired.

In the row behind the prosecution table sat the widower, Sheriff's Deputy Vincent Harrick, in full uniform. He sat between two other uniformed deputies, there to show support for their colleague and to triple down on the message to the judge that Harrick stood solidly behind the Sheriff's Department investigation, which still pointed the finger at Da'Quan Foster.

At times as he watched from the witness stand, Bosch wondered whether Haller was playing to the judge or the media. It was his practice to ask a question and when the prosecutor objected, to look at the judge first and then at the gathered members of the media in the gallery.

The deputy district attorney assigned to handle the hearing was named Brad Landreth. He was replacing Ellen Tasker for the announced reason that the 995 hearing conflicted with a trial she was finishing. But the inside word was that the District Attorney's Office viewed the case as a wounded duck that wasn't going to fly. They took one of their top prosecutors off it to keep her trial record blemish-free. Landreth's un-enviable job was to try to keep the case on the rails while the Sheriff's Department and the LAPD continued the glacier-like progress of their investigation. Bosch viewed Landreth as a talented and hardworking prosecutor but not one who would be a match for Mickey Haller.

With multiple objections from Landreth being routinely overruled, it took Haller almost two hours to lead Bosch through his testimony and the introduction of what was now called the Schubert recording. Since the hearing was only before a judge, Haller adopted an informal presentation and never stood during the examination. He remained sitting at the defense table next to Foster, who was clad in a blue jailhouse jumpsuit.

Haller and Bosch hit all the notes they had planned and rehearsed and then it was Landreth's opportunity for cross-examination. He rose from his seat and went to the lectern, choosing the more formal and perhaps more intimidating stance to question the former police detective.

Rather than attack Bosch's story on its merits, Landreth chose to potshot Bosch's methods, his skirting of legalities and shading of truthfulness. He adopted the timeworn strategy of attacking the messenger if the message is unassailable. The exchange regarding each person encountered during Bosch's investigation was repeated several times:

Landreth: "Did you tell this individual that you were a police officer?"

Bosch: "No, I did not."

Landreth: "But isn't it true that you did not dissuade him from his belief that he was indeed talking to a sworn law enforcement officer?"

Bosch: "No, not true. He didn't think I was a police officer because I never told him I was. I had no badge, no gun, and I didn't say I was a cop."

The strategy grew tiresome for everyone in the courtroom, especially Judge Sackville, who had allotted only the morning's hours for the hearing. He was soon ruling on objections before Haller could completely articulate them. He repeatedly ordered Landreth to move along and finally told the prosecutor that he was wasting the court's valuable time.

Landreth finally ended his cross and Bosch was able to step down and take a seat at the defense table next to Haller. Sitting there gave Bosch an uneasy feeling. He felt like he was on the wrong side of the room, as though he were driving a car with the steering wheel on the right.

Haller didn't notice his discomfort. He drummed his fingers on the table as he contemplated his next move. The judge finally prompted him.

"Mr. Haller, do you have another witness?"

Haller leaned toward Bosch and whispered in his ear.

"Let's roll the dice here, see if we can't get them to step into the bear trap."

He then stood up and addressed the court.

"No other witnesses, Your Honor. The defense is ready to argue the matter."

As Haller sat back down, Sackville turned his attention to Landreth.

"Does the state wish to call witnesses?" he asked.

Landreth stood.

"The state calls Sheriff's Detective Lazlo Cornell."

Cornell rose from his position at the prosecution table and walked to the witness stand. After being sworn in by the clerk, he began his testimony, with Landreth leading him through the steps of his own investigation of the Alexandra Parks murder.

Bosch leaned back at one point and glanced at his daughter. He nodded and she nodded back. He then glanced from Maddie to Mendenhall and they caught eyes. A small smile played on the Internal Affairs detective's face. Earlier, in the hallway outside the courtroom, Bosch had introduced Mendenhall to his daughter as the woman who had saved his life twice. It had embarrassed Mendenhall and maybe Maddie, but Harry was happy that he had made the introduction in the way he had.

Landreth used Cornell to hammer down the horror of the murder of Alexandra Parks and the painstaking detail of the crime scene investigation and subsequent autopsy. This eventually led to specific testimony detailing the collection of semen from locations on and inside the body and Cornell's professional opinion that the DNA material had been deposited during a brutal sexual assault and not planted.

Harrick remained in the courtroom through all of this testimony, his chin up and resolute, holding strong for his wife. His demeanor left no doubt that he believed he was sitting only twelve feet from his wife's killer. The machinations of the defense were just that to him. An attempt to manipulate the truth. He remained in solidarity with the official line.

Landreth concluded Cornell's testimony with a soft-ball roundup question about his final conclusions.

"I believe at this time and based on my lengthy experience investigating rape-murders that Ms. Parks was indeed raped and that the semen found on her thigh, on the sheets, and in her vagina was deposited by her attacker during the assault. It was not planted. It was not brought to the scene. I find that to be preposterous."

Landreth turned the questioning over to Haller.

"Detective Cornell, did any of the investigators or forensics people recover a condom at the crime scene?"

Cornell seemed to scoff at the question.

"No," he said. "There was a substantial amount of semen collected and no indication that a condom was used in this crime. The semen collected from the body and the sheets was indicative of no condom. It was the killer's mistake."

"The killer's mistake," Haller repeated. "This is a killer who you say carefully stalked his victim, correct?"

"That is correct."

"And carefully planned this murder, correct?"

"Correct."

"Knew that the victim did not own a dog despite the sign at the front of her house, right?"

"We think so."

"And broke in through a rear window while the victim slept, correct?"

"Correct."

"So it's your testimony based on your experience and knowledge of this case that the killer did all of these things, carefully selected and stalked this victim, then meticulously planned and carried out this murder, but then just forgot to bring a condom?"

"It's possible that he brought a condom but didn't use

it. It is quite possible that in the frenzy of the attack, he forgot to use it."

"The frenzy? So now you are saying it was a frenzied attack? I thought you testified that it was a carefully planned attack."

"All I know is that it was one of the most brutal I've seen in fourteen years with the Homicide Unit. The brutality indicated a loss of control during the assault."

The judge stepped in at that point and called for the midmorning break. He told all participants in the hearing to be back in place in fifteen minutes, then jumped up from the bench and disappeared through the door to his chambers.

54

As soon as the courtroom was back in session and Cornell returned to the witness stand, Haller moved in for the kill.

"Were the bathrooms in that house checked, Detective Cornell?" he asked. "The sink traps, I mean, or the toilets to see if the killer had flushed a condom?"

"No," Cornell said, a tone of annoyance in his voice. "First of all, that's TV. If somebody flushes a condom, that thing is gone. But there was no need. The suspect's semen was all over the crime scene and the victim. We weren't looking for a condom."

"I stand corrected, then," Haller said. "This semen that you said was all over the place, what did you do with it?"

"It was collected by forensics and then submitted to the Sheriff's Department's lab for analysis. From there it was submitted to the California Department of Justice for comparison to the state's DNA data bank."

"And that's how it was matched up with Mr. Foster, correct?"

"That is correct."

"So you just mentioned analysis. What kind of analysis are we talking about?"

"DNA is extracted from the submitted material. They analyze proteins, blood groupings, chromosome characteristics, several different factors. All of these characteristics or markers are what is put into the data bank."

Haller picked up a file and for the first time stood up and went to the lectern between the prosecution and defense tables. The teeth of the bear trap had just clamped on Cornell's leg, only he didn't know it yet.

"Detective Cornell," Haller said, "did your lab's analysis include checking the DNA material you submitted from this case for CTE?"

Cornell grinned like he was putting up with this annoying little tilt at a windmill from Haller.

"No," he said.

"Do you know what CTE is, Detective?" Haller asked.

"Condom Trace Evidence."

"So why didn't the lab check for CTE?"

"Checking for CTE is not part of the standard protocol for DNA analysis. It's an extra. If you want that, then it needs to be submitted to an outside lab."

"And you didn't want it?"

"As I said before, there was no indication at the crime scene, the autopsy, or anywhere else that a condom was used in the commission of this murder."

"But how would you know that if you didn't look for a condom or ask the lab to check the DNA for it?"

Cornell looked at Landreth and then at the judge and raised his hands palms up.

"I can't answer that," he said. "That doesn't make sense."

"It does to me," Haller said.

Moving faster than Landreth could object, Sackville admonished Haller not to editorialize.

"Ask questions, Mr. Haller," he said.

"Yes, Your Honor," Haller said. "Detective Cornell,

you are aware that this court ordered the state to share some of that collected DNA with the defense for its own analysis, are you not?"

"Yes," Cornell said.

Haller then made a motion asking the judge to allow him to submit the defense's DNA analysis report as an exhibit and to allow Cornell to read from it. This set off a protracted argument from Landreth, who attacked the report on two levels. In the first, he accused Haller of a discovery violation because the lab report he wished to introduce had not previously been turned over to the prosecution. In the second attack, Landreth objected to Haller's wish to have Cornell read from a lab report for which there had been no foundation established.

"He waltzes in here with this lab report we've never even heard of," Landreth said sarcastically. "Added to that, we don't know what lab even did it, what technician performed this analysis. Mr. Haller has laid no foundation whatsoever. As far as we know, he may have picked this report up at Walmart on his way into court this morning."

Landreth sat down proudly after assuming that he had hit it out of the park. What he didn't realize was that it is hard to round the bases when you're dragging a bear trap clamped to your ankle.

Haller stood and returned to the lectern. He first turned and looked at Landreth.

"Walmart?" he said. "Really?"

He then looked at the judge and proceeded to tear Landreth's objections to shreds.

"First, Your Honor, I would like to submit to the court a copy of an e-mail that shows that two days ago the lab report being questioned by Mr. Landreth was sent by me to Ellen Tasker, who at that time—as far as the defense knew—was the prosecutor assigned to this case."

Haller held a printout of the e-mail up over his head, waving it like a flag. Landreth objected but Sackville said he wanted to see the document. Haller walked to the bench and handed it over. As the judge read the e-mail, Haller continued his argument.

"The lab report was in the hands of the District Attorney's Office and the defense is not liable for that office's communication issues, Your Honor."

Landreth stood to object but Sackville cut him off.

"You had your objection on that, Mr. Landreth," he said. "We're moving on to foundation. Mr. Haller?"

"Your Honor, this is not a trial," Haller said. "This is a challenge to the findings of the court in a preliminary hearing. In that hearing the court allowed the state to offer hearsay testimony through Detective Cornell, who introduced its DNA report without establishing foundation through lab personnel. The defense simply wishes to have the equal opportunity."

It was true. Under the state's constitution, hearsay evidence was allowed into a preliminary hearing as a means of speeding the process. The prosecution could introduce hearsay evidence through its investigators, allowing them to summarize witness statements and avoiding the lengthy process of calling individual witnesses to testify.

The judge quickly made a ruling.

"Mr. Haller, you may proceed," Sackville said. "We can always hit rewind if I don't like where we're going."

Haller stepped up and gave copies of the lab report to Landreth, Cornell, and the judge, then returned to the lectern. After leading Cornell through several questions designed to identify the report and the independent lab that analyzed the DNA material, he asked Cornell to read a highlighted section of the summary regarding CTE. Cornell read the section with the same annoyed tone that had inflected most of his testimony.

"Test analysis of submitted genetic material contained condom trace evidence including particulate lycopodium and amorphous silica. Cited combination of CTE materials is found in condoms manufactured by Lessius Latex Products of Dallas, Texas, and distributed in its branded line called Rainbow Pride."

Haller paused after the reading for several seconds before proceeding.

"So, Detective Cornell, you previously testified you did not look for a condom at the crime scene because no condom took part in this crime. How do you explain the findings of this report?"

"I don't," Cornell said. "It's not our report. It's your report."

"Are you suggesting that this report is phony, that the findings are false?"

"I'm just saying it is not our report and so I am unfamiliar with it."

Cornell was losing his swagger. His tone was now more harried than annoyed.

"This case is still under investigation by a task force looking at all of the murders with some possible association with Officers Ellis and Long, correct?"

"Yes, but as I testified earlier, we have found no evidence connecting them to Alexandra Parks. Your client's DNA is the connection. He remains the suspect."

"Thank you for reminding the court, Detective Cornell. But as part of that joint investigation, have you looked at evidence, reports, and photos from all of these cases, or have you not bothered with that because you are so sure about Mr. Foster being your man?"

"We have reviewed all the evidence of all the cases."

"A moment, Your Honor."

Haller walked back to the defense table and reached under the table for a bag. He took it back to the lectern and then removed from it a large clear plastic container half filled with individually wrapped and different-colored condoms. As he placed it at the front of the lectern, Landreth stood and objected.

"Your Honor, what does counsel think he is doing?" he asked. "The state objects to this grandstanding and prejudicial display."

"Mr. Haller," the judge said sternly. "What is this demonstration?"

From his file Haller produced another document.

"Your Honor, this affidavit offers the sworn statement of a person named Andre Masters, who was a close friend of the murder victim James Allen. He states that this container of Rainbow Pride condoms was recovered from Mr. Allen's belongings after his murder. These are belongings the investigators of the murder did not collect. This is the same brand of condoms from which the CTE found in and on Alexandra Parks came. This is direct linkage between these two murders and it directly supports the defense theory that Da'Quan Foster was set up for this murder by Officers Ellis and Long."

Haller's response was punctuated by objections from Landreth but Sackville had not stopped Haller from finishing his explanation. After a pause, the judge responded.

"Let me take a look at that affidavit."

Haller walked a copy up to the bench and then gave one to Landreth. For the next few minutes the judge and prosecutor silently reviewed the statement. Bosch had found Masters and recovered the container of condoms a few days earlier when he finally returned to Haven House and paid the manager fifty dollars for Masters's cell-phone number.

"Your Honor," Landreth said. "The strange origin of this statement and the purported chain of custody of this, this, this condom container aside, the only evidence you have here is unreliable. Additionally, we once again have a discovery violation. The state was not provided with this affidavit until this very moment. Therefore, the state objects to its inclusion as an exhibit and moves that it be disallowed in the questioning of Detective Cornell. Smoke and mirrors, Your Honor."

As Landreth sat down, Haller countered.

"Your Honor, two things very quickly. First, I have here another copy of an e-mail, this one to the prosecutor previously assigned to this case. This affidavit from Mr. Masters was sent to her as well, meaning there was no discovery violation on the part of the defense. And second, Your Honor, the defense offers three exhibits from the LAPD murder book from the James Allen investigation. These are LAPD crime scene photographs that clearly depict the container of condoms in the victim's motel room on the day his murder was discovered. It is a match to what you see right here."

Haller walked the e-mail and photos up to the judge and then went back to the lectern. Bosch saw him wink at Maddie in the first row as he returned.

The judge took his time with the documents and the photos in front of him. The courtroom was so quiet Bosch could hear the air conditioner kick on above the ceiling.

Finally, the judge stacked the affidavits and photos together and leaned toward his microphone to speak.

"The court finds this evidence and the testimony brought by the defense compelling and exculpatory, while the state's own witness is unconvincing. The court hereby finds upon review of new evidence that the cause of the preliminary hearing is set aside. The charges against the defendant are dismissed. The state is free to reinstate the charges when and if it can meet the threshold of probable cause. Mr. Foster, you are free to go. You should be sure to thank your attorney for his thoroughness and zeal. Court is now adjourned."

And just like that it was over. The silence in the courtroom held as the judge stepped down from the bench and left through the door to his chambers. Then a burst of surprised conversation broke out throughout the room. Haller turned to Bosch first to shake hands.

"You did it," Bosch said.

"No, you did it," Haller said. "We make a good team."

Haller then turned toward his client and put an arm over his shoulder as he hugged and congratulated him. Bosch was left odd man out at the table and so he turned to look back at his daughter. She was beaming.

"Yay, Dad!"

He smiled and nodded, uneasy with the victory. He had to admit he was happy, and it was the first time he had ever felt that way after hearing charges of murder being dismissed. It would take some getting used to.

55

In the hallway outside the courtroom, the show belonged to Haller. Landreth didn't stick around. Cornell and Harrick didn't stick around. And Foster had to be processed out of custody and wouldn't actually be a free man for at least a couple more hours. That left Haller. The media from around the world surrounded him in an undulating circle of cameras, recorders, and microphones extended toward his face. He was like the guy who hit the walk-off home run at the World Series. They were three deep from all sides and Haller kept turning, looking high and low, giving everyone an opportunity to ask questions and hear his sage and sometimes wry responses. From his pocket he pulled a thick stack of business cards and handed them out as he spoke, making sure the reporters had his name right. The best advertising is free advertising.

Bosch stood off to the side with his daughter and watched the spectacle.

"This is amazing," Maddie said.

"Just don't get any ideas," Bosch said. "One defense lawyer in the family is enough."

"All right if I get closer up there to listen?"

"Sure, just don't get eaten by those sharks. It's a feeding frenzy."

Maddie rolled her eyes and went off to approach the media knot.

Bosch looked around and saw Mendenhall standing a few yards away in the secondary ring of hallway observers. She was fascinated by the media spectacle as well. Bosch sauntered over and they spoke while keeping their eyes on the center scrum.

"Thanks for coming today," he said.

"I wouldn't have missed it," she said. "By the way, your daughter is very proud of you. I can tell."

"For now."

"No, forever."

He smiled and nodded. He hoped so.

"I hope you have an unlisted number," Mendenhall said. "People are going to be calling you and Haller. Every innocent man in the system."

Bosch shook his head.

"Not me," he said. "I'm one and done."

"Really? You?" she asked. "So, what's next?"

Bosch shrugged and thought for a moment. Then he took his eyes off the circus and looked at her.

"I've got an old Harley. A nineteen-fifty panhead that needs its carburetor back in place. Actually, it needs a lot of things back in place. That's next. It's the same bike Lee Marvin rode in *The Wild One*. You ever see it?"

"I don't think so."

"You ride, Mendenhall?"

Now she took her eyes off the circus and looked at him.

"Not in a long time."

"Me neither. Give me a couple weeks and I'll call you. We'll ride."

"I'd like that."

Bosch nodded, then stepped away and walked over to get his daughter. It was time to go home.

ACKNOWLEDGMENTS

The author enjoyed the company and help of many fine people during the research, writing, and editing of this novel. Many thanks go to the real detectives—Tim Marcia, Rick Jackson, Mitzi Roberts, and David Lambkin—for their efforts to make Harry Bosch and his world as real as possible. Other readers whose help was just as important include Daniel Daly, Roger Mills, Henrik Bastin, John Houghton, Terrill Lee Lankford, Jane Davis, Heather Rizzo, and Linda Connelly. Additionally, thanks go to researcher Dennis "Cisco" Wojciechowski (watch-your-house-key). Three fine editors somehow made sense of the whole mess and to them the greatest debt of thanks is owed: Asya Muchnick, Bill Massey, and Pamela Marshall.

Many thanks to all.

ABOUT THE AUTHOR

Michael Connelly is the author of twenty-eight previous novels, including #1 *New York Times* bestsellers *The Crossing* and *The Burning Room*. His books, which include the Harry Bosch series and Lincoln Lawyer series, have sold more than sixty million copies worldwide. Connelly is a former newspaper reporter who has won numerous awards for his journalism and his novels and is the executive producer of *Bosch,* starring Titus Welliver. He spends his time in California and Florida.

New Job. Same Bosch.

Please turn the page for a
preview of

THE WRONG SIDE OF GOODBYE

Available in hardcover

*T*hey charged from the cover of the elephant grass toward the LZ, five of them swarming the slick on both sides, one among them yelling, "Go! Go! Go!"—as if each man needed to be prodded and reminded that these were the most dangerous seconds of their lives.

The rotor wash bent the grass back and blew the marker smoke in all directions. The noise was deafening as the turbine geared up for a heavy liftoff. The door gunners pulled everyone in by their pack straps and the chopper was quickly in the air again, having alighted no longer than a dragonfly on water.

The tree line could be seen through the portside door as the craft rose and started to bank. Then came the muzzle flashes from the banyan trees. Somebody yelled, "Snipers!"—as if the door gunner had to be told what he had out there.

It was an ambush. Three distinct flash points, three snipers. They had waited until the helicopter was up and flying fat, an easy target from six hundred feet.

The gunner opened up his M60, sending a barrage of fire into the treetops, shredding them with lead. But the sniper rounds kept coming. The slick had no armor plating, a decision made nine thousand miles away to take speed and maneuverability over the burden of weight and protection.

One shot hit the turbine cowling, a thock sound reminding one of the helpless men on board of a fouled-off baseball hitting the hood of a car in the parking lot. Then came the snap of glass shattering as the next round tore through the cockpit. It was a million-to-one shot, hitting both the pilot and co-pilot at once. The pilot was killed instantly and the co-pilot clamped his hands to his neck in an instinctive but helpless move to keep blood inside his body. The helicopter yawed into a clockwise spin and was soon hurtling out of control. It spun away from the trees and across the rice paddies. The men in the back started to yell helplessly. The man who had just had a memory of baseball tried to orient himself. The world outside the slick was spinning. He kept his eyes on a single word imprinted on the metal wall separating the cockpit from the cargo hold. It said Advance—the letter A with a crossbar that was an arrow pointed forward.

He didn't move his eyes from the word even as the screaming intensified and he could feel the craft losing altitude. Seven months backing recon and now on short time. He knew he wasn't going to make it back. This was the end.

The last thing he heard was someone yell, "Brace! Brace! Brace!"—as if there was a possibility that anybody on board had a shot at surviving the impact, never mind the fire that would come after. And never mind the Vietcong who would come through with machetes after that.

While the others screamed in panic he whispered a name to himself.

"Vibiana…"

He knew he would never see her again.

"Vibiana…"

The helicopter dove into one of the rice paddy dikes and exploded into a million metal parts. A moment later the spilled fuel caught fire and burned through the wreckage, spreading flames across the surface of the paddy water. Black smoke rose into the air, marking the wreckage like an LZ marker.

The snipers reloaded and waited for the rescue choppers to come next.

1

Bosch didn't mind the wait. The view was spectacular. He didn't bother with the waiting room couch. Instead he stood with his face a foot from the glass and took in the view that ranged from the rooftops of downtown to the Pacific Ocean. He was fifty-nine floors up in the U.S. Bank Tower, and Creighton was making him wait because it was something he always did, going all the way back to his days at Parker Center, where the waiting room only had a low-angle view of the back of City Hall. Creighton had moved a mere five blocks west since his days with the Los Angeles Police Department but he certainly had risen far beyond that to the lofty heights of the city's financial gods.

Still, view or no view, Bosch didn't know why anyone would keep offices in the tower. The tallest building west of the Mississippi, it had previously been the target of two foiled terrorists plots. Bosch imagined there had to be a general uneasiness added to the pressures of work for every soul who entered its glass doors each morning. Relief might soon come in the form of the Wilshire Grand Center, a glass-sheathed spire rising to the sky a few blocks away. When finished it would take the distinction of tallest building west of the Mississippi. It would probably take the target as well.

Bosch loved any opportunity to see his city from up high. When he was a young detective he would often take extra shifts as a spotter in one of the Department's airships—just to take a ride above Los Angeles and be reminded of its seemingly infinite vastness.

He looked down at the 110 freeway and saw it was backed up all the way down through South-Central. He also noted the number of helipads on the tops of the buildings below him. The helicopter had become the commuter vessel of the elite. He had heard that even some of the higher-contract basketball players on the Lakers and Clippers took helos to work at the Staples Center.

The glass was thick enough to keep out any sound. The city below was silent. The only thing Bosch heard was the receptionist behind him answering the phone with same greeting over and over: "Trident Security, how can I help you?"

Bosch's eye held on a fast-moving patrol car going south on Figueroa toward the L.A. Live district. He saw the *01* painted large on the trunk and knew that the car was from Central Division. Soon it was followed in the air by an LAPD airship that moved at a lower altitude than the floor he stood on. Bosch was tracking it when he was pulled away by a voice from behind.

"Mr. Bosch?"

He turned to see a woman standing in the middle of the waiting room. She wasn't the receptionist.

"I'm Gloria. We spoke on the phone," she said.

"Right, yes," Bosch said. "Mr. Creighton's assistant."

"Yes, nice to meet you. You can come back now."

"Good. Any longer and I was going to jump."

She didn't smile. She led Bosch through a door into a hallway with framed watercolors perfectly spaced on the walls.

"It's impact-resistant glass," she said. "It can take the force of a category-five hurricane."

"Good to know," Bosch said. "And I was only joking. Your boss had a history of keeping people waiting—back when he was a deputy chief with the police department."

"Oh, really? I haven't noticed it here."

This made no sense to Bosch, since she had just fetched him from the waiting room fifteen minutes after the appointed meeting time.

"He must've read it in a management book back when he was climbing the ranks," Bosch said. "You know, keep 'em waiting even if they're on time. Gives you the upper hand when you finally bring them into the room, lets them know you are a busy man."

"I'm not familiar with that business philosophy."

"Probably more of a cop philosophy."

They entered an office suite. In the outer office, there were two separate desk arrangements, one occupied by a man in his twenties wearing a suit, and the other empty and, he assumed, belonging to Gloria. They walked between the desks to a door and Gloria opened it and then stepped to the side.

"Go on in," she said. "Can I bring you a bottle of water?"

"No, thanks," Bosch said. "I'm fine."

Bosch entered an even larger room, with a desk area to the left and an informal seating area to the right, where a couple of couches faced each other across a glass-topped coffee table. Creighton was sitting behind his desk, indicating Bosch's appointment was going to be formal.

It had been more than a decade since Bosch had seen Creighton in person. He could not remember the occasion but assumed it was a squad meeting where Creighton had come in and made an announcement concerning the overtime budget or the department's travel protocols. Back then Creighton was the head bean counter—in charge of budgeting for the department among his other management duties. He was known for instituting strict policies on overtime that required detailed explanations to be written on green slips that were subject to supervisor approval. Since that approval, or disapproval, usually came after the extra hours were already worked, the new system was viewed as an effort to dissuade cops from working overtime or, worse yet, get them to work overtime and then deny authorization or replace it with comp time. It was during this posting that Creighton became universally known as "Cretin" by the rank and file.

Though Creighton left the department for the private sector not long after that, the "greenies" were still in use. The mark he left on the department had not been a daring rescue or a gun battle or the takedown of an apex predator. It had been the green overtime slip.

"Harry, come in," Creighton said. "Sit down."

Bosch moved to the desk. Creighton was a few years older than Harry but in good shape. He stood behind the desk with his hand held forward. He wore a gray suit that was tailor-cut to his taut frame. He looked like money. Bosch shook his hand and then sat down in front of the desk. He hadn't gotten dressed up for the appointment. He was in blue jeans, a blue denim shirt, and a charcoal corduroy jacket he'd had for at least twelve years. These days Bosch's work suits from his days with the department were wrapped in plastic. He didn't want to pull one of them out just for a meeting with Cretin.

"Chief, how are you?" he said.

"It's not 'chief' anymore," Creighton said with a laugh. "Those days are long ago. Call me John."

"John, then."

"Sorry to keep you waiting out there. I had a client on the phone and, well, the client always comes first. Am I right?"

"Sure, no problem. I enjoyed the view."

The view through the window behind Creighton was in the opposite direction, stretching northeasterly across the Civic Center and to the snowcapped mountains in San Bernardino. But Bosch guessed that the mountains weren't the reason Creighton picked this office. It was the Civic Center. From his desk Creighton looked down on the spire of City Hall, the Police Administration Building, and the Los Angeles Times Building. Creighton was above them all.

"It is truly spectacular seeing the world from this angle," Creighton said.

Bosch nodded and got down to business.

"So," he said. "What can I do for you...John?"

"Well, first of all, I appreciate you coming in without really knowing why I wished to see you. Gloria told me she had a difficult time persuading you to come."

"Yeah, well, I'm sorry about that. But like I told her, if this is about a job, I'm not interested. I've got a job."

"I heard. San Fernando. But that's gotta be part-time, right?"

He said it with a slightly mocking tone and Bosch remembered a line from a movie he once saw: "If you're not cop, you're little people." It also held that if you worked for a little department, you were still little people.

"It keeps me as busy as I want to be," he said. "I also have a private ticket. I pick up stuff from time to time on that."

"All referrals, correct?" Creighton said.

Bosch looked at him a moment.

"Am I supposed to be impressed that you checked me out?" he finally said. "I'm not interested in working here. I don't care what the pay is, I don't care what the cases are."

"Well, let me just ask you something, Harry," Creighton said. "Do you know what we do here?"

Bosch looked over Creighton's shoulder and out at the mountains before answering.

"I know you are high-level security for those who can afford it," he said.

"Exactly," Creighton said.

He held up three fingers on his right hand in what Bosch assumed was supposed to be a trident.

"Trident Security," Creighton said. "Specializing in financial, technological, and personal security. I started the California branch ten years ago. We have bases here, in New York, Boston, Chicago, Miami, London, and Frankfurt. We are about to open in Istanbul. We are a very large operation with thousands of clients and even more connections in our fields of expertise."

"Good for you," Bosch said.

He had spent about ten minutes on his laptop reading up on Trident before coming in. The upscale security venture was founded in New York in 1996 by a shipping magnate named Dennis Laughton, who had been abducted and ransomed in the Philippines. Laughton first hired a former NYPD police commissioner to be his front man and had followed suit in every city where he opened a base, plucking a local chief or high-ranking commander from the local police department to make a media splash and secure the absolute must-have of local police cooperation. The word was that ten years ago Laughton had tried to hire L.A.'s police chief but was turned down and then went to Creighton as a second choice.

"I told your assistant I wasn't interested in a job with Trident," Bosch said. "She said it wasn't about that. So why don't you tell me what it is about so we can both get on with our days."

"I can assure you, I am not offering you a job with Trident," Creighton said. "To be honest, we must have full cooperation and respect from the LAPD to do what we do and to handle the delicate matters that involve our clients and the police. If we were to bring you in as a Trident associate, there could be a problem."

"You're talking about my lawsuit."

"Exactly."

For most of the past year Bosch had been in the middle of a protracted lawsuit against the department where he had worked for more than thirty years. He sued because he believed he had been illegally forced into retirement. The case had drawn ill will toward Bosch from within the ranks. It did not seem to matter that during his time with a badge he had brought more than a hundred murderers to justice. The lawsuit was settled but the hostility continued from some quarters of the department, mostly the quarter at the top.

"So if you brought me into Trident, that would not be good for your relations with the LAPD," Bosch said. "I get that. But you want me for something. What is it?"

Creighton nodded. It was time to get down to it.

"Do you know the name Whitney Vance?" he asked. Bosch nodded.

"Of course I do," he said.

"Yes, well, he is a client," Creighton said. "As is his company, Advance Engineering."

"Whitney Vance has got to be eighty years old."

"Eighty-five, actually. And…"

Creighton opened the top middle drawer of his desk and removed a document. He put it on the desk between them. Bosch could see it was a printed check with an attached stub. He wasn't wearing his glasses and was unable to read the amount or the other details.

"He wants to speak to you," Creighton finished.

"About what?" Bosch asked.

"I don't know. He said it was a private matter and he specifically asked for you by name. He said he would discuss the matter only with you. He had this certified check drawn for ten thousand dollars. It is yours to keep for meeting him, whether or not the appointment leads to further work."

Bosch didn't know what to say. At the moment he was flush because of the lawsuit settlement, but he had put most of the money into long-term investment accounts designed to carry him comfortably into old age with a solid stake left over for his daughter. But at the moment she had two-plus years of college and then graduate school tuition ahead of her. She had some generous scholarships but he was still on the hook for the rest of it in the short term. There was no doubt in his mind that ten thousand dollars could be put to good use.

"When and where is this appointment going to be?" he finally said.

"Tomorrow morning at nine at Mr. Vance's home in Pasadena," Creighton said. "The address is on the check receipt. You might want to dress a little nicer than that."

Bosch ignored the sartorial jab. From an inside jacket pocket he took out his eyeglasses. He put them on as he reached across the desk and took the check. It was made out to his full name, Hieronymus Bosch.

There was a perforated line running across the bottom of the check. Below it were the address and appointment time as well as the admonition "Don't bring a firearm." Bosch folded the check along the perforation and looked at Creighton as he put it into his jacket.

"I'm going to go to the bank from here," he said. "I'll deposit this, and if there is no problem, I'll be there tomorrow."

Creighton smirked.

"There will not be a problem."

Bosch nodded.

"I guess that's it, then," he said.

He stood up to go.

"There is one more thing, Bosch," Creighton said.

Bosch noted that he had dropped from first name to last name status with Creighton inside of ten minutes.

"What's that?" he asked.

"I have no idea what the old man is going to ask you, but I'm very protective of him," Creighton said. "He is more than a client and I don't want to see him taken for a ride at this point in his life. Whatever the task is that he wants you to perform, I need to be in the loop."

"A ride? Unless I missed something, you called me, Creighton. If anybody's being taken for a ride, it will be me. It doesn't matter how much he's paying me."

"I can assure you that's not the case. The only ride is the ride out to Pasadena for which you just received ten thousand dollars."

Bosch nodded.

"Good," he said. "I'm going to hold you to that. I'll see the old man tomorrow and find out what this is about. But if he becomes my client, then that business, whatever it is, will be between him and me. There won't be any loop that includes you unless Vance tells me there is. That's how I work. No matter who the client is."

Bosch turned toward the door. When he got there he looked back at Creighton.

"Thanks for the view."

He left and closed the door behind him.

On the way out he stopped at the receptionist's desk and got his parking receipt validated. He wanted to be sure Creighton ate the twenty bucks for that, as well as the car wash he agreed to when he valeted the car.

2

The Vance estate was on San Rafael near the Annandale Golf Club. It was a neighborhood of old money. Homes and estates that had been passed down through generations and guarded behind stone walls and black iron fences. It was a far cry from the Hollywood Hills, where the new money went and the rich left their trash cans out on the street all week. There were no For Sale signs here. You had to know somebody, maybe even share their blood, to buy in.

Bosch parked against the curb about a hundred yards from the gate that guarded the entrance to the Vance estate. Atop it were spikes ornately disguised as flowers. For a few moments he studied the curve of the driveway beyond the gate as it wound and rose into the cleft of two rolling green hills and then disappeared. There was no sign of any structure, not even a garage. All of that would be well back from the street, buffered by geography, iron, and security. But Bosch knew that Whitney Vance, eighty-five years old, was up there somewhere beyond those money-colored hills, waiting for him with something on his mind. Something that required a man from the other side of the spiked gate.

Bosch was twenty minutes early for the appointment and decided to use the time to review several stories he had found on the Internet and downloaded to his laptop that morning.

The general contours of Whitney Vance's life were known to Bosch as they were most likely known to most Californians. But he still found the details fascinating and even admirable in that Vance was the rare recipient of a rich inheritance who had turned it into something even bigger. He was the fourth-generation Pasadena scion of a mining family that extended all the way back to the California gold rush. Prospecting was what drew Vance's great-grandfather west but not what the family fortune was founded on. Frustrated by the hunt for gold, the great-grandfather established the state's first strip-mining operation, extracting multi-tons of iron ore out of the earth in San Bernardino County. Vance's grandfather followed up with a second strip mine farther south, in Imperial County, and his father parlayed that success into a steel mill and fabrication plant that helped support the dawning aviation industry. At the time, the face of that industry belonged to Howard Hughes, and he counted Nelson Vance as first a contractor and then a partner in many different aviation endeavors. Hughes would become godfather to Nelson Vance's only child.

Whitney Vance was born in 1931 and as a young man apparently set out to blaze a unique path for himself. He initially went off to the University of Southern California to study filmmaking but he eventually dropped out and came back to the family fold, transferring to the California Institute of Technology, in Pasadena, the school "Uncle Howard" had attended. It was Hughes who urged young Whitney to study aeronautical engineering at Caltech.

As with the elders of his family, when it was his turn Vance pushed the family business in new and increasingly successful directions, always with a connection to the family's original product: steel. He won numerous government contracts to manufacture aircraft parts and founded Advance Engineering, which held the patents on many of them. Couplings that were used for the safe fueling of aircraft were perfected in the family steel mill and were still used today at every airport in the world. Ferrite extracted from the iron ore at Vance mining operations was used in the earliest efforts to build aircraft that avoided radar detection. These processes were meticulously patented and protected by Vance and they guaranteed his company's participation in the decades-long development of stealth technologies. Vance and his company were part of the so-called military-industrial complex, and the Vietnam War saw their value grow exponentially. Every mission in or out of that country over the entire length of the war involved equipment from Advance Engineering. Bosch remembered seeing the company logo—an *A* with an arrow through the middle of it—imprinted on the steel walls of every helicopter he had ever flown on in Vietnam.

Bosch was startled by a sharp rap on the window beside him. He looked up to see a uniformed Pasadena patrol officer, and in the rearview he saw the black-and-white parked behind him. He had become so engrossed in his reading that he had not even heard the cop car come up on him.

He had to turn on the Cherokee's engine to lower the window. Bosch knew what this was about. A twenty-two-year-old vehicle in need of paint parked outside the estate of a family that helped build the state of California constituted a suspicious activity. It didn't matter that the car was freshly cleaned or that he was wearing a crisp suit and tie rescued from a plastic storage bag. It had taken less than fifteen minutes for the police to respond to his intrusion into the neighborhood.

"I know how this looks, Officer," he began. "But I have an appointment across the street in about five minutes and I was just—"

"That's wonderful," the cop said. "Do you mind stepping out of the car?"

Bosch looked at him for a moment. He saw the nameplate above his breast pocket said Cooper.

"You're kidding, right?" he asked.

"No, sir, I'm not," Cooper said. "Please step out of the car."

Bosch took a deep breath, opened the door, and did as he was told. He raised his hands to shoulder height and said, "I'm a police officer."

Cooper immediately tensed, as Bosch knew he would.

"I'm unarmed," Bosch said quickly. "My weapon's in the glove box."

At that moment he was thankful for the edict typed on the check stub telling him to come to the Vance appointment unarmed.

"Let me see some ID," Cooper demanded.

Bosch carefully reached into an inside pocket in his suit coat and pulled his badge case. Cooper studied the detective's badge and then the ID.

"This says you're a reserve officer," he said.

"Yep," Bosch said. "Part-timer."

"About fifteen miles off your reservation, aren't you? What are you doing here, Detective Bosch?"

He handed the badge case back and Bosch put it away.

"Well, I was trying to tell you," he said. "I have an appointment—which you are going to make me late for—with Mr. Vance, who I'm guessing you know lives right over there."

Bosch pointed toward the black gate.

"Is this appointment police business?" Cooper asked.

"It's actually none of your business," Bosch replied.

They held each other's cold stares for a long moment, neither man blinking. Finally Bosch spoke.

"Mr. Vance is waiting for me," he said. "Guy like that, he'll probably ask why I'm late and he'll probably do something about it. You got a first name, Cooper?"

Cooper blinked.

"Yeah, it's fuck you," he said. "Have a nice day."

He turned and started back toward the patrol car.

"Thank you, Officer," Bosch called after him.

Bosch got back into his car and immediately pulled away from the curb. If the old car still had had the juice to leave rubber, he would have done so. But the most he could show Cooper, who remained parked at the curb, was a plume of blue smoke from the ancient exhaust pipe.

He pulled into the entrance channel at the gate to the Vance estate and drove up to a camera and communication box. Almost immediately he was greeted by a voice.

"Yes?"

It was male, young and tiredly arrogant. Bosch leaned out the window and spoke loudly even though he knew he probably didn't have to.

"Harry Bosch to see Mr. Vance. I have an appointment."

After a moment the gate in front of him started to roll open.

"Follow the driveway to the parking apron by the security post," the voice said. "Mr. Sloan will meet you there at the metal detector. Leave all weapons and recording devices in the glove compartment of your vehicle."

"Got it," Bosch said.

"Drive up," the voice said.

The gate was all the way open now and Bosch drove through. He followed the cobblestone driveway through a finely manicured set of emerald hills until he came to a second fence line and a guard shack. The double-fencing security measures here were similar to those employed at most prisons Bosch had visited—of course, with the opposite intention of keeping people out instead of in.

The second gate rolled open and a uniformed guard stepped out of a booth to signal Bosch through and to direct him to the parking apron. As he passed, Bosch waved a hand and noticed the Trident Security patch on the shoulder of the guard's navy blue uniform.

After parking, Bosch was instructed to place his keys, phone, watch, and belt in a plastic tub and then to walk through an airport-style metal detector while two more Trident men watched. They returned everything but the phone, which they explained would be placed in the glove box of his car.

"Anybody else get the irony here?" he asked as he put his belt back through the loops of his pants. "You know, the family made their money on metal—now you have to go through a metal detector to get inside the house."

Neither of the guards said anything.

"Okay, I guess it's just me, then," Bosch said.

Once he buckled his belt he was passed off to the next level of security, a man in a suit with the requisite earbud and wrist mic and the dead-eyed Secret Service stare to go with them. His head was shaved just so he could complete the tough-guy look. He did not say his name but Bosch assumed he was the Sloan mentioned on the intercom earlier. He escorted Bosch wordlessly through the delivery entrance of a massive gray-stone mansion that Bosch guessed would rival anything the DuPonts or Vanderbilts had to offer. According to Wikipedia, he was calling on six billion dollars. Bosch had no doubt as he entered that this would be the closest to American royalty he would ever get.

He was led to a room paneled in dark wood with dozens of framed 8 x 10 photographs hung in four rows across one wall. There were a couple of couches and a bar at the end of the room. The escort in the suit pointed Bosch to one of the couches.

"Sir, have a seat, and Mr. Vance's secretary will come for you when he is ready to see you."

Bosch took a seat on the couch facing the wall of photos.

"Would you like some water?" the suit asked.

"No, I'm fine," Bosch said.

The suit took a position next to the door they had entered through and clasped one wrist with the other hand in a posture that said he was alert and ready for anything.

Bosch used the waiting time to study the photographs. They offered a record of Whitney Vance's life and the people he had met over the course of it. The first photo depicted Howard Hughes and a young teenager he assumed was Vance. They were leaning against the unpainted metal skin of a plane. From there the photos appeared to run left to right in chronological order. They depicted Vance with numerous well-known figures of industry, politics, and the media. Bosch couldn't put a name to every person Vance posed with but from Lyndon Johnson to Larry King he knew who most of them were. In all the photos, Vance displayed the same half smile, the corner of his mouth on the left side curled up, as if to communicate to the camera lens that it wasn't his idea to pose for a picture. The face grew older photo to photo, the eyelids more hooded, but the smile was always the same.

There were two photos of Vance with Larry King, the longtime interviewer of celebrities and newsmakers on CNN. In the first, Vance and King were seated across from each other in the studio recognizable as King's set for more than two decades. There was a book standing upright on the desk between them. In the second photo Vance was using a gold pen to autograph the book for King. Bosch got up and went to the wall to look more closely at the photos. He put on his glasses and leaned in close to the first photo so he could read the title of book Vance was promoting on the show.

STEALTH: The Making of the Disappearing Plane
By Whitney P. Vance

The title jogged loose a memory and Bosch recalled something about Whitney Vance writing a family history that the critics trashed more for what was left out than for what it contained. His father, Nelson Vance, had been a ruthless businessman and controversial political figure in his day. He was said but never proven to be a member of a cabal of wealthy industrialists who were supporters of eugenics—the so-called science of improving the human race through controlled breeding that would eliminate undesirable attributes. After the Nazis employed a similar perverted doctrine to carry out genocide in World War II, people like Nelson Vance hid their beliefs and affiliations.

His son's book amounted to little more than a vanity project full of hero worship, with little mention of the negatives. Whitney Vance had become such a recluse in his later life that the book became a reason to bring him out into public light and ask him about the things omitted.

"Mr. Bosch?"

Bosch turned from the photos to a woman standing by the entrance to a hallway on the other side of the room. She looked to be almost seventy years old and had her gray hair in a no-nonsense bun on top of her head.

"I'm Mr. Vance's secretary, Ida," she said. "He will see you now."

Bosch followed her into the hallway. They walked for a distance that seemed like a city block before going up a short set of stairs to another hallway, this one traversing a wing of the mansion built on a higher slope of the hill.

"Sorry to keep you waiting," Ida said.

"It's okay," Bosch said. "I enjoyed checking out the photos."

"A lot of history there."

"Yes."

"Mr. Vance is looking forward to seeing you."

"Great. I've never met a billionaire before."

His graceless remark ended the conversation. It was as though his mention of money was entirely crass and uncouth in a mansion built as a monument to money.

Finally they arrived at a set of double doors and Ida ushered Bosch into Whitney Vance's home office.

The man Bosch had come to see was sitting behind a desk, his back to an empty fireplace big enough to take shelter in during a tornado. With a thin hand so white it looked like he was wearing a Latex glove, he motioned for Bosch to come forward.

Bosch stepped up to the desk, and Vance pointed to the lone leather chair in front of it. He made no offer to shake Bosch's hand. As he sat, Bosch noticed that Vance was in a wheelchair with electric controls extending from the left armrest. He saw the desk was clear except for a single white piece of paper that was either blank or had its contents facedown on the polished dark wood.

"Mr. Vance," Bosch said. "How are you?"

"I'm old—that's how I am," Vance said. "I have fought like hell to defeat time but some things can't be beat. It is hard for a man in my position to accept, but I am resigned, Mr. Bosch."

He gestured with that bony white hand again, taking in all of the room with a sweep.

"All of this will soon be meaningless," he said.

Bosch glanced around in case there was something Vance wanted him to see. There was a sitting area to the right with a long white couch and matching chairs. There was an office bar that a host could slip behind if necessary. There were paintings on two walls that were merely splashes of color.

Bosch looked back at Vance, and the old man offered the lopsided smile Bosch had seen in the photos in the waiting room, the upward curve on only the left side. Vance couldn't complete a full smile. According to the photos Bosch had seen, he never could.

Bosch didn't quite know how to respond to the old man's words about death and meaninglessness. Instead, he just pressed on with an introduction he had thought about repeatedly since meeting with Creighton.

"Well, Mr. Vance, I was told you wanted to see me, and you have paid me quite a bit of money to be here. It may not be a lot to you, but it is to me. What can I do for you, sir?"

Vance cut the smile and nodded.

"A man who gets right to the point," he said. "I like that."

He reached to his chair's controls and moved closer to the desk.

"I read about you in the newspaper," he said. "Last year, I believe. The case with that doctor and the shoot-out. You seemed to me like a man who stands his ground, Mr. Bosch. They put a lot of pressure on you but you stood up to it. I like that. I need that. There's not a lot of it around anymore."

"What do you want me to do?" Bosch asked again.

"I want you to find someone for me," Vance said. "Someone who might never have existed."

3

After intriguing Bosch with his request Vance used a shaky left hand to flip over the piece of paper on his desk and told Bosch he would have to sign it before they discussed anything further.

"It is a nondisclosure form," he explained. "My lawyer said it is ironclad. Your signature guarantees that you will not reveal the contents of our discussion or your subsequent investigation to anyone but me. Not even an employee of mine, not even someone who says they have come to you on my behalf. Only me, Mr. Bosch. If you sign this document, you answer only to me. You report any findings of your investigation only to me. Do you understand?"

"Yes, I understand," Bosch said. "I have no problem signing it."

"Very good, then. I have a pen here."

Vance pushed the document across the desk, then drew a pen from an ornate gold holder on his desk. It was a fountain pen that felt heavy in Bosch's hand because it was thick and made of what he presumed was real gold. It reminded Bosch of the pen Vance used in the photo to sign the book for Larry King.

He quickly scanned the document and then signed it. He put the pen down on top of it and pushed both back across the desk to Vance. The old man placed the document in the desk drawer and closed it. He held the pen up for Bosch to study.

"This pen was made with gold my great-grandfather prospected in the Sierra Nevada goldfields in 1852," he said. "That was before the competition up there forced him to head south. Before he realized that there was more to be made from iron than from gold."

He turned the pen in his hand.

"It was passed on from generation to generation," he said. "I've had it since I left home for college."

Vance studied the pen as if seeing it for the first time. Bosch said nothing. He wondered if Vance suffered from any sort of diminished mental capacity and if the old man's desire to have him find somebody who may never have existed was some sort of indication of a failing mind.

"Mr. Vance?" he asked.

Vance put the pen back into its holder and looked at Bosch.

"I have no one to give it to," he said. "No one to give any of this to."

It was true. The biographical data Bosch had looked up said Vance was never married and childless. Several of the summaries he had read suggested obliquely that he was homosexual but there was never confirmation of this. Other biographical extracts suggested that he was simply too driven by his work to keep up a steady relationship, let alone establish a family. There were a few brief romances reported, primarily with Hollywood starlets of the moment—possibly dates for the cameras to put off speculation about homosexuality. But for the past forty years or more, Bosch could find nothing.

"Do you have children, Mr. Bosch?" Vance asked.

"A daughter," Bosch answered.

"Where?"

"In school. Chapman University, down in Orange County."

"Good school. Is she a film student?"

"Psychology."

Vance leaned back in his chair and looked off into the past.

"I wanted to study film when I was a young man," he said. "The dreams of youth…"

He didn't finish his thought. Bosch realized he would have to give the money back. This was all some kind of derangement, and there was no job. He could not take payment from this man even if it was only an infinitesimal drop from Vance's bucket. Bosch didn't take money from damaged people, no matter how rich they were.

Vance broke away from his stare into the abyss of memory and looked at Bosch. He nodded, seeming to know Harry's thoughts, then gripped the armrest of his chair with his left hand and leaned forward.

"I guess I need to tell you what this is about," he said.

Bosch nodded.

"That would be good, yes."

Vance nodded back and offered the lopsided smile again. He looked down for a moment and then back up at Bosch, his eyes deeply set and shiny behind rimless glasses.

"A long time ago I made a mistake," he said. "I never corrected it, I never looked back. I now want to find out if I had a child. A child I could give my gold pen to."

Bosch stared at him for a long moment, hoping he might continue. But when he did he seemed to have picked up another string of memory.

"When I was eighteen years old I wanted nothing to do with my father's business," Vance said. "I was more interested in being the next Orson Welles. I wanted to make films, not airplane parts. I was full of myself, as young men often are at that age."

Bosch thought of himself at eighteen. His desire to blaze his own path had led him into the tunnels of Vietnam.

"I insisted on film school," Vance said. "I enrolled at USC in 1949."

Bosch nodded. He knew from his prior reading that Vance had spent only a year at USC before changing paths, transferring to Caltech and furthering the family dynasty. There had been no explanation found in his Internet search. Bosch now believed he was going to find out why.

"I met a girl," Vance said. "A Mexican girl. And soon afterward, she became pregnant. It was the second worst thing that ever happened to me. The first was telling my father."

Vance grew quiet, his eyes down on the desk in front of him. It wasn't difficult to fill in the blanks but Bosch needed to hear as much of the story from Vance as he could.

"What happened?" he asked.

"He sent people," Vance said. "People to persuade her not to have the child. People who would drive her to Mexico to take care of it."

"Did she go?"

"If she did, it was not with my father's people. She disappeared from my life and I never saw her again. And I was too much of a coward to go find her. I had given my father all he needed to control me: the potential embarrassment and disgrace. Even prosecution because of her age. I did what I was told. I transferred to Caltech and that was the end of it."

Vance nodded, as though confirming something for himself.

"It was a different time then...for me and for her."

Vance looked up now and held Bosch's eyes for a long moment before continuing.

"But now I want to know. It's when you reach the end of things that you want to go back..."

A few heartbeats went by before he spoke again.

"Can you help me, Mr. Bosch?" he asked.

Bosch nodded. He believed the pain in Vance's eyes was real.

"It was a long time ago but I can try," Bosch said. "Do you mind if I ask a few questions and take some notes?"

"Take your notes," Vance said. "But I warn you again that everything about this must remain completely confidential. Lives could be in danger. Every move you make, you must look over your shoulder. I have no doubt that efforts will be made to find out why I wanted to see you and what you are doing for me. I have a cover story for that, which we can get to later. For now, ask your questions."

Lives could be in danger. Those words ricocheted inside his chest as Bosch took a small notebook from the inside pocket of his suit coat. He pulled out a pen. It was made of plastic, not gold. He'd bought it at a drugstore.

"You just said lives could be in danger. Whose lives? Why?"

"Don't be naive, Mr. Bosch. I am sure you conducted a modicum of research before coming to see me. I have no heirs—at least known heirs. When I die, control of Advance Engineering will go to a board of directors who will continue to line their pockets with millions while fulfilling government contracts. A valid heir could change all of that. Billions could be at stake. You don't think people and entities would kill for that?"

"It's been my experience that people will kill for any

reason and no reason at all," Bosch said. "If I find you have heirs, are you sure you want to possibly make them targets?"

"I would give them the choice," Vance said. "I believe I owe them that. And I would protect them as well as is possible."

"What was her name? The girl you got pregnant."

"Vibiana Duarte."

Bosch wrote it down on his pad.

"You know her birthdate by any chance?"

"I can't remember it."

"She was a student at USC?"

"No, I met her at the EVK. She worked there."

"EVK?"

"The student cafeteria was called Everybody's Kitchen. EVK for short."

Bosch immediately knew this eliminated the prospect of tracing Vibiana Duarte through student records, which were usually very helpful, since most schools kept close track of their alums. It meant the search for the woman would be more difficult and even more of a long shot.

"You said she was Mexican," he said. "You mean Latina? Was she a U.S. citizen?"

"I don't know. I don't think she was. My father—"

He didn't finish.

"Your father what?" Bosch asked.

"I don't know if it was the truth but my father said that was her plan," Vance said. "To get pregnant so I would have to marry her and she would become a citizen. But my father said a lot of things to me that weren't true and he believed a lot of things that were...out of step. So I don't know."

Bosch thought about what he had read about Nelson Vance and eugenics. He pressed on.

"By any chance, do you have a photograph of Vibiana?" he asked.

"No," Vance said. "You don't know how many times I've wished for a photograph. That I could just look at her one more time."

"Where did she live?"

"By the school. Just a few blocks away. She walked to work."

"Do you remember the address? The street, maybe?"

"No, I don't remember. It was so long ago and I spent so many years trying to block it out. But the truth is, I never really loved anybody again after that."

It was the first time Vance mentioned love or gave an indication of how deep the relationship had been. It had been Bosch's experience that when you looked back at a life, you used a magnifying glass. Everything was bigger, amplified. A college tryst could become the love of a lifetime in memory. Still, Vance's pain seemed real so many decades after the events he was describing. Bosch believed him.

"How long were you together with her before all of this happened?" he asked.

"Eight months between the first and last times I ever saw her," Vance said. "Eight months."

"Do you remember when she told you she was pregnant? I mean, what month or time of year?"

"It was after the start of the summer session. I had enrolled just because I knew I would see her. So late June 1950. Maybe early July."

"And you say you met her eight months before that?"

"I had started in September the year before. I noticed her right away working at the EVK. I didn't get the courage to talk to her for a couple months."

The old man looked down at the desk.

"What else do you remember?" Bosch prompted. "Did you ever meet her family? Do you remember any names?"

"No, I didn't," Vance said. "She told me her father was very strict and they were Catholic, and I was not. You know, we were like Romeo and Juliet. I never met her family and she never met mine."

Bosch seized on the one piece of information in Vance's answer that might advance the investigation.

"Do you know what church she went to?"

Vance looked up, his eyes sharp.

"She told me she was named after the church where she was baptized. St. Vibiana's."

Bosch nodded. The original St. Vibiana's was in downtown, just a block from the LAPD headquarters, where he used to work. More than a hundred years old, it was badly damaged in the 1994 earthquake. A new church was built nearby and the old structure was donated to the city and preserved. Bosch wasn't sure but he believed it was an event hall and library now. But the connection to Vibiana Duarte was a good one. Catholic churches kept records of births and baptisms. He felt this bit of good information countered the bad news that Vibiana had not been a USC student. It was also a strong indication that she might have been a U.S. citizen, whether or not her parents were. If she was a citizen, she would be easier to track through public records.

"If the pregnancy was carried to full term, when would the child have been born?" he asked.

It was a delicate question but Bosch needed to narrow the timing down if he was going to wade into records.

"I think that she was at least two months pregnant

when she told me," Vance said. "So I would say January of the following year would be the birth. Maybe February."

Bosch wrote it down.

"How old was she when you knew her?" he asked.

"She was sixteen when we met," Vance said. "I was eighteen."

It was another reason for the reaction of Vance's father. Vibiana was underage. Getting a sixteen-year-old pregnant in 1950 could have gotten Whitney into minor but embarrassing legal trouble.

"Was she in high school?" Bosch asked.

He knew the area around USC. The high school would have been Manual Arts—another shot at traceable records.

"She had dropped out to work," Vance said. "The family needed the money."

"Did she ever say what her father did for a living?" Bosch asked.

"I don't recall."

"Okay, going back to her birthday, you don't remember the date but do you remember ever celebrating it with her during those eight months?"

Vance thought a moment and then shook his head.

"No, I can't remember a birthday occurring," he said.

"And if I have this right, you were together from late October till June and maybe early July, so her birthday would have likely been somewhere in July to late October. Roughly."

Vance nodded. Narrowing it to four months might help at some point when Bosch was going through records. Attaching a birth date to the name Vibiana Duarte would be a key starting point. He wrote the spread of months down and the likely birth year: 1933. He then looked up at Vance.

"Do you think your father paid her or her family off?" he asked. "So they would keep quiet and just go away?"

"If he did, he never told me that," Vance said. "I was the one who went away. An act of cowardice I have always regretted."

"Have you ever looked for her before now? Ever paid anybody else to?"

"No, sadly, I have not. I can't say if anyone else has."

"Meaning what?"

"Meaning that it is quite possible such a search was conducted as a preemptive move in preparation for my death."

Bosch thought about that for a long moment. He then looked at the few notes he had written. He felt he had enough to start.

"You said you had a cover story for me?"

"Yes, James Franklin Aldridge. Write it down."

"Who is he?"

"My first roommate at USC. He was dismissed from school in the first semester."

"For academics?"

"No, for something else. Your cover is that I asked you to find my college roommate because I want to make amends for something we both did but he took the blame for. This way, if you are looking at records from that time, it will seem plausible."

Bosch nodded.

"It might work. Is it a true story?"

"It is."

"I should probably know what it is you both did."

"You don't need to know that to find him."

Bosch waited a moment but that was all Vance had to say on the subject. Harry wrote the name down after checking the spelling of Aldridge with Vance and then closed his notebook.

"Last question. The odds are Vibiana Duarte is dead by now. But what if she had the child and I find living heirs? What do you want me to do? Do I make contact?"

"No, absolutely not. You make no contact until you report to me. I'll need thorough confirmation before any approach will be made."

"DNA confirmation?"

Vance nodded and studied Bosch for a long moment before once more going to the desk drawer. He removed a padded white envelope with nothing written on it. He slid it across the desk to Bosch.

"I am trusting you, Mr. Bosch. I have now given you all you need to trick an old man if you want. I trust you won't."

Bosch picked up the envelope. It wasn't sealed. He looked into it and saw a clear glass test tube containing a swab used to collect saliva. It was Vance's DNA sample.

"This is where you could be tricking me, Mr. Vance."

"How so?"

"It would have been better if I had swabbed you, collected this myself."

"You have my word."

"And you have mine."

Vance nodded and there did not seem to be anything else to say.

"I think I have what I need to start."

"Then I have a final question for you, Mr. Bosch."

"Go ahead."

"I'm curious because it wasn't mentioned in the newspaper stories I read about you. But you appear to be the right age. What was your status during the Vietnam War?"

Bosch paused a moment before answering.

"I was over there," he finally said. "Two tours. I

probably flew more times on the helicopters you helped build than you ever did."

Vance nodded.

"Probably so," he said.

Bosch stood up.

"How do I reach you if I have more questions or want to report what I find out?"

"Of course."

Vance opened the desk drawer and removed a business card. He handed it to Bosch with a shaking hand. There was a phone number printed on it, nothing else.

"Call that number and you will get to me. If it's not me, then something is wrong. Don't trust anyone else you speak to."

Bosch looked from the number on the card to Vance, sitting in his wheelchair, his papier-mâché skin and wispy hair looking as frail as dried leaves. He wondered if his caution was paranoia or if there was a real danger to the information he would be seeking.

"Are you in danger, Mr. Vance?" he asked.

"A man in my position is always in danger," Vance said.

Bosch ran his thumb along the crisp edge of the business card.

"I'll get back to you soon," he said.

"We have not discussed payment for your services," Vance said.

"You've paid me enough to start. Let's see how it goes."

"That payment was only to get you to come here."

"Well, it worked and it's more than enough, Mr. Vance. All right if I find my way out? Or will that set off a security alarm?"

"As soon as you leave this room they'll know it and come to meet you."

Vance registered Bosch's puzzled look.

"This is the only room in the house not under camera surveillance," he explained. "There are cameras to watch over me even in my bedroom. But I insisted on privacy here. As soon as you leave, they will come."

Bosch nodded.

"I understand," he said. "Talk to you soon."

He stepped through the door and started down the hallway. Soon enough Bosch was met by the nameless man in the suit and escorted wordlessly through the house and out to his car.

4

Working cold cases had made Bosch proficient in time travel. He knew how to go back into the past to find people. Going back to 1951 would be the farthest and likely the most difficult trek he had ever made but he believed he was up to it and that made him excited about the challenge.

The starting point was finding the birth date of Vibiana Duarte and he believed he knew the best way to accomplish that. Rather than go home after his meeting with Vance, Bosch took the 210 freeway across the northern rim of the Valley and headed toward the city of San Fernando.

Barely bigger than two square miles in size, San Fernando was an island city within the megalopolis of Los Angeles. A hundred years earlier all of the small towns and cities that comprised the San Fernando Valley were annexed into Los Angeles for one reason: the newly built Los Angeles Aqueduct offered bountiful supplies of water that would keep their rich agricultural fields from drying up and blowing away. One by one they were added and Los Angeles grew and spread north, eventually taking in the area's entire sprawl. All except for the 2.3 square miles of the Valley's namesake, the city of San Fernando. The little town didn't need L.A.'s water. Its ground supplies were more than adequate. Avoiding the overture of the big city that now surrounded it, it stayed independent.

A hundred years later it remained so. The Valley's agriculture pedigree may have long ago given way to urban sprawl and urban blight, but the city of San Fernando remained a quaint throwback to small-town sensibilities. Of course, urban issues and crime were unavoidable but they were nothing the tiny town's police department couldn't routinely take care of.

That is, until the financial crash of 2008. When the banking crisis occurred and economies constricted and spiraled downward around the world, it was only a few years before the tidal wave of financial pain hit San Fernando. Deep budget cuts occurred and then occurred again. Police Chief Anthony Valdez saw his department drop from forty sworn officers, including himself, in 2010 to thirty officers by 2016. He saw his detective squad of five investigators shrink to just two—one detective to handle property crimes and one to handle crimes against persons. Valdez saw cases start to pile up unsolved, some not even initially investigated fully and properly.

Valdez was born and raised in San Fernando but was seasoned as a cop with the LAPD, putting in twenty years and rising to the rank of captain before taking his pension and checking out, then landing the top spot at his hometown's department. His connections to the bigger department that surrounded his own ran deep, and his solution to the budget crisis was to expand SFPD's reserve program and bring in more officers who worked part-time hours but for free.

And it was this expansion that led Chief Valdez to Harry Bosch. One of Valdez's early assignments when he was with the LAPD had been in a gang-suppression unit in the Hollywood Division. There he ran afoul of a lieutenant named Pounds, who filed an internal complaint and unsuccessfully attempted to have Valdez demoted or even fired.

Valdez avoided both and just a few months later heard about a detective named Bosch who himself got into an altercation with Pounds and ended up throwing him through a plate-glass window at Hollywood Station. Valdez always remembered that name, and years later when he read about a now-retired Harry Bosch suing the LAPD for forcing him out of his job on the cold case squad, he picked up the phone.

Valdez couldn't offer Bosch a paycheck, but he could offer him something Bosch valued more: a detective's badge and access to all of the tiny city's unsolved cases. The SFPD's reserve unit had only three requirements. Its officers had to maintain their state training standards as law enforcement officers, qualify once a month at the department's shooting range, and work at least two shifts a month.

It was a no-brainer for Bosch. The LAPD didn't want or need him anymore but the little town up in the Valley certainly did. And there was work to be done and victims waiting for justice. Bosch took the job the moment it was offered. He knew it would allow him to continue his life's mission, and he needed no paycheck for that.

Bosch easily met and surpassed the reserve officer minimums. It was rare that he didn't put in at least two shifts a week, let alone a month, in the detective bureau. He was there so often that he was permanently assigned one of the cubicles that had been left open when the squad was trimmed in the budget crunch.

Most days he was working in the cubicle or across First Street from the police station in the old city jail where the cells were repurposed as storage rooms. The former drunk tank now housed three rows of standing shelves stocked with open case files going back decades.

Because of the statute of limitations on all crimes but murder, the great majority of these cases would never be solved or even examined. The small city didn't have a lot of murders, but Bosch was meticulously going through them, looking for ways to apply new technologies to old evidence. He also took on a review of all sexual assaults, nonfatal shootings, and attacks resulting in major injuries within the statute of limitations for those crimes.

The job had a lot of freedom to it. Bosch could set his own hours and could always take time away if a case came up for him in private investigation. Chief Valdez knew he was lucky to have a detective with Bosch's experience working for him, and he never wanted to impinge on Bosch's ability to take on a paying job. He just stressed to Bosch that the two could never mix. Harry could not use his badge and access as a San Fernando cop to facilitate or further any private investigation. That would be a firing offense.

5

Murder knows no bounds or city limits. Most of the cases Bosch reviewed and pursued took him into LAPD turf. It was only expected. Two of the big city's police divisions shared borders with San Fernando: Mission Division to the west and Foothill Division to the east. In four months Bosch had cleared two unsolved gang murders—connecting them through ballistics to murders in L.A. for which the perpetrators were already in prison—and linked a third to a pair of suspects already being sought for murder by the larger department.

Additionally, Bosch had used MO—modus operandi—and then DNA to connect four sexual assault cases in San Fernando over a four-year period and was in the process of determining whether the attacker was responsible for any rapes in Los Angeles as well.

Driving the 210 away from Pasadena allowed Bosch to check for a tail. Midday traffic was light and by alternately driving five miles below the speed limit and then taking it up to fifteen above it, he could check the mirrors for vehicles following the same pattern. He wasn't sure how seriously to take Whitney Vance's concerns about the secrecy of his investigation but it didn't hurt to be alert to a tail. He didn't see anything on the road behind him. Of course, he knew that his car could have been tagged with a GPS tracker while he was in the mansion with Vance, or even the day before while he met with Creighton at the U.S. Bank Tower. He knew would need to check for that later.

In fifteen minutes he had crossed the top of the Valley and was back in L.A. He took the Maclay Street exit and dropped down into San Fernando, where he turned onto First Street. The SFPD was located in a single-story building with white stucco walls and a red barrel-tile roof. The population of the tiny town was 90 percent Latino and its municipal structures were all designed with a nod to Mexican culture.

Bosch parked in the employee lot and used an electronic key to enter the station through the side door. He nodded to a couple of uniform cops through the window of the report room and followed the back hallway past the chief's office toward the detective bureau.

"Harry?"

Bosch turned and looked through the door to the chief's office. Valdez was behind his desk, waving him in.

Harry stepped into the office. It wasn't as big as the LAPD chief's suite but it was comfortable and had a sitting area for informal discussions. Hanging from the ceiling was a black-and-white toy helicopter with SFPD painted on its body. The first time Bosch had been in the office Valdez had explained that this was the department's helicopter—a joking reference to the fact that the department didn't have its own bird and had to call in air support when needed from the LAPD.

"How's it going?" Valdez asked.

"Can't complain," Bosch said.

"Well, we certainly appreciate what you're doing around here. Anything happening on the Screen Cutter?"

It was a reference to one of the serial cases Bosch had identified.

"I'm about to go check on responses to our e-mail. After that I'll get with Bella to talk about next moves."

"I read the report from the profiler when I approved the payment. Interesting stuff. We gotta get this guy."

"Working on it."

"Okay, well, I won't hold you up."

"Okay, Chief."

Bosch glanced at the helicopter for a moment and then left the office. The detective bureau was just a few paces down the hall. By LAPD or any standards, it was quite small. It had once consisted of two rooms, but one room had been subleased to the County Coroner's Office as a satellite office for two of its investigators. Now there were three detective cubicles crammed into one room with a closet-size supervisor's office adjoining.

Bosch's cubicle had five-foot walls that allowed him privacy from three sides. But the fourth side was open to the office door of the squad's supervisor. That post was supposed to be a full-time lieutenant's slot, but it had been vacant since the budget crunch and the supervisor was currently the department's only captain. His name was Trevino and he had so far not been convinced that having Bosch on premises and handling cases was a good thing. He seemed suspicious of Bosch's motives for working so many hours for no pay and kept a careful watch over him. For Bosch, the only thing that alleviated this unwanted attention was that Trevino wore multiple hats in the department, as is often the case with small agencies. He was running the detective bureau and was also in charge of interior operations in the station, including the dispatch center, the indoor firing range, and the sixteen-bed jail built to replace the aging facility across the street. These responsibilities often drew Trevino out of the detective bureau and off Bosch's back.

Bosch checked his mail slot upon entering and found a reminder notice that he was overdue qualifying this month on the range. He moved into his cubicle and sat down at his desk.

Along the way he saw that Trevino's door was closed and the glass transom above it was dark. The captain was most likely in another part of the building carrying out one of his other duties. Bosch thought he understood Trevino's suspicion and lack of welcome. Any success he had in clearing cases could be seen as a failing on Trevino's part. After all, the detective bureau was currently his domain. And it didn't help when word got around that Bosch had once thrown his LAPD supervisor through a plate-glass window.

Still, there was nothing Trevino could do about Bosch's placement in the office, because he was part of the police chief's effort to overcome personnel cuts.

Bosch turned on his computer terminal and waited for it to boot up. It had been four days since he was last in the office. A flyer for a department bowling night had been left on his desk and he immediately transferred this to the recycle bin beneath it. He liked the people he worked with in the new department, but he wasn't much of a bowler.

Using a key to open a locked file cabinet in his desk, he pulled out a few folders pertaining to open cases he was working and spread them on his desk so it would appear he was engaged in SFPD business. He noticed when he reached for his Screen Cutter folder that it wasn't there. He found it in the wrong spot in the drawer. It had been misfiled under the first victim's name rather than under the unknown suspect's moniker: Screen Cutter. This immediately alarmed and annoyed Bosch. He didn't believe he could have misfiled the case. All of his career he had carefully managed his case files. The file—whether it was a murder book or a manila folder—was the heart of the case and it always needed to be neatly and thoroughly put together and safely stored.

He put the folder on his desk and considered that someone with a duplicate key might be reading his files and checking his work. And he knew exactly who that might be. He reversed himself and returned all his files to the drawer, then closed and locked it with his key. He had a plan for smoking out the intruder.

He sat up straight to look over the partitions and saw that both of the other detective cubicles were empty. Bella Lourdes, the CAPs investigator, and Danny Sisto, who handled property crimes, were probably out in the field following up on crime reports. They often went out to handle much of their fieldwork together.

Once he was logged into the department's computer system, Bosch opened up the law enforcement databases. He got out his notebook and began the search for Vibiana Duarte, knowing he was breaking the one rule the police chief had given him: using his SFPD access to supplement a private investigation. Not only was it a firing offense at SFPD but it was a crime in California to access a law enforcement database for information not pertaining to a police investigation. If Trevino ever decided to audit Bosch's use of the computer, there would be a problem. But Bosch figured that would not happen. Trevino would know that if he made a move against Bosch, he was making a move against the police chief, and that was most likely career suicide.

The search for Vibiana Duarte was short. There was no listing of her ever having a driver's license in California, no record of her ever committing a crime or even getting a parking ticket. Of course, the digital databases were less complete the farther back the search went but Bosch knew from experience that it was rare not to find any reference to an entered name. It supported the possibility that Duarte had been an illegal and possibly returned to Mexico in 1950 after becoming pregnant. Abortion in California was against the law back then. She might have crossed the border to have her baby or to have the pregnancy terminated in one of the backroom clinics in Tijuana.

Bosch knew the law on abortion back then because he had been born in 1950 to an unmarried woman and, soon after becoming a cop, he had looked up the laws so that he would better understand the choices his mother had faced and made.

What he was not familiar with was the California penal code in 1950. He accessed it next and checked the laws about sexual assault. He pretty quickly learned that in 1950 under penal code section 261, sexual intercourse with a female under age eighteen was considered a chargeable offense of rape. Consensual relations were not listed as an exclusion to prosecution. The only exclusion offered was if the woman was the wife of the offender.

Bosch thought about Vance's father believing the pregnancy was a trap set by Duarte to force a marriage that would bring her citizenship and money. If that was the case, the penal code gave her a solid piece of leverage. But the lack of any record of Duarte in California seemed to belie that angle. Rather than use her leverage, Duarte had disappeared, possibly back to Mexico.

Bosch switched the screen, went back to the DMV interface, and typed in "James Franklin Aldridge," the cover name Vance had given him.

Before the results came up, he saw Captain Trevino enter the squad room, carrying a cup of coffee from

Starbucks. Bosch knew there was a store located a few blocks away on Truman. He often took a break from computer work in the bureau and walked over himself. This was not only to give his eyes a rest but to indulge in a recent addiction to iced lattes that had developed since he began routinely meeting with his daughter at various coffee shops near her school campus.

"Harry, what brings you in today?" Trevino said.

The captain always greeted him cordially and by his first name.

"I was in the neighborhood," Bosch said. "Thought I'd check e-mail and send out a few more alerts on the Screen Cutter."

As he spoke, he killed the DMV screen and pulled up the e-mail account he had been given by the department. He didn't turn around as Trevino went to the door of his office and unlocked it.

Bosch heard the door open but then felt Trevino's presence behind him in the cubicle.

"In the neighborhood?" Trevino said. "All the way up here?"

"Well, actually, I was in Pasadena seeing somebody and then I just took the Foothill across," Bosch said. "Thought I'd just send out a few e-mails, then get out of here."

"Your name's not on the board, Harry. You have to sign in to get credit for your hours."

"Sorry, I was only going to be here a few minutes. And I don't have to worry about making my hours. I put in twenty-four last week alone."

There was an attendance board by the entrance to the detective bureau on which Bosch had been instructed to sign in and out so Trevino could chart his hours and make sure he hit the reserve officer minimum.

"I still want you signing in and out," Trevino said.

"You got it, Cap," Bosch said.

"Good."

"By the way…"

Bosch reached down and rapped his knuckles on the file drawer.

"I forgot my key," he said. "You have a key I can open this with? I need my files."

"No, no key. Garcia turned in the only one. He said that was all he got from Dockweiler."

Bosch knew that Garcia was the last detective to occupy the desk and that he had inherited it from Dockweiler. Both were casualties of the budget crunch. He'd heard in the office scuttlebutt that both men left law enforcement after being laid off. Garcia became a schoolteacher and Dockweiler saved his city paycheck and pension by transferring to the Public Works Department, where they had an opening in code enforcement.

"Anybody else have a key around here?" Bosch asked.

"Not that I know of," Trevino said. "Why don't you just open it with your lock picks, Harry? I heard you're good with those."

He said it with a tone that implied that Bosch was somehow skilled in the dark arts because he knew how to pick a lock.

"Yeah, I might do that," Bosch said. "Thanks for the idea."

Trevino stepped into his office and Bosch heard the door close. He made a mental note to check with Dockweiler about the missing key. He wanted to make sure the former detective didn't have it before he took any steps toward proving Trevino was the one secretly checking his files.

Bosch reopened the DMV portal to run Aldridge's

name. He soon pulled up a history that showed Aldridge had a California driver's license from 1948 until 2002, at which point it was surrendered when the license holder moved to Florida. He wrote down Aldridge's date of birth and then entered it with his name on a check of the Florida DMV database. This determined that Aldridge had surrendered his license in Florida at age eighty. The last address listed was in a place called The Villages.

After writing down the information, Bosch checked for a website and found that The Villages was a massive retirement community in Sumter County, Florida. Further searching of online records found an address for Aldridge and no indication of a death record or obituary. He had likely surrendered his driver's license because he no longer could or needed to drive, but it appeared that James Franklin Aldridge was still alive.

Curious about the incident that supposedly got Aldridge kicked out of USC, Bosch next ran the name through the crime database, doubling down on his firing offenses for the day. Aldridge had a DUI on his record from 1986 and that was it. Whatever had happened back in his freshman year of college remained hidden from Bosch.

Content that he had sufficiently chased down the name as needed for a possible cover story, Bosch decided to check through the e-mail that had accumulated on the Screen Cutter case. It was the investigation that had consumed most of his time since he had joined the ranks of the San Fernando Police Department. He had worked serial murder cases before during his time with LAPD and most, if not all, had a sexual component to them, so the territory was not new to Bosch. But the Screen Cutter case was one of the more puzzling cases he had ever encountered.

6

*S*creen Cutter was the case name for a serial rapist Bosch had identified among the department's open sexual assault reports. Combing through the files in the old city jail, Bosch had found four cases since 2012 that were seemingly related by MO but previously not seen as connected.

The cases shared five suspect behaviors that alone were not unusual but when taken as a whole indicated the strong possibility of one perpetrator at work. In each case the rapist had entered the victim's home through a rear door or window after cutting the screen rather than removing it. All four assaults occurred during the day and within fifty minutes before or after noon. The rapist used the knife to cut the victim's clothes off rather than ordering her to remove them. In each case the rapist wore a mask—a ski mask in two attacks, a Freddy Krueger Halloween mask in a third, and a Mexican Lucha Libre wrestling mask in the fourth. And finally, the rapist used no condom or other method to avoid leaving his DNA behind.

With these commonalities in hand, Bosch focused an investigation on the four cases and soon learned that while the suspect's semen had been collected in rape kits in three of the four cases, only in one instance had the material actually been analyzed in the L.A. County

Sheriff's crime lab and submitted for comparison to state and national DNA databases, where it found no match. Analysis in the two most recent cases was delayed because of a backlog of rape kits submitted to the county lab for examination. In the fourth case, which was actually the first reported rape, a rape kit was collected but no DNA from the rapist was found on the vaginal swab because the victim had showered and douched before calling police to report the assault.

The county lab and the LAPD lab shared the same building at Cal State L.A., and Bosch used his connections from his cold case days to speed up analysis of the two recent cases. While he awaited the results he thought would solidly connect the cases, he began requesting follow-up interviews of the victims. Each of the victims—three women in their twenties and a now-eighteen-year-old—agreed to meet with the detectives. On two of the cases he would have to turn over the questioning to Bella Lourdes because it was noted that the victims preferred to do the interviews in Spanish. It underlined the one drawback for Bosch in working cases in a city where nine out of every ten citizens were Latino and had varying capabilities when it came to English. He spoke Spanish passably, but for an interview with a crime victim, where subtle nuances of storytelling might be important, he needed Lourdes, who understood it as a first language.

To each meeting Bosch brought a copy of a victim questionnaire used by LAPD investigators who worked violent crimes. It was nine pages of questions designed to help identify habits of the victim that might have drawn the attention of the offender. The questionnaires were helpful in serial investigations, particularly in profiling the offender, and Bosch had cadged a copy from a Hollywood Division sex crimes investigator who was a friend.

The questionnaire became the stated purpose of the new round of interviews, and the stories that emerged were equal parts sad and terrifying. These were undoubtedly stranger rapes and the attacks had left each woman recovering both mentally and physically as long as four years after the crime. They all lived in fear of their attacker returning and none had recovered the confidence they once had. One of them had been married and at the time was trying to conceive a child. The attack changed things in the marriage and at the time of the follow-up interview, the couple were in the midst of divorce proceedings.

After each interview Bosch felt depressed and couldn't help but think about his own daughter and what sort of impact such an assault would have on her. Each time, he called her within the hour to check that she was safe and okay, unable to tell her the true reason he was calling.

But the follow-up interviews did more than reopen wounds for the victims. They helped focus the investigation and underlined the urgent need to identify and arrest the Screen Cutter.

Bosch and Lourdes adopted a conversational approach to each victim that started with assurances that the case was still being investigated as a priority by the department.

They scheduled the interviews in chronological order of the assaults. The first woman was the victim from whom no DNA evidence had been collected. The initial report on the crime explained that the woman had taken a shower and douched immediately after the attack out of fear that she would become pregnant. She and her husband at the time were trying to conceive a child and she knew that the day of the attack was also the day that she was most fertile in her ovulation cycle.

The second victim was still separated by almost four years from the attack, and while the psychological trauma persisted, she had found coping mechanisms that allowed her to talk more openly about what was the worst single hour of her life.

She described the attack in detail and revealed that she had attempted to dissuade the suspect from raping her by lying and saying she was having her period. The woman told Bosch and Lourdes that the man replied, "No, you're not. Your husband's coming home early to fuck you and make a baby."

This was new information and it gave the investigators pause. The woman confirmed that her husband was scheduled to come home early that day from the bank where he worked so that they could have an evening of romance, with the hope that it would result in her pregnancy. The question was, how did the Screen Cutter know that?

Under questioning from Lourdes the victim revealed that she had an app on her cell phone that tracked her menstrual cycle and told her the day of the month when she was ovulating and most likely to conceive. It was then her practice to transfer this information to a calendar kept on the refrigerator door. Each month she marked the day with red hearts and phrases like "Baby Time!" so her husband would be reminded of its significance.

On the day of the attack the woman had gone out to walk her dog in the neighborhood and was away from her home no more than fifteen minutes. She had her phone with her. The Screen Cutter had gained entrance to the house, and when she returned, he was waiting for her. At knifepoint he made her lock the dog in a bathroom and then took her into a bedroom, where the assault took place.

Bosch wondered whether those fifteen minutes she was walking the dog were enough time for the Screen Cutter to break into the house, see the calendar on the refrigerator, and understand its meaning to the point that he could make the comment to her about knowing what she and her husband had planned for the day.

Bosch and Lourdes discussed this and both felt it was more likely that the rapist had been in the house previously, either as part of stalking the victim, or because he was a family friend or relative or a repairman or someone who'd had some other business there.

This theory was supported when the other victims were interviewed and an eerie new component to the Screen Cutter's MO was established. In each case, there were indicators inside the victim's home that revealed details of her menstrual cycle. In each case as well, the assault had taken place during what would have normally been the ovulation phase of each woman's cycle.

The second and third victims revealed during the interviews that they used birth control pills that were dispensed from push-through pill cards. One of the women kept her pill card in a medicine cabinet, and the other in her bedside table. While the pills suppressed the ovulation cycle, the cards and color-coding of the pills could be used to chart when that five-to-seven-day phase would normally occur.

The last victim had been attacked the February before. She was sixteen years old at the time and home alone on a school holiday The girl reported that at fourteen she had been diagnosed with juvenile diabetes and her menstruation cycle affected her insulin needs. She tracked her cycle on a calendar on the door of her bedroom so she and her mother could prepare the proper insulin dosage.

The similarity in the timing of each of the attacks

was clear. Each victim was assaulted during what would normally be the ovulation phase of their cycle—the time when a woman is most fertile. For this to have occurred in four out of four cases seemed beyond coincidence to Bosch and Lourdes. A profile began to emerge. The rapist had obviously carefully chosen the day of each attack. While information about each victim's cycle could be found inside her home, the attacker had to know this information beforehand. This meant he had stalked his victims and likely had previously been in their homes.

Additionally, it was clear from descriptions of the attacker's body that he was not Hispanic. The two victims who spoke no English said he gave them orders in Spanish but it was clearly not his first language.

The connections between the cases seemed stunning and raised serious questions about why the cases had not been linked before Bosch arrived as a volunteer investigator. The answers were rooted in the department's budget crisis. The assaults occurred while the detective bureau was shrinking in size and those left in the squad had more cases to work and less time to work them. Different investigators initially handled each of the four rapes. The first two investigators were gone when the second two cases occurred. There was no cohesive understanding of what was going on. There was no constant supervision in the squad either. The lieutenant's position was frozen and those duties were assigned to Captain Trevino, who had responsibilities in other areas of the department as well.

The connections Bosch identified between the cases were confirmed when the DNA results came back linking the three cases in which semen had been collected. There was now no doubt that a serial rapist had struck at least four times in four years in tiny San Fernando.

Bosch also believed that there were more victims. In San Fernando alone, there was an estimated population of five thousand illegal immigrants, half of them women and many who would not call the police if victimized by crime. It also seemed unlikely that such a predator would operate only within the bounds of the tiny city. The four known victims were Latinas and had similar physical appearances: long brown hair, dark eyes, and a slight build—none of them weighed more than 110 pounds. The two contiguous LAPD geographic divisions had majority Latino populations, and Bosch had to assume that there were more victims to be found there.

Since discovering the connection between the cases, he had been spending almost all of his time on the SFPD job making contact with investigators from LAPD's burglary and sexual assault squads throughout the Valley as well as in the nearby departments in Burbank, Glendale, and Pasadena. He was interested in any open cases involving screen cutting and the use of masks. So far nothing had come back but he knew it was a matter of getting detectives interested and looking, maybe getting the message to the right detective who would remember something.

With the police chief's approval, Bosch had also contacted an old friend who had been a senior profiler with the FBI's Behavioral Analysis Unit. Bosch had worked with Megan Hill on several occasions when he was with the LAPD and she was with the Bureau. She was now retired from the FBI and working as a professor of forensic psychology at the John Jay College of Criminal Justice in New York. She also kept her hand in profiling as a private consultant. She agreed to look at Bosch's case for a discounted rate and he sent her a package on the Screen Cutter. He was keenly interested in knowing the motivation and psychology behind the attacks. Why did the Screen Cutter's stalking pattern include determining his intended victim's ovulation phase? If he was trying to impregnate his victims, why did he choose two women who were taking birth control pills? There was something missing in the theory, and Bosch hoped the profiler would see it.

Hill took two weeks to get back to Bosch, and her assessment of the cases concluded that the perpetrator was not choosing the attack dates because he wished to impregnate his victims. Quite the opposite. The details of the stalking and subsequent attacks revealed a subject with a deep-seated hatred of women and disgust toward the bodily ritual of bleeding. The day of the attack is chosen because the victim is considered by the offender to be at the cleanest part of her cycle. For him, psychologically, it is the safest moment for him to attack. Hill added to the profile of the rapist by describing him as a narcissistic predator with above-average intelligence. It was likely, however, that he had a job that did not involve intellectual stimulus and allowed him to fly below the radar when it came to the assessment of his employers and coworkers.

The offender also had a high degree of confidence in his skill at eluding identification and capture. The crimes involved careful planning and waiting and yet were marked by what seemed to be a critical mistake in leaving his semen in the victim. Discounting that this was part of an intention to impregnate, Megan concluded that it was intended to taunt. The offender was giving Bosch all the evidence he needed to convict him. Bosch just had to find him.

Hill also focused on the seeming incongruity of the offender leaving probative evidence of identity behind—his semen—and yet committing the crimes while masking his visual identity. She concluded that the offender might be someone the victims had previously met or seen, or he intended to make contact with them in some manner following the attacks, possibly deriving some of his satisfaction from getting close to the victims again.

Megan Hill's profile ended with an ominous warning:

If you eliminate the idea that the perpetrator's motive is to give life (impregnate) and realize that the attack is urged by hate, then it is clear that this subject has not concluded his evolution as predator. It is only a matter of time before these rapes become kills.

The warning resulted in Bosch and Lourdes upping the game. They started by sending out another set of e-mails to local and national law enforcement agencies with Hill's assessment attached. On the local level, they followed up with phone calls in an effort to break through the typical law enforcement inertia that descends on investigators who have too many cases and too little time.

The response was close to nothing. One burglary detective from LAPD's North Hollywood Division reported that he had an open burglary case involving a screen cutting but there was no rape involved. The detective said the victim was a male Hispanic twenty-six years old. Bosch urged the investigator to go back to the victim to see if he had a wife or girlfriend who might have been attacked but was afraid or embarrassed to report the assault. A week later the LAPD detective reported back and said there was no female living in the apartment. The case was unconnected.

Bosch was now playing a waiting game. The rapist's DNA was not in the databases. He had never been swabbed. He had left no fingerprints or other evidence behind other than his semen. Bosch found no other connecting cases in San Fernando or elsewhere. The debate over whether to go public with the case and ask for the help of citizens was simmering on the back burner in the office of Chief Valdez. It was an age-old law enforcement question: Go public and possibly draw a lead that breaks the case open and leads to an arrest? Or go public and possibly alert the predator, who changes up his patterns or moves on and visits his terror on an unsuspecting community somewhere else?

In the Screen Cutter case Bosch and Lourdes had conflicting views. Lourdes wanted to go public, if only to chase the rapist out of San Fernando if the move produced no leads. Bosch wanted more time to quietly look for him. He felt that going public would indeed chase him out of town but that it would not stop the victim count. Predators didn't stop—until they were caught. They just adapted and continued, moving like sharks to the next victim. Bosch didn't want to move the threat to another community. He felt a moral obligation to chase the suspect down here where he was active.

But there was no right answer, of course, and the chief appeared to be waiting, hoping that Bosch would come through and break the case before another victim was attacked. Bosch was ultimately relieved not to have the decision on his shoulders. He figured this was why the chief made the big bucks and he made none.

Bosch checked his e-mail now and saw he had no new messages in his queue with *Screen Cutter* in the subject line. Disappointed, he shut down the computer. He put his notebook back in his pocket and wondered if Trevino had looked down on it while hovering in the cubicle. It had been opened to the page with James Franklin Aldridge's name written on it.

He left the squad room without bothering to say good-bye to Trevino or write his time down on the board at the front door.